THE
FALLEN
KINGDOM

THE

FALLEN
KINGDOM

BOOK THREE OF THE FALCONER TRILOGY

ELIZABETH MAY

CHRONICLE BOOKS
SAN FRANCISCO

First published in the United States of America in 2017 by Chronicle Books LLC.
First published in Great Britain in 2017 by Gollancz.
Gollancz is a division of The Orion Publishing Group.

Copyright © 2017 by Elizabeth May.

Library of Congress Cataloging-in-Publication Data available.

ISBN 978-1-4521-2883-2

Manufactured in China.

Typeset in Requiem.

10 9 8 7 6 5 4 3 2 1

Chronicle Books LLC
680 Second Street
San Francisco, California 94107

Chronicle Books—we see things differently.
Become part of our community at www.chroniclebooks.com.

For my readers
Who sent me emails and messages that made me smile
Who told their friends about my books
Who stayed with this series from start to finish
Who knew me long before that,
and who have encouraged me all these years
I wrote this last one for all of you.

—Elizabeth May

CHAPTER 1

AM THE beginning of a girl: her throat filled with ash, desperately clawing her way from the earth with weak, trembling limbs and an urgent message on her lips.

I surface. I open my eyes to see the wide gray sky. A howling scream pierces the air—I realize it's *mine*.

My fingernails sink into the damp soil as I heave the rest of my body out of the ground. I collapse onto my stomach, my cheek pressed to the dirt. I gasp out words that catch in my throat, a litany on my tongue with no thought, no memory, no reason attached. The message grows ragged with my breathing, more and more incoherent as I come back to myself. As thoughts begin to form. As they cloud my mind, too many at once.

Where am I? How did I get here? I don't remember.

I stagger to my feet, grasping a nearby branch to steady myself. I blink against the light, my vision clearing as I take in the sight before me.

I'm in a forest that has burned black, every tree uprooted and fallen. Twisting branches cage me in, reaching for the sky like gnarled fingertips. I cough at the overwhelming stench of smoke from a recently extinguished fire. The air is so saturated with it that I have to press the back of my hand to my nose. It's hardly any better. My bare arms are covered with soot and grime. The black dress I'm wearing is caked with dirt.

I swipe a hand down the silky fabric. *How did I come to wear this?* It's not even familiar. *Nothing* is familiar. I have no memory of my life before now.

My breath hitches in alarm. "Think." My voice is rough, jarring. I press a hand to my chest as if it could slow my heartbeat. "There has to be *something*."

I try reaching for some scrap of memory, desperate to quiet the panicked thoughts that come again. *Who am I? Where am I? How did I get here?* But nothing comes. My mind is empty. An endless void where I know—*I know*—there ought to be a lifetime of memories.

Something rustles behind me. A few feet away, a crow lands on a blackened branch and beats its wings. Its small, inky eyes fix on me, unblinking. The sound it makes is a cross between a growl and a squawk. I step back, my skin breaking out in gooseflesh.

Eyes black as pitch. Withered skin stretched over bones. *I'll find you. Wherever you go, I'll find you.*

I flinch at the quick, fleeting image in my mind—a cacophony of ebony wings and cawing laughter that fills me with dread. Disturbing flashes of long, sharp beaks dripping with something. Blood? Then a voice that rises up from the shadowed parts of my mind, one that is old and trembling, yet filled with malice.

After this, you're on borrowed time.

Who did that voice belong to? I don't remember, and something tells me that I *need* to, that the message she gave me—the one I recited when I fought my way out of the ground—is important. And whatever it was, it scared the hell out of me.

The voice comes again, fainter this time. Fading, dying.

I came to make you an offer.

She dissolved into ash in my arms.

I pull out of the memory with a startled jerk that scares the crow away. It takes off in a flurry of plumage, coming in too close as it swoops past. I step back so quickly that one of the pointed tree branches slices through my palm. A hiss of pain escapes my lips as I stare at the welling blood beginning to snake down my fingertips.

Before I can stop myself—before I realize what I'm doing—power surges through my veins. It rushes down my wrist to where the blood pools along the palm of my hand. The energy is insistent, demanding. It hovers in the air as if asking for a command, anything I desire. I can make it real.

I don't want anything. Just something familiar. A memory.

I watch in shock as the branch that cut me is warped into metal as sharp as the pointed edge of a dagger. It's unsettling. I recall the shape of it, deep down in the blank space of my memories. As I'm trying to draw up the image, metal spreads along the tree, its limbs turning into a thousand twisting blades. A nightmarish sight, drawn from thoughts of a place I don't ever, *ever* want to recall. Where monsters with serrated teeth hid in the shadows of a dark forest.

Turn it back to what it was. Burn it down again. Please.

Black, scorched branches replace metal—but my power doesn't stop there. It bursts out in startling, vivid blue flames that lick the air and consume the contorted, dead trees around me.

Gasping, I shut my eyes as fear knots my stomach. *I have to get out of here. I have to get out before I make it worse. I have to—*

An ear-splitting crack fills the silence. I open my eyes just as the trees all collapse to the ground, sending cinders into the sky that extinguish one by one like a thousand dying stars.

Now what's left is a perfectly cut path through the remains of the twisting branches.

Pull it in. Pull it in now. My power settles back in my chest, a painful, solid weight that leaves me doubled over with a gasp. As if it's stretching out the bones of my body, twisting itself into a space that doesn't fit—that wasn't made for it.

As if it never belonged to me to begin with.

I hear that voice again, the one that sounds like a crone in her last, precious moments before death; filled with a tired, sad awareness of mortality. *You are my only blood.*

Remember, I tell myself. I desperately search my mind, but the few memories there are too tenuous, delicate.

"I can't." I can barely say the words. *I can't, I can't, I can't.*
Try harder.

I begin to walk the burned tree path, tearing through string after string of fleeting memories. They disappear as if they were grains of sand falling through my fingertips. *Focus.* I try to redirect my thoughts to something simple. How I came to be here. Where I am.

My name.

My name. I don't know my name.

A hot rush of panic hits me hard. That's not possible. Who forgets her own bloody name?

It feels like it should come easily. It's *right there*, within my reach: the letters, the sound of it, the way my lips form the syllables. But when I push for the memory, it won't come.

Fear makes me walk faster. My bare feet pad across the ash-covered ground at a speed that makes my legs burn with the effort, but I'm too upset to care. Up ahead, at the far end of the forest, a sliver of sunlight peeks through the clouds and reflects across the surface of a loch.

I pause as an image of that loch flutters across my mind, swift as bird wings. I was flying—no, I rode a horse over the landscape so quickly, it *felt* as if I were flying. I was racing after a dark-haired man and a woman who were also on horseback. We were headed into a battle, defending people I cared about. But where are they? *Who* were they?

Maybe my reflection will help me remember.

I break into a run, tearing through the line of dead trees, ignoring the sharp pain when my feet are cut by twigs. I burst through the forest and sprint down the rocky beach, heading for the remains of a dock. The wood looks just sturdy enough to walk on.

My name is on my lips; I'm trying to form the sounds. It's something several syllables long—but there's another one, shorter. A single rough note that's concise, direct.

It comes with the memory of the man who rode into battle with me. God, my chest aches at the thought of him. He whispered that shortened name like he loved the sound of it. Like he was telling me a secret. As if it meant *I love you* and *I want you*. As if it were a promise on his lips, a declaration. A vow.

My feet hit the dock. The whole structure groans beneath my weight. I take those last steps tentatively, so the wood doesn't collapse. Then I lie down on my stomach, peer over the edge, and look into the still water.

Those aren't my eyes.

It's the first thing I notice. They should be different— hazel, I think. A mixture of brown and deep, deep green. Now they're the light amber of raw honey. The color is rich and vibrant and unsettling.

Those aren't my eyes. They can't be.

I study my features for anything else that stands out. My face stares back at me, and it looks familiar. Beneath the fine layer of dirt and soot, ginger freckles are scattered across the bridge of my nose, along my cheekbones and the tops of my shoulders where the dress has left them bare. My curly, copper-colored hair dips closer to the water, a single ringlet barely touching the surface. I know my face, just as I'd know my name if I heard it.

The rest of me is ordinary, normal. Human features in a human face. My attention returns to my eyes. Not *mine*. Not human. A chill goes through me when I see a glimmer beneath the irises, like a shadow crossing water.

Compelled, I reach out to touch my reflection. The moment I make contact with the water, it tugs at the power inside me. God, it hurts. The pain eases only when I free it again from its prison in my chest.

Ice forms around my fingertips—but it doesn't stop there. It spreads quickly across the surface of the water, fanning out in tendrils of frost. The sleek, smooth surface is as clear as a mirror. It's so beautiful that I can't help but admire it.

Until I realize the ice isn't stopping. I try to draw it back, but it's too late. I can't. My powers won't be caged now, they won't be contained or slowed. The frost keeps spreading across the loch, reaching the rocks along the far shore.

Slow down. Slow down—

Thunder claps in the distance and I start. Overhead, the shaft of sunlight that lit up the silver waters of the loch disappears behind dark storm clouds that weren't there a moment ago. A sudden icy wind slices through the delicate fabric of my dress.

"Stop it," I tell my power in a choked whisper, struggling to pull it back into that too-small space in my chest. "Stop stop *stop*."

My power snaps back so fast and painfully that I cry out. I scramble to my feet, pulse quickening. The loch and the beach are covered in a thick layer of ice.

What did I just do? The power is like my eyes—it doesn't feel right. It's not mine. How can it be? I can't control it.

Accept. You must accept now.

A skeletal hand wrapping around mine in a hard, bruising grip. A withered body embracing me, and a sudden agonizing, searing pain.

I remember how I threw back my head and screamed and screamed and screamed.

Staggering at the memory, I hurry away from that damned dock before I can do something worse than freezing the water and bringing a storm.

Just what the bloody hell was that? What am I?

My thoughts whisper a word. A horrifying suggestion that makes me go still with dismay. *Fae.*

No, I'm not fae. I stare down at my feet, swollen and cut up from walking through the forest. Fae don't bleed this easily. The realization is a small comfort. A memory comes fast: me curling my fingernails into my palms to recall what pain felt like.

Pain that said *I'm still human. I'm still me. Bleeding is what mortals do.*

I'm still mortal.

The sharp beat of horse hooves draws me out of my thoughts. The rhythm is a faint, steady staccato against the earth. It isn't just the sound—I can *feel* it. In the rocks, the same way my power connected to the water. It's coming from the living forest at the far end of the loch.

Three horses. Each with a rider and . . .

Power. It has a weight to it, the way air does on humid days. A heaviness accompanied by a wild, earthy scent that's vaguely floral. It calls to something inside me that *knows*— with certainty—that those riders are my enemies. Their power grows closer, gliding across the land in tendrils as dark as shadows cast by trees.

They're searching for someone.

I flick a glance down at my hands, still cold from the water. They must be looking for the source of power. For whoever burned the forest to the ground. For whoever froze the surface of the loch.

Me. They're looking for me.

CHAPTER 2

I TAKE OFF running. My bare feet slap against the smooth beach rocks and up the bank until I reach the soft, charred dirt of the dead forest. Power barrels out of me in a burst through the branches, bending them in an arched path to let me pass. I sprint toward the towering trees farther up the beach, where the forest was left untouched by my destructive abilities.

The riders are getting closer. As if they sense I'm nearby, the rhythm of horse hooves grows faster, louder. It matches the beat of my heart, the roar of my breath.

The living forest is full of tall Scots pine, the perfect kind of place to hide—or attack. The trees have grown so densely that little is visible beyond the first line of the thicket. The canopy of lush, vibrant leaves greedily absorbs the sunlight before it can touch the ground, leaving the trunks shrouded in impenetrable shadows. The branches creak and groan, the air growing colder as I approach.

I run for the cover of darkness, an inexplicable thrill going through me. This is comforting—the familiarity of it, the way setting up an ambush is second nature. I've done this before. Many, many times.

As I near the line of trees, the sticks and rocks in the soil here are sharper against my bare feet. I speed up and leap the last few feet into the thicket as if I were diving into a cold stream. With no light to reach the ground, even the air is frigid and harsh against my skin.

I find a dark space between the pines, then wait for the fae to come.

The horses are right behind me at the entrance to the woods. One of the fae riders lets out his power in a soft, searching stroke as they dismount and head through the trees. A tendril of it brushes the hair along my neck, followed by a voice at the back of my mind saying, *Found you.*

I hope he hears my silent challenge: *Then come and get me.*

I move against a tree, pressing my back firmly to the trunk and slowing my breath. My power recedes into my veins and I tamp it down further, ignoring how much it hurts. It pulses in my chest, unsettled; the space where it's being kept is too small, too confining. It longs to be freed.

Not yet. Soon.

In this dense thicket with my power contained, they can't see or sense where I am. I'm invisible. I smile at the excitement building in my chest. Almost. They're so close now; I can feel them.

I peek around the trunk to see the riders. Their skin shines even in the shadowed grove. Though their faces don't trigger any memories, my power senses theirs and identifies it easily. *Daoíne sith*, the most powerful fae in the Seelie and Unseelie Courts, capable of controlling the elements. They specialize in entering humans' minds, and are able to manipulate them with a single thought.

These are Unseelie. I can tell. Even as they search for me, their hunger for human energy is insatiable, a demanding roar at the backs of their minds. My power can sense it.

"Here," one of them says. From my hiding place I can glimpse the blood red of his hair, the slope of his strong jaw. "The trail ends here."

"Is it the Queen?" says another.

"Doesn't feel like it," the first says in a low voice. "But she might have sent someone to kill for her."

The Queen. A memory stirs inside me, but it's gone the moment the fae edge closer to my tree. They move through the woods like ghosts, every step so controlled that not a single sound gives them away.

But they don't know I'm only a few feet from them. I can tell by the cautious way they hold themselves, eyes searching the distance. They don't sense me pressed against the tree as if I were a part of it.

I look around me for a weapon, pausing when I notice the foliage at my feet. I think of what happened at the loch, the way my blood mixed with power to turn wood into metal. I can make my own blade.

A smile curves my lips as I pluck a branch from the ground to slice open the skin of my arm. I hold back a flinch at the cut. My power flows down my wrist in a subtle pulse the fae soldiers won't notice. The anticipation of battle keeps me focused, intent. Unafraid. There's no time for fear.

A thin line of melted metal forms around the branch, warping and flattening to form a fine edge. Then it lengthens into a point sharp enough to break easily through skin. The blade is beautiful, perfectly suited to me, with its own internal, fiery glow. An object of power. Made from my blood. Created to kill fae.

I move with the sword in my grip, slipping forward in agile, silent steps across the ground. I don't need to remember my past to know that I've done this many times before. My body recalls it for me. The way my knees bend to keep my motions swift. The way my toes touch the soil and take my weight. The way I stall my breath to exhale as quietly as the air around us.

So the faery at the back of the trio never even realizes I'm there—until the moment I hook an arm around him, press my palm to his lips, and slide my blade across his throat.

He dies before he can make a sound.

His energy fills me. My blood sings in response, a hymn of death that only I can hear. The other two fae pause, as if sensing something, but they don't turn. They're confident he's behind them, ready to defend their backs. Ready to protect them.

That is their mistake.

The one at the front motions with two fingers to move forward. *Perfect.*

I gently set the faery's body on the ground and loop around a tree, pressing my back to it as I approach the second.

I was wrong about having hunted like this before. It's efficient and brutal and familiar—but different. My power hums. It muffles my steps. It makes my joints move as fluidly as water across rocks. There's a wildness that I'm sure I've never felt before, as if I'm aware of the entire forest, and every move my enemy is about to make.

I slip behind him like a shadow. One palm to his lips, just like the other. A joyful, savage whisper in his ear that scares some part of me from the life I've forgotten: *Got you.*

My arm snakes around the faery as if to embrace him, and then I plunge the sharp end of the blade through his ribs and into his heart. His muffled scream presses to my palm. I jerk my head up to see if the last one noticed.

Our eyes lock.

He watches with horror as I pull the sword out of his companion and drop his body to the ground. His blood drips from my blade, a *tap, tap, tap* against the dirt.

As the second dead faery's energy fills me, I smile. In that moment, I know I look like death.

His expression changes to one of recognition. He manages a single word: "*You.*"

Minutes ago, that would have made me pause. It would have been enough to break through my haze of confusion. But I'm too far gone now. My power is finally calm, sated, singing the words *finish it finish it finish it* in a blood-pounding roar in my ears. After all, he's not running.

That is his second mistake.

My fingers grip the hilt of the blade. I flick my wrist and the blade flies through the air. It strikes the faery through the neck. His legs curl beneath him, the way a stag's would after being shot on a hunt.

We are all the stag.

Who had told me that? I wince at the sudden pang of vulnerability those words bring. *Stop it.* Nothing matters but the feel of his power through my veins. Mine now. He needed to die. He would have killed me.

Curling my lip, I stride over and yank the blade out of him.

My head comes up as I sense another source of power. This one is less substantial; it doesn't have as much weight to it, or the same deep, insatiable hunger. It's more like rays of sunshine that break through the haze of my own power and call to something vulnerable inside me.

Something human. The idea makes me want to cry with joy.

I turn, the blade hanging limply in my grasp. There he is: a small glow in the thicket of trees. A halo of light that would fit neatly in the palm of my hand.

He whispers a name, no more than a breath of a sound. As if saying it hurts.

"Aileana."

CHAPTER 3

AILEANA. That name is a burden, something painful and sharp-edged and thorny. Seven letters and four syllables that scratch and scratch and scratch at something inside me, peeling it away like a layer of skin to see the blood beneath.

Aileana.

My memory of this faery is so strong I can practically feel his tiny dragonfly wings rustling beneath my fingertips, soft and smooth as silk. His musical laughter in my ears, clear as a bell.

Aileana.

No. No, I don't want it. Whatever it is that comes with that name—whatever this crushing burden is—it's too much, too oppressive. It's a crippling weight, more than any one person should bear.

"Aileana," the faery says again in delight. "I felt a burst of power and it felt like you and—" He pauses and tilts his head slightly. "Your eyes look different. How can you be—"

Then he's flying toward me, his movements so quick that I'm jarred from my memories. I slide back into the comfort of instinct, of battle-readiness. It's the only thing I know. It's the only thing that's felt right since I clawed my way out of the dirt and cracked my eyes open to find myself alone in a scorched forest.

I don't know you. I don't know that name. You weren't there. No one was.

"Stop!" My blade slices through the air between us, the tip halting a pinpoint away from the pixie's wee face. "Stop," I say again, lower this time. "Don't come near me."

He puts up his hands, but his eyes narrow. "Put that down. What is *wrong* with you?"

Nothing. Everything. *I don't remember.*

He tries to fly around the sword, but I put it between us again. "I said don't come near me." My body is poised in a fighting stance. "Don't make me hurt you."

For some incomprehensible reason, I feel guilty saying that.

"Have you gone barmy?" The pixie flickers a glance at my faery victim and he looks irritated. "What are you going to do, stab me?" When I don't reply, he lets out a huff. "For god's sake. I watched you die. At least let me sit on your shoulder and plait your hair before you threaten me."

Sit on my shoulder? *Plait my hair?* What?

Then his earlier words sink in: *I watched you die.*

A sudden phantom pain shoots through my chest—just over my heart. It feels real enough that I press a hand there, almost expecting to find a blade sticking out of my ribs.

Instead, there's only the puckered skin of a fresh scar, long and thin.

I look down and drag a finger across the mark, assessing the shape, the depth of the injury that would have caused such a thing. Three smaller marks form a semicircle around it—the design of the underside of a sword hilt, thrust hard enough to leave an impression behind.

With enough force to rip through skin, bone, and heart. A killing blow.

"I died?" I can barely contain my horror. Is that why I was in the ground? *Then what brought me back?*

A whisper at the back of my mind once more, as soft as a rustle of feathers. *Accept. You must accept now.*

The pixie's impatient snort interrupts my thoughts. "*Yes.* Now can we get to the part where you give me a damn hug?"

I almost smile, but then another voice brushes across my mind, quick as a heartbeat. A young woman's words, filled with grief: *I can't heal this.* I blink back the sting of tears at that. "How long have I been dead?"

The pixie's hands fist at his sides as if he's resisting the urge to touch me. "Two months, nineteen days. I've kept count."

Two months, nineteen days. And I can't recall any of that time, or my life before that.

I search my mind again, and all I can grasp are impressions, remnants of profound joy and grief. Of chasing monsters through the night. Of intimate touches and whispered promises. Nothing that tells me who I am, or how I came to be in a forest, surrounded by miles of dead trees, with no memory.

I lower my blade and slide my fingers down my bare, blood-and-dirt-coated arms. As if I would find the answers there. As if everything should suddenly become so clear.

Nothing.

Beneath the grime is smooth, unblemished skin. And yet . . . that seems wrong. I may only remember fragments, but my fingers recall the feel of uneven skin, marred with half-moon marks. The shape of teeth. Dozens and dozens of bites that speak of loss and loneliness.

"I can't remember," I whisper.

"You're going to have to be more specific," the pixie says. He plants his hands on his hips. "Do you remember dying?"

"No."

"How you got those freaky eyes?"

"No."

"How you gained the power to level a whole forest?"

I let out a small laugh despite myself. "Still no. Listen—"

"You remember me, right?" the pixie bursts out. When I shake my head, his face falls. "But . . . I'm Derrick. I lived in your closet. You're my companion." He waves his hands frantically. "I made your dresses!"

I frown down at my dress. "You made this?"

Now Derrick looks insulted. "No, I did not make that. *That* is hideous. I made you things with ribbons and flounces and you looked like you belonged on the top of a fancy cake."

When I just blink at him, he takes my moment of uncertainty to fly over to me. Then, before I can even protest, Derrick is tangled in my hair.

I almost push him away. I open my mouth to tell him, *Stop touching me*, because I'm starting to feel things. Too many things. Killing is easy, it's instinctive. It doesn't require thoughts or memories or regret over my empty mind. It doesn't come with a name that's more like a burden.

Then the pixie's hands slide through the strands of hair just behind my ear, his cheek presses briefly to mine, and I can't say the words. Each touch is enough to break through my violent urges to speak to the parts of me I've forgotten. Something in me that knows he's doing this to make sure I'm really here. Alive.

How long have I been dead?

Two months, nineteen days. I've kept count.

One inhalation, another, as he breathes in my scent. Derrick frowns. "You smell different."

His wings fluttering against my skin are so utterly familiar that I shut my eyes. My body relaxes. All my fighting instincts and roaring power are calmed by the immediate comfort his scent and touch brings, a sense of *home*. I can't help but reach up to stroke his wings. *I'm home. I'm home. He's my home.*

"What do I smell like?"

"*You*, but not." Derrick sniffs again and scowls. "I don't like it. It reminds me too much of—" He presses his lips together, the halo around him flashing crimson.

"Now, now," I say gently. He looks upset, and something tells me an upset pixie is never a good thing. But I have to know. "You can't start a sentence like that and not end it."

"Fine," he bites out. "You smell like *him*."

I suddenly find it painful to swallow and I don't know why. "Him?"

Derrick's wings are fanning gently, his jaw tight. "There's a lot you've missed. Let's save that conversation for later. I just got you back." He looks me over, pausing at the mix of soot and dirt on my face. Suddenly, his light goes dim and he looks stricken. "Oh, god. Please don't tell me you've been wandering around all this time—"

"*No*," I say quickly. Then, more quietly: "I came out of the ground and couldn't remember how I got there." *And there was no one there to remind me.* "You didn't leave me behind?"

Derrick's shocked eyes meet mine. "Of course I didn't—" Then he realizes what I just said. "You came out of the . . . ? Bloody hell. Bloody *hell*. No wonder you pointed that sword at me. No one else was here except those goddamn Unseelie."

Now he's prodding my temple with his wee fingers, checking for injuries. "Are you hurt? Did you hit your head when you came back?" Derrick asks, all concern now. "You humans have very fragile heads. Your brain isn't about to leak out of your ears, is it?"

I wince when he touches a shallow cut along my hairline where a branch must have snagged me while I was running. "Um. I don't think so."

"Good. Can you count to five?" He waves a hand in front of my face. "How many fingers am I holding up?"

I pull away. "Stop that. I'm not an idiot and I don't have a visual impairment."

"Well, how am I supposed to know?" he asks, clicking his tongue. After another minute of inspection, he says, "The good news is, you have no serious injuries and your head isn't broken. Congratulations."

"And the bad news?"

"You came out of the ground, you don't have a memory, and you're standing there staring at me like a fuddled sheep. Also, you smell. Just a bit."

I glare at him. "Any other helpful observations? Theories about why I can't recall anything?"

Derrick pulls back, tapping a finger against his lips. "I've never heard of someone coming back after being dead as long as you, especially not one who didn't have a body to return to. That, and your fragile human brain, is probably to blame for the memory loss." He snaps his fingers. "I know someone who can help you."

"Who?"

"Aithinne, of course." When I just stare at him, he sighs. "She's the Seelie Queen. She talks a bit like she's outrageously drunk most of the time, but she's harmless unless she wants to kill you. But first things first." He motions to the bodies at our feet as if I should know what to do with them. "We need to dispose of these. Quickly. We've spent too much time here as it is."

Derrick dives to the ground and starts digging with a combination of his hands and small bursts of power. He moves the heavy dirt and rocks with surprising speed and efficiency for such a small creature, heaping them in a pile on the forest floor. In no time, the hole grows a few feet deep and wide and he just keeps going.

When he catches me staring, he says impatiently, "Well? Don't just stand there. You slaughtered them, you help bury them."

I shake my head and grasp one of the dead faeries, grunting as I pull him across the ground. With all that armor on, the faery is heavier than he looks. "Is there a reason we're hiding them? Why can't we just leave them behind?"

"Because, my forgetful friend, unlike the rest of the *sithichean, daoine sìth* don't decay. We're in the middle of a tense accord between the Seelie Queen and the Unseelie King, and once he discovers the bodies of his dead soldiers, things are bound to become terrible very, very fast." Derrick says it evenly, but there's a note of worry beneath his words. An urgency. "The King is going to assume Aithinne has declared war. Burying his scouts will buy us enough time to warn her."

I just came back from the dead and I've already started a war between two monarchs. Brilliant. "I didn't mean to—"

"There's nothing to apologize for," he says shortly. "One of them has to kill the other, and they've been delaying it in the hope that another solution will present itself. It hasn't. This was inevitable."

No wonder the other faeries were talking about territories and the Queen sending someone to kill for her; we must be on the King's land. That pricks at a memory at the back of my mind, another important one I can't recall.

It's to do with the monarchs. The King. I may not remember his name, but the emotions I feel when I think of him are strong. I cared for him. Deeply enough that Derrick's words fill me with dread.

Ask something else. "They have to?"

"They don't have a choice," he says.

"Then I need to speak with the King." I need him to know I'm alive. "I'll tell him it was me. It doesn't have to be inevitable." I know it doesn't have to. There has to be something else—

"No," Derrick says.

"Derrick—"

"It won't make any difference," he says sharply. "We're running out of time." The ground rumbles and his power tosses so much dirt that it smacks into a nearby tree. "We have to accept that one of them is going to die and *she's* the better, kinder monarch. She should be the one to live."

In the middle of dragging the third body toward the pit, I freeze at his words. *She should be the one to live. We're running out of time.*

He sees my expression and slows his digging. "Hell," he mutters. "I'm sorry. I shouldn't have said that."

I don't reply. Blurred memories surface. They're an assault of images and words, none of them clear except for an urgency that leaves me trembling. A desperate sense that it isn't too late, that we can save them both. But when I try to see how, pain slams through my temples so hard that stars flash in my vision. I bite my tongue to keep from crying out.

"Running out of time?" I ask, voice hoarse. I shake my head in frustration. What's the point of being brought back if I can't remember anything?

"You'll see. The land is crumbling just beyond the forest border." Derrick returns to his rapid digging, only this time his movements are more agitated. The pit is at least six feet deep now, but the fae would be able to smell their dead past that. He keeps going. "Our realm is breaking apart because they refuse to kill each other. If one of them doesn't die, we all will."

Our realm. There it is again; the voice in my memories is whispering something about curses and power. When I push for more, my head starts pounding again. I wince and press my fingertips to my temples.

When I glance at Derrick, he looks away. But I'm nothing if not persistent. I want to know who the Unseelie King is. Why I feel so strongly. "If you think he should die," I say quietly, "shouldn't I at least speak with him before the end?"

Derrick's mouth presses into a hard line. "You weren't here to see the things he's done," he says quietly. "He's so far gone, he might not give a damn about you."

I blanch at that, blinking back the tears that suddenly prick at my eyes. I don't have a response; there's nothing from my memories to insist that Derrick is wrong. Only what I feel. And I don't know if I can trust that, either.

So I roll the corpses into the pit and help Derrick cover them up with dirt.

CHAPTER 4

ERRICK URGES me through the forest at a demanding speed. If I slow to a jog, he pushes me to go faster. "The farther we get from those bodies before nightfall, the better," he says. "I've got people to warn."

I almost stumble over a tree root. I'm breathing so hard I can't say anything at first. Finally, I manage: "Fly ahead?"

Derrick's mouth sets in a line. "No."

"But—"

"I'm not leaving you." His wings flick in agitation. "Not when I'm half convinced you're the product of either some insane dream or my overactive imagination. And I just got my shoulder seat back. Now, move your arse."

I pick up my pace, sprinting until my muscles burn. Neither of us speaks, not even hours later, when we find an abandoned cottage deep in the woods. Derrick decides we're far enough from the dead forest to rest for the night.

And not a moment too soon, because I am about to keel over.

The thatched roof is sturdy enough to keep out most of the rain. The air inside is musty. A single hole in the corner of the stonework lets in enough rain that water and moss have spread along the walls.

My feet ache. Carefully, I lower my sore body to the cold stone floor and sit while Derrick rummages in a trunk on the far side of the room. The blankets he finds inside are moth-eaten and dirty, the old wool riddled with holes. With a contented sigh, he pulls a needle and thread from his coat pocket and starts stitching up the fabric.

"Derrick." I test the weight of his name on my tongue, hoping to use it to conjure a memory. The sense of home returns, the comfort, but no memories. No images of my former life.

"Aileana." I try my own name, reaching to the dark parts of my mind. I have to know why I came back. *How* I came back. I whisper my name over and over until it's a breath on my lips. Until it's no more than a sound. That feeling of immense burden rises again and I try to weather it. I let the storm build and see where it takes me, but beyond it, there's still nothing.

Oh, confound it. I give up.

"I had another name," I say, irritated by my inability to recall even the most basic things. "Didn't I? It was shorter. One syllable."

Derrick goes quiet, and his fingers are suddenly still. He's avoiding my gaze. "You did." He jabs the needle through the material and bites his lip. He's thinking hard, that much is obvious.

I narrow my eyes. "I may not have my memories of you, but I know that look. You don't want to be honest with me."

"Fine." He shrugs. "If you want honesty, I prefer *Aileana*. It's distinctive, rolls off the tongue in a pleasant—"

"Tell me or I won't let you sit on my shoulder."

"Kam," Derrick finally says in a short sigh. "*He* called you Kam, short for your surname, Kameron. There. Are you happy now?"

Kam. That's the one. I recall the sound of it between wild kisses, as if he would never tire of saying it. *Kam.* I love that name. I can feel him whispering it against the pulse at my throat. It meant everything. It *said* everything.

But with those memories comes a reminder of the urgent message I came back to deliver. It's to do with him. It's why I'm here.

"Derrick," I say softly. He looks over at me, cautious now. "Is *he* the Unseelie King?"

He's quiet for the longest time. "Aye."

"Did I love him?"

"More than anything."

It hurts to swallow. "Did he love me?"

Rain taps against the roof. A breeze rattles the wooden door. When Derrick speaks, his voice is so soft, I strain to hear him. "He loved you so much that when you died, he might as well have died with you."

The next morning, we continue our journey through the woods, with a pace just as grueling as before. The forest has grown so shadowed that I can barely see the ground in front of me. Beyond the far-reaching tops of the trees, the slate-gray clouds are heavy with rain, dark enough to appear shaded with ink.

I notice with some bewilderment that the sky is not the only part of the landscape that's monochrome. The farther we travel, the more the forest seems entirely bled of color, like I'm walking through a charcoal drawing. The minimal traces of green among the trees are faded, as if coated with a layer of fine dust. The leaves are all withering, the branches brittle.

The entire forest is dying.

When I brush my fingertips against the trunks of the trees, the life force there quivers faintly beneath my touch—a slow, fading beat. The pulse of a living thing in its last days, as it struggles to take its final breaths. Just like the voice from my memory.

Accept the offer, child.

That small flash is enough to make my heart slam painfully against my chest. She had a voice of destruction. One I can still feel viscerally, a stroke of cold fingertips down my spine.

The only thing that works to lessen my unease is when Derrick tells me about my past. About how I grew up in Edinburgh as the daughter of a marquess. About how he and I met after my mother was murdered. He regales me with tales of the nights I spent killing faeries, until the day they rose up from the mounds beneath the city and raided Scotland. They destroyed every village and township—and then they continued their destruction elsewhere. All this while I had been captured and imprisoned in their realm.

Derrick talks and talks, but his account of my life is missing the details of the Unseelie King. Who he was, how he and I met, how I came to love him. The things he's done since my death. Every time he almost comes up, Derrick changes the subject.

So I don't mention him again. Derrick is content to sit on my shoulder and tell stories about our misadventures. He seems amused by the fact that my previous life summed up is basically death, destruction, and murder—in that order. What a miserable existence.

"So you thought I was dead once before, and then I *did* die?" I ask in disbelief. "This is something I do often? Die and come back?"

Now I'm not certain I *want* my memories. No wonder I've blocked it all out. Maybe my burden became too much and I decided to bid goodbye and good bloody riddance to Aileana Kameron. She was a girl who lived for vengeance and became blinded by it. By the time she realized that, it was too late to change anything.

Only she wasn't a different girl. She was me, and I had the chance to save the world and failed.

Maybe I wanted to start over.

Derrick's hands are in my hair again, plaiting, plaiting, always plaiting. He said he would only do one strand and now there are about fifteen braids lost in my curls. Later, when I take them out, my hair is going to look like a bird's nest, I'm sure of it.

I wonder if it's because Derrick enjoys the task, or if he touches me to remind himself that I'm not a figment of his imagination. Or if he's deliberately trying to make my hair look ridiculous. The former, I hope.

"You know how a cat has nine lives?" he asks.

I sigh when I feel him start on another strand. "No."

"Well, they have nine and you have . . . well, I don't know how many at this point. At least twelve. More than any other human I've ever met, certainly." His hands move deftly as he braids. "So I kept searching for you because I thought that maybe, like a cat, you'd just show up one day and start making demands."

I step over the trunk of a felled tree as we cross a forest glen. "You thought I'd just show up? Even after you burned my body and buried my ashes?"

After he'd told me about fae funeral rites, the way I came back made more sense. No wonder it felt like my throat was lined with ash, my body was covered in soot, and I had to claw my way out of the ground. My body was burned on a pyre. My ashes were put into the ground. My death was final.

Bringing me back after all that must have required a great deal of power. I had to be rebuilt—bone, muscle, blood, heart, and mind. All of it.

Derrick goes quiet. "Aye." I know he wants to say more, but instead he clears his throat and quickly adds, "After all, you're my companion. I can always sense you, even when you don't feel the same, and even when you smell of death and misery."

My feet are silent on the ground as I slip through the trees, my movements light, my pace quick. I may not know where he's leading me, and I may be reluctant to remember the difficult parts of my past, but something in my memories is demanding that I hurry. I need to get my memories back before . . .

Before what?

That trembling, ancient voice is whispering in my ear again, but I can't make out the words.

At my second frustrated breath, Derrick puts his chin in his hands and says, "So are you going to share what's going on in that silly mind of yours or shall we play a guessing game? Does it involve murdering something?"

"No." My head hurts. "Don't you wonder what brought me back? Why I'm here?"

"Of course I do," he says in a tone that sounds like *I'm not a bloody idiot.* "Your memory is shite. You smell weird, your eyes are weird, your scars are gone, which is weird, your skin is—"

"Weird?" I guess.

"*Feverishly hot.*" He makes an exasperated sound. "That's not normal. Don't humans die if they get too hot?" When I open my mouth to reply, he shushes me. "Never mind. And stop asking the other questions, because once they're answered, it's going to ruin everything. I just know it."

"Fine. Then tell me why you looked for me when you knew I was dead."

Derrick flinches and looks away. It wasn't my intent to bring up something so painful. And it must be—his wings have drooped and he has finally stopped plaiting my blasted hair.

After a few minutes, he finally says, "I wished for you. I spent two and a half months wishing for you. To see you one last time."

"Before what?"

"I don't know yet."

I almost tell him I'm not the Aileana he deserved, the one he wanted. He hoped for his friend, and instead he got me—a not-quite-human creature whose mind is empty. Maybe when the dead come back, they're always wrong. Different. Maybe it's not something Aithinne can fix.

"I don't know if I believe in wishes," I murmur, almost to myself. It's like believing in hope. They make you want things you can't have. Wishes are dangerous things.

"Maybe you should." He sounds almost defensive. "Wishes hold power. We believe that if you love someone and wish for them hard enough, they'll return to you. Here you are. I loved you enough; we all did. I'm guessing *he* did, too."

He. Him. As if by Derrick not saying his name, the Unseelie King ceases to be who he was, someone I loved. I know the power names hold better than anyone. Yesterday, I was a girl without an identity, someone risen from the ashes of a dead forest.

A girl whose only memories were the movements her body made during a slaughter.

Now I have a name. And with that comes the expectation that I'm unchanged, still the same Aileana killed by a sword to the chest while she tried to save the world. Derrick believes I can be fixed—and I don't have the heart to suggest that maybe you can't fix what's already dead.

Just like maybe I can't save the Unseelie King. Perhaps Derrick is right and the parts of the man I loved died with me and he can't be fixed, either.

Another memory is tugging at the dark corners of my mind; insistent, demanding. I can't help but follow it. In my mind I'm standing next to a shadowed figure in a forest like this. That ruinous voice echoes in my thoughts again, sharp this time. Angry. Desperate. *There's nothing you can do. One of them has to die.*

Something about that memory is important. Vital. When I try to chase it again, it slips through my fingers. "Damn it," I breathe. "Derrick—"

A flicker of something in the woods slows my pace. Like before, when the other fae found me: a taste of power.

Damnation. It's just as Derrick said: They've come looking. Only I didn't think they would find us this far out or this quickly. They must have followed our trail; we never strayed from the forest. Have they found the other bodies yet? I can only hope not.

They might be silent, but I can *feel* them moving through the woods. The pressure of their feet in the dirt. The cadence of their breath. They're close.

I murmur a curse and say Derrick's name again.

"What?" He flicks his wings hard against my cheek. "Look, don't finish that sentence if it's about what brought you back. I just know it's going to make me unhappy."

I ignore him and slip behind a tree. The cloth of my tattered dress scrapes against the bark and it sounds like fingernails scratching wood. I cringe.

"What are you doing?" Derrick asks.

I put a finger to my lips and motion with my hands to indicate we're not alone. He goes still, his expression intent. He's listening.

Derrick's eyes widen a fraction. He senses them, too.

"Soldiers. A dozen of them," he breathes against my ear.

CHAPTER 5

I F THEY'RE here because they found the bodies, we have to hurry and warn Aithinne they're coming," Derrick says.

"Can we reach her before nightfall?"

"If we're quick. Shh." Derrick presses a restraining hand to my neck, an indication to be still.

The other fae are almost upon us. They move through the trees, fanning out in a quick, efficient formation. They are dressed in black, their skin shining opalescent in the low light. They pause every so often, as if they sense something isn't right. Their power snakes through the trees, searching— not just for me, but for their fellow soldiers. The ones I killed.

"Are we still in the King's territory?" I ask in a low whisper. I see Derrick nod out of the corner of my eye. "They haven't found them yet. I can feel them searching."

A few feet from us, the fae go still. I press a hand over my mouth to muffle my breathing.

Derrick whispers in my ear, his voice so low I strain to hear it. "We'll hide. No killing. The King will know if this many don't come back soon." He peeks around my shoulder. "Edge to the other side of the trunk. Now. Go, *go*."

I don't argue. I ease around the trunk, pressing my body against it. Then my foot crunches a twig. Derrick presses his hand to my skin again. *Wait. Stop.*

The fae haven't moved. When I peek around the tree, I notice they're in attack formation, listening and waiting for any enemy. They're so still, as if they're not even breathing.

I reach out with my abilities—nothing more than a searching stroke through the air—and I sense that they're connected. A web of power links each soldier into a cohesive unit. It keeps the darkness of their hunger for human energy at bay, a burden shared by the group.

Unseelie. Just like the other fae.

I could try to send them somewhere else. I brush their minds with my power, a slight suggestion, a nudge: *Maybe you should go back the other way.*

As if he can sense what I'm doing, Derrick turns sharply toward me. I stroke a finger down his wings to reassure him, but he shakes his head rapidly, fingernails sinking into my neck. I can't help the startled jerk that causes me to lose control over my powers.

The small nudge I had intended to give the fae becomes a *shove*. An obvious declaration: *I'm right here.*

Oh, bloody hell.

A ripple of awareness moves through the group. Their powers search the air, grasping at mine and prodding to find its source—

My power retaliates. It fills me, the ache in my chest growing. It *screams* at me to *let it out let it out let it out.* I'm dimly aware of Derrick whispering things in my ear, saying my name to try to bring me back. His power attempts to wrap around mine.

Mistake. My power shoves him out, and Derrick tumbles from my shoulder. His wings barely beat in time to save him from slamming into the ground.

"Aileana!"

His startled cry isn't enough to break through the pounding, unrelenting power roaring to get out. I can't stop it. I can't control it.

I let it go.

It wraps me in a cloak of darkness, thick and impenetrable. I am suddenly calm, my pulse a steady cadence. My mind slides right back into the instinct of a hunt. It's so easy. My power assures me that I am perfect. I am untouchable. Without my memory, it's the only thing that can help me feel complete again.

I ease away from the tree, ignoring the pixie attempting to grasp at my hair. He says a name—my name—but I'm too far gone to care. I don't remember that name. I don't remember that girl. I flick him away with my power so easily.

Then I'm moving fast. To the next trunk, then the next, an unseen predator stalking her prey. I move as if I were part of the shadows. As languid and easy as smoke through the trees.

The fae never even see me as I whirl between them. Not when I whisper in their ears, counting down the moments until their deaths. *You first. Then you. I'll save you for last.*

The Unseelie stir, their breath coming fast. Their fear is an elixir.

Until another thread of energy—of fright—makes me pause. Derrick. He's afraid of me. Just the sick, rancid taste of it makes me lose my concentration. I brush against the tree with an audible *scratch*, and the nearest fae turns with a blade in his hand.

He strikes high and I barely move in time. He slices me across the shoulder.

That's all it takes. I throw back my head with a rough, savage hiss. My blade is in my hands before he can move again. I lash out, catch his throat. I feel the eyes of the others on me, taking in the sight of my dripping blade, shadows rising around me, the body at my feet.

One of them screams—a sharp cry that echoes through the forest. As one, they dive for me.

My sword whistles through the air, nothing more than a blur. Skin breaks beneath my blade; blood splatters across the ground. I am faster than they could ever hope to be. I move like a dancer, in graceful whirls and kicks and rapid slashes.

I am powerful. I am merciless. Each kill fills me up, gives me more energy. My massacre is as swift as spreading darkness.

Something comes at me, a light out of the corner of my eye. I grasp it before I even know what it is, a small body in my hand, my fingers closing over tiny bones and soft, breakable wings.

"*Aileana!*"

That's Derrick's voice. Derrick's scream. I stare down at him in shock, catching his stricken expression before he flies off into the trees.

I drag in a breath as I survey my kills. I did this. Derrick saw me do this. He saw me lose control.

Why don't I feel anything?

Not even pride or accomplishment—and something tells me I felt those things about battle once. That later, I fought only out of necessity, survival. Kill or be killed. Either way, I felt *something*.

I gaze at the dozen dead fae across the forest floor and I know this: I didn't do this out of necessity. I could have forced them away. I could have run and they wouldn't have captured me. If I disarmed them, none could have defeated me. I slaughtered them all, because I could.

I would have killed Derrick, too.

A rough sound escapes Derrick's throat. He's settled on a branch in a nearby tree, examining the bent tip of his wing.

Then he turns and stares down at me through a glistening veil of tears. He doesn't say anything, but I feel his fear again. The taste of it is foul, bile down the back of my throat.

I did that. I injured his wing. *I did that.*

"You hurt me," he says, his voice trembling with anger and . . . something else. Something like betrayal. "You *hurt* me."

I know from his voice that I've never hurt him before. Not once.

That's all it takes for me to rein in my power. To stuff it back into its too-small bone case and let it settle inside me with the ache that I deserve. And when I do, I'm suddenly aware of Derrick's thoughts. I can hear them so clearly, as if he were saying the words aloud.

She slaughtered a dozen fae in under a minute.

She's a monster wearing the skin of a girl.

She came back wrong.

Is that how he sees me?

Without thinking, I shove into Derrick's mind. His thoughts are prismlike, a cacophony of colors and images. At first they're unclear, difficult for me to understand. My mind doesn't work this way; even now, it's still too human, too simple.

Each thought is layered, never one at a time. It's a complex intermingling of observations and smatterings of gold and red hues and images. His sounds have taste. His tastes have texture. His colors evoke feelings and desires.

The color he had given me—the old Aileana—was amber; the texture and taste is like honey. His favorite thing in the world other than me. A girl with wild copper hair and a smile as devious as his own. A girl whose bravery he admired. A girl he felt so close to that she became his family when all the rest had died.

I've eclipsed that Aileana and become something less than human. Because that's what I am: a creature. Not human, not fae—a girl in-between, powerful and formidable. Someone dangerous. Someone who could easily hurt him without meaning to.

I bite back a gasp when I see myself through Derrick's eyes. He sees his friend—the girl he searched for these last two months, wishing that she'd come back from the dead. And here I am, right in front of him: dripping with blood, my face covered in it. My eyes glow fierce and bright and inhuman; *freakish* eyes. As uncanny as any fae. Shadows gather around me like a cloak, a shroud.

And beyond the images and colors and textures, a single thought of Derrick's rings as clear as a bell: *She's not my Aileana.*

That thought makes my chest ache. Not his Aileana. Not his friend. I'm just a monster who doesn't remember where she came from or who she is.

I don't care what she looks like, his thoughts continue. *She's not my Aileana.*

"Get. Out. Of. My. Head," Derrick says through clenched teeth.

I hadn't realized I had forced him to stay unmoving while I read his thoughts. I used my powers against him effortlessly, without giving any thought to them at all. First I hurt him, then I broke into his mind.

He's right: You are a monster. I shut my eyes and pull away.

The moment my power leaves him, Derrick's breathing turns ragged, as if he's trying to find his bearings. His lips tremble. He smooths the thin line of his left wing. It's straightened slightly, healing.

I'm sorry, I almost say. But I swallow my apologies down because I don't deserve his forgiveness. I read his thoughts without permission. I could have killed him.

I wonder if, in the heat of battle, I would have even cared.

"I'm different from the girl I was," I say, trying to keep the tremor out of my voice. *She was in control of herself. She didn't hurt you. She loved you.*

Without memories, the feeling of home isn't enough. Without them, I've learned nothing, been nowhere. I have no parts of myself to remind me of what I've lost, what I've overcome, who I am, who I've been.

An apology is on my lips again. *I'm sorry. I'm sorry I'm this shadow creature who doesn't remember the girl you loved and lost. I'm sorry you wished for her and got me instead.*

Derrick's fear turns to anger. His power is as sharp as blades on my tongue. "How dare you?" he snaps. "I could forgive you hurting me—I know how easy it is to lose yourself in battle. But how *dare* you invade my mind like that? You didn't even try to stop yourself."

"I know." My words are barely audible, but he hears them anyway. "I'm sorry. I am."

"Don't," he grits out. "You don't know and you're *not* sorry. How the hell could you be?" He rakes me with a glare, hard and accusatory. "The friend I knew had someone break into her mind, day after day, for months. If you were her, you would *never* have done that to anyone. Not after what Lonnrach did."

After what Lonnrach did.

Teeth biting me over and over. They sank in so deep that blood slid down my skin and dripped onto the floor. *Drip, drip, drip.* Thirty-six human teeth. Forty-six fangs that descended from his gums, pointed at their tips like a snake's.

They left behind hundreds of scars that dotted my arms, shoulders, chest, and neck. They were a declaration: *You're mine. I own you.*

But when I feel for those scars, they're not there. They're on that other body, the one burned on a pyre by the loch. Whoever brought me back left behind the only scar that mattered: the one that had killed me.

Those other scars held memories. They held parts of the Aileana I was and now all that's left of her are flashes in my mind, pieces of a puzzle I can't put back together.

Unable to stop myself, I tell Derrick again, "I'm sorry."

"Stop saying that," he grits out. His wings buzz with agitation, as quick as a dragonfly's. He runs his hands through his hair. "God, I can still feel you in my head." When I don't respond, he says, "You were empty inside. Like you're just some *thing*, not her—"

"I don't have my memory," I snap. "You think my mind was empty? *Try living it.*"

We're both breathing hard, staring at each other like two strangers. Derrick's light has darkened to a shadowed halo around him. He looks stricken, as if he just realized what he called me.

You're just some thing.

"I don't know what I'm doing," I tell him, my voice almost breaking. "I don't know who I am or where I belong; I just know that when I woke up I had this power inside me that I couldn't control. The only thing that felt right was killing *them*." I gesture to the bodies at my feet. "When you called me by my name, a part of me didn't want to remember anything else. It hurt too much."

"Aileana."

"Wait." I hold back my tears. I don't want him to see me cry. "I know I'm not the same. I injured you. I broke into your mind. You wished for someone else and got me and I'm all wrong. But the moment I saw you, I was home. I didn't need to have memories of you to know that I trust you and I need your help." When Derrick doesn't respond, I whisper, "Please. Help me."

He stares at me, unspeaking. I have the sudden urge to hold him close, to stroke my fingers down his wings as if that would help calm him. Because I can't tell him over and over again, *I am her*. The only difference is that I came back broken.

You're just some thing.

"I'm sorry," I say. Again. A damn echo. *Sorry sorry sorry. Sorry I'm a disappointment. Sorry I'm all wrong. Sorry I'm a remorseless killer. Sorry I'm a thing. Not human.*

I look down at the bodies littered across the forest floor and feel a sudden sense of helplessness, a burden more overpowering than my name.

I hold my breath when I hear the flutter of Derrick's wings. He lands on my shoulder, his touch gentle. "I didn't think about what it was like for you." At my surprised expression, he explains, "I wished for you, and you came back, and I'm the ungrateful bastard who couldn't accept that you weren't exactly the same. How could you be? Why *should* you be? Just because I wanted it?"

"That doesn't justify what I did."

"No," Derrick agrees. "But after what you've been through . . ." He shakes his head.

I finally allow a tear to fall. "You're lovely. I can see why I never murdered you."

Derrick's smile is small. "Oh, please. As if you ever could." He notices my tears and sighs, murmuring, "You should know, I never can stay mad at you when you're crying." His wing brushes against my cheek, but he keeps his distance. He's not angry with me, but whatever he saw in my mind scared him. When I try to catch his gaze, he turns away. "Help me bury them. If we hurry, we'll reach Aithinne's camp before nightfall."

We begin to dig.

CHAPTER 6

NCE WE leave the woods, Derrick leads me around a fissure that stretches for miles.

Waves crash against the rocks deep at the bottom, rolling against the escarpment. Each swell comes with a soft sigh of grinding stone—the steady breath of the ocean. I don't dare stray too close to the unstable edge. Every few minutes, I see massive pieces of the rock break off and tumble into the chasm. The earth is falling apart, little by little.

The sight is unnerving; I've seen it somewhere before, in the missing pieces of my memories. But it wasn't here. It was in that place I recalled by the loch, where there were forests full of demons and metal trees with branches as sharp as blades.

When I open my mouth to ask Derrick about it, he flies off and I hurry after him. I should keep my eyes ahead, but my attention is drawn back to the landscape. To the dull color of the sky and trees—even more apparent here than in the forest.

The sky is a single, unending slab of slate gray. There is no texture to the clouds, not a single ray of sunshine or a heaviness to indicate rain. In contrast, the trees are etched in deep black hues, as if they've been scorched by flames. Only the smallest traces of pigment show beneath the drab, ashen landscape. Even the hills, which should be at the very least a deep brown at this time of year, are the somber shade of dust.

Derrick darts around some boulders against a particularly rocky part of the ravine and I follow him, scrambling up the rough granite. "Where are we?" I finally ask, tired of the silence.

Derrick hasn't spoken since the forest. When he thinks I'm not looking, I catch him staring, studying me. As if he's thinking about what he saw when my mind invaded his. Maybe he's wondering if I can ever be fixed.

I don't miss the way he looks away sharply, guilt flashing in his features, as if he suddenly realizes how quiet he's been. He might have forgiven me for what I did to him back in the woods, but I can sense how tense he is, like he's waiting for me to lose control again.

"Skye," he says mechanically. "We're still on Skye. We never left."

"Still?" I ask lightly, so as not to upset him.

In the hours we've been walking, I have taken care not to move like I did back in the forest. I keep my powers reined in so tightly that it's painful. I don't want Derrick to see that monster again. That *thing*.

I want him to see me like I'm a human—the way I used to be. His Aileana. His friend.

"You died on the island," he says. "We could have gone somewhere else, but there's not much point when it's all falling apart." He gives me a smile that doesn't reach his eyes. "Any plans before that happens? You could always get blackout drunk with me. We could sing inappropriate songs, dress like pirates, and dance over the entrails of our enemies."

I wrinkle my nose. "Is that something I enjoy?"

"Not yet. But only because you've never tried it. I assure you, it comes highly recommended."

"By whom?"

"By *me*." He huffs. "Honestly, Aileana, everyone ought to dress up like an inebriated pirate at least once. It's much more fun killing things in costume."

I can't help but smile when he calls me by my name. It's the first time he's said it since the forest, and the sound of it wraps around me like a warm blanket. In the past few hours I've begun to remember feelings associated with that name. Stirrings of memories that include Derrick's wee body curled against the crook of my neck, hands tangled in my hair because he'd fallen asleep plaiting it.

"Then I'll try it," I say, approaching the edge of the fissure. "We'll dress like pirates, and we'll dance, and you'll sing me a song before the end. And maybe we'll stab a few things with cutlasses."

He flies over to my shoulder as I inch closer to the ledge, careful lest the rocks fall. "Are you all right?"

I shake my head. My memory stirs again, with images from that nightmarish place that are so overshadowed by fear that I can't see beyond it. I try to trigger other thoughts by kicking a large rock over the lip of the crag. It tumbles down the escarpment and into the sea below.

There it is. A man's voice somewhere in the shadows of my past. *The land was whole and now it's cracked right down the middle. It's all falling apart.*

I was on an island floating in the air within a vast chasm, like a leaf on a river stream. It drifted endlessly through an alien landscape even more colorless than this one. It had been full of buildings set atop platforms made of jagged rocks hanging in empty space.

That memory comes with teeth. With a sense of helplessness that makes me sick to my stomach. A name floats to the top of my memory. "This looks like the *Sìth-bhrùth*," I say to myself.

Derrick turns sharply. "What makes you say that?"

I don't know.

When I search my memories for something about the *Sìth-bhrùth*, the only thing that comes up is an overwhelming sense of despair and grief and desperation. Whatever my reason for being there, it was not of my own free will. I was trapped there.

"I think it was like this." I stare out at the colorless landscape. "It didn't always look this way here, did it?"

"No. It started shortly after—" Derrick bites his lip and I know what he was about to say. *After I died.* He continues as if he never stopped. "First it was just the color. Then one day the land started breaking apart all across the island and the mainland. I expect it's only a matter of time before this whole bloody place crumbles into the sea."

I glance at the escarpment, at the sea below. "What then?"

Derrick's laugh is short, strangely bitter. "What then? The end of the world, unless Aithinne kills Ki—the King. If she doesn't, I hope my end is swift and painless. By then, we'll have collapsed on the ground in our pirate costumes, I hope."

The end of the world. The message I have to recall tugs at me in that dark trembling voice again. *Remember,* I tell myself. *Remember. You have to remember.*

Accept the offer, child.

And if I don't?

Skeletal arms wrapping hard around me. Agonizing pain as if every bone in my body were being pieced back together again, muscles and sinew being formed anew.

A woman's voice amid the torment. *Our realms will be destroyed.*

"She died," I whisper, finally realizing what that memory meant. "The woman in my memories. When she died, it caused all of this." I don't know how to explain who *she* was, except that she was someone important. Someone who held power over these realms.

"You're not making any sense," Derrick says. "You're not fuddled, are you? Is this something to do with your broken mind?" Then he puts up a hand hastily. "Never mind. Don't answer that. I keep forgetting you've—"

"Derrick." My voice is breathless. At his questioning look, I say, "I think she told me how to save the realms."

CHAPTER 7

ITHINNE'S CAMP is in the middle of the woods, where the trees are so colorless, they're almost black.

Lit torches form a massive circle through the trees, the flames flickering high. Beyond the light are three stone cottages. The structures have been hastily and haphazardly built, the walls composed of larger stones interspersed with smaller rocks and uneven, thrown-together thatched roofs. The dwellings form an arc around a massive fire-pit burning high enough to bathe the camp in a dim, golden glow. Though the sun hasn't set yet, the rest of the forest is so dark that it might as well be night.

There are three people sitting on logs by the fire, speaking in hushed tones. One of them is a girl with blond hair, her delicate features illuminated in the light. She's sitting close to a muscular young man wearing an eye-patch, who leans closer and whispers in her ear. She laughs, nudging the other man with her elbow.

He looks so much like her. My fae powered senses can make out the details of his features even from here: the same hair color, the same blue eyes. I can see the scars that frame one side of his face around his eye. When he laughs, it's quieter, more restrained.

Something about the scene makes me swallow back a lump in my throat, makes me want to apologize for something, and I'm not certain what.

Just when I'm about to step forward into the light, Derrick flutters in front of me and puts up his hands. "Not yet. Not until we see what can be done about your memories." His expression is firm, no-nonsense. "Stay here while I get Aithinne."

Derrick flies off in a flurry of wings, zooming right past the people around the bonfire. He ignores their surprised greetings and makes for one of the structures. He shoves his way through the rickety wooden door and it closes with a slam.

From the shadows of the forest, I watch the trio around the fire with a longing that aches. I know them. I'm positive I do.

I loved you enough; we all did.

I might be the Aileana who came back from the dead, but I'm not *their* Aileana. I don't have memories of how each of these people loved me. I don't recall how much I loved them in return.

Despite that, I can't ignore the impulse to tell them *I'm here. I'm alive.*

The feeling is so strong that I shift on my feet, about to move forward, when I see a faery—the Seelie Queen, it must be—throw open the cottage door Derrick just went through. He trails behind Aithinne as she strides past the fire.

One of the humans asks if everything is all right. Aithinne responds with a quick, distracted nod, and hurries through the trees at Derrick's direction. I stand still under the dark cover of the branches until she sees me.

Her eyes meet mine, and she makes a sound in her throat. "*Trobhad seo*," she says. Before I can do or say anything, her arms are around me in a crushing embrace. Then she's murmuring in another language, one I've heard before but don't understand. "*Chan eil mi tuigsinn, agus chan eil e gu diofar.* You're back! You're alive!"

Aithinne's power calls to mine, wraps around me as warm as her physical embrace. It's like an old coat I've worn a thousand times. I've used that power before, in the life I don't remember. I know I have.

Aithinne pulls back and grins, taking in the state of me. "Oh, my goodness, look at you!" she says in delight. "You look wonderful for someone who just came back from the dead. All of your limbs are exactly where they should be."

Derrick flutters beside us, clicking his tongue. "She doesn't remember you, you ninny. Can you fix her or not?"

Aithinne tilts her head, never losing her smile. "Maybe. Do you know, I've never fixed anyone's mind before," she says brightly. Then she leans in, as if to tell a secret. "I hope I don't make your head explode. It's rather nicely shaped."

"Aye," I say dryly. "Especially since I need it."

"Fix her scent," Derrick says, "She doesn't smell the same and I don't like it. My shoulder seat isn't nearly as pleasant and it's making me unhappy."

"Well, her scent might be different, but the lack of memories hasn't changed her scowl. Such a magnificent murderous glare you have," she tells me. "I love it. Teach me."

"For god's sake, Aithinne," Derrick says. "Admit it, you got into my honey stash and now you're completely foxed, because she's not—"

"Can we focus on the task at hand?" I ask impatiently. "I'd like my memories back."

Aithinne moves closer, her nose nearly touching mine. Her eyes are an exquisite, bright silver, the color swirling. Suddenly, she sniffs and wrinkles her nose. "You smell like my mother."

Derrick pauses right in the middle of another agitated loop around the trees. "Your mother? As in the Cailleach, the deranged former monarch, your mother?"

"I'm afraid so." Aithinne is standing so close that my first instinct is to step back and preserve some semblance of personal space. That is, until she says, "I'll need to go into your mind for this. Will you let me?"

After Derrick's response to what I did to him, I hesitate. I can only hope it's different if you give permission. I don't want to lose control over my powers again. But if this is the only way to regain what I lost . . .

I shut my eyes and nod.

Aithinne places her hands on either side of my head and I feel her power extend toward me. The touch of it is light at first, as gentle as a summer breeze. Then all at once, it pricks me with a hard, swift sting.

My power shoves back at hers and Aithinne flinches.

"Blimey." Her energy unfurls toward me again, more careful this time. Stroking, dancing around mine with a prodding touch. "Well, that's . . . not good."

Something about the way she says that knots my stomach in dread. "What?"

Aithinne shakes her head once. "Let me in. I need to see."

My power resists at first. It's defensive; it doesn't like someone else touching or manipulating it. Aithinne soothes it the way one might calm a wild animal: by proving she's not a threat. She coaxes it to relax in gentle touches. Then, after several moments, it does and she's through.

Bursts of memory come so fast that I can barely keep up. Me on a cliff at sunset with a touch of cold fingertips along my spine. The skeletal woman stands next to me, her body trembling with her last breaths.

The woman is speaking about a book. What book?

I cry out as Aithinne delves further into my mind, tearing through memories like she's scratching at my skin. It hurts. It hurts. *It hurts.*

My power surges, all heat and bluster—a clear message to *back off.* I'm aware of Aithinne clinging to me, her fingers digging into my shoulders hard enough to bruise. She manages to pull up the memory we need—the one I've tried to recall all this time.

Leabhar Cuimhne. The Book of Remembrance.

My power slams into her. With a startled gasp, Aithinne is thrown into the air. She smacks hard into a nearby tree, landing in a heap on the ground.

Derrick flies over to help her. "What the hell happened?" he asks me.

I don't know.

My head is pounding. Memories flash across my mind—too fast for me to grasp. As if Aithinne broke open a door and didn't shut it behind her. I'm assaulted by feelings and images and thoughts and words and it's too much. There are too many.

Me running through the streets of Edinburgh at night. Me in a mirrored room, helpless and at the mercy of Lonnrach. Me impaled through the chest and my vision fading as I died just in time to see—

Kiaran.

Kiaran. That's his name. *Him. The Unseelie King.* Kiaran.

He loved you so much that when you died, he might as well have died with you.

Dimly, I hear the distant clamor of footsteps. "Aithinne?" a familiar voice calls. Then: "Bloody hell. What happened?"

The blond woman by the fire. Catherine, my best friend. *I remember. I remember.*

Catherine sees me and freezes. Her voice is ragged with emotion when she finally speaks. "Aileana?"

"Don't go near her." Derrick shoves his way between us, his halo flashing crimson. "Until Aileana has a hold over her powers, she might hurt you. So don't move."

My heart squeezes at his words. *She might hurt you.*

Derrick has never said that about me. Ever. I'm his companion, his friend. Our history repeats behind my eyes and each instance is like a blade twisting a little deeper in my gut. Even at my darkest, he trusted me. He always has. Until now. .

Catherine seems uncertain until her eyes meet mine. Her expression softens. "Are you all right?"

"Did you miss the part where she threw Aithinne into a tree?" Derrick demands. "Do *you* want to be tossed around like a sack of potatoes?" He throws up his hands. "Humans. You don't listen."

I step back, wishing I knew what to say. I almost tell Derrick that I recall everything now. How we met. The day he claimed his closet. Him and me and our misadventures. But then the memories of Lonnrach return, and the torture I endured in his prison. Lonnrach forced his way into my mind. He read my thoughts. He stole my memories.

And I did that. I did that to Derrick.

"She just surprised me," Aithinne says before I can speak. She manages to pull herself into a sitting position, looking a bit dazed. "See? I'm excellent."

Aithinne must have a demented definition of *excellent*; I don't think I've ever seen a faery try three times to get to her feet and still end up on her arse.

"*Surprised you?*" Derrick's sharp gaze assesses her. "Your nose is bleeding. You're wobbling like a tavern drunkard."

Aithinne touches her nose, and her fingers come away with blood. I can't help but wince at the sight of it. I did that, without meaning to. I wounded the Seelie Queen.

"Oh. Well, that's interesting," she says. "I don't have many occasions to see my own blood." And she isn't at all bothered by it, or her inability to stand.

"You're absolutely ridiculous," Derrick says, shaking his head. Then he looks at me. "Now you. Did she—"

"I remember," I say quietly. *I'm sorry for what I did. I'm so sorry.* "Everything." Derrick squeals in glee and is about to fly to my shoulder, but I avoid him to crouch next to Aithinne. I can't face him yet. "You promise I didn't hurt you?"

Aithinne grasps my hand and I haul her to her feet. "Nothing worse than I've received in battle."

"Someone is going to have to explain this to me," Catherine says. Then she puts up a hand before anyone speaks. "But first . . ." She steps forward and pulls me in for a tight embrace. "I'm so glad you're back," she whispers.

"I am, too," I murmur.

Derrick finally loses all patience and swoops onto my shoulder, his halo brighter than a blasted street lamp. "Catherine, you've had your hug. Now shove off and give me a turn."

Catherine rolls her eyes. "So demanding."

Regret lances through me as I stroke my fingers around his wings. "I'm sorry," I breathe. "About what I did—"

"Hugs now, apologies later." I smile as he leans away and sniffs me. "Damn it. That smell is *still* there. Aithinne, why is the foul odor of your homicidal mother still plaguing my companion?"

Aithinne shifts, as if uncertain. "Aileana has the power of the Cailleach."

Derrick goes silent then. He looks at me sharply and so many emotions cross his features at once: dawning realization, pity, and then—finally—sadness. "Well, shit," he mutters. "*Shit.*"

My eyes meet Aithinne's. There's a question in her gaze. I know what she's thinking, what she wants to ask.

I can bring you back to life, but eventually my powers will kill you.

Don't tell them. I know my message is clear. *Please don't tell them they will lose me again.*

We both saw the memory. We both know the Cailleach's powers—these destructive abilities I can't control—are slowly killing me. It's only a matter of time. That's my curse. The gift of life will be taken away again if I can't find that book. But at least this time I can save them all.

And if we do find that book, they never have to know.

"My turn," Aithinne murmurs, wrapping her arms tightly around me. I don't move when she whispers in my ear, "My mother's dead, isn't she? I thought she might be when the forest started falling into the sea, but I thought . . ." She pulls away and I see a glimpse of her wet eyes. "Just that I'd see her one last time."

I'm scared, mo nighean.

The Cailleach held me until her skin tore away and turned to dust. And she did it so I would have one final chance to make things right. Just one.

This is my final gift to them.

"Do you know anything about the book she referred to?" I ask Aithinne.

Aithinne hesitates. "It's a child's story among my kind. You know better than anyone how warped those tales can become." She shakes her head. "Some of the older *sìthichean* in my territory might know more. I didn't even believe it was real."

"Your mother seemed to think it was. She wanted me to save you," I tell her gently. "Both of you."

Save them from an unchangeable fate: two monarchs born to power—one to rule the Seelie, the other to rule the Unseelie. The most powerful of the two would trigger a war, kill the other, and take the place of the last Cailleach . . . and so it had always been, until Aithinne and Kiaran refused to fight, and created the ripple effect that's fracturing both fae and human realms. A destruction that will stop only when one of them becomes the new Cailleach.

Unless I find that blasted book.

Aithinne's body tenses. "I don't know if Kadamach can be saved." My throat tightens when I see the message in her face, as clearly as if she had spoken it aloud. *I don't know if you can be saved, either.*

CHAPTER 8

M Y MEMORIES come with the kind of ache that feels as if my head is being taken apart and stitched back together again.

Catherine went off with the man in the eye-patch—her husband, Daniel—to find herbs to help with the pain. Aithinne hurried to check the boundary for any signs of other fae after Derrick told her about my kills back in the forest. She left so damn fast that I didn't have time to ask her about Kiaran.

And me . . . I scrubbed away the worst of the grime and changed into the trousers, thin shirt, and boots Derrick scrounged up for me on such short notice. Now I'm sitting by the fire, trying not to vomit from the nausea.

I pull the blanket tighter around my shoulders and flinch as another group of images bursts through my mind—this time from further back in my childhood: me and my mother;

our inventions; the way she sang during Sunday services. Little things that remind me that I've lost her.

Think of something else. Something that'll hurt less.

My mind doesn't obey. This time, my thoughts are filled with Kiaran. Me, kissing him like I couldn't get enough. Tracing my fingertips across the swirled marks on his body, physical remnants of the fae vows he made. The largest one was a penance he bears for all the deaths he's caused.

The way he looked at me when he said, *Aoram dhuit. I will worship thee.*

Each repetition hurts more than the last. Aithinne thinks I lost my memories because my body was destroyed. That when the Cailleach's magic brought me back, my mind took longer to piece together. When Aithinne's power connected with mine, she opened the floodgates.

Catherine's brother Gavin settles on the log beside me. "You look miserable."

His blond hair is longer now, almost touching the base of his neck. Stubble has grown along his jaw, obscuring part of the scar that begins just below his eye.

How different he is from the boy I knew growing up. Gavin went from the perfect, titled gentleman to this—one of the few humans left alive, thanks in no small part to his gift of the Sight, the natural ability to see the fae. We earned our abilities the same way: by dying and coming back.

All things considered, Gavin is taking my miraculous return rather well. When he saw me, all he did was smile and say, "You really intend on stretching the definition of *dead* until it loses all meaning, don't you?"

What would he say if I tell him my borrowed magic is all that's keeping me alive? That none of us will survive if I don't find the Book of Remembrance?

His response would probably be like Derrick's. *You're like a cat: You'll just gain another life.*

I sigh. "My head is splitting. I may vomit."

"Ah. Well, then this will either help or make it infinitely worse." Gavin presents a bottle of whisky. "You look like you could use a dram. Just don't throw up on my shoes."

"Good god, Galloway," I say with a laugh. "Only you would manage to have whisky on hand after everything's been destroyed. What's the occasion?"

Gavin shrugs. "You're alive. What you see here is probably the last bottle in existence, and I want you to enjoy it with me before the world ends."

I make a face. "Morbid."

"Appropriate."

A voice rings out from behind us. "There had better be some for me." Derrick flies over from one of the cottages and settles on my shoulder. "I'm out of honey," he grumbles, wings flicking my hair. "That foul-smelling peated shite is all that's left to help me achieve my goal of complete oblivion."

My body relaxes with Derrick there. Now that my memories are intact, I feel more in control. You don't realize how important even the smallest interactions are until your mind has been emptied of them all. It was as if I had never lived.

Gavin looks at the pixie and raises his eyebrow. "If you want me to share, don't insult my drink."

"*Shiiiite*," Derrick sings. "Go on, then. Give us a toast."

Gavin uncorks the bottle and raises it in a salute. "To Aileana's return, just in time for the inevitable war and our probable demise. But until then, *slàinte*." He takes a long swig. I can tell by his face that it burns. "Fair warning," he says hoarsely, passing me the bottle, "this is not going to go down smoothly."

I take the bottle from him, but I don't drink. "Probable demise? I don't suppose you or Daniel have had a vision that gives us some hope of winning?" My smile is forced. "If not, I'm hoping for a relatively painless death this time."

Aside from seeing faeries, those with the Sight have other abilities. Gavin has premonitions of the future, and Daniel hears voices that contain prophecy—about *me*, specifically. According to those voices, I'm the girl whose gift is chaos, who can either save the realms or end them.

I lived up to my gift: I'm the one who broke the world.

Gavin shakes his head. "No visions. Daniel hasn't heard any voices either. Everything has gone quiet, which I'm taking to be something of a bad omen." He winks at me. "So drink up, darling. Might as well drown our woes while it's still calm."

The whisky scorches a path down my throat and I swear I've lost all feeling in my tongue. The sound I make is somewhere between a cough and a choke. "That is absolutely vile," I say, passing it back.

"Last bottle of whisky on earth"—Gavin grimaces at another sip—"and it tastes of despair. You can thank the pixie for finding it."

Derrick looks offended. "So ungrateful. See if I bother bringing you another bottle if I find one. I'll light it on fire in front of you and watch you weep."

Gavin smiles. "Complain, complain, complain."

He offers me another swig and I shake my head. "So." I look pointedly at Gavin as I lean forward to feed another log into the fire. "I take it from *your* silence on the matter that you're not allowed to mention Kiaran." I tilt my head to Derrick. "This one just spent two days refusing to call him by name."

"He deserves it," Derrick grumbles. He drops a sewing thimble in my palm. "Pour some of that piss in here, will you?"

I roll my eyes and fill the thimble with whisky. "Don't think I haven't noticed you changed the subject."

"I didn't change the subject. I'm celebrating your return by sampling this miserable beverage. Welcome back! You still owe me a dance in a pirate costume."

Gavin looks interested. "Pirate costume?"

I relax as the new log blazes and sends a blissful wave of heat toward me. "Don't ask. For god's sake don't ask."

"Oh, but now I must know. In fact, I find myself keenly interested."

Derrick happily opens his mouth and I shush him. "Don't you dare. Gavin, stop indulging his deranged fantasies. He'll probably make you a gown."

Derrick brightens. "Oh, my giddy aunt, I never thought of that." He immediately gives Gavin a long, assessing look, as if sizing him for a gown. "You would look *so beautiful* in flounces and lace, Seer. I think blue is just your color. I'd even make you a corset—"

Gavin makes a choking sound at the back of his throat.

"—with little bows. And then I'll make you fancy undergarments—"

"Aileana, make him stop."

"You're the one who encouraged him. You deserve it after not telling me about Kiaran. Now speak up. Tell me everything."

Gavin hesitates and looks at Derrick. "Aithinne might not have threatened my life," he finally says, "but she was very clear: She wanted to be the one to talk to you when she gets back." He rests his elbows on the log and leans back. "Frankly, I was hoping you'd take the whisky and pass out."

"I was hoping you wouldn't remember Kiaran at all," Derrick grumbles.

I make a sound of frustration. Fine, then. I have plenty of other things to ask. "Then tell me what happened to Lonnrach and Sorcha."

Gavin shrugs. "No one has seen Lonnrach since . . ." I notice the way his eyes linger just below my collarbone, as if he's searching for the scar that killed me. Then he looks away. "You wounded him and he fled after the attack. Sorcha, too."

"Don't remind me," Derrick says. "I'd like to skin that pointy-toothed hag alive after what she did to Aileana. And I'd settle for keeping her brother's head." He pauses. Then: "He'd make a good trophy for the garden."

Gavin looks confused. "What garden?" He gestures around us with the bottle. "We're in the middle of the damned woods on the brink of an apocalypse."

Derrick's halo flashes red. "The garden I intend to make from the corpses of our enemies," he hisses. "I can't help it if your human mind lacks vision."

While they natter on, my fingers curl into my palm. So Sorcha and Lonnrach got away. Of course they did. Sorcha had planned the attack for months: to find the crystal from the Old Kingdom and use its power to break Aithinne's binding over Kiaran's power. To turn him into the Unseelie King again. Sorcha saved me more than once to ensure that happened. She betrayed her brother. And then she killed me.

I don't know which of them I hate more. Her, for stealing my life and taking my mother from me. Or him, for breaking my spirit and making me wish for death.

I'd murder them both if I could. But Lonnrach is Aithinne's kill, and I couldn't slay Sorcha even if I had the opportunity. Thousands of years ago, when Kiaran ruled over the Unseelie throne, Sorcha was his consort. They spoke a vow that bound their lives together. If Sorcha dies, so will he.

"What about the other fae?" I interrupt. "The ones under Lonnrach's command and the ones with the humans in Derrick's city. Was there any word from them?"

Derrick goes quiet and Gavin stares into the fire. Shadows play along his face, across the scars he received from a fae attack while I was imprisoned by Lonnrach. I'll never forget the haunted look in his eyes when I saw them for the first time. Gavin had been running and hiding from the fae for years by the time I escaped the faery realm. Almost all traces of the person I knew growing up had gone, replaced by a man hardened by grief and war.

"The humans are fine," Gavin finally says. "A few of the fae on the ship come to us for supplies, and they're holding out near the Western Isles for now. It's not safe enough here. Not with—" He glances at me. "Some of the fae who were with Lonnrach deserted the others, but most chose sides. An overwhelming majority didn't choose Aithinne's."

Derrick looks annoyed. "You'd think some of those who became Seelie again after Kiaran's powers were restored would remain loyal to their Queen, but they turned on her. Never seen anyone turn their back on their own Court." Then he grumbles, "Goddamn traitors."

When Kiaran chose to give up the Unseelie throne, Aithinne took out the part of his power that required feeding on humans in order to survive. He once had the same hunger I sensed in the Unseelie I fought in the forest, only his role as King made it more insatiable. Aithinne didn't have a vessel to pass his power to—another faery willing or able to accept it, the way I accepted the Cailleach's. So that power went into every faery in the two Courts, until even Seelie became Unseelie.

With Kiaran's Unseelie powers now returned, those fae would be Seelie once more. But changing back into what they were doesn't mean they would forgive their Queen for making them just like the Court they once loathed—even if she did it by accident—or for trapping them for thousands of years in a prison beneath Edinburgh so they could no longer harm humans.

Gavin rolls his eyes at Derrick. "Let's be honest, shall we? They turned on Aithinne to save their own skins." He leans back and tips the whisky bottle to his lips. "We're the losing side and you know it."

The losing side. That means Kiaran is winning.

Derrick is shaking his head and clicking his tongue at Gavin. *You have to ask. You have to.* But first . . . I steal the bottle and take a big swig. *Bloody hell* it burns.

"All right," I say. "Tell me about Kiaran. Both of you. Either of you. I don't want to wait for Aithinne." When they remain silent, I bite out, "Stop trying to protect me, or pretending you know what's best for me. It's ridiculous and insulting after everything I've been through."

Gavin and Derrick look at each other again. Derrick swears softly and is about to speak, but Aithinne's voice cuts him off. "Wait."

I look over to see her at the edge of the woods. Her eyes meet mine and something sad flashes in them. "There's something you need to see first."

CHAPTER 9

'M POSITIVE I won't like what she's about to show me. "Is this to do with the Book?" I ask as she leads me through the trees. *Please let this be about the damn Book.*

We've been walking for a good ten minutes, farther and farther from the warmth of the camp and into the frigid air of the forest. There is no light up ahead, nothing to indicate where she's taking me.

Aithinne shakes her head. "I've sent the word out with *sìthichean* still loyal to me to find out what they can about the Book. I can't risk trusting what I know." She gestures to a turn in the path. "This way."

My breath exhales in white mist. It would be almost spring by now; at this time, snowdrops ought to be covering the forest floor—hints of flower buds breaking through the icy ground. A sign that the deep, dark Scottish winter is almost over.

There are no flowers. No leaves. Just cold, biting wind and black branches under a starless sky.

Aithinne stops so quickly I almost run into her. Surprised, I peek around her to see a cottage just up the path, nestled away in the darkest parts of the woods beyond a small, quiet meadow. It's larger than the dwellings back at Aithinne's camp and just as hastily erected. Only, this structure has no windows or other doors, nothing to bring the light in except the single entrance before me. The door itself is carved into a massive boulder with fae marks etched into the stone.

I'm tempted to step back. It isn't welcoming. There is no blazing fire, no greeting. Nothing to indicate this is anything more than another abandoned place in a country now full of them.

We Scots would call a place like this haunted. Because one look at it sends a chill right through you.

"What do the markings mean?" I ask hesitantly.

"*Fois do t'anam*," Aithinne murmurs. "It's an offering of peace." She nods toward the cottage. "Go. I'll wait for you out here. And then I'll tell you everything you want to know."

No, I think as I take those first shaky steps toward the door. *No, no, no. Turn back. Don't go in. Don't see what she has to show you.*

It'll change everything.

But I have to. My pulse fills my ears as I twist the knob and push open the heavy wooden door.

The first thing I see are beds. Dozens of them, taking up almost every inch of space, like a hospital when it's filled to capacity. The only room left is in the aisles between each row, the gaps only just wide enough to walk through. Every bed has a table next to it with a single lit candle, casting a dim, shadowed glow across the cottage.

On each bed is a human in repose. Some lie so still that I wonder if this is where Aithinne keeps her dead, but when I look closer, I see that they're alive.

If you can call whatever the hell this is alive.

Their eyes are wide open, but with no apparent awareness of their surroundings. Not one of them seems to notice I'm there, not even as I pass by their beds. Their expressions all remain the same: in joyous, twisted awe. As if they've just glimpsed something beautiful—or something terrifying.

Something they would crawl for. Something they would die for.

I've never seen people so malnourished, so shockingly thin and emaciated that their cheekbones are sharp as blades. If I lifted those blankets, I could count their ribs. And their wrists . . . god, how delicate those are. How easily breakable. I can't help but compare the visible bones of their hands to fragile, injured bird wings; their fingers clench and unclench as if they were in pain.

Each human has a small faery settled on the pillow beside them, wings curled up around their bodies as if they were sleeping—but they're not. Every faery is biting into their human victim's throat hard enough to draw blood.

My instinct is to attack, to grab those faeries and kill them all. But when I step forward, a will-o'-the-wisp goes still, looks up at me, and pulls its teeth out of the woman's skin.

She seizes. Her too-thin arms grasp at the air as if trying to bring the wisp back. She makes a sound in her throat, a howling desperate cry like an animal caught in a snare. Her limbs start to thrash so violently I fear she'll hurt herself.

I back away, slamming my ankle painfully into a nearby bed. I barely notice. A gasp escapes my throat and I cover my mouth at what I see when the blanket slips back from her body.

Marks on her arms and legs—scars too large to be caused by a wisp. Thirty-six human teeth. Forty-six thin fangs. Over and over and over. Not a single part of her body spared.

Oh god. Oh god oh god.

The small faery's eyes meet mine as it settles its tiny teeth into her neck once more. It sinks its fangs in so deep that blood drips down to her collarbone.

And the woman settles back against her pillows with a sigh—and a smile.

My stomach heaves. I turn, shove the door open, and get out of that cottage. Away from those beds, those faeries, those humans.

Don't look back. Forget everything again. Forget what you saw.

My toe catches a rock, but I manage to catch myself before I hit the ground. Someone calls my name just as I cross the clearing and empty the contents of my stomach into the bushes.

I rest my elbows against my knees, my breathing ragged. I shut my eyes as if that could somehow erase the image of that woman, alive with the desire for only one thing: a faery's bite.

Kiaran once told me about what happens when the fae take humans. *They waste away from it and still yearn for more. When a* sìthichean *decides to take a human, it's not something they walk away from. Not ever.*

I've never seen it before. I've never seen a human so addicted to the touch of a fae that it's all that keeps them alive. I've experienced death and war, but there was something about *that*—about seeing humans wither and fade in beds, the fight taken out of them.

They might as well be dead.

"Aileana." Aithinne's voice is gentle behind me. She steps closer. "Are you—"

"*Don't.*" I put my hand out and wipe my mouth with my shirt. "Please. I need a moment."

Her expression is patient, understanding. "Very well."

I support my body against a nearby tree and ease down until I'm sitting on the cold soil. I still feel sick. So damn sick that I can't even stand. It takes a few minutes for the nausea to pass, for me to speak.

"I want you to tell me the truth," I say, my voice flat, mechanical. "No faery half-lies. No riddles. Are those . . ." I swallow hard, because the words stick in my mouth. "Are those Kiaran's victims?"

Aithinne says nothing. Her silence speaks for her. But as if that weren't bad enough, she finally answers with a whispered, "Aye."

I press my palm to my mouth. The vow Kiaran made to a Falconer he fell in love with thousands of years ago prevents him from killing humans, or he'll die himself. Once a faery makes a vow, he's bound to it forever.

But as the Unseelie King, his purpose is death, destruction. Without feeding on human victims, he dies. When Kiaran asked Aithinne to remove the part of himself that required human victims, she was able to help him, but only at a price: She had to bind the powers that made him the monarch of the Unseelie Court.

When Sorcha murdered me, she used the Old Kingdom crystal to override Aithinne's binding and restore his abilities. And this is Kiaran's fate. To kill a human and die, or feed on them and leave them like this.

"Why are they here?" I press the heels of my hands to my eyes, as if that could help me forget. *Why are you keeping them?*

"Kadamach leaves them on the border between our territories," she says, her voice low. "Derrick told me that putting a blade through them would be a mercy. Either that, or I could take those fae from their veins and let them fade, but I can't. I just . . . I can't." I swear I see pity in her expression. Pity for *me*. "You can try to save him, but I don't know if he's your Kiaran MacKay anymore."

He leaves them there. Like when the *sluagh* used to bring Aithinne Kiaran's gifts. A cruel taunt, a message. *I'm going to win.*

No, he can't be like that. He can't. There has to be a part of him that can still be reached, that's still worth saving.

So many feelings lance through me, each one worse than the memory of Sorcha's blade through my chest. I should never have come to care for Kiaran. I should never have let myself. Because I can't be objective. I can't give up on him.

He's in my heart and I'm in his, and I think it's going to destroy us both.

As if she has read my mind, Aithinne kneels beside me and puts her hand over mine. "You have to understand," she says. "The curse of becoming too attached to a human is something my kind learn from an early age, because we can't help but be drawn to human beauty. To its fragility."

She continues, "My mother always said that loving a human was like loving a butterfly. When I was young, she used to ask me the same question every day—'What do humans do best?'—and she was never satisfied until I found the answer."

"What was it?" I say, dreading what I'm about to hear.

Aithinne looks at me. "You die."

Of course. The Cailleach *would* teach something like that. She once told me that she could forgive Aithinne for creating the Falconers—a line of human women gifted with a small amount of Aithinne's power specifically to help kill her enemies—but she could never forgive Kiaran for loving a human.

One of them has to die, she'd said. *It should be Kadamach.*

My fingernails bite into my palms. A small pain to ease my thoughts. "Why are you telling me this?"

"This is the price of immortality. We're doomed to watch the humans we love die, and each time, it kills some of the empathy in us." Aithinne's hand squeezes mine. "Don't you understand now?" she whispers sadly. "You were his butterfly."

His butterfly. His breakable human girl. One sword to the heart and I died like a butterfly that lost its wings. So easily. "Aithinne, where is he?"

Aithinne looks away. She's quiet for so long that I wonder if she'll even answer. Then, in a voice barely above a breath, she says, "Come with me."

CHAPTER 10

AITHINNE OPENS a faery portal, an easy way of traveling long distances in an instant. The one she creates is a bright path that emerges through the trees as if she had willed it into existence. One minute it wasn't there, the next . . . there it is.

When we step through, we're standing at the top of a cliff over the raging sea. The landscape is familiar; I recognize the line of trees just off the rocks and the shape of the hills in the distance. We're on the bay that bordered the pixie kingdom—across from where Sorcha killed me.

"There," Aithinne whispers, gesturing toward the water. "He's in there."

I turn, expecting to see the old crystal in the ruins of Derrick's city, the crystal Lonnrach wanted so badly that he'd destroyed the pixie city to find it. What's there instead makes me suck in a shocked breath.

Where the bloody hell did that come from?

Right off the coast is an island supporting a dark, pointed palace. It looks as though it was carved into the rock, a single, massive shard of crystal that has twisted around itself to form a tall, serrated building that towers over the water. It's sharp, bladelike. I sense its power: a terrible, unsettling dark energy as cold as the bite of winter wind.

There is almost no nature on that island. The earth is scorched black and cracked, completely devoid of moisture despite being surrounded by the sea. The few trees scattered across the land are composed of sharp, bare branches that arch toward the palace's twisting crystal shard. They are needle-like, thorny and beckoning, every bit as ominous as something I'd see in the fae realm. Every bit as frightening.

The palace looks like it was erected as a threat, a warning.

"Kadamach raised the island out of the sea," Aithinne says in a low voice. "He built it around the crystal, a perfect replica of his palace in the Unseelie Kingdom." She hesitates before adding, "No doubt as a deliberate message to me that I was unwelcome. He even made new soldiers to replenish his ranks when I killed them."

Made new soldiers? "He can do that?"

"Using the crystal." Aithinne's smile is bitter. "Why do you think he wanted it so badly that he slaughtered your pixie's kingdom to find it? It would have guaranteed him an easy victory against me when our kingdoms were at war. He would have been unstoppable."

The crystal that Sorcha used to restore Kiaran's powers. I remember it being the height of an Edinburgh tenement, towering and forbidding. This castle is made of the same gleaming material—dark rock that is lit from within, fire inside black obsidian.

As if the structure weren't intimidating enough, dozens of soldiers stand guard just outside the massive gates. They're in perfect formation. Prepared for an attack. It's a blasted fortress.

"Have you gone to see him?"

"Of course I have." Aithinne's voice is bitter. "I've tried at least a dozen times to get that stubborn arse to speak with me, and he refuses to let me in."

I look at her in surprise. "He won't? Why?"

"He's preparing to go to battle with me," she says softly. "The first thing he does is close himself off." Her expression is impassive, but her tense shoulders betray her emotions. "I've seen it before."

My heart aches for her. "When?"

"It's what our mother did after we grew into our powers." I notice her hand trembles when she pushes her hair back. "Among the *daoine sìth*, there's no difference between Unseelie and Seelie at a young age," she explains. "We're born with the same rudimentary abilities. We all even have fangs, though Seelie have no need to use them."

Daoine sìth are the most powerful fae in the Courts. They're also the most human-looking, though their level of beauty is beyond compare.

I never realized they all had teeth like Sorcha and Lonnrach, a second level of sharp fangs that descended from their gums to make it easier to feed on human blood and energy. I had always assumed it was their lineage, but perhaps the legend of the vampiric faery called a *baobhan sìth* simply grew from the centuries when Sorcha slaughtered humans while the rest of the *daoine sìth* were trapped beneath Edinburgh—in a prison of Aithinne's making.

"Since my mother couldn't have known which Court we'd eventually lead," Aithinne continues, "Kadamach and I were raised together for centuries. When we finally came into our mature powers and he couldn't stop himself from killing his first human, I knew what he was. What it meant."

"That you'd be separated," I say.

Aithinne nods. "It happens. Siblings belonging to the same Court are more common, but separations aren't unheard of. Kadamach and I tried to hide our respective abilities at first; we didn't want to be apart. He'd kill human after human, and each time he would be his usual self for just long enough that I'd forget what he was . . . then he'd turn into someone I barely recognized before he hunted again." She shrugs. "Eventually he couldn't hide it from our mother. So she took us to our respective Courts and refused to allow any contact. She said it would be easier for us to go to war one day if we stopped thinking of each other as brother and sister."

I look again at the dark palace Kiaran built. "So he's using her tactics," I murmur.

I edge closer to the cliff and peer over the crag. The fall is straight to the bottom. I've leaped off this bluff before and would have died if Kiaran hadn't been with me. I can't get to that island by myself. Even with the Cailleach's abilities, I'm still human. The rocks below would break me.

"Open another portal," I say to Aithinne. "He'll speak to me." He'd *better* speak to me.

Aithinne studies the palace and the soldiers guarding it, assessing how I'd go about getting in. She gives a small shake of her head. "I believed that once," she tells me. "I just hope he doesn't do to you what he did to me."

"What did he do?"

"It was years after we were first separated. My mother had taught me to despise him and I never could. So I went to him." She gestures down to the island, her expression almost cold. "It was exactly like that—right down to the same number of soldiers. Kadamach is a creature of habit."

"Did he speak with you?" *You don't want to know, and yet you ask anyway. The price you pay for truth is knowledge.*

"No," she says flatly. "He timed how long I stood outside the gates. For each minute I waited for him to see me, he had his *sluagh* capture my most vulnerable subjects. And then every day, for five hundred days, he sent me their bodies." Aithinne's hands are fisted at her side. "They were his first *gifts*."

I flinch. *Now you know. You are a damned fool.*

"Why do you think he leaves those people at my border?" Aithinne flushes with anger. "He's telling me he'd kill them if he could. He's provoking me."

The Cailleach showed me some of the worst parts of Kiaran's past, things I'll never be able to forget. I won't excuse what he did. Some things are so terrible that the price of forgiveness becomes insurmountable.

But Kiaran has spent two thousand years trying to atone. I have to believe that there's still a part of him that is seeking redemption, the part of him that chose a human name. The part of him that I came to care for.

When Lonnrach kept me prisoner, Kiaran never gave up on me. I won't give up on him, either.

Fool that I am.

"He saved my life," I tell her. "I owe him a debt."

Aithinne nods once, her expression conflicted. "All right." She steps back abruptly from the cliff. "All right. When I hear back about the Book, I'll make you a portal. If you're right, and he is still your Kiaran, he'll want to help."

"And if he isn't?"

She lowers her eyes, but not before I see the regret there. She doesn't say anything; she doesn't have to. I can see the answer in her features as surely as if she had spoken the words aloud.

Then I'm going to have to kill him.

CHAPTER 11

THAT NIGHT, I sleep next to the fire, and I dream of Kiaran.

We're in a bed in an unfamiliar room, as opulent as anything that might grace a royal palace. Above us hangs a chandelier formed from teardrop pieces of dark opal, alight from within with red flame. The gleaming walls of the room are sculpted from obsidian, etched with elaborate designs like those on Kiaran's skin. Reaching up from floor to ceiling, the pattern stretches in elaborate, pointed branches.

The bed is a massive four-poster carved from the seared wood of an alder tree. It smells of ash, smoke, and heather.

I'm tracing the scars covering Kiaran's bare back, the intricate series of raised swirls and lines and loops that appear scorched onto his flesh, then sliced inch by agonizing inch. It represents his oath not to kill humans, his penance for the ones he murdered. Each of his victims has a place on his skin, their own separate mark.

This was his atonement. This was the vow that made him Kiaran.

"Are you still you?" I ask him. "Or are you . . ." *Kadamach. Someone else. Someone beyond redemption.*

He stirs beside me, his arm slipping around my waist to gather me closer. We are pressed together, skin to skin, and in that moment, there is nowhere I'd rather be.

"Sometimes," he says. "It depends."

"On?"

"On whether or not I can pretend, for a few minutes, that you'll still walk into a room and ask me irritating questions."

I laugh. "You sound like you."

"Aye. Until I remember that you won't walk into the room. You never will again."

I say nothing. I just hold him tighter because I don't want to let go of this. Of us.

"I wish I would stop dreaming about you," he tells me in whispered words against the base of my neck. He presses his lips there once, twice.

"Do you?" When I run my fingers down the length of his spine, a slight shudder runs through him. That hint of a physical response reveals the effect I have on him, something he can't hide. "Are you trying to forget me, MacKay?"

Kiaran looks up at me, his beautiful lilac eyes oddly vulnerable. "Say that name again." His voice is rough with emotion. He does feel. And if he still feels, then he's Kiaran. And he's worth saving.

I smile. "MacKay."

His fingers slide down my ribs. Lower. "Again."

"Kiaran MacKay."

His name barely leaves my lips and then he's kissing me, long and slow. I breathe it out again, his name. A chant. A prayer. Again. Once more.

He rewards me with another kiss, another. He trails his fingertips across my skin in slow, exploring strokes that leave me aching. That make me *want*.

As he covers my body with his, before I forget myself, I tell him something else. "I'm going to save you."

Kiaran goes still. "Save me, Kam?" His low, bitter laugh is cold enough to freeze my heart. His next words are whispered against the pulse at my throat. "If you were alive, you'd wish you had killed me."

Then he sinks his teeth into my skin.

* * *

I wake with a gasp caught in my throat. The phantom pain of Kiaran's bite is so strong that I can't help but slip my fingers up to brush the skin above my collarbone. The warmth of his tongue against my pulse was so real. Too real.

My heart pounding, I sit up and look around—half expecting to find myself in that massive bed in my dream—but I'm still by the fire in Aithinne's camp.

The animal pelts I had slept beneath slip down to my lap and I shiver in the cold air. The bonfire has long since gone out and now only glowing, charred wood is left. The first vestiges of predawn light peek through the forest trees.

Gavin and Daniel are on the other side of me, still fast asleep. Derrick is curled up on my coat at my feet, his hands clutching the fabric. He's snoring loudly for such a wee thing.

Catherine and Aithinne. Where are they?

I shove the pelts aside and scramble to my feet. I don't know what compels me to go in the direction of the cottage Aithinne showed me yesterday, but I find myself on the path through the woods, moving quickly. Only now do I notice there are no birds in the trees here, welcoming the morning light with their songs. No animals rustle in the thicket. There is only the lonely, unnerving groan of branches swinging in the icy breeze.

As I walk farther from the camp, I can still smell the fire on the air. I can't help but think of that bed made of dark wood. My hands stroking Kiaran's marks. His whispered words against my neck: *If you were alive, you'd wish you had killed me.*

I move faster, trying to put his words out of my mind. I swear I still feel his teeth breaking the skin at my neck, the blood warm down my collarbone. Faster. My boots pound against the path.

You'll never forget what you've seen. Why do you want to go there again?

I don't know why I've come to the cottage that houses Kiaran's victims. I don't know why I put my hand on the doorknob and push my way inside.

Catherine looks up in surprise when I enter—then her expression shows something else. Pity? Sadness? I can't tell. "Hullo." She dips a rag into the bowl next to her.

She's sitting at the bedside of the woman I saw yesterday, still lying there with her eyes fixed on the ceiling. I wince when I notice the unsettling serene smile on her face hasn't budged. The will-o'-the-wisp remains with its teeth in her neck, though it appears to be fast asleep. There are three marks beside its mouth. Each one of them is still bleeding.

Compelled, I feel for the scars Lonnrach left on me. But when I trace my fingertips down my wrist, I find only smooth, unmarked skin. A blank slate. My scars are like Aithinne's now: down in the darkest parts of me, hidden from view. Some scars go more than skin deep.

I'll never forget being that helpless.

My gaze takes in the other beds, the fifteen other people there. Kiaran's discarded victims. I have to swallow back the bile in my throat.

Are you still you?

I don't know.

I flinch, unable to look at them anymore. "What are you doing in here?" I ask Catherine, my voice low. As if those people could hear me. As if they weren't so far gone they were beyond caring. "You should be asleep."

Catherine wrings out the cloth and presses it to the woman's forehead. "I don't sleep much anymore. Not since the pixie kingdom was destroyed."

I put a comforting hand on her shoulder. Catherine has been my best friend since we were children; we grew up together. While Lonnrach kept me prisoner, she took care of the surviving humans. She's stronger than I had ever given her credit for.

She smiles at me gently, but I don't smile back.

I think about everything she's been through. She watched as the fae slaughtered people she loved. Then she tried to create a home in the pixie kingdom, until the fae came and destroyed that, too.

My fault. The guilt I experienced when Derrick first said my name comes rushing back. The same overwhelming sense of responsibility for every damn thing that's happened. As if it were a physical weight pressing down on my shoulders and growing heavier with each passing moment.

"Stop it," Catherine snaps, as if she reads my mind. "Stop blaming yourself. You think I don't see it? You look at me like I'm a burden. Like we all are."

"You're not a burden," I say. "Not ever." *You're stronger than I am.*

Catherine pulls away from me. "I don't believe you. You've managed to convince yourself that every terrible thing is your fault. And it's absolute *bollocks.*"

She always manages to see right through me. Even when I hid being a Falconer from her, she still knew something was wrong. "Bad habit," I murmur.

"The worst," she agrees.

My laugh is low, forced. "You know those stories where the lone hero saves the world?" I ask. "Do you ever notice that they don't talk about what happens if the hero fails?"

Catherine looks impatient. "That's where it began, wasn't it? Thinking it was *your* duty to protect us all." She shakes her head. "We're not your responsibility, Aileana. This world isn't your burden. It belongs to all of us." She gestures to the beds in the room. "Even them."

All I can do is stare at Catherine, watching how she dips the cloth in the water and presses it to the woman's face again. "Is this you doing your part?" I ask.

Catherine looks startled by the question. "I suppose. I come here every morning and spend some time with each of them. I don't know their names, but I talk with them as if I did."

I study the woman on the bed. Bloody hell, she's so far gone, I could probably cut her with a blade and she wouldn't even react.

"Why?" I can't help how harsh I sound when I add, "It's not as if any of them can tell you're there." The woman is dead. Kiaran found a way to kill humans without stopping their hearts.

If you were alive, you'd wish you had killed me.

Stop it, I tell myself. *Stop thinking about it.*

Catherine doesn't seem offended. If anything, she just looks sad. "These people didn't choose this," she says. "Isn't that what separates us from *them*? *They* treat us like we're cattle. Like we're expendable." She holds the woman's hand in a gentle grip. "If it were me, I'd want someone to treat me with dignity before I died. I'd want someone to believe I mattered."

I wish I were more like Catherine. Even now, after everything she's gone through, she's still kind. She still cares. She didn't lose those she loved and turn to vengeance.

Her strength isn't physical. She wouldn't go onto the battlefield for a slaughter. She'd go to aid the wounded, the vulnerable. It takes a rare, exceptional sort of bravery to lose everything and still give so much of yourself. That's the kind of courage most people lose in a war.

I did.

I sit on the edge of another bed across the aisle, occupied by a young man about my age. His smile is peaceful. His eyes are tearing up, as if caught in an emotional memory.

I wonder if, deep down, he knows I'm here. I wonder if he wishes someone still cared.

Hitching a breath, I lean down and grasp a cloth, dip it into the bowl of water, and raise my eyes to meet Catherine's. "Tell me what to do," I whisper.

I don't remember how to care for anyone.

Catherine comes over and sits down next to me. "You don't have to do anything," she tells me. "Just being here is enough."

An hour later, Aithinne bursts into the cottage. The humans must sense her there—her power, or perhaps the light of her skin shining like a beacon in the darkness. They start writing, unsettled. It's the first time I've seen any sort of lucidity in their gaze, any awareness at all.

The woman in the bed next to me gasps low in her throat at the sight of Aithinne. "Beautiful," she murmurs. Her hands reach for Aithinne, fingers grasping.

Aithinne ignores their cries. "Come with me," she tells me urgently. "I have news about the Book."

CHAPTER 12

FOLLOW AITHINNE out of the cottage, matching her pace as she strides through the forest in the direction of the camp.

"Quickly," Aithinne says. She crosses a clearing in a half-run. "Derrick went back to weave another cloaking ward on those soldiers you killed, and they were gone."

The way she says it fills me with dread. "I take it that means Kiaran found them."

"He'll think I've declared war. If he hasn't sent his soldiers already, he will now." She shakes her head. "We need to prepare."

"Can't you just refuse to fight?" She's walking so fast that I have to jog to keep up.

"No," Aithinne says simply. "Kadamach isn't going to give me a choice. If I don't kill the soldiers, they'll slaughter my subjects. There are a few camps scattered across my territory that have wards against opening portals. I won't be able to get to them in time."

We reach the edge of the camp and head for the line of cottages. "How long do we have?"

"A few hours at most," she says. "Hopefully enough time to send you through a portal to see Kadamach." She shoots me a glance. "Do whatever you can to get through to him. Use threats if you have to."

What if I can't get through to him at all? What if that dream was just wishful thinking?

I don't tell Aithinne my doubts. Instead I try to be nonchalant. "Threats? Too easy. If he doesn't listen, I'll challenge him to a duel and beat him a few times with a blunt instrument. He likes that sort of thing." In fact, I seem to recall it being Kiaran's idea of flirting.

Aithinne grins. "One day I pray I'll meet a woman who engages me in combat as a way to say, *I love you*. Be still my heart."

I raise an eyebrow. I've known ladies who fancied each other, but they only spoke about it in whispers. "A woman, you say?"

Her laugh is short. "Did you think Kadamach was the only one whose weakness was ladies in armor? If you weren't his, I'd ask you to be mine."

"Aithinne, I think that might be the nicest thing you've ever said to me."

"Don't you dare tell my brother. He'd never stop teasing me." She nods to her cottage. "In here. I have a few things for you and then I'll tell you what I know about the Book."

Aithinne pushes open the door and grabs some clothes off the bed. "Put these on."

I glance down at my own clothes, the ones Derrick hastily stitched together when I arrived at the camp. "What's wrong with the things I'm wearing?"

Aithinne is strapping on her weapons: small blades attached to her wrists, one at her boot. "They look terrible," she says, checking the point of her blade.

Oh, for goodness' sake. "I'm preparing to fight either Kiaran or a very large group of soldiers. Not attend a ball."

Aithinne looks me over from head to toe and smirks as if to say, *Aye, but you look like shite.* "When my brother sees you, do you want to be wearing those dirty, stinky clothes riddled with holes?" She wrinkles her nose. "Wait, don't answer that. He might still be demented enough to find it romantic."

I roll my eyes, but start removing my wool shirt and trousers. The breeches Aithinne has given me are made from the softest leather, molding to my legs as if they were made for me. They match the tall, soft leather boots she provided.

The coat is probably the finest I've ever seen: a stunning brocade with a faelike design of intricate swirls, with golden stitches sewn right in. It cinches at the waist, closing with buttons made of fine, polished gold. It's a coat made for royalty—made for a queen.

I hesitate before putting it on. "Derrick made this for you, didn't he?"

"He seems to have the misinformed notion that I ought to wear it to a coronation that is never going to happen." Aithinne's shrug is flippant, but I see the hint of worry there.

"I'll probably be wearing it for my own funeral rites if we don't find the Book."

"Aithinne—"

"Aileana," she says with a sigh, "it's just a coat. Put the damn thing on."

I do as she says, keeping quiet when she passes me the sheath with my blood-made sword already tucked inside. I put it on the bed next to my discarded trousers. "What if Kiaran doesn't listen to me? Do we have an alternate plan?"

"Use your powers on him." Aithinne straps another blade to her wrist. "Throw him into a tree like you did me."

"Didn't we already establish that Kiaran finds that sort of thing attractive? He'll thinks it's—" I wave a hand, unable to come up with a delicate word for what I mean. *Oh, for heaven's sake. How can I possibly be thinking about propriety now?*

"You, hinting at him to take off your clothes?"

"*Aithinne!*"

She flashes a smile. "When you saw me in the clearing, my power called to yours, didn't it?" At my nod, she says, "Kadamach's will be the same. The Cailleach's power recognizes its own." Then, more quietly, "And it's easier because he's your lover."

I can't help but touch my neck, pressing my fingers there. The memory of the dream still hasn't faded. The warmth of Kiaran's lips on my throat. The pressure of his teeth sinking into my skin. His whispered words against my neck.

If you were alive, you'd wish you had killed me.

"You're distracting me, Aithinne. Enough about your brother's lunatic ideas of romance." I can't think of Kiaran, not after that dream. *I can't.* "Tell me about the Book. Did your contacts say where it is?"

Aithinne looks thoughtful. "Something like that." She makes a face. "Apparently it's not anywhere."

I pause in the middle of buttoning the coat. "I beg your pardon?"

"That is to say, it's not anywhere *here*. The Book"—now she's grinning, so this ought to be good—"is elsewhere."

Confound it. I'm going to kill her. The fae passion for riddles is something I will never understand. "Are you purposely trying to annoy me?"

"Did you know that when you get impatient, you make these clicking noises with your teeth like an irritated cat? It's rather delightful." My glare would be enough to sear the skin off an ordinary person, but Aithinne is anything but ordinary. "What I mean is that the Book is in a realm outside this one."

"Not the fae realm?" I ask, thinking of where Lonnrach kept me. It's not somewhere I'd like to revisit. I barely made it out the first time.

"No. According to my source—who, granted, is a very old, very inebriated will-o'-the-wisp with a bigger honey problem than your pixie—the Book was hidden in another realm for its own protection. According to our stories, any faery who managed to get its hands on it would be unparalleled in power. They'd be able to alter time."

I freeze. "Alter . . ." I seize Aithinne's wrist. "Can it do that or not?"

"I don't know. I—"

"What did the wisp say?" I demand.

I sound half-crazed, but I have to know. Doesn't she realize? If that were true, it would change everything. We could reverse the course of fate, prevent all of Scotland and elsewhere from being destroyed. We could bring Edinburgh back. We could bring *everyone back*. My father. Gavin and Catherine's mother. *My* mother.

"Aileana." Aithinne's voice is calm. "I know what you're thinking and I don't know for certain. The only thing the wisp could tell me was that if someone controlled the Book, it would make them more powerful than my mother."

The original Cailleach was believed to have created the realms—both human and fae. The dramatic landscapes of Scotland were born of her incredible power; some claimed she formed the mountains and the streams, that she blessed the Scottish people with fertile lands.

That power was passed down through her lineage all the way to the last Cailleach, who gave her power to me, a human she despised. And she did it because she was dying: She needed to pass it to *someone*, and both of her children loathed her.

So I just happened to be a convenient vessel to hold her powers, which are slowly killing me. I release Aithinne. "Tell me everything the wisp said."

"He said that long before the first Cailleach became monarch of the fae, the Old Kingdom was ruled by another queen. She was the Cailleach's sister."

I sit on the bed to buckle my boots. "Why do I have the feeling this doesn't end well?"

Aithinne looks amused. "My kind makes a lot of noise about being better than humans, but when it comes to power, immortals aren't immune to greed. We're not like lobsters."

That makes sense. After all, I've met plenty of fae who—"Wait, what?"

"Lobsters," Aithinne says again, just in case I misheard her, and I rather hoped I had. "I hear they're biologically immortal," she explains, "and exempt from greed. And they're funny looking, so I've decided they're my favorite."

"First of all," I say, "I don't think that's true. Second of all—"

"So maybe it isn't true, but what do you think of a lobster for a pet?" Aithinne asks suddenly, as if she's thought long and hard about this. "I used to have a falcon—"

"Aithinne." I pinch the bridge of my nose. Those two thousand years she spent underground really affected her focus. One minute she's intense, the next minute she's talking about lobsters and driving me insane. "You're distracting me again. What was her name?"

"The falcon? Oh, her name was—"

"*The Cailleach's sister.*" Blast it all. "Soldiers coming. Impending war. Our possible demise. Talk quickly."

Aithinne waves a hand, as if it's a minor detail. "She was called something different then, but her name has lived on as the Morrigan."

That name is not a minor detail. *That name* does not deserve a hand-wave, as if to say, *oh, it's just So-and-So from Such-and-Such.*

What little I know about the Morrigan is only from legends, but they were certainly enough to leave a terrifying impression. Like the Cailleach, the Morrigan was considered a goddess—a powerful creature of war. Though the Cailleach was capable of brutality, there were plenty of stories that spoke of her small acts of kindness.

The Morrigan had no acts of kindness. She was renowned in stories for the death and destruction she wrought.

She was the faery who almost wiped out the human race.

CHAPTER 13

EMEMBER THAT not-good feeling?" I ask Aithinne. "The one you had a moment ago?"

"Right. That feeling. It just got worse." I draw in a long breath. "Let me guess—and I am saying this purely on it being the worst thing I can come up with since I have a habit of attracting disaster. The Morrigan wrote the damn Book, didn't she?"

"I'm afraid so." Aithinne looks at me, concerned. "You're not going to vomit again, are you? Would you like a bucket?"

"Just tell me about the Morrigan and the Book."

She moves to sit next to me on the cot. "It started out as a history of the fae. How we were created, our great families, the geography of the Old Kingdom. When the Morrigan became monarch, she began to use it as her spell book." She smiles sadly. "The Morrigan was the first Seelie Queen, you know? She loved knowledge. But the more she wrote, the more the Book became a creature independent of its creator."

I swallow hard. I don't like the sound of that. "What does that mean?"

"We have a belief," Aithinne says, "that if you put enough power and importance into an object, over time it can take on a life of its own. It can become a force, capable of being used for great things—or terrible things." Her eyes meet mine, intent. "You saw this with the crystal. How Sorcha was able to project enough power through it to overtake mine. If that's done enough times, the object becomes infused with that power."

The crystal. It was once a part of the Old Kingdom, the only relic of its kind left. Believed to have been lost, it was actually buried beneath the pixie kingdom. It was so powerful that the pixies were able to create small worlds within their city, built at the whims of their creators.

I can't help but feel for the scar beneath my shirt, my fingertips grazing the upraised skin. When Lonnrach discovered where the crystal was, he demolished the pixie kingdom to unearth it, hoping to use its power to steal mine. Instead, Sorcha used it to turn Kiaran back into the Unseelie King.

I tried to destroy the crystal the night I died. I failed.

"Did the Cailleach use the crystal against the Morrigan?" I ask, trying to keep the emotions out of my voice. Sometimes my memories are too much to bear. "Did she overthrow her?"

"No." Aithinne shakes her head sharply. "As long as she had the Book, the Morrigan was much too strong. She grew more cruel, with an insatiable desire for war. The Seelie powers she had were twisted into something darker, and she became the first Unseelie. She gifted loyal subjects with the same abilities. They grew into the Unseelie Court.

"I know you thought my mother was merciless, but she was considered by many to be a fair monarch. For all her faults, she brought prosperity to both Courts when she came to power. The Morrigan's kingdom was forged in darkness. Her rule was absolute. And with the Book by her side, no one could challenge her."

"But the first Cailleach did."

"She had no choice," Aithinne explains. "Dissent grew in the kingdoms. There was talk of rebelling, and my ancestors knew they would all be slaughtered if they tried. The Cailleach was the only one strong enough to slay the Morrigan."

Her own sister. Just like every other Cailleach after her, sibling killing sibling. Exactly as Kiaran and Aithinne are expected to do. "And did she?"

"This is where the story becomes unclear. It's not known whether the Morrigan's own consort betrayed her or was used by the Cailleach to lure the Morrigan into a prison between worlds, but the Book was hidden somewhere in that place. Some say the Morrigan found the Book and is still alive there. Others say the disappearance of the Morrigan means the Cailleach must have succeeded in killing her." Aithinne lifts her shoulders in a shrug. "The wisp wasn't certain. He just knew that . . ."

Aithinne looks away. I don't have to see her expression to know her eyes are wet. "Aithinne? Knew what?"

"Before the Book disappeared, the Morrigan used it to make the Cailleach suffer," Aithinne says flatly. "The last thing she wrote was a curse: Each Cailleach shall give birth to two children of power, one with the gift of death, the other with the gift of life. The most powerful shall inherit the throne only when they have killed the other. Over and over and over, forever. And if they try to escape the fate written for them in that Book, they will rip the realms asunder."

Aithinne stands in anger, her back to me. Her hands fist at her sides. "In every version of the story, the last lines she wrote were the same." Aithinne looks at me, her jaw tight. "*As it begins in death, so shall it end in death, until the day a child of the Cailleach confronts their fate with a true lie on their lips and sacrifices that which they prize most: their heart.*"

A true lie on their lips. No circumvention. No manipulation. And the fae can't lie. "So never," I say. "She might as well have said *Nothing can undo this curse.*"

"In order to create a curse, you have to provide a way to break it," Aithinne says bitterly. "As you've already surmised, we *sithichean* have come up with creative ways around our limitations. The Morrigan was very clever."

"The worst fae usually are."

"So we'll find it." Aithinne grabs my sword in its sheath and presses it to my palm. Her eyes are intense, molten silver. The way Kiaran's get just before a battle. "We'll find that damn Book and change your realm back to the way it was, and we'll write out that curse."

I look down at my sword, afraid to ask the next question. "If we don't?"

Aithinne winces. "If it comes down to him or me, the curse dictates it's going to be me," she says. Then, more softly, "But I spent two thousand years being tortured and imprisoned. I'm not ready to die. Not when I feel like I've barely lived."

"I won't let that happen," I tell her firmly. "Did your wisp tell you how to find it?"

She hesitates. "You're not going to like this."

Before I can ask what she means, Derrick barrels through the door. He comes to a hard stop, the tips of his wings lit red. "The soldiers have crossed the border and they're coming too fast to send Aileana before they get here." He looks at me. "Now is a good time for you to unleash those scary powers and kill them all."

Aithinne is already strapping her sword around her hips. "Is Kadamach with them?"

Derrick's wings are buzzing, as agitated as a dragonfly's. "I don't know. I sure as hell hope not."

I don't miss the way Aithinne flickers a glance at me, a fraction of concern there. If Kiaran is out there with his soldiers, that means the war starts here. Right now. I may be the element of surprise, and my being there might be enough for him to call it off, but the moment he sees me with Aithinne—alive and ready for battle—he'll assume I've chosen my side.

"There's no helping it if he is," Aithinne says.

"We should get Catherine, Gavin, and Daniel somewhere safe," I say.

Aithinne slips on her coat and looks at me in amusement. "Where would they go?" she asks me. "If it starts, nowhere is safe from the Wild Hunt." When I don't say anything, she grips my shoulder. "The humans are going to take the horses out and draw the soldiers away from the other camps. This is their fight as much as ours."

This world isn't your burden. It belongs to all of us.

I *know* that. I know it. But if they're forced into combat, they won't survive. Helplessly, I look at Derrick.

His features soften. "I'll bring them back here alive. All right?"

I reach out and stroke his wings in thanks. "Be careful."

"If you leave before I'm back, *you* be careful." He sighs before adding, "Don't get yourself killed trying to save him."

Gavin meets us outside the cottage. I notice he's carrying weapons, as if he's been training for this.

He glances at my sword and his lips quirk up. "Now this sight brings back fond memories. Though I admit, I miss the torn dresses. Trousers just don't have the same touch of reckless insanity."

I roll my eyes. "Trust you to flirt with me right before a battle. What happened to Brooding Gavin?"

"Brooding Gavin had a city to protect," he says. "All I have now is my own arse. Oh, and this whisky." He pulls open his coat and the bottle is right there in the inside pocket. He's actually determined to save that shite single malt.

"You're ridiculous," I tell him.

Aithinne, however, brightens when she sees it. "Thank god," she says. "Save a dram for me. I always like a spot of whisky after I murder things."

God help me. Or kill me now. Just put me out of my misery.

I hear the quick clamor of hooves behind me. It's Catherine and Daniel, hurrying out of the trees with three fae horses saddled and ready to go. "Stick by me," Daniel says to Gavin. "Don't do anything bloody stupid, all right? Not like last time."

"You know me, old chap," Gavin says, swinging up onto his horse. Derrick settles on his shoulder with his wings tucked in. "Bloody stupid is only my Plan B."

Daniel looks over at me, his one eye assessing. "Good to have you back," is all he says. Then he mounts his horse and Catherine does the same. We all say our goodbyes before the fae horses take off, so fast they blur. I don't even hear them as they disappear into the dark woods.

Aithinne and I wait and listen.

In the span of minutes, I feel the soldiers moving through the forest. I send out a tentative, searching stroke of power. A few soldiers take off in the direction the humans and Derrick went, but Kiaran isn't with them. *Thank god.*

The soldiers must sense me, though, because their power pushes against mine, a warning: *We're coming for you.*

Out of the corner of my eye, I see Aithinne's grim smile in response. *We're ready.*

CHAPTER 14

S THE soldiers draw closer, their power is hot against my skin, a combined energy that makes the air torrid, heavy.

Unlike the fae I encountered in the woods, they aren't trying to hide their presence. They're announcing it with every step. They're screaming it. It's the cocky entrance of fae who have no idea what they're up against. They don't understand that they're about to be the first casualties of war. They're about to be the declaration.

My power unfurls, a darkness at the back of my mind just waiting to be unleashed. Waiting to kill.

Come closer.

When the fae reach the outskirts of the camp, my power roars. It demands. It paces inside its too-small bone cage. When they finally step through the trees, I can barely hold it back.

Wait . . . wait . . .

Aithinne puts a hand on my arm as if she senses my struggle. Her power wraps around mine to hold it in place. There's a steadiness to her gaze, a patience I hadn't expected before a battle. *Hold.*

The fae in the forest surround us, their eyes glowing like beacons in the darkness. My power senses twenty heartbeats. Twenty inhales and exhales, breathing as one.

Twenty stupid, suicidal faeries who won't live to see the morning.

I step forward, but Aithinne's grip tightens. "Wait," she says to me in a low voice. Then louder, so the others can hear: "You're trespassing in my territory."

An Unseelie at the front laughs. It's a low, rough scrape at the back of his throat. "We know."

"I see." Aithinne sounds calm. So calm. Almost like she feels sorry for them. "Then you must be aware that Kadamach intends for you to be killed."

They remain unmoving, impassive. Maybe they haven't learned how to feel yet. Maybe Kiaran taught them what he learned in the Unseelie Court himself: that emotions are a weakness.

"You're young," she says dismissively. "Just made."

"What's that supposed to mean?" one of them asks.

Aithinne shrugs. "It's not your fault he sent you to your deaths. He can just make more soldiers. You're expendable."

I look sharply at Aithinne. *What are you doing?*

Her expression says everything. She's giving them an opportunity to switch sides. To save themselves. They're taking their place in a war they never started, one that began thousands of years ago.

Aithinne is the kinder monarch. She's the better monarch. He's just the stronger one. The one meant to live.

None of the fae answer. Their composure never falters; they're ready to die if necessary. Kiaran must have trained them well. Apparently he never lost his ruthlessness.

A faery at the front slides her blade out of its sheath and the others follow. They've declared their allegiance. The female soldier charges toward Aithinne like a damned fool with a death wish.

Aithinne doesn't hesitate. She grabs the soldier around the neck like an errant child and holds her effortlessly in place. I wince at the gargled choke the soldier makes.

"Last chance," she tells the others. "Choose my side and live, or die right here. Right now. As your king's cannon fodder."

Their silence is her answer. When none of them steps forward, Aithinne tightens her jaw. "Fine."

She snaps the soldier's neck and rams her sword into her gut. Then she lunges for the other fae. Aithinne is spectacular in battle. She cuts one down, whirls, cuts another.

I take my place alongside her. And it's like I've come home.

Death is in my blood. I breathe it in like oxygen. The darkness inside me roars in response, powering each thrust of my sword, forcing my blade through sinew and bone. Their energy fills me, one right after the other. I feed on every kill. Each one makes me stronger, more powerful.

The battle happens so quickly, it's as if time is suspended. Derrick wanted me to become the creature I was in the forest, but with my memories I'm something different. I'm *me*, only faster, more efficient. I kill with the speed of a brush fire through a forest. Nothing can stop me. They never even have the chance to scream.

The darkness inside me grows. Each thrust of my sword makes it roar in response, makes it scream. The Cailleach's power is a battle cry in my blood, in my bones. My heart is singing.

I have the last faery in my sight, the blade at her throat—

"Aileana!"

Something about that voice makes me pause.

"Aileana," she says again, slowly. Carefully. Like I'm an animal in the wild—a deadly one.

I'm breathing hard as the darkness clears from my vision.

It's Aithinne I have pressed against a tree. Aithinne who I'm about to kill. Aithinne I have at the end of my blade with a stream of fresh blood down her neck—a reminder of how close I came to killing her.

"It's all right," she says when she sees the look on my face. "It's all right. You're all right."

No. No, I'm not. I almost killed you and I almost killed Derrick before and I'm not all right. I'm not—

A searing pain bursts through my temple. I stagger back. The oxygen leaves my lungs, and suddenly I can't get in enough air.

"Aileana!"

I'm on the ground, fingernails digging into the dirt as I come back to myself. It takes a moment for my blurred vision to clear.

A sudden wetness crosses my lips. I dart out my tongue and taste the overwhelming coppery tang of blood coming from my nose. "Aithinne," I breathe. That's all I can manage. Fear speeds up my pulse.

I can bring you back to life, but eventually my powers will kill you.

It's started. I can feel it. The way my body is weakening. Now that the darkness has left and my power is contained, I'm trembling from its use, tired. So tired I can't move.

What do humans do best? They die.

Aithinne crouches next to me and gently lifts my chin to get a better look. "You'll have to be more careful when you search for the Book. Use your powers sparingly or they'll rip you apart."

I pull away from her touch. "How long do I have?"

"That depends," she says carefully. "If you keep using them like this, not long. If you don't, you might have more—"

"Aithinne." *Breathe, girl. Just breathe.* "How long?"

She looks away. "A few days."

A few days. And then I'm dead all over again.

I had laughed in the Cailleach's face when she told me her powers would eventually kill me. Of course there was a price to being brought back. There's always a price. I didn't consider that this time around, the repercussions for not finding the Book wouldn't just be my death: It would be everyone I love having to grieve me once more.

Maybe that's your curse, Aileana Kameron. Anyone who loves you is doomed to watch you die over and over again.

CHAPTER 15

FOCUS ON *something else. Something in your control.* I look at the fae Aithinne and I just slaughtered. "Did you mean what you said before? That Kiaran created them just to be killed here?"

"Did you think that just because he took the title *King* that it would undo two thousand years of him hunting his own kind?" At my frown, Aithinne's expression hardens. "He hates them."

I made you the same as me. Kiaran said that to me once, and now I wonder if he was wrong. Maybe he didn't make me the same. Maybe I made him hate the fae more.

"He doesn't have to be King," I say. I hate how childish that sounds. How dangerously naïve. I know better than anyone what it's like to be forced into a role I never wanted. He didn't choose to be King. I didn't choose to be a Falconer. It was nothing more than an accident of birth.

From Aithinne's pointed expression, I'd wager she believes me naïve, too. "When Sorcha restored his powers, she stole his choice. He and I can't ignore it any more than we can ignore the fact that one of us has to die." She pushes to her feet and offers me her hand. "And now I need you to delay our war."

I take her hand and follow her into the woods. Though Aithinne's pace is fast and determined, her small frown betrays her concern. I almost tell her that I'm sorry. If I had my memory when the Cailleach brought me back, I would never have killed those other fae. Now I've forced Aithinne to go to war with Kiaran.

She is the girl whose gift is chaos. Wherever she goes, death follows.

I suppose I can't help it, can I? I broke the world, and now I've started the war. It's my *gift*. My purpose. It's what I was made for.

"Tell me what I need to do," I say. I ignore the trembling weakness in my body and push through the pain.

"You'll have to get Kadamach's attention. He ought to be in something of a listening mood." She pauses, considering. "I think."

"You *think?*"

Aithinne sighs and looks away. "He left another human for me this morning. So he's recently fed." Her voice is low, thick. "He'll be more . . . in control."

Another human added to the cottage. Another life gone. "For how long?"

"He might hold on longer because he loves you, or not at all because you're human. I'm not certain." Aithinne's gaze catches mine. "No matter how normal he might appear at first, his hunger will always win out. Always. Remember that."

I ignore the tremor of fear her words bring. I have to focus on the task at hand. "How do I get his attention?"

Aithinne's smile is slow, brilliant; she's clearly relieved to be back to a more comfortable topic. "Well, if you want my advice, slaughter his soldiers. He's bound to notice when they're all dead outside his gates. He'll probably watch and fall in love with you all over again."

"Bloody hell, I'm never asking you for advice on romance in the future. *'Just kill all the soldiers, Aileana,'*" I mock in falsetto, rolling my eyes. "Tell me about finding the Book."

She looks amused. "The good news is, the way to the Book is through the palace. You can use the power of the crystal to open the doorway."

"And the bad?" *I'm not going to like this.*

Aithinne forges ahead. "You'll have to find some way to abduct Sorcha. Only her lineage can find the portal that leads to the Book."

"Aithinne." I say her name very, very carefully. "You're saying I'm supposed to enlist—against her will—the faery who killed me to help me find this Book?"

"Well, yes. The Morrigan's consort was a relation of Sorcha and Lonnrach's. The wisp was very clear that her blood was the key to the prison. You'll need her—alive, regrettably."

I curse. Loudly. Of course it would be their relative. Of course. *Terrible things. Always. Happen. To me.*

"Even if Kiaran agrees to this plan, I'll never convince Sorcha to help."

"You don't need to convince her. Chain her up. Drag her along." Aithinne shrugs. "If she starts getting irritating, punch her in the face. When the time comes, use your power to send word to me and I'll help you with her. I'm quite anxious to smash my fist into her nose."

"You and me both," I mutter.

Sorcha and Lonnrach have both destroyed me in different ways. Sorcha murdered my mother and, eventually, murdered me. I used to have nightmares about her. I used to track her kills. She was the reason I gave up everything to become what I am.

But Lonnrach . . . he almost did what she couldn't: He tried to break my very soul—and he nearly succeeded. The marks of his teeth might no longer be on my skin, but their effects haven't waned.

I only spent two months imprisoned by him in the fae realm, the equivalent of three years in the human world. But each day had stretched so vast that I had no concept of time. He broke into my mind for information to use against me, an extraction that required my blood. He'd pierce my skin with his teeth, day after day, over and over again. His bites left hundreds of scars down my arms and across my throat. Indentations that contained precious memories.

Over time, those memories faded in my mind, like old etchings that had been sanded away. To bring them up again,

I had to scrape my fingernails over the scars, digging them in just to bring up the memories of who I was. They were all I had left.

I shut my eyes briefly. I have to do this for Kiaran and Aithinne. For Catherine and Gavin and those people in Aithinne's cottage who didn't choose their fate. I have to do whatever it takes to find the Book and give them their lives back. I won't fail them again.

"I hate this," I mutter.

"Really? I'm having a grand time," Aithinne says brightly.

"That's because you're barmy."

"I believe you just mispronounced *magnificent*."

She leads me back to the edge of the cliff. This time when I peer down at Kiaran's castle, the soldiers are still in formation. As if they're waiting for instruction. We have to act now.

"You don't intend to open the portal halfway down, do you?"

Aithinne looks like she's considering it. At my outraged expression, she winks. "I'll do it here." She gestures to the soldiers. "Be ready. As soon as they sense power, they're going to attack. Make sure you don't lose control and almost murder my brother like you nearly did me." She smiles. "Easy."

Right. Just battle four dozen soldiers to get the attention of my lover, who may or may not be evil depending on what mood he's in.

"You know," I say lightly, "I think we need to rethink your use of *easy*. Just a suggestion."

"I have taken your suggestion under consideration and decided to ignore it." She steps back with a smile. "Ready?"

I recall another portal Aithinne opened for me to cross between islands. "You're not going to have me nearly crushed by tree branches again, are you?"

"No, no. Crushed by water."

With that, she lifts a hand as if she's beckoning something. Water rises from the sea, up and up toward the sky, until it's flowing with the force of a waterfall. The stream wraps around me, the water rushing past like a river suspended in air. It encloses me, mist spraying my clothes, my skin.

Just before it closes entirely, Aithinne says, "Good luck. I'll await your word."

Then I'm surrounded by water. The current is so deafening that any sound beyond it is muffled. I grip my sword tightly, ready to engage. My body is in fighting stance.

Then, suddenly, the water clears. Aithinne has dropped me right in the middle of the soldiers, no doubt on purpose. A hush goes through them. They all tense.

My power gives a mocking tap on their shoulders. *Right here.*

They attack as one. *God, they're fast.* Faster than the fae in the forest. These must be Kiaran's better soldiers, because they move like I do. Like they've been trained for this— trained for *me.*

The Cailleach's powers urge me to use them. All I have to do is let go and I could destroy these soldiers in a minute—a few seconds, if I wanted to show off. It would be so easy. All I'd have to do is—

Use your powers sparingly.

Aithinne's no-nonsense instruction brings me back from the brink.

Stay focused, Aileana. Don't give in. Don't die yet.

I might be slower without it, but I've never needed the powers of the Cailleach to win my battles in the past. I have to relearn how to use my body with its human limitations.

Every movement is a discovery. It's my limbs on fire as I block and lunge and swipe. It's the breath in my lungs bursting with exhilaration. It's my fist slamming across a faery's face so hard that my knuckles bleed. It's remembering what I can do with a sword and how graceful I am. And it's showing off for Kiaran. *Remember this? Remember us? You once said I was exquisite in battle. Let me show you. Let me remind you.*

My sword sings. I battle as if I'm in a dance, tempting him, beckoning him. For Kiaran—for us—this is how we seduce. And I can feel him watching.

This is me. Entering a room. About to ask you annoying questions.

When it's all over, I stare up at the castle, my breath coming fast. *Now let me in, you stubborn arse.*

The doors to the castle open with an echo that can probably be heard across the sea.

I smile. *Got you, Kiaran MacKay.*

CHAPTER 16

F THE castle had appeared nightmarish from the lookout point on the cliffs, it's even more desolate up close. My boots crunch through the dry, cracked soil as I enter the gates. They tower on either side of me, massive doors carved out of black rock that lead to the dark interior.

A frigid breeze ruffles my hair and I resist the urge to shiver. This place is unsettling. Not a single thing is recognizable as being formed from the remains of Derrick's home, a pixie city that was bursting with life. This castle was erected right over the rubble.

Nothing is left of that city. It's as if it never existed.

Inside, it's a cavern. The antechamber is vast, with great arched columns that lead up to a ceiling lit by flickering candles suspended in the air. Every inch of the black rock walls is covered in fae symbols. There's an aura to the room, a strange glow of energy that casts a shimmer along the stone archways, like when sunlight strikes water at a certain angle.

The walls breathe as if they were alive, as if this entire place were living, a sleeping creature. It's unnerving and beautiful, terrifying and darkly lovely. A million different dichotomies. Like everything fae.

"MacKay?"

No response.

You invited me in, and now you're stuck with me, Kiaran MacKay. You'll have to speak to me if you want me to leave.

I cross the antechamber and head toward a massive oak door that connects the great hall to another room, equally vast and deserted. An empty dais occupies the far end, indicating this as the throne room. But there is no throne there, no sign that anyone rules from the palace at all. My skin is covered in gooseflesh as I pass the vacant dais.

I swear I can feel the age of this place as if it were written along the walls, a tapestry of power depicting the rise and fall of the original palace that the crystal came from. This is an extension of the Old Kingdom, then. Not a replacement palace, but the Morrigan's home, created anew.

I wince as my footsteps echo across the floor. It's so loud: the only sound in this empty place. Despite the candles floating near the ceiling, the air is cold. Like the ruins of an old cathedral, desolate and filled with memories long lost. An old fallen kingdom risen out of the rubble and destruction of another.

"MacKay," I call again. Still no response. "Fine, if you won't speak then I will: I killed your soldiers in the woods.

Your sister didn't do it." Nothing. Not even footsteps. "I would apologize, but I'm not sorry."

I sigh in irritation when there's no response. *Bloody hell, MacKay.*

Fine. If he won't speak to me, I'll make myself feel welcome. I'll shout annoying questions down the halls if I have to.

I stride across the throne room and through another door, pausing just beyond the threshold. Now this looks more lived-in. It's an intimate space, furnished. At the far end of the room is a window that spans from floor to ceiling. Right in front of it is a single black leather chair. I almost smile at the memory of Kiaran's flat in Edinburgh, what seems like so long ago now. The only furniture he'd had in that place was a chair, a table, and a bed with warm wool blankets. Practicality and small comforts over opulence.

Aithinne was right: He is a creature of habit.

I approach the window. The view overlooks the cliffs of the mainland down to where the waves crash against the rocks just below the palace. I slide my fingertips across the back of his chair. I can picture him sitting there so easily, listening to the sea raging below. Kiaran always found solace in stillness; we both did. It's one of the reasons we trained so well together.

To my left, I notice the bed. *The bed.* It's exactly the same as it was in my dream, right down to the carvings in the headboard. How is that possible?

Aithinne's words brush across my mind. *The Cailleach's power recognizes its own. And it's easier because he's your lover.*

When my memories came flooding back, it must have helped our connection. My fingertips graze my neck. Despite the smooth, unmarked skin, the pressure of his teeth hasn't faded. Nor has my memory of this room. It wasn't entirely a dream, then. Somehow, my power linked with Kiaran's and I saw this room before ever setting foot in it.

The only difference is a massive table constructed of heavy oak on the far end of the room, set right in front of the grand fireplace. From here, I can see a scattering of objects on it.

I approach the table slowly.

A map is laid out there, branded into what looks like tanned leather and topped with old chess pieces carved from ivory. I trace the lines of the map and recognize the curve of the bay just beyond the castle, the forest I traveled through with Derrick that stretches eastward along the isle. Each piece is set very deliberately across the map.

Pawn. Pawn. Pawn. Three of them fallen like trees in a forest.

I swallow hard when I realize they mark different camps on Aithinne's land. The ones he's planning to attack first. Right in the center is the Queen.

And her crown is broken off.

The heavy wooden door behind me closes and I go still. I sense him standing there, as surely as if he were touching me. I hold my breath and turn.

Kiaran.

CHAPTER 17

KIARAN IS even more uncanny than I remember, every inch the faery King he was born to be. His luminous, pale skin stands out in contrast to his gleaming dark hair. The candlelight casts him in a halo of red and gold, an effect that's unsettlingly angelic. But an angel could never look that dangerous, that savagely beautiful. An angel wouldn't look at you as if torn between desire and violence, between yearning and something else. Something primal. Something dark.

I go still when our gazes meet. His once vivid lilac eyes are now cold and ringed with black, like ink spattered across flower petals.

I can't recall the last time I was so uncertain about him, so torn between fighting or running or *want*. The memory of his lips against mine surfaces, unbidden. I recall it perfectly now. White-hot kisses and trembling hands sliding down my arms, my back, my hips. The sounds he made, his whispered encouragements against my skin.

Kiaran lets out an uneven breath. I wonder if he's remembering, too. If he's thinking about every word we've ever said to each other, every promise we've ever made. I wonder if he sees that space inside me that belongs to him and always will. And he didn't take it by force or coercion. He wore away small pieces of it until so much was taken up with *him* that before I realized, I had given him the whole of my heart. I had given him my soul. I had given every part of me that was mine to offer.

Kiaran turns his head away sharply, his entire body tense. As if he's getting himself under control—or, at least, trying to.

Then he looks at me again, and his expression is too even, too composed and unreadable. I grip the table. Not ready to run. Unable to step back. Uncertain about stepping forward.

Aithinne's voice in my mind is a reminder to remain cautious. *No matter how normal he might appear at first, his hunger will always win out. Always.*

Is he Kiaran right now? Or is he Kadamach? "Hullo," I say softly.

Then he's striding toward me with a hard glint in his gaze, purposeful. Threatening? I can't tell. *I can't tell.* I grasp the hilt of my sword in warning, but he doesn't even glance at it.

His hunger will always win out. Always.

I pull the blade from its sheath. In the space of a breath, the tip is pressed to the base of his neck.

Kiaran goes still. His eyes lock with mine, his features softening. "Kam," he whispers.

That's all I need to hear. The single syllable is a declaration between us, an admission. *I missed you* and *I'm still here* and *I'm still me.*

I drop the sword and it clatters to the floor, forgotten.

My first words are spoken through tears. "I walked into this room to ask you irritating questions. Are you still *you?*"

Kiaran says something under his breath. A prayer? Then he steps forward, presses his forehead to mine, and wraps his arms around my waist. "I don't know yet. Ask me another irritating question. Pester me with them."

I let out a choked laugh. "Oh, thank god. I was concerned I'd have to challenge you to a duel."

"You still might." He shuts his eyes, as if he's savoring the sound of my voice. "I enjoy a good duel, don't you?"

"Swords or fisticuffs, MacKay?"

His smile is the most beautiful thing I've ever seen. "Both. Either. I don't care. I just want you." He cups my cheek. "Kam." He says my name like he can't say it enough. Like it's his prayer. Like I'm his salvation. Then, in a voice just below a whisper, "Touch me."

I slide my fingertips across his jaw, my thumb brushing his lower lip. Buying time before I explain everything. I have so much to say. "So you're probably wondering—"

"Don't finish that sentence yet," Kiaran says, pushing me gently against the table. He pulls the collar of my shirt aside to press a kiss to my shoulder. "I prefer this instead."

"You have no idea what I was about to say."

"Something about how you're alive, why your eyes look that way, and why your power feels different." Kiaran's lips trail to my collarbone as he begins unbuttoning my shirt. Kissing lower, until he finds the scar over my heart. When he pulls away to look at it, the black ring around his irises bleeds into the color and the fine hairs on my body rise. I've never seen his eyes do that before. "And it'll involve our realms hanging in the balance, both our lives, and an inevitable exhausting battle. Do I have the right idea?"

"I'm afraid so."

Kiaran's irises become lilac again. "Then don't tell me yet. I would rather pretend, for just this moment, that the world can fix itself." He leans in, fingertips grazing my scar and sliding down, down, down, unbuttoning. "Touch me more. Kiss me. Say my name." Each request brings another hot touch of his lips, his hands, a new button undone. Another. Another. "I need to be sure."

"Of what?"

"That you're real." Then he presses an achingly soft kiss against my lips, one I barely feel. Then another, harder. "Tell me you're real."

"I'm real," I whisper. "I'm still here. I can ask you more questions, if you'd like."

"Later," he says.

Then Kiaran's lips are on mine. Hard. Desperate. Like he can't get enough of me; like I'm going to disappear. As if at any moment, he's going to wake up from this dream and I'll be gone.

Kiaran kisses me like he's about to lose me all over again. He isn't gentle. There's no softness, no hesitancy, no delicate touches. And I don't want kind. I don't want gentle. My desire is just as fierce, just as demanding. I grasp the back of his shirt, digging in roughly with my fingernails. *More.* I want more. I need this. I need *him*.

I pull back only briefly to yank off my shirt, the rest of my clothes, his. Then it's Kiaran's skin against mine and we're both burning, kissing, biting, clawing. It's a physical urgency, a devouring need, a benediction of *yes, now, more.*

Kiaran lifts me onto the edge of the table. Pawns scatter across the map; the Queen falls onto the floor with a sharp knock.

Then Kiaran eases into me, hands gripping my thighs hard. When he presses his lips to my throat, I have a brief flash to my dream. To his teeth biting down, drawing blood. I stiffen slightly, uncertain.

But he only whispers, "Don't disappear again, Kam. Don't disappear."

CHAPTER 18

LATER, WHEN my eyes are heavy with sleep, I say to Kiaran, "Shall I finish that sentence now?"

Kiaran embraces me from behind, dragging his fingertips across my shoulder blades. We're in his bed and it feels as if we're back in my dream. As if none of this is real and we're in a safe space separate from the world. Cocooned in a beautiful lie.

Across the room, a shaft of light pools beneath the window from the full moon outside. The muffled roar of the waves crashing against the rocky isle fills the vast, silent space. And it's so soothing. I could stay like this with him, in this bed, forever.

If we had that long. I wish we did.

"MacKay?" I look over my shoulder at him. When my eyes meet his, something in his expression makes me go still. Hunger.

He jerks away from me, breath hitching. Kiaran doesn't answer. I watch as he struggles with himself, his features taut. His lips move, as if he were counting. Gaining control again.

"Are you all right?" I whisper uncertainly.

"Fine." He shakes his head once, and then the tension leaves his body. "I'm fine. Don't finish your sentence yet. It's going to lead to me slaughtering things."

"You *like* slaughtering things."

"Compared to this? No." He touches me again, his fingers grazing my arm. Tentative, hesitant. When I tell him he's usually the practical one, he replies, "It must be your influence. I'm actually about to make several suggestions, and all of them are impractical."

I smile. "Ooh, *several* suggestions, is it? My, my. Impractical Kiaran MacKay is . . . dare I say it? Adorable."

Kiaran looks at me in disgust. "I am not."

"You are and you don't even know it. Adorable."

"*Adorable* is something we call foolish humans right before we kill them."

"*Adorable* is what we call adult men who love to cuddle and swear on their lives that they don't." Kiaran makes a sound in his throat. "You can growl at me all you want. I know your weaknesses, MacKay. Cuddling. Neck kisses. That ticklish spot just above your—"

I laugh as he grabs me around the waist and pulls me against him. He kisses me fiercely enough to make my toes curl. Then he pulls back with the smug expression of someone who has had thousands of years to perfect seduction and knows exactly how to use it against me.

* * *

Between touches I whisper that soon we'll have to go back out into the world and face our fates. Kiaran doesn't answer. He just kisses me like I'm going to die all over again. I haven't been able to tell him yet that I still might.

"Let me tell you a story," I say instead. "Once upon a time, there was a girl whose life was saved by the faery king—"

"This story sounds distinctly familiar. I think I might have heard it somewhere before."

I shush him and say not to interrupt. "If anyone asked her how she felt about the king, she would have said she loathed him. He ruthlessly trained her to fight his own kind. He taught her to kill. She learned from his lessons how to quiet the rage that burned inside her. But she had already decided that one day, when she had grown strong enough and learned everything she could about battle, she was going to murder him."

Kiaran goes still, his eyes glittering in the darkness. He says nothing.

"Her opportunity came one night when he decided she was ready to hunt her first faery. It was a skriker that had been terrorizing a nearby village, slaughtering children in the night. The king handed the girl his sword and ordered her to kill the goblin-like creature.

"She barely won. But in the end, as she thrust the sword deep into the monster's gut, she felt something so profoundly that she thought it would consume her. So she told the king. She whispered the words and meant them with every part of her rage-filled soul: 'I hate you. I hate *all* of you.' When she lifted the sword again, she intended to pierce it right through his heart.

"That was the first time the girl had ever seen the faery king smile."

I lift my hand and press my palm to Kiaran's cheek. "You'll have to finish the story. She never knew why he smiled. Just that one day, she wanted to see him do it again. So she dropped the sword and spared his life. And she never told the king what really happened that night."

Kiaran looks amused. "The king knew the girl's plan all along. He smiled because he decided he liked her. She kept things interesting."

I stare at him. "So the faery king is a deranged sort. As the girl always suspected."

"How about his side of this story?" He pulls me close, his lips soft on my shoulder. "He never told the girl that during a hunt, when she ran alongside him with the wind in her hair and the moonlight behind her, that she was the most magnificent thing he had ever seen and he wanted her."

Then Kiaran's hands are in my hair, lips brushing mine. "And when the king watched her in battle, she'd look over at him with a smile and he desired her.

"It was never at once," he continued. "It was after everything they had gone through and then it was the king and the girl facing an entire army together. And he knew the truth. His heart was hers. It always was. It always will be."

A shadow crosses Kiaran's irises. A reminder that he's still fighting. Just to be here. With me. He shuts his eyes, expression strained. Before I can ask if he's all right, he pulls me against him and holds me close.

His next words are spoken under his breath, so low I wonder if I heard them at all. "The girl helps the king keep his darkness at bay."

* * *

In the hours before dusk, I know it's time to tell him everything. "Don't go to war with Aithinne."

He sighs. "Kam—"

"She doesn't want it," I interrupt. "I'm the one who killed your soldiers."

"I gathered that when you announced it in my hallway," Kiaran says dryly. "And when you made quick work of my men outside." He's counting my vertebrae, fingers sliding up one at a time, inch by inch. His touch is gentle. When he kisses my back, his lips are as light as moth wings.

"I had to get your attention. It was Aithinne's idea."

"I thought that dramatic entrance had suggested-by-Aithinne all over it." His fingertips sweep down, down across my spine. So slow that I shiver. "I can feel the pulse of power straining beneath your skin," he murmurs. "I know it's not yours. You've made a terrible decision, haven't you?"

"How do you know?"

"Easy. You have a knack for attracting mayhem."

"I think it was a wonderful decision, all things considered. I'm here, aren't I?"

"You're using my affections to garner sympathy. It won't work." He pulls back and looks down at me, serious now. "Tell me what you did."

"What I had to do," I say.

There was no other choice. The decision between death and one final goodbye isn't truly a choice. The Cailleach gambled on me saying yes.

She placed her bet and she won.

I tell him about what happened after Sorcha killed me. "If we find the Book, you don't have to kill Aithinne," I say softly. "It'll end the curse. We can change everything back to the way it was before all of this. All the people we failed to save will have their lives back, their homes back." When he doesn't respond, I press closer, whispering in his ear, "You and I will run through the night again. We'll dance in the rain and watch the sun rise over the sea. This time I won't even mind if you show up unannounced at my house as long as you don't break my father's vases again."

Kiaran doesn't return my smile. He gently pushes me away, eyes searching mine. "What haven't you told me?"

My heart thuds in my chest. I let out a breath. "The Cailleach gave me her powers as a short-term solution. My body wasn't meant to hold them."

As he stares down at me, I know he understands. But I have to say the words. They stick in my throat at first and I shut my eyes.

Outside, the waves crash against the rock. The wind rattles the windows. Then everything goes quiet and all I can hear is my pulse in my ears. "I'm dying, MacKay," I whisper. "If we don't find that Book—"

Kiaran doesn't let me finish. He kisses me, pressing me into the pillows, and the words disappear on my lips.

I never get the chance to tell him that each time I use the Cailleach's powers, they kill me a little more. I never get the chance to tell Kiaran about needing Sorcha to find the Book. Each kiss interrupts my words. His hands pave a path of heat down my body. He touches me like he wants to forget the world. Forget our fates. Forget everything. Like he wants to drown in this, in us, in me.

I let him.

I let myself drown in him, too.

CHAPTER 19

I WAKE TO find myself alone in Kiaran's room. The side of the bed where he slept is cold to the touch; he hasn't been there for hours. The duvet is even undisturbed, as if I dreamed the whole thing.

It's early morning. The first vestiges of daylight spill through the open window and I can hear the faint crashing of ocean waves as the tide rolls in—the only sound in the still, massive room.

I rise from the bed and grab my discarded clothes from the floor. It's so drafty in that empty space that I slip on my coat and boots as I head to the door. I don't know if Kiaran wants me wandering the vast halls of this nightmare palace, but I'm not comfortable staying in his room alone, either.

I push the door open and slip into the great hall.

"MacKay?"

My call is met with silence. The candles that were floating overhead when I arrived have gone; the only light is from the flickering torches that line the obsidian walls. I didn't notice before that the walls have been shined and buffed to such perfection that they look like deep, dark pools. My footsteps echo as I cross the great hall and step into another corridor.

I'm greeted by a row of doors that seems never-ending. Dozens of them, and every single one is made of the same dark ash wood as Kiaran's bed. I would never have time to search through them all.

There is something disquieting about this place, about the way the stones feel as if they're pressing closer together. It doesn't help that the air is heavy and still. My breath hitches at a memory of the mirrored room where Lonnrach kept me imprisoned after he destroyed Edinburgh. How those mirrors seemed to close in, too. Until it felt as though I didn't have enough space to breathe.

That's how the blackened walls feel. Like it isn't a palace, but a tomb—one that belonged to the Morrigan.

Stop wasting time. Find Kiaran. Tell him about Sorcha. Then make her help you find the Book.

I start down the hall, purposeful now. If I make enough noise, he's bound to hear me—at least, that's what I assume until I realize how bloody vast and empty this castle is.

So I tap into my power to find Kiaran. His power calls to mine like a rope pulling me in. A bond I can't fully describe. I break into a run, my heels pounding against the floor. The walls stretch farther and farther, twisting and turning, a labyrinth constructed of obsidian.

I follow his power past another bedroom, then down an equally long hallway. Nothing about this place changes, as though each door has been replicated a thousand times, every detail perfectly mirrored.

Just before I make another turn, I spot a shaft of light on one of the walls. *There.* An open door, the first since I left Kiaran's bedroom. I slow to a walk, approaching it cautiously. I pause when I see what's on the other side.

It isn't another room, but a meadow at nightfall. A full moon hangs low on the horizon, ringed with purple and blue, in a twilight sky. Colors of teal, sapphire, and ebony glow in a gradient that starts at the horizon and extends upward. Beneath the beautiful sky, the meadow is as vast as the ocean.

Kiaran stands some distance from me, grooming a faery horse. The animal is semitransparent, the metal of its coat thin enough that its organs are visible. Even from here, I can see the gold blood pumping through its veins, the rapid pulse of its real horse's heart. I know from experience that despite being made of metal, the creature is soft to the touch, like nothing human-created. I watch as Kiaran slowly strokes the brush across its back. Over and over.

With my faelike senses, I notice little things about Kiaran's reaction that I might not have detected without the Cailleach's power. His breathing is so steady, but it hitches slightly when he realizes I'm behind him. He murmurs a curse.

He keeps brushing the horse in easy strokes. He's pretending I'm not there. No doubt he came out here for some time alone after what I told him earlier. Kiaran has a tendency to distance himself when he feels too strongly, and he's already seen me die twice.

Well, he's just going to have to deal with me. I'm here now. I came back. We have to find the Book. And now I need Sorcha.

I cross the meadow, walking briskly. Grass breaks beneath my boots, and my fingers brush the thigh-high flowers as I head toward Kiaran. The air here is damp but comfortably warm, like the coast on a misty summer morning. The scent of heather and rain grows stronger the farther in I go.

Kiaran doesn't look up as I approach, but I notice the way his fingers grip the brush harder. His breathing slows as if he's carefully controlling each inhale, exhale.

"Let me guess," he says when I come up beside him, "you tracked me."

I shrug. "Serves you right for all the times you did it to me in Edinburgh. Showing up randomly at the park, at my *home* . . ."

Kiaran's smile is small as he smooths the brush down the horse's neck. "You offered me your foul human tea. I wanted to strip off that ridiculous clothing you were wearing and you asked me to destroy it instead." He finally looks up at me from beneath his eyelashes. "Believe me, I remember. I wanted you then. I had for a long time."

I look at him in surprise. "You did?" I'm suspicious. "You kept telling me I was a silly human girl. You were so condescending and superior about it."

"Well, you were a silly human girl I happened to want."
He shrugs. "And I won't argue the rest."

The horse nudges my shoulder with its muzzle in a clear
hint for attention. I gently reach out to stroke my fingertips
down its nose. It makes a sound of contentment and
I smile—until I notice the saddle on the ground next to
the horse.

Kiaran was about to leave.

"Are you avoiding me?" I ask him, not bothering to hide
my irritation. "Is that why you were about to ride off somewhere? Be honest."

His jaw tightens. "No," Kiaran says. "I was leaving so I
could prepare for finding that Book."

"To prepare . . . ?"

I glance sharply at the faery horse, at the saddle again. It's
covered in familiar markings. Where have I seen those
particular symbols before? I remember the grooves of them
beneath my fingertips—

During the battle for Edinburgh. Those are the symbols
of the Wild Hunt.

"You were going to hunt for a human victim." When he
doesn't respond, I ask more sharply, "Weren't you?"

When Kiaran looks at me, his expression is distant.
Almost cold. "Then Aithinne showed you. And you still
came."

I hold back a flinch at the reminder of the thin woman in
the cottage, the panicked sounds she made when the faery at
her neck lifted its teeth away. "Of course I came," I say. "I'm

the one who was supposed to stop Sorcha from using the crystal—"

"Don't," Kiaran snaps. "Don't talk like this is something you allowed to happen to me. This is who I *am*. It's who I was for thousands of years before I ever met you. It's who I was born to be."

My fingernails bite into my palms. "It's who you were forced to be."

"Semantics, Kam." He resumes brushing the horse. "If I don't do this, I won't be in a position to help anyone, not even you."

I think of his victims in the cottage, and what he's reduced them to. But the faery in front of me seems calm, not evil. Not beyond saving. Kiaran laughed in bed with me. He made love to me, and he let me tell him my silly story. He's not Kadamach.

Or so I believe until the moment I touch his shoulder and the meadow wind blows back the collar of my coat. He looks over at me, gaze flickering to the exposed skin at my throat.

And I see the hunger in his eyes.

Kiaran's body tenses. He looks away and strokes the brush down the faery horse's coat. He's getting himself under control. Stroke. *Control*. Stroke. *Control*.

The black around his irises begins to bleed into the color. Unlike the fae in the forest, I don't sense his insatiable desire to feed. But I can hear the way his breathing has become uneven. Rough.

"Go back inside, Kam." His voice is sharp. The lilac of his irises is but a small interior ring.

Be still. Be calm. My heart slams against my chest. The way he's looking at me is so raveous that I barely recognize him. "I need something from you."

The air grows colder. "So you showed up for ulterior motives, then."

I hate the way he says that, like I came here and laughed with him and kissed him and it was all for a favor. "Stop it, MacKay."

"Just tell me what you want."

I hesitate. "I need Sorcha."

When he looks at me, his eyes are black. Brutal. The cold air bites my skin and my lungs constrict. "No," he says in a voice I've only ever heard once before.

That voice as frigid and sharp-edged as a river in winter, one I could drown in. Kadamach's voice. The voice of the Unseelie King.

I don't move. I don't even blink. "I wouldn't be asking this if it weren't important. You know that. Not when it comes to *her.*"

"I said *no.*" His words are a dangerous warning.

Don't make me use my powers against you. "Her ancestor was the Morrigan's consort," I say. "I need her blood to find the Book."

"Then take her blood. Drain her dry, for all I care." I hate that voice. I hate the way it rolls over me, makes me shiver in dread. "But she stays where she is."

I swallow hard, afraid to ask. "Where did you put her, MacKay?"

Kiaran's smile sends chills down my spine. "Exactly where she belongs. She's where I should have kept her two thousand years ago, and she deserves every second of it."

The air is so brutally icy that it hurts. I can feel my power rebelling, demanding to defend itself. But I keep it tamped down. I embrace the pain because I know how easily I could lose myself to it—and how easily Kiaran could do the same. Right now, his powers are barely contained. His eyes have become as hard and dark as obsidian, emotionless. Unyielding.

As if Kiaran senses my power stirring, his own rises in response. Shadows gather along the ground at his feet. My skin is covered in a fine layer of frost, so pale from cold it's almost blue.

"Stop this," I whisper. "I don't want to hurt you."

I see the moment my words sink in. Kiaran flinches, turning away. All at once, the temperature rises—so fast my skin stings with the warmth. The shadows recede into the ground and the meadow looks as it once did: as welcoming as a summer morning.

"We'll discuss Sorcha later." I hear the strain in his voice. His knuckles are white around the brush. "I need to go. Don't get in my way."

"Help me understand. The longer you go between feeding, the worse you get?"

Kiaran drops the brush to the ground and grabs the saddle. His movements are stiff as he positions it on the horse and secures it in place. "You wouldn't recognize me at my worst. I don't want you to see me like that."

Just as he's about to swing into the saddle, I move to stop him, but he pulls back from my touch. I drop my hand. "How many people will you hunt before you decide you're prepared to find the Book? One?" His fingers tighten on the saddle, but he doesn't answer. *Not one. More.* "How many people are you asking me to let you kill, MacKay?"

"I'm not—"

"You *are*," I say through clenched teeth. "I've seen them. You may not stop their hearts, but you take their lives. What you do to them is worse than death. *How many?*"

Kiaran looks away, but not before I see his expression. Shame. Guilt. Regret. He doesn't answer, not even when I put my hand over his. "You don't have to do this. When we find the Book, we'll use it to break this curse."

His laugh is hard, bitter. "Do you think that matters to me? I was ready to kill Aithinne and get this over with. You saw the map on my table. Then you came back and told me I was about to lose you all over again." This time, when his eyes meet mine, they're so bleak I almost can't bear to look at him. "You're asking how many people I'm prepared to kill? The answer is however many it takes. However many it takes to save you."

I step back. "Don't you dare say you're doing this for me. Don't put that on me, MacKay."

"You don't know what you're asking. You want me to go with you to find this Book and I can barely stand next to you right now."

"Why—"

"Because I don't trust myself with you," he snaps. When he looks over at me, the lilac of his eyes is almost completely enveloped. "You're still human," he says in a low voice, "and my control isn't limitless. Do I need to remind you what happened to the last woman who trusted me not to harm her?"

I shut my mouth. Catríona. The Falconer he fell in love with thousands of years ago. He stopped feeding on humans and couldn't stop himself killing her.

This time, when Kiaran steps closer, his touch is cold. Brutally so. "Shall I tell you the truth? What I haven't been able to stop thinking about since yesterday?" His fingers brush the artery at my neck. "How when I kiss you there, I can feel your blood moving through your veins. I could sense the power inside you. It runs from here"—he presses a cold palm to my chest—"down to here." Kiaran's touch trails slowly down my arms to my fingertips. I shut my eyes at the shiver that runs through me. "And it should be a deterrent, but it isn't. You only burn brighter." Then he dips his head and presses his lips to my throat. Raggedly, he whispers, "Here. I would bite you right here."

When his teeth scrape the length of my neck, I freeze. *Don't. Please don't. Not that.*

With a soft sound, Kiaran abruptly pulls away. "And that's why I don't trust myself with you. That's why I need to go."

I reach out to grip his hand, noticing how his eyes darken slightly. Not like before, but just enough to tell me that I need to be careful.

"When I saw your human victims in the cottage," I say, "Aithinne said she didn't know if you were my Kiaran MacKay anymore."

There it is, the flicker of guilt in his gaze. So quick I almost miss it. I press on, knowing I'm right this time. "I thought of your *gifts*. How you used to have your *sluagh* deliver Falconers' bodies to Aithinne. And I thought she might be right. I thought you might be tormenting her again the way you used to."

"Good," he says coldly. "It's easier that way."

I raise my hand to touch his face. "But then I remembered the one time you felt guilt, when you killed Catríona, you delivered her yourself. You're the one who takes those humans to Aithinne's camp, aren't you? Because she's not the one you're tormenting." *You're tormenting yourself*, I think. *You are.* As if he reads my mind, he says nothing. But I notice how his gaze softens. Because he is still my Kiaran MacKay. He is. "Don't do this to save me, MacKay. Not when you're the one who taught me that I need to save myself."

"Kam," he whispers.

I keep going, because I know I only have seconds to get him to listen. "When you did that, you taught me how to endure," I say softly. "I'm asking you to do the same. I'm asking you to be stronger than your curse."

This time, when he looks at me, I know he's made his decision. "Then I need you to make me a promise before we do anything else. Before I take you to Sorcha."

I swallow. "All right."

"If I go with you and I become someone you don't recognize, don't let me hurt you. Leave me behind if you have to." When I hesitate, he says it again. "Promise me."

Then I do something I've never done in all the time I've known Kiaran: I lie to his face. "I promise."

CHAPTER 20

'VE BARELY walked through the door where Kiaran is keeping Sorcha before I have the urge to run in the other direction. Now I understand what Kiaran meant when he said Sorcha was exactly where she belongs. Why he said she was paying for the things she's done.

Since my time in the *Sìth-bhrùth* I've become well acquainted with the fae's creative methods of imprisonment. They employ power against their victims. Everything they do is intended to break you down little by little each day, each hour, each second. They make you decide which is easiest: death or handing over your soul.

"What the hell is this?" I breathe to myself.

Sorcha's prison is a crossroads at night. She's chained between two trees, one on either side of the road, and the shackles are so tight that her body is splayed and mostly immobile. The trees bend toward her, as if caging her in. The combined scents almost make me gag. Iron. Flesh. Something burning.

She looks so broken.

Along Sorcha's arms and legs are long, jagged cuts that drip down her pale skin and onto the ground—where a pool of blood gathers so deep in a pockmark that it covers her to her ankles.

I should be satisfied to see Sorcha suffer—the way she made my mother suffer when she tore out her heart and left her to die in the street. I might have been, once, in the months after my mother's death when I cared for nothing except vengeance. That Aileana wouldn't have given a damn about compassion. Not for Sorcha.

But now . . .

Maybe it was the *daysweeksmonthsyears* Lonnrach had me. Helpless. When he kept me in the mirrored room, he tortured me like this, with control and isolation. A punishment to fit my crimes. I had spent a year hunting the fae, and in my time with him, I was no longer the hunter. I was the prey. He made certain I never forgot that.

Lonnrach's words echo in my mind, a terrible reminder of my own worst days. *Now you know precisely how it feels to be that helpless.*

No one deserves to be under someone else's complete control, unable to fight back even if they wanted.

Maybe I've grown too soft. Maybe I'm just tired of death. Maybe it's compassion that separates us from monsters. *Does that make me better than them or does it make me a fool?*

"Kam?" Kiaran's touch is light on my arm, but I pull away. As if he reads my thoughts, his gaze darkens. "Don't look at me like that."

"Do you come in here just to . . ." *make her bleed? Like Lonnrach did when he visited me?*

Some punishments are so terrible that they are beyond justification. But the fae operate under a moral code that gives little thought to empathy. Especially when that faery is the Unseelie King.

"I have many faults," Kiaran says in a hard voice, "but I don't torture for amusement."

"You did once."

Like you loved it. Like you lived for it. Because you believed emotion was a weakness.

His expression shutters. "If I ever reach that point again"—a flicker of a glance at me—"that's when you'll know I'm gone." He gestures to Sorcha with a nod. "These are her memories. Her torture is self-inflicted."

"Her memories?"

"This is what she did to people when she lured them to crossroads at night." Kiaran leans against the doorframe, his features shadowed in the moonlight. "The chains are dipped in water infused with *seilgflùr* so her powers are bound. The power here forces her to endure the deaths of those she's killed. It's considered a fair punishment."

A breeze picks up, gently rustling the trees that line the road, and the faint scent of blood reaches me. Sorcha's chains clink softly together, an eerie sound.

She still hasn't looked up.

I don't realize I've stepped back until I bump into Kiaran. "You think me cruel." When I don't respond, he says, "This is what she did for thousands of years to your kind. Every night. She doesn't deserve any pity."

"What about what you did?" I can't help but ask. He may wear the penance of his kills on his skin, but it's nothing like *that*. "What was your punishment?"

He's unreadable, frustratingly so. I hate when I can't tell what he's thinking.

Kiaran drops his hand from my arm. "I gave my heart to a human." He walks away before I can respond.

After a moment's hesitation, I follow.

Sorcha never even looks up as we approach. Her dark hair shines in the moonlight, hanging down to her hips. It hides her face like a shroud. She wears a thin black dress that covers her from wrists to ankles, like something a woman would wear to a funeral. She looks so small like this; her shoulders are hunched forward, hands hanging weightlessly. The chains are the only thing holding her upright.

It's such a macabre sight that another jolt of pity goes through me. That only grows as we draw closer and her short, wheezing breaths fill my ears. I shudder when I hear them.

I hate that sound.

They're the quick, panting exhalations of an animal in so much agony that it's all they can think about. If I'd heard that during a hunt, I would have killed the creature quickly. It would have been the right thing to do. It would have been a mercy.

I know that pain firsthand. I breathed like that after Lonnrach's interrogations.

We stop in front of her, and beneath the cascade of her hair, I see Sorcha's bloody lips curve into a smile. One that doesn't fool me.

"Have you come to gloat, Kadamach?" Her voice is rough, like she's been screaming. "Or are you simply here to watch and enjoy my punishment? I don't know why you ever gave up your crown. Unseelie suits you."

"Do you think I enjoy this?" Kiaran sounds tired. "I never wanted to be your King."

"You did once." Sorcha's laugh is more of a choke. "You were willing to kill for it. The old you would have looked at all this blood and told me it was a waste. That I should have bled them all dry."

A sudden image bursts across my mind. Sorcha at my mother's neck, teeth buried in her skin. Her pulling away, lips covered in my mother's blood. It marked her pale skin as starkly as oil on porcelain.

I can't hold back the sound that escapes my throat.

Sorcha jerks her face up, and her eyes narrow at me through the veil of her deep black hair. Then she throws back her head and laughs, a throaty scratch of a noise that echoes in the night, half-crazed.

"For a human, you don't know how to stay dead, do you?" Her smile slices through me like a blade. "I should have cut out your heart and eaten it. Like I did with your mother's."

I'm struck by memories of everything Sorcha has ever done. The night she killed my mother. The pain of her driving a sword into my chest. The jarring, ugly scrape of metal through the sinew, muscle, and bone of my body to strike right through my heart. And Kiaran looking up at me through it all. She took from him the one choice he had made for himself: not to be King.

My thoughts must be so clear; Sorcha only laughs harder, an arrogant, mocking laugh that says: *I don't feel for you. I don't care about you. I am remorseless.*

"You were right," I tell Kiaran tightly. "She does deserve this."

Sorcha's rough chuckle is self-satisfied. "Oh, don't tell me," she says. "You saw me hanging here and you felt sorry for me. How sweet."

"A momentary lapse in memory, judgment, and sanity that won't happen again."

"She's such a mouthy little human, Kadamach. And here I thought you preferred your pets silent."

"They were never silent," Kiaran replies casually. "You couldn't hear them over the constant noise coming from your wide-open trap."

"Maybe not silent, then," she says with a sweet smile. "But always on their knees."

I take a sharp step toward her, but Kiaran stops me with a restraining hand on my shoulder. He's back to calm, practical Kiaran. I'm grateful for that, at least. Especially now that we're in the worst possible situation.

Kiaran leans in, turning his head so Sorcha can't hear him or read his lips. "She's trying to get a rise out of you. Sorcha doesn't respond well to pity."

"What would you suggest?"

He puts a finger under my chin so I'm forced to meet his eyes. I can't help but wince. Those beautiful lilac irises are never going to be the way they once were. Never as clear. They're a reminder that the Unseelie inside him is always there, barely contained. "Don't let her see your weaknesses. Find out what she wants."

I tighten my jaw and glance over at Sorcha to find her watching us with unabashed interest. "How soft you've become, Kadamach. Talking to your pet as if she were an equal. She ought to be crawling at your feet like the worthless animal she is." Her gaze rakes me over. "Unless she's one step above a pet. Which would make her your whore."

Kiaran's hand grips mine in a silent message: *Don't dignify that with a response.*

I squeeze his hand and release it to take a step toward her. Sorcha raises her chin, as if waiting for a blow that won't come. "You make the mistake of defining me by his ownership," I say softly. "You don't seem to understand that he's mine every bit as much as I'm his."

Sorcha drops her arrogant smile just long enough for me to see something vulnerable in her expression. Something that longs for *him.*

As if she realizes what she almost showed me, she clenches her jaw. "Is there a reason you're here, Falconer? Unless you've come to triumph over my misery. Let me assure you: I would rather be tortured here for a thousand years than listen to you for another moment."

"The Book of Remembrance," I say, voice tight. "Tell me how to find it without the usual cynical commentary. Now."

Sorcha goes still, as if she's surprised by the question. If I hadn't been watching for her response, I might not have noticed the fleeting emotion in her eyes. Even so, it's gone so quickly I wonder if I imagined it.

Her armor of smug indifference is firmly back in place. "Oh. That," she says, in the same casual tone one might use to say, *Oh that old thing.* "I understand it was lost a long time ago." Her slow smile is no doubt deliberately meant to anger me. "But I might be persuaded to help you find it. For the right price, of course."

I will tear you apart limb from limb and make you help me.

Maybe when the Cailleach revived my bones and gave me her power, a small piece of her lived on inside me. Or maybe she made me less human and more fae. That's the only explanation I have for what I do next: I grasp Sorcha by the throat and *squeeze* until I know she can't breathe.

Behind me, I sense Kiaran step closer. "Kam—"

"Don't," I say sharply, without looking away from Sorcha. "We're running out of time and options, and I'm losing my patience. You said to find out what she wants. So let me do this."

It's my turn to smile smugly. It's my turn to have the power.

It's my turn.

"Do what?" I can hear the uncertainty in his voice.

This time, when my power leaves its cage and the darkness takes me over, I let it consume me. I let it wash away my emotions, my concerns, my worries. I let it take my compassion, too. If compassion is for humans, brutality is for fae.

And I'm both.

My eyes meet Sorcha's. "Nothing she hasn't already done to me."

CHAPTER 21

I KNOW SORCHA senses my power thickening in the air, sharp as electricity. It gives off the heady stench of iron and ozone.

She's afraid of me. I see it in her eyes; I can taste it. *Good.*

When I touch my fingers to her temple, she struggles, as if she knows what I'm about to do. Her throat convulses in my grip as she chokes for breath, pricking at something human in me. Something that forces me to remember Derrick's harsh words to me in the forest.

The friend I knew had someone break into her mind, day after day, for months. If you were her, you would never have done that to anyone.

I can't be that Aileana anymore. I can't be her and find the Book. I can't favor my humanity when my realm is crumbling to dust and so many lives hang in the balance. Compassion won't help me right now—Sorcha doesn't give a damn about pity. She'd use it against me.

A part of me still doubts. *Do this, and there's no going back. You'll be the dark creature Derrick saw in the woods, and this time you have no excuses. Your memories are intact. Do this, and you're no better than her. No better than Lonnrach.*

Sorcha looks at me and I see how much she hates me. I make my decision. *So be it.*

I tear into her mind like a sword ripping through flesh. She's so surprised that she puts up no resistance. I catch the first glimmers of color in her thoughts, similar to Derrick's. Only hers are all red-rimmed with sharp black edges, thorny branches of ivy that cover her memories in a protective shield.

Sorcha recovers from her initial shock and her mind slams into mine. She shoves at me with so much force I see stars beneath my lids. I grit my teeth. Her power is an onslaught of teeth and claws bucking against me.

You'll have to kill me first, she's thinking. *You'll have to kill Kadamach.*

The assault of her power is tremendous—but it's no match for mine. I surge through, catching a glimpse of the memories beyond the thorns. I can see the outer fringes of them—images that flicker by so quickly I can't keep up.

She puts up another fight, frantic now. Desperate. *Don't.*

My fingers tighten around her throat. *Surrender,* I think to her. That inner voice is as harsh and cold as any fae. I sound powerful. I sound like the Cailleach.

I shove into her mind again just as my fingernails break through her skin. *I said, surrender.*

Sorcha's struggles grow fainter now, her defenses weakening. I can't help the small stir of triumph that she's finally helpless against me. Finally. *Finally.*

Don't, I think to myself as revulsion knots my stomach. *Don't become so much like Lonnrach that you forget why you're doing this.*

I focus on my task: to find information. Like with Derrick, my human mind can't comprehend the stream of images that make up the span of Sorcha's experiences. There are thousands of years of thoughts, events, and emotions to sift through. Each one is perfectly intact, all of it happening at once. As if time is different for her, meaningless.

When Lonnrach did this, he sorted through my memories with care and precision, as if he were running a thread through a needle. I try his tactic of calling memories forth, coaxing them out of the stream of images based specifically on what I want.

The Book of Remembrance. Show me what she doesn't want me to see. Show me. Show me.

Sorcha uses the last ounce of her strength to resist and send me off in another direction, but I hold firm. I bend her to my will. Her last vestiges of resolve vanish under the force of my command, my power. I feel her body go slack in its chains and I loosen my grip on her throat.

Her mind opens, and I walk into her memory.

I'm standing in a glen just after twilight, beside a tree that reaches for the sky with sharp, bare branches. The beautiful, fresh scent of spring flowers is fragrant in the air. Beads of water have collected along the bark, signs of a recent rain. Etched in the tree is a fae symbol I've never seen before. When I reach out to touch it, my fingers go right through the trunk.

It might look real, but it's only a memory—so perfectly intact I can see every groove in the bark.

Sorcha is standing next to me and I'm shocked by her appearance. *What's wrong with her?*

She looks sickly and too thin. Beneath the gossamer glow of her fae skin, she has a fevered flush to her cheeks. Sweat glistens along her brow, and her hand trembles as she pushes her hair back. Her eyes are filled with depths of emotion I've never seen from her. Desperation?

I flinch at Lonnrach's voice behind me. "I can't come with you."

I turn, expecting the same harsh gaze I'd seen so much of while he kept me prisoner. But, like Sorcha, he doesn't resemble the Lonnrach I've come to know. This isn't the cold faery who bit me every day just to read my memories and discover my secrets.

In contrast to his sister, Lonnrach's skin is startlingly beautiful, glittering in the moonlight. His pale hair is gathered at the nape of his neck, the salt-white strands shining in a halo around the crown of his head.

As he regards his sister, Lonnrach's expression is stern, but sympathetic. I'm startled by how open he is, how readable. He often tried to hide his feelings from me in the mirrored room, especially when he searched through my mind. Sometimes, when he pulled up memories of me and my mother together, I think he felt sorry for me. Those glimpses of his true self were always overshadowed by what he'd done to me and Aithinne.

But in this memory . . . his eyes aren't the same battle-weary ones that settled on me with disdain every day between his torture sessions.

Sorcha's mind tells me why: This happened before Lonnrach was imprisoned. Before both kingdoms fell. Before Kiaran killed his Falconer and gave up his throne.

"*Bheil thu eagal?*" Sorcha's question is teasing. At Lonnrach's sudden sharp look, she smiles. "So you *are* afraid. It's only a book."

"*Bi sàmhach*," Lonnrach snaps. He glances around, as if he expects to be attacked. At Sorcha's laugh, Lonnrach scowls. "I heard the Cailleach never really killed the Morrigan. You'd better hope she's not trapped in there."

"Oh, stop it. Those stories are for children." Sorcha waves a dismissive hand. "Even if they *were* true, the Morrigan was weakened. While imprisoned, she's—"

"Still stronger than you," Lonnrach interrupts. "You have no idea what you're getting yourself into."

"If you're so worried, then come with me." She sounds teasing again, but I hear the hint of worry beneath her words. I can sense from her thoughts that she *needs* the Book, not just to own it for the power.

Why then?

"I promised I'd help you find the door. Now I have," he says. "If I go with you, my Queen—"

"Would execute you for your betrayal." Her lip curls in disgust. So she loathed Aithinne even then. "I know. You told me."

Lonnrach stares at the tree for a moment, as if he's tempted to help her even at the risk of death. "Maybe you should let him die," Lonnrach says, his voice so low that I barely hear him.

Sorcha looks at him sharply. "No," she says. "He's my friend and my consort."

"Sorcha—"

"*Mo chreach!*" She throws up her hands. "Do you realize what you're asking? I won't stand aside and let Aithinne become the Cailleach." Sorcha spits out Aithinne's name like it's a curse. "She'd execute me on sight."

Lonnrach's expression grows cold. "I'll beg for your life."

"It won't matter and you know it." Sorcha shakes her head. I hear her thoughts: *You are so naïve, Lonnrach. You always have been.* "We're at war. If Aithinne takes the throne, she'll slaughter my people until the rest bow to her. I can't let that happen."

"That's not what this is about, though, is it?" he asks. "Do you think I haven't heard the rumors? That I can't see for myself that you're wasting away?" Sorcha stiffens at that and her brother laughs bitterly. "You might as well admit the truth: Your friend and consort is letting his kingdom rot because he fell in love with some human and won't kill them now."

"*Tha sin gu leòr,*" she bites out.

"No. I'm not done." He exhales, his features softening. "What are you risking your life for, Sorcha? Do you think if you break his curse he'll choose you over her?"

His curse. Oh god, she was looking for a way to save Kiaran?

"Finding the Book won't change anything." Lonnrach's words are surprisingly gentle. He reaches to grip her arm, as if to make her understand. "He won't love you back. Do you understand that?"

Sorcha stiffens, but she doesn't pull away. "He's my king."

"Not what I asked."

Sorcha is silent for the longest time. Emotions flutter across her face: grief, uncertainty, and finally, longing. As if she's already lost him. I didn't realize she felt so strongly for Kiaran.

"I understand," she whispers. "He's worth everything."

Lonnrach stares at her in disbelief—and when her expression confirms the truth of her words, he grimaces.

Then, in the deep lingering thoughts from this memory, I hear one so clearly: *I don't make a vow unless I mean the words.*

I almost pull out of her mind with a surprised curse. Sorcha never told Lonnrach about the vow she made to Kiaran, the one that entwined their lives. Kiaran once said it was a vow the fae made to their consorts, but perhaps it was only observed in the Unseelie Kingdom.

I assumed she made her vow for the reasons Kiaran had, out of obligation or tradition. But she hadn't—she had meant it with every piece of her soul.

Sorcha *loved* Kiaran. She loved him once the way *I* love him. It radiates in her memory, pure and untainted.

No wonder she looked at Kiaran and me the way she did; it hurt for her to see us like that. No wonder Sorcha betrayed Lonnrach back during the battle over the crystal.

She chose Kiaran over her own brother. Because she loves him still. I always assumed what she felt for him wasn't real. I was wrong—maybe this is what thousands of years of unrequited affection and tragedy and war do to love. They destroy it. They turn it into something dark and ugly and corrupted.

"You can't really mean that," Lonnrach says.

"I do," she tells Lonnrach firmly. "But it doesn't have to be only about me. If we find the Book, we can use it to end the war. Simple."

"And then what?" Lonnrach's voice is brittle. "Do you think Aithinne and Kadamach will rule happily, side by side? That the Courts can forget thousands of years of slaughter and live in peace together?"

"It has to start *somewhere*. Why can't it start with us?" Her expression is pleading. "Don't abandon me, Lonnrach. Do this with me and I'll forgive you for everything."

I'll forgive you for everything. What does that mean?

Lonnrach gazes up at the branches of the tree and for a moment I think he'll say yes. I can see his features softening, the first signs of battle-weariness that I saw when I was in the mirrored prison are there, left by centuries of bitter war between their kingdoms.

But then Sorcha whispers, "Help me save them both."

"No." Lonnrach steps back. "You don't want to save them both, you want me to save *him*. And I won't help him live. I won't betray my Queen and my Court, especially not for—" He shuts his mouth.

"For what?" Sorcha's eyes darken. "A filthy Unseelie? Just like our mother."

His intake of breath is subtle but noticeable. When he speaks again, it's through his teeth. "This is the way it is, Sorcha. We can't change it."

"You don't want to change it," she hisses. "I should have known that when you turned your back on me the first time. You'll regret this."

"I doubt it."

"I'll *make* you regret this."

"Sorcha—"

"Dutiful knight," she mocks. "Enslaved to his beloved Queen. I hope I free her from the curse and save her life, just to watch Kadamach rip out her heart anyway." Her pointed teeth flash in the nightmarish smile I know all too well. "And when he does, I'll beg him to spare you. So that you'll know, for the rest of your pathetic eternity, that it was your misguided sense of duty that got her killed."

"If you weren't my sister," Lonnrach growls, "I'd kill you for that."

Sorcha flashes her teeth in a snarl. "And if you weren't my brother, I would have killed you after you showed me how to find the door." She steps closer. "No, a long time ago. I should have hunted you down and killed you when I earned my freedom."

Earned my freedom. Something must have happened in their past. Something awful. Something irreconcilable. She wasn't free?

Lonnrach's flinch is so quick, I barely catch it. "You're going to die in there," he tells her flatly.

"Better to die in there than be like you." She pulls out her blade, but keeps it by her side. "You're a sniveling, mindless coward. This time, I won't forget it." Then she slices the skin of her palm and slams her hand against the tree trunk.

Before I can see what happens next, Sorcha surprises me by pulling back and slamming into my mind. The force is so strong that I cry out and stagger back, wrenched out of Sorcha's thoughts.

When I open my eyes, I'm on my knees in the dirt road.

CHAPTER 22

I TOUCH THE wetness leaking from my nose to my lips. Blood. Aithinne's chastising voice rises in my mind. *You'll have to be more careful when you search for the Book. Use your powers sparingly.*

"Kam? Are you all right?"

Kiaran kneels next to me and I swipe my sleeve across my nose before he can see. "Fine," I say, waving him off to stand on my own. I don't want Sorcha to see him help me up.

She went in search of the Book to save him.

"*Nighean na galla*," she snaps, spitting on the ground. "I hope that hurt. I'll never forget the feel of your disgusting little human mind—"

"Oh, you didn't like that?" I cross my arms. "A terrible thing, isn't it? Having someone else in your head, manipulating your thoughts."

Sorcha snarls. "Whatever borrowed powers you're using don't make you fae, little girl. Let me out of these chains and I'll feed you your insides before I kill you—"

My powers cut her off, and her sentence dies in a garbled choke. Aithinne's warning doesn't stand a chance against the rising tide of darkness inside me, demanding to be released. Demanding bloodshed. Demanding battle.

Just a little bit of pain.

I twist my fingers to cut off her air. My power slides down my veins, ready to kill.

Just a little bit more—

Kiaran grips my shoulder. "Stop."

I shake him off. "I'll never forget her sword." My hand fists and blood pours out of Sorcha's mouth. "It felt like *this*."

"Kam." Kiaran turns me to face him. His hands are on either side of my face, his voice gentle. "Look at me. *Look at me*." He speaks through the darkness to something human in me.

"She went to find the Book, MacKay. She knows where the door is." I can't help the power in my voice, the low, dangerous pitch that doesn't sound like me anymore. That barely sounds human. "I can *make* her help me."

I can make her do anything. I could make her dance until her feet bled. Whatever I want.

"Not if she's dead."

My lip curls. "I know that."

"Do you? Because you're killing her," he tells me, voice hoarse. "I can feel it."

Shock courses through me, just enough clarity to force my powers back down. To lock them up in the tight space of my chest and keep them from spilling out again.

Sorcha immediately gulps in air, her chest heaving with the effort.

It hurts so damn much to hold all that power. I feel like I'm dying. I *am* dying. But Kiaran is studying me too closely, so I shutter away the pain. I ignore the ache. After his willingness to kill people to help save me, I can't tell him that every time I use my powers, I die faster. I can't risk what he might do.

Don't let him see.

"I'm sorry," I say to him, shaking my head. "I can't—I'm sorry."

"You should be sorry," Sorcha gasps behind us. Her voice is barely above a whisper. "If there was even a chance I was willing to help you before, I take it back. I'd rather hang here for eternity."

I make a threatening step toward her, but Kiaran stops me. He's staring at Sorcha with an intense, considering look. I know that expression: He's making a decision. Weighing the alternatives. Kiaran is careful like that.

That's how I know that whatever he's about to propose is either incredibly foolish or very dangerous, and probably both.

"MacKay—"

"You said you'd do it for a price," he finally says to Sorcha, avoiding my gaze. "Name it."

"No." I put my hand against his chest to push him back. "Don't you dare."

But the stubborn arse won't even look at me. He says to Sorcha: "Just tell me what you want."

Sorcha's smile is slow. It cuts through me quicker and more painfully than any blade. And when she looks at me with that arrogant, mocking hint of a fang between her lips, I know. I know what she's considering.

Whatever will hurt me the most.

"She knows exactly what I want," Sorcha says in that cheerful, singsong voice of hers. The one from my nightmares. "Don't you?"

Kiaran. She wants Kiaran.

My fingers curl into fists. "Go to hell."

Sorcha laughs, a throaty, seductive sound. "Been there, done that," she says. "And I'm prepared to go again. For that, my price is steep."

I blanch. *And I'm prepared to go again.* Through the door. What did she experience on the other side?

The Morrigan. Sorcha's expression says it all. The Morrigan is still alive.

Sorcha doesn't wait for my answer. "You'll need my blood to open the Book, too. You can even have it when we find it. But you, Kadamach? You'll be mine, wholly and forever. She'll never see you again. Those are my terms."

I rake her with a look. "This is a disgusting deal, even for someone like you."

"Oh, but I was so moved and inspired by your earlier words." Her melodic voice is back, mocking me. "*He's mine every bit as much as I'm his.* You said I didn't understand that. Now I will, won't I? Kadamach won't be yours anymore; he'll be *mine.*"

My control is fraying at the edges, barely there. Kiaran's restraining hand on my arm is the only thing keeping me from snapping Sorcha's neck. Then he slides his fingers down my arm and presses his palm to mine, a calming touch.

He whispers in my ear, "Don't let her see. Remember?"

I try. I try so hard to hide it all. That awful spiraling helplessness I haven't experienced since I lost my memories is returning and pulling me down, down, down again.

Sorcha's teeth flash in a grin. "What say you, Falconer? Does saving the world mean more to you than your precious *Kiaran*? How desperately do you need my help?"

She knows how few options we have. And she's mocking us for it.

When Kiaran looks at me, I see he's actually considering this. And the thought of what he'd endure during an eternity by her side makes me ill. I'm so close to letting my powers take over, close to hurting her, *killing* her—

"Kam." Kiaran's voice, cutting through the darkness.

My name. Just my name. Like he's asking me to understand that he's willing to give up himself—no, his soul—to Sorcha in order to save me.

That's all it takes to regain my focus. I can't let him do this. *No.* Kiaran isn't some bloody piece of property. You don't make someone love you by owning their soul.

And Sorcha is doing this because she knows he owns all the bits and pieces of my heart.

She's doing this because she loves him just as much as she hates me.

"Aye, how about it, *Kam?*" My fingernails bite into my palm when Sorcha says my name. "Do we have a deal?"

"No," I say through gritted teeth. "No, we don't have a *fucking* deal."

But when Kiaran's eyes meet mine, I can see he's already made his decision. He's weighed the options, and our alternatives.

And he's decided we really are that desperate.

When he speaks, it's in a low voice that kills something inside me. "If I do this, you'll agree to my terms. No circumvention. You'll make a promise not to harm Kam."

"The same goes for you. If she tries to use the Book to break the vow, you die. If she tries to put another mark over it, you die. If she ever sees you after we find it, consider the part of my vow not to hurt her null and void. You know me, Kadamach. I learned my lesson about the language of vows."

I look at her sharply. *What does* that *mean?*

Kiaran nods once. "The Book is Kam's. And don't even think about getting around killing her by putting her in a state of permanent sleep. No games. No twisting terms." He studies her with a harsh gaze. "I learned my lesson about the language of vows, too. From you."

Her laugh is another sword to my chest. "Believe me, I want her to live out a very, *very* long life. Fully conscious and aware she'll never see you again."

That does it. I grasp Kiaran's shirt to pull him away from Sorcha before something in me snaps. "I need to speak with you. Now."

Kiaran lets me lead him far enough from Sorcha that I know her enhanced fae hearing can't pick up our words. The only sound between us is the breeze rustling through the trees that line the road, the distant garble of a nearby creek.

Kiaran doesn't say anything when we stop; he just looks at me with that silent, stoic expression.

Hiding his feelings. Hiding everything.

Once, that was the only way he looked at me. When we hunted together, when I lived half my life in secret. Back then I assumed all the fae were emotionless, that they weren't capable of feelings. After he and Aithinne saved me from Lonnrach's prison, Kiaran was different. He wasn't reserved anymore. His longing mirrored my own.

But now Kiaran hides his emotions from me when he feels the most. When he doesn't want me to see how much he hurts.

Stop trying to protect me, MacKay.

"What are you doing?" I hiss.

His expression doesn't change and that makes me angrier. I want to see emotions from him. Longing, regret, grief, guilt—*something.*

"What are my alternatives, Kam?" he asks. "Aithinne's death? *Your* death? Sorcha has the advantage and she knows it."

"Then we'll hunt down Lonnrach."

Kiaran's eyes meet mine. "How long do we have before you die?"

I almost stagger at the question. "Don't make this about—"

"Don't ask me to overlook it," he snaps. "We don't have time to find Lonnrach, do we?"

I look away and give a small shake of my head. He sighs, a sound of frustration and a bone-deep tiredness that I understand only too well. I wonder if he's thinking about our time together in bed, when it seemed so easy to forget everything else. If he's tempted to go back there and let us drown in each other all over again.

I'm tempted, too.

"Offer her something else," I whisper. "Anything." I press my hand against his chest, over where I know Sorcha's mark is hidden beneath his shirt. "Then when we find the Book you won't be bound by your vow to her anymore."

"She won't take another offer. Not when she knows we wouldn't be asking her for this if we had another choice."

"You're not a possession," I tell him sharply. "Just because you wear her mark doesn't mean she owns you."

At that, his expression softens and he touches me. His fingers run along my arm, tracing down until he reaches the back of my hand. "Do you know what I'll miss most about you, Kam?"

I shake my head. *Don't tell me now. Not when you're considering giving up your life to her.*

But he slides his hand up to cup my cheek and force me to look at him. "I never had to wear your mark to know that I'll always be yours."

Then he's kissing me, his lips soft against mine. "One day, you'll tell people the story of the faery king and the human girl," Kiaran whispers. "And how he watched from afar as she lived out twenty thousand human days. And if she listened closely during winter, when the wind was cold and the nights were longest, she could hear him whisper that he cherished her so much he was willing to give her the world."

I shut my eyes before tears fall. "What if I don't want the world?" I ask him. "What if I just want you?"

"You already have me. This doesn't change that." Another kiss, and then he pulls away and I feel his absence like an ache. "I'm not asking your permission. I'm telling you to let me go."

Let me go.

He said that to me before on the battlefield in Edinburgh. I had been willing to do it then. But now?

A part of me wishes he hadn't changed. That he had some uncaring ruthlessness left in him that would tell Sorcha to take her deal and burn it. But then he wouldn't be Kiaran. He wouldn't be *my* Kiaran.

Don't say the words. Once you say the words, you'll lose him.

I can't. Every instinct in me is screaming. I could use my powers. I could make her more willing. But every time I use my powers I know that I have less time. Less time with him.

"Kam," he says softly. "You have to let me go."

"I know that." I can barely speak. "But I can't stand here and listen while you sell her your soul."

I turn my back on him and walk away.

CHAPTER 23

KIARAN FINDS me in the bedroom later, sitting in the great leather chair by the window. The fireplace is blazing—a small comfort I allowed myself.

I don't look over as he approaches. I watch the ocean waves around the island swell and retreat, swell and retreat. I time my breathing with the sound, needing to control something. Anything. Because I know that if I don't, I'm going to walk out of this room, find Sorcha, and put a blade through her.

I sense his warmth directly behind me, but he makes no move to touch me. "You made the vow." It isn't a question. My voice sounds calmer than I feel. I keep my breath even, as even as those ocean waves.

"Aye," Kiaran says quietly.

My fingernails prick the skin of my palm painfully. "And Sorcha?"

"She's resting. She'll take us to the door tomorrow."

I stand, struggling to maintain my last vestiges of control. "She doesn't need to rest," I say, turning to face him. "Let's just get this done."

When I try to sweep past him, Kiaran's hand shoots out to grip my arm. "Kam."

Don't let him see. Control your breathing. Control your expression. Don't let him see.

If I don't leave now, I won't be able to hold back my tears. The second my eyes meet his, it's going to break me. "Let go, MacKay." The first signs of emotion are creeping into my voice. "The sooner we find the Book—"

"I need one last night with you."

I look at him, surprised to find his expression laid bare and vulnerable. Like he's begging me. *Stay. Stay with me.*

One final night together before we go to find that Book and I lose Kiaran, one way or another. That vow he made to Sorcha is somewhere on his body. She's marked him. Twice.

"Let me see it," I say, voice hoarse. "Show me her vow."

"Don't," he whispers. "Don't do this."

"*Show me.*"

With his jaw set, Kiaran roughly removes his coat and drops it to the floor. Then his shirt.

I suck in a breath when I see the new marks on him.

Kiaran's torso is a map of swirled designs carved into his flesh and healed over into scars. The one that spans his entire back is the vow he made to Catríona, the Falconer he fell in love with thousands of years ago: his vow never to kill humans.

Sorcha's mark used to lie over his heart in a mess of spiky branches that reached across his skin, expanding to the tops of his shoulders as if it wanted to cover every inch of him. As if it wanted to consume him.

And now it does.

His vow to Sorcha has woven itself around and inside his other vow, across his rib cage, up and up around the muscular flesh of his upper arms and shoulders.

I step around him to see that it continues across his back, disappearing beneath the waistband of his trousers, continuing high up toward his neck where it dips beneath his hairline.

Kiaran tenses when I touch him, but he doesn't move, doesn't say anything. I try to sense his powers, but all I can feel are Sorcha's. As if she's wrapped herself around him, forced herself beneath his skin.

This isn't just a vow: It's a mark of ownership. It says, *You're mine forever and I'm never letting you go.*

I pull away from him, as if his skin burns. "I'm going to find a way to get that off of you," I tell him tightly. "Whatever it takes."

Before I can even blink, Kiaran takes me by the arms and he's kissing me. It's heartbreakingly slow at first, his lips light, tentative. But I want more. I kiss him harder. I put everything I feel into it, every part of me. Everything I can't say in words.

"I'm yours," he rasps against my lips.

He drags me against him, his fingers frantically pulling at my shirt to feel my skin beneath. I pull away only to let him lift it over my head and then his hands are everywhere, touching, stroking.

"I'm yours," he says again.

His lips trail down to my neck, my shoulder. Each touch burns. His lips sear a path of heat down my body as he whispers those two words over and over and over again. A reminder. A promise. A vow to me, this one marked on his soul.

"I'm yours."

It feels like he's saying goodbye.

CHAPTER 24

K IARAN AND Sorcha are waiting in the antechamber of the palace the following morning. Their heads are bent and they're in something of a heated discussion. Their voices are low, urgent. They both look up when my footsteps echo across the dark onyx floor.

Sorcha is wearing a stunning red brocade gown and boots with pointed heels, as if we were on our way to an assembly. She even looks like she's wearing jewelry.

Good Christ, she is. It's an elaborate necklace dripping with rubies. Like something royalty would wear.

"Are we intending to battle an ancient evil or going to a ball?" I ask as I approach.

Sorcha's smile is slow, lazy. Victorious. It says, *I have everything I want and I don't care what you think.* "I go into a war dressed for the outcome."

I glance at her ruby necklace. *I hope the Morrigan chokes you with it.*

Sorcha glances at my sword and I hear her thoughts: *I hope the Morrigan stabs you with it.*

If I didn't hate her so much, I'd laugh. *One day I'm going to destroy you,* I think to her. *I'm going to burn your life to the ground.*

She grins. "Someone's feisty this morning. You must be well rested. Unlike Kadamach, who appears this close"—she raises her thumb and forefinger—"to tearing open your throat."

I jerk my head around. When Kiaran's eyes meet mine, I almost step back in alarm. The black part of his irises has bled even more into the lilac. Worse, he has a wild look to him, a savageness barely contained. He's straining to control himself around me.

I should have sensed it last night when he left the bed. Just before dawn, I heard him murmuring something to me, the cadence of it lulling me back into my dreams. He'd pressed a kiss to my shoulder, and then I thought I felt the light scrape of his teeth against my skin.

When I stirred, he pulled back sharply. *"Falbh a chadal,"* he'd whispered from the bedside, breathing heavily. "Go to sleep."

The bed felt cold after that.

As if reading my thoughts, Kiaran looks away. Sorcha laughs. "Ah, then you're denying yourself on her account. I should have guessed. So noble. So righteous. So very human."

"It's better than being a morally bankrupt harridan," I say.

"His needs have nothing to do with morality, you naïve little girl." She rolls her eyes and then studies her fingernails.

"If the Morrigan doesn't kill you before you find the Book, Kadamach probably will. He won't be able to help himself. How do you think his first little Falconer pet died?"

Kiaran narrows his gaze. "If you went three entire seconds without saying something vile and cold-hearted, you'd perish on the spot, wouldn't you?"

"What you call vile and cold-hearted, I call honest." Sorcha shrugs. "You keep blaming me for her death, but I never had to do anything. I just had to shove her in a room alone with you."

This time he flashes his teeth in a hiss and I see a hint of fangs descend from his gums—until he notices my soft gasp. I can't entirely hide my expression of unease at those fangs, like the ones that had marked my arms, my neck, my shoulders, my chest. Just like that woman in the cottage.

"Kam," he whispers. Then he shuts his mouth.

I shake my head. "I'm sorry I ever asked you to bring her into this."

"I regret listening to you, but here we are."

Sorcha's laugh is melodic, unnerving enough to make me shudder. "Oh, come now. I thought we were all friends."

"Funny," I say. "I thought we were bitter enemies."

"Isn't that what I just said?" She holds up her wrist where her vow has marked her skin in a design like Kiaran's. "Now you have my vow to help you find the Book, and Kadamach doesn't belong to me until it's yours. You won't have to worry about me stabbing you again. I'd say that makes us even better than friends."

"Take us to the door before I strangle you," Kiaran says, gesturing to the doorway that leads to the labyrinthine halls.

With a sweep of her long brocade dress, Sorcha starts for the hallway. Just as Kiaran turns to follow, I stop him. "Wait." At his frown, I say, "I'm bringing Aithinne."

"Oh, a reunion," Sorcha says in delight. "I love reunions with all the people I've tried to kill. It's so cathartic, don't you think?"

I pinch the bridge of my nose. "MacKay? Any chance you could reword that vow to enforce silence for the rest of her very long life?"

Kiaran ignores that. "I didn't agree to bring Aithinne."

"You didn't disagree either. We never discussed it."

Kiaran looks over at Sorcha, who is watching us in amusement. He takes me by the arm and leads me to the other side of the vast antechamber for some semblance of privacy. "The pixie. Not Aithinne."

"If Sorcha is telling the truth about the Morrigan, we're going to need your sister with us."

Kiaran's grip on my arm tightens. "If I lose control in there and hurt you, I don't trust Aithinne to make the right choice. She's too soft, Kam."

I frown. "What choice, exactly?"

"You already swore you'd leave me there."

"That's not what you're talking about, though, is it?" At his silence, my voice dips lower. "What, MacKay? You want me to kill you?"

"Whatever it takes." His voice is a rough hiss. "The Book is our priority. If it comes down to me or finding it, I trust you to make the right decision." He releases me. "My sister would choose me. She always has. Sometimes I suspect she'd let the goddamn world destroy itself over me."

It's not coming to that. I'll never let it come to that.

But we're doing this to stop Aithinne's curse, too. She ought to be there, by our side. She ought to be there to help us through it, to end it all. And if I die before we find the Book, she has to be the one to reverse the destruction in our realms. I'm not certain the Book can resurrect me if I die with the Cailleach's powers, but at least Aithinne will be able to give back Catherine, Daniel, and Gavin everything they lost in the war. They deserve a better life than this.

I back away from him. "And if the worst happens and you turn on me? Then what?" I lower my voice. "Do you expect me to subdue you? I've only bested you once. And that was before—"

Before you. Before us. Before everything.

"If you think I'll be more objective than Aithinne," I say instead, "then you're an idiot. And that isn't a word I'd use to describe you."

I've tried not to let my feelings for Kiaran blind me, but it's too late. I already have. Doesn't he know I'd do whatever it took to save him? Just as he would for me? Neither of us is objective. We're too far gone.

I try to appeal to Kiaran's practical nature instead: "Derrick doesn't have enough power to fight the Morrigan, and he's better off at the camp where he can help the others in case the land starts falling apart. You know that."

That does it. Kiaran steps back, his expression shuttered again. "Fine. Send word to Aithinne."

I hesitate before tapping into my power, cautious not to let it become too overwhelming. It's too tempting to let it take me over, to lose myself in it.

It slides down my veins and into my palm and I direct it with a quick stroke of my wrist. *Find Aithinne.*

The response is almost instant. She's back at her camp with Derrick and the others—I give myself a moment of relief that they're unharmed. The flames of their bonfire burn high, and they're all sitting on the ground with old wool blankets over their shoulders. Gavin has resumed drinking that terrible whisky, while Derrick natters on to Catherine and Daniel about nothing in particular.

Aithinne's head comes up when she senses me. I leave a lingering thread of power to hint at her to follow it. "It's about bloody time," she says with cheer. "I'll make a portal. Tell Kadamach to open the gates."

I pull back and give Kiaran her message. He crosses the room to reach for a massive lever near the double doors that I hadn't seen. With a swift yank, he pulls it to the side and the heavy oak entrance splits open.

Derrick flies through the portal first. "Look at you," he says, stopping to study me. "Alive. Unscathed. Good. If you hadn't been, I would have lopped his fingers off."

Kiaran moves to stand beside me. "I would have pulled off your wings."

"Ignore him, pixie." Aithinne strides into the room, her long coat billowing behind her. "I should have figured he'd be sullen and moody."

Kiaran's emotionless gaze flickers to her. "*Phiuthair.*"

"*Bhràthair.*" She stops and studies him. "You look like hell. I suppose you haven't fed in a few days, if the lack of gifts is any indication."

"Don't." Kiaran's voice dips in warning.

"I'm wonderful, by the way," she continues, as if he hadn't spoken. "Do you like my coat? Don't I look lovely? Aren't I the best sister for standing here, still willing to talk to you after you've ignored me for months, you *stubborn* bastard?"

"Well, this is fun," Derrick says. "I'm really feeling the love in this room. It's beautiful. Aileana, isn't it beautiful?"

"You're here because Kam wanted your help. Not because I did."

"Damn it, MacKay—"

"You might not have wanted me," Aithinne says, ignoring my attempts to stand between them, "but look how quickly I came. Because I still care about you. Though god only knows why, since you're such an obstinate pain in my arse."

"I love it when Aithinne curses at people." Derrick says to me. "I say we let them fight it out. A round of fisticuffs. No killing. I'll go and find refreshments."

"Oh, for god's sake," Sorcha says from behind us. "If you're all going to squabble, I'd prefer to be back in my prison. That wasn't torture. *This* is torture."

Derrick peeks through my hair. "What's that murderous arsehole doing here?"

Sorcha blinks at him. "What did you just call me?"

"You heard me, pointy-toothed hag."

"Sorcha can find the Book," I interrupt. "And we need her blood to get there. It was her or Lonnrach."

"So given a choice between murderous arseholes you chose the one who killed you." Derrick's laugh is dry. "That's interesting."

"I chose the one who was conveniently chained up, rather than the one in hiding."

Derrick doesn't look convinced. "And we're just supposed to believe she's helping out of the goodness of that black hunk of rock in her chest that she calls a heart?"

"I'm standing right here," Sorcha says sharply.

"Wish you weren't," Derrick sings. Then, to me: "Let me give you some advice, friend. If you're going to take her along, make her go first. That way you don't have to worry about her shoving a blade into your back."

"Sweet little pixie," Sorcha says. "If there's one thing you should have learned, it's that I'm perfectly willing to stab her in the front." She turns on her heel and heads toward the great hall, the fabric of her brocade dress sweeping across the ground like a cloak. "If you're coming, the door is this way."

Derrick starts to follow, but I stop him. "I need you to stay at the camp."

"But I won't get to kill anything there," he whines.

"I'd take you with me if I could, but I can't leave the others unprotected. Not with the realm falling apart."

Derrick sighs. "Fine. *Fine.* Just be careful, will you? Don't do anything foolish. And whatever you do, don't let Sorcha get her hands on a blade."

"I won't." He hugs me and I rest my cheek against him briefly. "Make me a pirate costume."

I feel his smile against my skin. "Only if you save me a dance."

With that, Derrick flies out of the palace and I turn to follow Sorcha.

CHAPTER 25

KIARAN FOLLOWS closely behind Sorcha—no doubt to keep an eye on her—while I walk with Aithinne. The long, obsidian hallway is still eerily silent. The lights seem dimmer, the corridor cast in shadows that appear to be growing, moving. *Breathing.*

Beside me, Aithinne shivers. "I hate this place," she whispers. "Just once, I'd like to go through a portal beneath a rainbow, or near a litter of kittens."

I snicker.

Sorcha pauses and presses her palm to the bricks, her fingers lingering there in an almost loving caress. She shakes her head once and keeps moving, her heels snapping decisively against the floor.

Aithinne leans in. "I'm still convinced she's leading us to our demise."

"She made a vow to help me find the Book," I say. "She's bound to it."

Kiaran is a master at faery half-lies and manipulation. He would have made certain the terms of their vow were as strict as possible. But I also know this: Sorcha will be looking for ways to turn it against me. Just because the fae can't tell lies doesn't mean they're honest, and the limitations of a vow doesn't make them incapable of deception. I haven't met a single person Sorcha hasn't betrayed, even those she loves.

Right now, she has all the advantages. She's found the door before; she knows its secrets; she's seen the Morrigan. And somehow she's still alive.

"In my Court we have a saying for ones like her." Aithinne lets out a small laugh. "You'll think you won the fight until you step back and she cuts your ankles out from under you."

"I can hear you." Sorcha presses her palms to another wall. Her smile is small. She probably likes that saying. It was probably made *just* for her.

"Can you?" Aithinne asks in delight. "Oh, good. Now that I have your attention, I'll add that I often amuse myself by imagining what it would look like if you were tossed off a cliff into the sea. By the way, nice dress."

"What purpose does it serve to have you here?" Sorcha's green eyes glitter with irritation. "Other than being a crazed little baggage who lost her mind somewhere in the bowels of Edinburgh." Aithinne's smile falters and Sorcha sees it. "Tell me, how long did it take my brother to break your sanity? How many times did he have to shatter your bones and burn your body before you became this pathetic? Did it take a hundred years? Five hundred?" Sorcha's smile is merciless. "Or is that too generous?"

Somewhere in the midst of Sorcha's cruel questions, Aithinne's eyes go blank. Dead. I've seen it before.

I gently grasp her hand. "Aithinne." I murmur her name again, until I see a flicker of recognition in her eyes.

"You shouldn't bother," Sorcha says to me. "Aithinne is broken. The Morrigan is going to destroy her easily."

Kiaran jerks Sorcha to him. *"That's enough."* There's something wild in his expression, something mad. Something dark. "Speak to my sister like that again, and the next torture I come up with will leave you begging me to end us both." His knife is in his hand before I can blink. "Perhaps I should start now? How about one of these lovely green eyes?" He taps her cheek with the edge of the blade.

I back away. His voice is unrecognizable. Unfamiliar. That voice is how I imagine death to sound: a low, dangerous voice that freezes me to my bones.

Sorcha's expression doesn't change, but a small tremor goes through her body. "Come now, Kadamach. You made a vow—"

"And it doesn't come into effect until we find the Book. Now move." Then he roughly shoves her away.

Sorcha just looks at Aithinne, lifts her chin, and keeps searching. She might be an expert at hiding how she feels, but I'm not fooled. Kiaran just scared the hell out of her.

He scared the hell out of me, too.

As we continue through the hall, Aithinne doesn't speak. Every so often, her fingers clench and unclench around the hilt of her sword; what Sorcha said is getting to her. I lean over and whisper in Aithinne's ear that being vulnerable doesn't mean she's broken. Aithinne's hand grips mine, squeezes in understanding. Lonnrach tried to shatter us both.

After a while, Sorcha stops again, fingertips skimming along the wall. I feel her power in the air, only for a moment, before she pulls away again with a soft, frustrated curse.

"If you found the door before this castle existed, why are we searching through it now?" I ask.

"When Lonnrach found the Morrigan's prison for me the first time," Sorcha says, "it was through the *Sìth-bhrùth*. And since the *Sìth-bhrùth* has withered away to practically nothing, we need to find it here. I'm using the crystal to direct my powers, but the damn door moves."

"It moves?" I ask skeptically.

"Why do you think I had to ask for my brother's help the first time?" She sounds annoyed now. "Since it required our blood, it was easier with two of us."

"Or finding it required someone with a skill beyond subterfuge and betrayal," Aithinne mutters, sounding more like her old self.

Sorcha flicks out her hand and I feel her power build. A moment before it strikes, Aithinne shoots out her hand and disintegrates Sorcha's power as easily as if she were tearing a piece of paper.

"Don't embarrass yourself," Aithinne says with a sweet smile. "I may be broken, but if I wanted to, I could make your heart explode in your chest."

With a scowl, Sorcha turns down another long hallway. She puts her hands out, fingertips brushing the stone walls, and I can feel her power in the air again. It tastes like iron and has an abrasive texture, rough as pumice.

She presses her palms to the wall, her face a mask of concentration. "The door exists between our worlds," she murmurs. "In the right space, I can conjure it forth, the same way we'd travel between this realm and the *Sìth-bhrùth.*"

"Why didn't you find the Book?" I ask. "If you wanted it so badly, what made you walk away?"

Why give up on ending his curse and saving him? If you loved him so much?

When Sorcha looks at me, her eyes are glazed over, her power still searching. "That's where you have it wrong, Falconer. I didn't walk away; I got on my knees and crawled. With my life."

Her brow creases into a frown and she takes a few steps from us. Then she comes to a hard stop, her head jerking to the left. She's staring at the wall, as if she sees something the rest of us don't.

I reach out with my powers and sense a shadow of . . . something there. But it's so slight that I can't make it out. Power, but a mere glimpse of it—as faint as a waft of heather on the air.

"Kadamach," Sorcha says in a low voice. "Give me your blade. Quickly."

Before I can protest Sorcha being in charge of something pointy, Kiaran slips a knife from the sheath at his wrist and passes it to her, hilt first. Without any explanation or hesitation, Sorcha slices the weapon down across both palms in two quick swipes. Then she passes back the blade and smears her blood across the obsidian wall.

She slams her palms against the stones. I watch as the blood gathers along the smooth rock, glistening like molasses. Only it doesn't drip down as it should. Instead, it curves across the stone to form a pattern. Like something from one of Kiaran's marks, a swirling design that loops and loops around itself, becoming smaller and more intricate.

"There you are," Sorcha whispers. "*Fosgail.*"

A startling crack resounds through the hallway, so loud that my hand immediately goes for the hilt of my sword. Before us, a fissure forms in the wall, stretching from floor to ceiling. The stones disintegrate, tearing away to reveal a pitch-dark hollow that I can't see beyond—an opening just large enough for a single person to fit through.

Sorcha blinks and steps back from the fissure. "There you have it. One portal to hell."

I stare at the dark opening with an impending sense of alarm. *What could the Morrigan have done to make Sorcha decide Kiaran wasn't worth it?*

"You never said what made you give up," I say to her.

I'm surprised by the small hint of humanity in the depths of her usually cold green eyes. I've seen moments of her emotions before, when she looks at Kiaran with longing. But this is something more, a sense of loss I recognize from having keenly felt it for so long.

"The Morrigan will do whatever it takes to break out of there," she murmurs. "The moment we go in, she's going to decide which of us are the pawns, and which one of us is the key to her escape."

I swallow hard. "Which were you?"

Sorcha's smile is both bitter and brutal. "Neither. I was her entertainment."

With that, she steps back and gives me a look as if to say, *How about it, Falconer? Is he worth it?*

Kiaran's eyes catch mine. His expression is unfamiliar, unsettling. A glimpse of something dark and hungry just beneath the surface, barely contained. His curse. The curse I have one chance to undo.

Save me, Kam? You'll wish you'd killed me.

I look away sharply, and step through the portal.

The hallway on the other side is similar to the one we've left—a wide, shadowed passage. Only there are no doors—at least, none that I can see through the swaths of dead ivy that snake across the stones from floor to ceiling. Not a single green leaf remains on the foliage, just withered brown vines that extend down to the dark end of the corridor.

I shiver in the chill from the old damp stones, my breath exhaling in white mist. The cold is a bone-deep kind that comes not from the temperature but the atmosphere. The walls feel too close and too far away at the same time. As I stand there, the hallway grows darker, colder, longer.

Somewhere in the ivy—in this dead, empty space—someone is watching me.

I turn in dread. Kiaran, Sorcha, and Aithinne step out of the portal—and it disappears, closing up like a quickly healing wound. Then it seals shut as if it had never been there at all.

"Well, this isn't a good sign," Aithinne says, studying the ivy. She slides her finger along a branch. "This place feels wrong. Dead." Then she mutters: "Why couldn't it have been kittens? Just once?"

Sorcha stares at the hall, going pale with fear. "It didn't look like this before." A soft curse on her lips. She's realized something. "The Cailleach was holding this place together. Now that she's dead and her powers are in the body of an incompetent human, this realm is falling apart just like ours." She glances sharply at Aithinne. "I should push you onto Kadamach's blade myself. I'm not going to die because he's grown too soft to kill you."

"Not helpful," I snap.

"I don't care. This changes things. Do you realize how desperate the Morrigan will be to escape? This is her last chance." She steps back toward the portal we just came through. When she finds it closed, she shuts her eyes. "Kadamach, just murder your idiot sister and become the next Cailleach. Save us the trouble."

"I'd rather kill you. Now find the Book."

Sorcha straightens. "If it were that easy, it wouldn't still be here, would it?" she snaps. Then, to me: "Pray you survive to make it yours, Falconer."

She pushes past us, and the rest of us follow. As we continue through the dead vines, the hallway keeps stretching ahead. It never changes. The vines blur together in a seemingly endless branch, withered and dead. Leaves litter the floor, the only indication that this place had once been bursting with life.

Were the plants a cruel taunt the Cailleach left for the Morrigan, a reminder that she would never, ever see true nature or the world again? Or perhaps they were a small kindness the Cailleach gave to her sister before shutting her in here and throwing away the key: a garden to grace her prison walls.

As we push through a jumble of leaves, I cast my senses out slightly, enough to search the hallway without exhausting myself or becoming consumed by my powers. A sudden chill glides across my skin and I pause. There are eyes on me again, in the walls, beyond those leaves.

A voice stirs across my mind—one similar to the Cailleach's, but not old and frightened and dying. This voice is powerful. It sounds like a promise of death.

I see you.

The air in the hallway thickens, rippling as if a small pebble had been tossed into a pool of water. We all come to a sudden halt. Next to me, Kiaran whispers a foul curse.

"I take it you all felt that?" Aithinne asks. We nod. "Anyone else get the sense they're about to be gutted and strung up by their intestines?" she says. When we nod again she adds, "I've never felt trousers-pissing terrified before."

Kiaran grasps his blade. "Aithinne," he murmurs, his eyes on the dead vines. "That's more information than I cared to know."

"You're so delicate," Aithinne says lightly, but she steps closer to me with her sword out, too.

A scrape of rock against metal from somewhere in the hall makes us all jump. Sorcha's breathing turns uneven. "I say we kill the Falconer," she says. I don't miss the tremble in her voice. "Old magic loves a good sacrifice."

I glare at her. "Does it? You do realize everyone here hates *you*, aye?"

Before she can reply, the hallway shudders again, this time more violently. The stone around us groans. Something crashes. I whirl to see a chunk of ceiling has fallen and shattered to the floor. And when I look up . . .

Thick vines crash through the roof, bearing thorns as sharp as blades.

CHAPTER 26

IARAN GRIPS my arm and pulls me so hard I almost lose my balance. "Run!"

We fly down the hallway, our boots pounding through the dead leaves. Something tugs at my foot to hold me back, but I surge forward. Another tug, harder. Another. Another. Something grasps me hard by my ankle and when I look down, my stomach lurches with alarm.

Vines. Bursting up through the onyx slabs and growing fast around my legs. Holding me in place.

Oh, god. A burst of panic brings back unwanted memories of the mirrored room where Lonnrach kept me. The vines there held me in place, tightened if I struggled. Held me while his teeth bit into my wrists. My arms. My shoulders. Neck—

"MacKay." I just manage to whisper.

"Shit." Kiaran seizes my hand again with a rough yank.

The vines snap, but I still can't move, can't think, can't do anything. *Move and it'll only hurt worse. Move and the vines will cover my mouth to muffle my screams—*

Kiaran's hands are rough around my waist as he pulls me. "Kam, you have to run!"

You're not there. This isn't the mirrored room. Go!

I try. God, I try. Vines sprout around our feet, rising from the floor. They grab for my ankles, but I break through. I rip. I claw. I tear. But when the vines wrap around my wrists, I can't fight anymore. My limbs slacken.

Can't. Can't, can't, can't. Teeth at my wrist. Teeth at my throat. Half-moon marks. Don't move or it'll hurt more.

I'm consumed by my memories. I couldn't fight back. It feels real. It *is* real.

Teeth at my wrist. Biting down. Drawing blood. Breaking into my mind.

Can't move. Can't scream. Can't think—

Kiaran jerks me forward, slashing his blade through the growth. "Kam!" His hands are on either side of my face. "I'm here. I'm right here with you."

"It's her fear," Sorcha pants from behind us. "The Morrigan read her."

"I'm here," he whispers again. "I'm here."

That's all it takes to get me moving once more. Kiaran's touch anchors me. It reminds me that I can still fight. I'm not a prisoner.

Somewhere behind us, another chunk of the onyx ceiling crashes to the ground. Another, another. Vines spring up on either side of us, closing us in. Trapping us.

Aithinne wipes at the bleeding gash on her face. "If anyone has any ideas, now might be a good time to share with the rest of us."

Kiaran shakes his head sharply. "We're going to have to force our way out." He looks behind us, assessing.

"Kadamach," Sorcha says, raising her palm, "wait—"

Kiaran rounds and slams his fist into the wall. An impact that should have shattered the bricks to dust.

His hiss of pain startles me. When Kiaran pulls his hand back, his knuckles are bleeding. The wall broke his near-invulnerable fae skin. How on earth is that possible?

Amid the chaos, he stares hard at Sorcha. Though his gaze is calm, I can see something simmering there. Something wild again. His expression is dark and slightly on edge.

"Kam," he says slowly. "Can you blast this wall apart?"

Aithinne steps in front of me. "I'll do it—"

"No." Kiaran's voice is hard. He nods to me. "I need it to be Kam." His expression leaves no room for questions.

Aithinne presses her lips together and, as if she's projecting her thoughts to me, I can hear her in my mind. *Tell him.*

I give the barest shake of my head.

If I tell Kiaran, his attention would be split between finding the Book, and worrying that every small burst of power will be the one that kills me. He'd stop me from using my abilities to find the Book—and against the Morrigan, I won't have a choice. I'm going to need them.

"Stand back."

My powers are a storm building inside me. Electricity crackles in the air. I throw back my head when energy rushes down my veins, through my blood. My heart slams faster and faster, filling my ears with a dull roar.

Vines break through the stone around my feet and I smile grimly. *Stop.* When the vines cease, I command them to die. They begin to break apart around us, falling to the ground and withering. *That ought to give us enough time to get out of here before the Morrigan attacks again.*

Seconds seem like minutes. The fine hairs on my arms rise and the feeling of a storm builds and builds and builds within my chest until it becomes a painful pressure there.

Breathe it out like air, I tell myself. *Easy.*

I let my power go in a blast that turns the wall to rubble— and all that's behind it is a hallway identical to this. *Well, so much for that.*

Another vine breaks through the wall behind us with a thunderous *crack.* Out of the corner of my eye, I see leaves growing beneath the old dead ones. They shoot out of the walls and the floor faster than before, shattering the stonework all around us. The foliage is bigger and thicker and stronger, with thorns long enough to impale.

"Great work, Falconer," Sorcha says. "You made the Morrigan angry."

We'll have to take our chances in the next hallway. The archways behind us are crumbling, pierced by thorns. A wall next to me shatters and a massive vine comes straight for us.

"Go!" I yell.

We clamber through the hole in the stonework just before the hallway behind us buckles and the plants begin to close in. Brick shatters to the ground, detritus dusts the air. My breath comes out in a cough. I can't *see*—

Rebuild. Quickly.

I clench my fist and raise my hand, directing my power to stack the stones, throwing them in place so there's something stable enough to hold for now. We just need enough time to run. The makeshift wall forms to cover any cracks the vines might come through, and then . . . silence. Only our strained, tired breathing fills the space.

A burst of power pushes against mine. God, the Morrigan is so strong—

"Hold it, Kam."

Hold it? Is he mad? I shut my eyes, my body straining as the Morrigan's power fights mine, shoving hard against my makeshift wall.

"MacKay," I say. "Now isn't a good time—"

"I need a moment," he says. Some cold and brutal emotion darkens his expression. "Aithinne, feel for your power."

Aithinne shuts her eyes. Almost immediately, she frowns. When she opens her eyes, it's the first time I've ever seen her look scared. "It's there but I can't . . . I can't reach it." Aithinne holds out her hand, like she's expecting something to happen. "I can't even conjure a flame. A bloody child's trick." She looks at Sorcha with accusation. "What did you do to us?"

"Our powers are bound," Kiaran says shortly. He pulls Sorcha to him.

I gasp as the Morrigan's powers crash against mine again. The hallway shakes. Above us, a small portion of the wall crumbles and falls. *Hold. Hold, damn it.*

"MacKay," I say warningly.

But Kiaran ignores the chaos around us. His gaze is focused on Sorcha, his grip bruising around her arm. "You knew, didn't you?"

Sorcha tries to look nonchalant. "I knew that little girl needed the Book."

Kiaran slams her into the wall and Sorcha gasps in pain. "Explain. For every answer I'm not satisfied with, you'll lose a finger. Try growing it back without any powers."

Fear flares in Sorcha's eyes. "All right," she says roughly. "*All right.*"

The Morrigan's power slams into mine and I bite back a cry. My body is trembling now, my vision hazing. The hallway starts to sway. A brick tumbles from the top of the makeshift pile. "MacKay, *hurry.*"

Kiaran releases Sorcha. "Talk fast."

"It's part of the prison's design. The Cailleach was able to kill the Morrigan's body, but she was too strong. The prison dampens her abilities enough that she can't rebuild her body and escape it." Sorcha looks at me, at where I patched the hole in the wall. "The Falconer must be immune because it wasn't created to hold a human. The effect on less powerful fae is almost completely binding."

"What does that mean?" My voice is hoarse from the effort to hold the wall in place. I shut my eyes briefly against another push. Another. I start to sway on my feet, dizzy.

Kiaran's curse is loud in the quiet hallway. He pulls away from Sorcha and studies his knuckles. Thin cuts dot his pale skin from when he punched the wall. Blood is dripping across the back of his swelling hand.

His wound isn't healing.

"It means," Kiaran says through gritted teeth, "that we can all die in here. And Sorcha didn't bother to tell us."

"An opportunity presented itself, so I took it." Her smile is familiar, terrible and dark. "I wouldn't be me if I didn't. I wanted you and I *hate* her."

Kiaran's laugh is low, dangerous. It makes me shiver. "Ah, *laoigh mo chridhe*," he murmurs to her, brushing two fingers down her cheek. "I'm going to live out the rest of my existence imagining all the different ways I'd slaughter you if I could." His voice dips. "Does that sound familiar? How does it feel to be no better than your former master?"

What does that mean?

Sorcha draws in a sharp breath. "Kadamach," she whispers. Her hand trembles as she reaches for his arm. "Listen—"

The Morrigan slams into the shield of power I'm holding with enough force that I cry out. "I don't mean to interrupt—" She shoves again, and this time I grit my teeth against the onslaught.

Vines snake their way through the cracks in the rubble. The Morrigan's power is building around us like an oncoming storm, pushing through mine with an almost mocking delight.

A voice whispers in my mind, cold as ice on the wind. *A human with my sister's powers. Now that is interesting.*

Now she knows my weaknesses. She knows I'll die if I keep trying.

Kiaran is next to me. "Kam?"

I try to concentrate but my muscles hurt. My body strains with the effort to keep the Morrigan at bay, to keep the wall up. "I can't hold it."

"Let it go and run when I say," he tells me. Then he counts in my ear. One. Two. Three. Go.

I drop my powers and we race down the long hallway, my boots hitting the onyx floor hard. Behind us, the wall bursts open. Vines crawl along the ceiling, thicker now. Thorns tear through the bricks like paper.

As we speed past cracks forming along the stonework, the Morrigan is in my mind, digging, digging, digging. Reading me. Assessing my powers and looking for another weakness. I can't stop her. I can't keep her out entirely, not after holding her power at bay. She knows that and—

I swear I can feel her smile.

The hallway shakes and I'm thrown off balance. Something slams into the bricks. "Do you feel that?" I say to Kiaran, panting hard.

He shakes his head once as if to clear it. His answer is strained. "Aye."

A moment later, the ground beneath me gives way.

CHAPTER 27

M Y STOMACH drops. I bite back a scream as I plunge through the floor and into the darkness. Broken bricks crash into the walls below me. I feel the rough grasp of Kiaran's fingers on my clothes, pulling me closer. He says my name and it echoes around us.

I manage to open my eyes to see below and . . . there is nothing—*nothing*. Just a pit, endlessly black, with no visible bottom. I had taken a risk, made a wager that I was going to find the Book, and now my only thoughts are that I'm going to die and fail the people I care about. Only this time, I'll be gone for good.

This time, there's no coming back for me.

"Kam." Kiaran's sharp voice draws me out of my thoughts. He has a bruising hold on my arm, and jerks me to him in a rough embrace as the air rushes around us. *How far have we fallen? How far do we have left?*

"Keep your body straight."

How the bloody hell can he sound so calm at a time like this? He's mortal now, for god's sake.

"What?"

Kiaran's hands slip around my waist, fingers digging into my coat to keep me from struggling. How can I not struggle? We're falling fast, weightless, down down *down*—

"Can't you smell it?"

Focus. Calm.

I inhale. And through the musty odor of stone all around us, I breathe in the crisp, clean scent of water. As if we were falling to the bottom of a well or a cave. It's a chance of survival. A blessing in the form of an underground lake. Do this right, and we might live. Do this wrong, and we die.

"Do you remember the cliffs on Skye?" Kiaran's breath is soft on my throat. I can barely hear him over the air rushing around us as we fall, fall, fall. "Push with your power to lessen the impact." I shiver when his fingers brush just beneath my ribs. "From there. Do you feel it?"

I feel it. A pulse across my skin. A cadence: *Trust your body. Trust your mind. Trust your power.*

But how can I? We're still falling. This cave is endless. As if we're plunging through the stars, through space, into the ocean. I try not to be distracted by my trembling body, my panicked thoughts. I concentrate on the feel of my powers, coiled and ready as if just waiting for my command. I let them calm me.

I am fearless. I am powerful. Trust.

"Now let it out, Kam."

I let all that power out. Before, it was like trying to breathe through a fire, with smoke in my lungs and everything tight and constricted. It's becoming easier each time, less painful. Now it's like trying to inhale on a cold winter's day. Just a press of my lungs and then . . . in and out. In and out.

"That's it." As if Kiaran can't help himself, he presses a kiss to the underside of my jaw. "Now build an updraft to slow us down."

I do exactly as he says. I never realized how much of a faery's power was simply manipulating the existing elements, like air or water or earth. Bending them to your will and using them to your advantage.

My power commands the air around us to thicken and create an upward gale so harsh that it slows us down, exactly as Kiaran did for us when we fell from the cliffs on Skye. Only when he did this, it had been graceful. He made it seem effortless.

In the space of a few seconds, my control begins to wither. *Trust your power. Trust your body. Trust—*

My chest tightens. I draw a gasping breath but I can't get in air. My mental chant isn't enough when my lungs are burning with the effort to control all that power. My vision begins to blur.

Kiaran must sense there's something wrong. "Kam?"

Focus on the water. Your safety net.

Your only chance of survival.

One last breath. One final push. A weak pulse of power before the end. My concentration shatters the moment before we hit the water.

I can't move. My limbs are suddenly too heavy, dead weights dragging me farther into the cold water. There's no current to wash me away, nothing but a still pool without a bottom.

I must have lost consciousness, because the next thing I know, I'm hearing Kiaran saying my name. Repeating it over and over like a prayer. His fingers clumsily press a few times to my neck to seek my pulse. And I hear his small gasp for breath, a betrayal of his normally calm façade.

"*Kam.*" Fear in his voice.

Kiaran doesn't have to tell me. I can hear the slow, heavy pulse in my ears. An uneven drum that reminds me: *You're dying. You're dying. You're dying.*

I open my eyes. With my fae senses, I can see Kiaran's shadowed features in the pitch blackness of the cavern, the way his pale skin is glistening with water.

"What the hell was that?" His voice is rough as stone.

Lie. "Nothing," I say, my voice hoarse. *Lie better.* "The Cailleach's power just takes some getting used to, that's all."

Kiaran stares at me hard, his thumb softly brushing my upper lip. "Your nose is bleeding." His words are uneven. He suddenly jerks away, swimming fast to put distance between us. That few feet of separation feels vast.

I don't know what else to do but dab at my nose. With my fae-powered eyes, I can see the light mix of blood and water. It would barely have been noticeable to a human, but with Kiaran's Unseelie nature . . .

Kiaran flinches and looks away. His features are strained, his jaw set. My movements are slow as I dip my head into the water and blot the blood. The same way I would when encountering a predator in the wild: No sudden movements. Back away an inch at a time.

Don't look like prey.

"Being mortal now doesn't make a difference?"

He shakes his head once. "My powers are bound, not nonexistent. Being temporarily mortal doesn't make me human any more than having powers makes you *sìthiche*."

Kiaran's words are even, emotionless, and almost a touch harsh. As if he were blaming me for bleeding—but that's not it. We've hunted together for so long that I can read his thoughts as clearly as if they were my own: Kiaran blames himself for being tempted.

Here. I would bite you right here. And that's why I don't trust myself with you.

After a long stretch of silence between us, I speak. "Are you all right now?" My voice is faint, hesitant. Careful. He knows what I'm asking. *Are you Kiaran or are you Kadamach?*

"Not yet. Talk. Distract me."

I try to focus on our surroundings, staring up at the hole we fell through. It's so high up it looks like a small, bright star amid the black. "Do you think they're still up there?"

I hear Kiaran's soft inhale as he looks up, too. "If they were, my sister is foolish enough to have dived down with us."

"Do you think they're all right?"

"I hope so." When I don't respond, he rasps, "Tell me what you see."

My eyes adjust to the near-pitch-black cavern and I tell him. The only light comes from the hole so far overhead, such a small break in the thick rock surrounding us. I swim to a small alcove and ease around a boulder raised out of the underground loch. The crack in the wall on this side of the loch is dark; for all I know it leads deeper into an underground cave system. It looks dangerous, and too tight for Kiaran to fit through.

My hands trail along the slippery walls. No way to climb up, anyway. And despite the sections of smooth rock within the loch, there are no other tunnels—at least, none above water.

No way out.

Hesitantly, I look over at Kiaran. Should I tell him that? His eyes are closed, as if he were lulled by the sound of my voice. "Keep talking. Just for a few more minutes."

"What should I say?"

"Anything." His voice is raw. "Anything. Tell me another story."

I force out a breath and say the first thing that comes to mind. "The faery king and the girl used to train in the earliest hours of the morning," I say, keeping my tone soft, steady. "They sparred until the predawn light came up over the North Sea. On rare mornings when the sky was clear of rain clouds, the girl would look over at the king just as the first rays shone through the buildings and bathed the city in a beautiful, golden glow.

"Because, you see, that was when the king tipped his head back and closed his eyes and the girl allowed herself, for those brief moments, to think about things she could never admit to him aloud. Like how with each passing day, she hated him less and less. Until the morning came when she watched him greet the sun and knew she didn't hate him at all, not anymore. She understood then that one day, she would be there when the sun rose over the sea, and she'd look at him, and realize she loved him."

I almost say it. The words are on my lips and the darkness seems to hold its breath, waiting, waiting for me to say them.

I love you, I love you, I love you.

Then I hear something. A breath next to my ear, almost inaudible. I jerk my head to the side and Kiaran looks over, about to speak.

I press a finger to my mouth, listening hard. "Shh."

A whisper, faint—as if it were coming from far away. I whirl sharply, but there's nothing there. *Did I imagine it? Am I going mad?*

No, there it is again. A voice so low that I can't make out the words, spoken in an unfamiliar tongue.

I turn again, my hand reaching out, but there's nothing but air. "MacKay," I say warningly. "Did you—"

Kiaran is at my side in an instant, his shoulder against mine. He swears, low and foul. "I don't know."

There's another murmur to my left, quiet and dark, and I press closer to Kiaran. "I definitely heard that," he says.

We both listen again, but the cave is silent. Too silent. There is no soft *tap tap tap* of dripping water or anything to indicate we're in a cave at all. It's as if we've been dashed into space, drifting in a desolate lake with no light or sound— nothing but our breathing.

And something else. Someone in the cave that I can't see, watching us from the shadows. Someone that most certainly can see *us*. My senses might be enhanced now, but I'm still human. My body has its limitations. And Kiaran's powers are bound.

We're both vulnerable. Both mortal. Both almost human.

There's a small splash behind us. Someone is moving through the water. A whisper to my left, then a sudden searing pain across my cheek. I cry out, more out of shock than pain, and press my palm to my skin.

It comes away wet with blood.

CHAPTER 28

ON'T MOVE." Kiaran's voice is low, ragged. He makes a sound in his throat, something like a growl. I tense. He smells my blood.

"Breathe," I say sharply. "Goddamn it, just breathe." I grasp his arm and pull us through the water until there's a boulder at our backs and we're tucked away in the alcove.

Only a minute. If the Morrigan is going to attack, we only have a minute.

"Any ideas?" When he doesn't respond, I bunch his shirt in a fist and force him to look at me. "Don't make me smack some sense into you, Kiaran MacKay. *Ideas. Now.*"

Kiaran's eyes focus on mine and he breathes through his mouth, his features strained. "The Morrigan was known for her ability to mentally influence other fae. She could break into their minds, make them do whatever she wanted." I nod. *Keep going. Keep talking.* "If the Cailleach destroyed her body, maybe she can only manipulate our surroundings or take the form of other fae."

The Morrigan will do whatever it takes to break out of there. She's going to decide which of us are the pawns, and which one of us is the key.

Which are we?

"If she's taking another form, then what faeries live in the water? Who also like the dark? Faeries who—"

"Are you going to keep listing?"

"I'll keep listing if you don't give me a bloody answer. Think!"

A whisper to my left, mocking laughter. A laugh right behind me. I whirl. She's circling, a predator ready to leap. "MacKay—"

I cry out as the Morrigan slashes at my arm. This time it hurts worse, as if the faery used a red-hot knife. I shove away from Kiaran before he can smell the blood. I scan the water, but I see nothing. I hear nothing. My powers are beckoning, tempting, but if I use them, I risk blacking out again.

No way out. Nowhere to go.

"MacKay," I say, somewhat desperately. "Her form?"

Something is moving through the water; I can't even see impressions anymore. It's as if the darkness is thickening, the cave misting over. The air turns hot and humid.

Kiaran inhales sharply and I know the Morrigan must have struck him. "Water-horse." The suggestion of a fae form falls from his lips with contempt, like he's saying something foul. He continues listing: "Fuath. Fideal. Afanc—"

I yelp in pain as claws drag across my back, deep and sharp. The Morrigan's whisper at my ear again: "It's been a long time since I've seen a human."

I swing my arm out in an attack, catching strands of long hair that dissipate like smoke. There's a flash of her bright sapphire eyes before the Morrigan tears away into the shadows. Her laughter spreads around me in a rush of sudden cold that breaks through the humidity of the cave.

"She's a faery form with claws and long hair," I tell Kiaran. "She just evaporated into the damn shadows and—"

Kiaran's head snaps toward me in the dark. "What did you just say?"

"—I'm going to *kill* her—"

"She evaporated into the shadows?" Before I can even blink, Kiaran seizes my wrist. "We're getting out of here. Now."

"MacKay, I already told you. There's no way out."

His answer is spoken through gritted teeth. "Then I'll shove you through that small tunnel if I have to."

Kiaran is pulling me so forcefully to the other side of the loch that I have to swim or end up with a mouthful of cave water. "Wait—"

The Morrigan rips me out of Kiaran's grasp and throws me violently across the water. I hit the surface, only inches away from smacking into the cave wall. I emerge, gasping for breath.

"Kam!" Kiaran dives for me, his strokes fast.

Something strikes him hard. Kiaran hits the wall with a rough jolt that makes him growl. He whirls, but the darkness is complete. I push myself through the water to reach him. His hands find mine in a crushing grip.

A laugh echoes around us and something flickers in the corner of my gaze, but it's gone so fast. Then her voice is at my ear, claws grazing my neck softly. "What do you think? Does he love you enough, human?"

I take the risk. I draw on my powers, building them like a storm inside me and fighting through my blurring vision. But before I can defend myself, the Morrigan slashes her claws down my arm in a quick, painful swipe. My power dies, leaving behind a dull ache at my temples.

Kiaran's harsh intake of breath fills my ears and he releases me.

"MacKay." When I reach for him, I seize nothing but air.

"Don't come near me. She's doing this on purpose. She's a water wraith."

"*What?*"

It sounds as if his words are spoken through a grimace. "And she's playing with us."

I can't remember his lessons. Not now. Not with the darkness pressing in, suffocating. My legs burn from treading water. "Water wraith?" I pant.

"They draw lovers together and turn them against one another. She's using this form to find our weaknesses. She *wants* me to hurt you."

The Morrigan's laugh is in my ear. "Hurt you?" she whispers with a laugh. "He wants to *kill* you."

I lash out to slam my fist into the creature's face, but she's too fast. She's already behind me, breathing cold, biting words into my ear. "He can't hide his thoughts from me. I was the first Unseelie. His blood is my blood."

I whirl, lashing out again.

She's at my back, a devil filling my head with terrible doubts. *Where is Kiaran?*

As if she senses me looking for him, the hot cave mist clears just enough for me to see him in profile. He's so still. Not moving. Listening?

"It's in his nature to hunt your kind." I feel her shift around me, pressing closer. "He can only resist my curse for so long before he gives in. He can't help but want to feed on you."

That's when I know, unquestionably, that the Morrigan isn't just speaking to me. She isn't only at my ear.

She's at his.

I say his name, low and urgent. And when he looks at me . . . *Oh god.*

I go still. Kiaran is looking up at me through his lashes, his gaze dark, hooded, and intense.

Are you Kiaran or Kadamach?

Something flickers in his eyes. *I don't know.*

"Do you see the way he looks at you?" The Morrigan sounds like a victor on the battlefield, walking through the bodies. "Right now he can hardly breathe without being tempted by your blood. That's my curse." Her lips are close to my ear. "That's the punishment of his lineage."

Snarling, I turn to grab the Morrigan, but just when I think I've connected with something solid, she turns into mist, slipping away with a throaty laugh.

"*MacKay*." I surge through the water toward him. "Listen to me," I say sharply when I reach him. "Listen to my voice. You're the Unseelie King. Now snap the hell out of it and help me. How do we kill her?"

Kiaran shakes his head once, but the darkness doesn't leave his face. We swim to another set of boulders jutting out of the water; he's as close as he can get without touching me.

His voice dips just low enough for me to hear, his words uneven, forced. "If she takes physical form, you might be able to overpower her and prevent her from going incorporeal again."

"How do we make her take physical form?"

Kiaran exhales in a shuddering breath, then rests his palm on my cheek. "Trust me."

As he bends in closer, I can see the hunger in his gaze. His pupils are dilated like a predator ready to attack its kill.

Then, with aching softness, he presses his lips to mine.

It takes all my effort to stay still, to stop myself from pulling him closer. My fingernails bite into the skin of my palms. *Stay still. Don't move. Don't breathe. Don't even think.* I know his control is tenuous. I sense it when his lips tremble against mine. In the slow, deliberate way he breathes as if he's trying to keep calm.

For us, it's a chaste kiss. I don't know how such a simple touch leaves me shivering, but I'm not the only one.

Kiaran's fingers trail down my wet coat, a touch of fire through the cold material. Then his hand slips underneath to find my waist, fingers brushing the skin where my shirt and trousers meet. My mind whispers a simple word. *Yes*, I think. *Yes*.

Claws slash across my back, ripping through the fabric and deep into my skin, and I cry out. But my instincts don't fail me. I twist out of Kiaran's arms, raise my palms, and unleash my power.

Stay, I command with all the force of the Cailleach. *Be still*.

The Morrigan in the wraith's body thrashes, sloshing water everywhere. Her sapphire eyes flash with rage and disgust. "*Filthy* human."

"This filthy human has you trapped," I say. "MacKay." When he doesn't move to strike, I glance at him. "MacKay?"

A soft curse escapes me.

He's staring at me—no, not at me. At my back, where the Morrigan slashed her wraith claws through my skin so deeply that I can smell my blood mixing into the water.

Kiaran's lips part. Then I see the small flash of fangs descend over his teeth. When his eyes meet mine, the normally bright, uncanny lilac of his eyes is shadowed by something darker.

Something ravenous.

"There it is," whispers the Morrigan. "My beautiful Unseelie curse."

"Shut up," I say sharply.

Already, the energy to keep her corporeal is taking its toll. I'm growing lightheaded, dizzy. My temples pound, and dots flash across my vision. My human body can't take it and I've had no chance to mend since last using my powers. I'm afraid that if I move to kill her, I'll black out again.

Trust him. Trust him.

The Morrigan comes closer, straining against the limits of my powers. She senses an opportunity. "I can read his thoughts. Shall I tell you?"

"*Stop.*" My vision is fading.

"He's fighting between his feelings for you and his will to survive. Which do you think will triumph? Do you think he can go against what he was made for? What *I* designed him to do? My curse always wins."

His hunger will always win out. Always.

"MacKay," I say, his name barely a whisper as I fight to stay conscious. "Look at me. Listen to my voice."

Are you Kiaran or Kadamach?

He's closer, moving through the water like a great shadow. It makes him seem bigger, more formidable. Even with his powers bound, Kiaran isn't human. He's a creature of darkness, fae in every way. That Unseelie in him that I always saw lurking beneath the surface is no longer hidden.

And the focus of his attention—of that towering build and those deep, dark eyes—is me. There's nothing in his gaze to indicate that he sees me as anything other than a means of his survival.

Trust him. Trust him.

His name is on my lips, a pleading whisper. *Look at me. Come back to me.*

The Morrigan laughs.

Trust him. Trust him.

He's so close. His fangs flashing, reaching for me, to choke the life out of me—

Kiaran grabs the wraith by the throat and with a swift jerk of his hand, snaps her neck. Gasping, I stare at the wraith's slouched, lifeless form as I draw my powers back inside me. I ignore the pounding headache at my temples and stare at Kiaran, but he won't look at me.

He doesn't have to.

To my left, the cave wall begins to crumble as easily as dried mud to reveal a portal. Small bits of stone splash around us. I swat at the water in my face, braced for another fight—for the Morrigan to return. But through the portal, all I see is a forest below the magnificent stars of a night sky. A way out of the cave.

Just beyond the line of dark trees, I swear I see a glimpse of a girl with long hair and pale skin silhouetted against the moonlight.

But when I look again, she's gone.

CHAPTER 29

OUTSIDE THE cave, the forest towers high with trees as thick and dark as soot-covered columns. A bright full moon hangs high, the light illuminating the tops of the branches in a dusky, glowing haze. I tilt my head back at the cool breeze, shivering a bit in my wet clothes.

Who was that girl?

"Did you see . . ." My voice trails off when I glance over at Kiaran.

His breathing is slow and steady, as if he's counting the seconds to calm himself down. He lifts a trembling hand to push back his hair. "See what?" His rolling accent is uneven.

"Nothing. Never mind." I press my lips together, uncertain what to say. "Should we go through the forest?" I ask instead. "Won't the Morrigan find us easily here?"

"Even the Morrigan would have to recover from an attack like that," he says. "Taking physical form would have required a great deal of power. We'll use the opportunity to rest."

Kiaran tosses me his coat. "Here. There's a roll of bread for you in the inner pocket. You need to eat something."

The bread is wrapped in leaves that kept it dry. I gratefully murmur my thanks that Kiaran is so practical. Between the Morrigan's attacks and worrying over the Book, I didn't even notice how famished I was.

Kiaran gathers wood for a fire and I light it with my powers. A small bit of energy I'm willing to risk because I'm so bloody tired and I've never seen Kiaran look this rough, either.

Now you know how I feel, I think wryly as I move to sit near the flames. *No invulnerable, shining fae skin. No immediate healing. Just the deep bone-tiredness of mortality.*

Kiaran sits opposite, as far from me as possible. The scent of burning wood must mask the scent of my blood, at least a little. His eyes flicker to me in a quick, controlled assessment. "Your wounds need binding."

I can't help but smile. "First the bread, now my wounds. Is this the Kiaran MacKay way of fussing over someone?"

"I don't fuss," Kiaran says. "I give stern instructions, like: Bind your goddamn wounds."

"I don't like overbearing men."

His mouth quirks into a sly smile. "And yet I love assertive, stubborn women."

I laugh in surprise. "God, I adore you."

I ease my coat from my shoulders to check my injuries. There are a few superficial scratches down my arms. The deepest ones, along my shoulders, will need stitching. But I don't have the luxury of such things now. All I have for dressing my wounds is the fabric from my coat. Brocade isn't exactly ideal, but anything is better than bleeding out.

As I peel the sopping coat the rest of the way off, Kiaran's sharp voice startles me. "Burn it."

I glance up in shock. "I beg your pardon?"

"Burn. The. Coat." This time he says the words through his teeth. "Wear mine to cover up your scent. I can smell your blood and it's driving me mad." Then he says something I never would have expected in a thousand years: "Please."

Please. In all the time I've known Kiaran, he has never, ever said that. Along with *Sorry,* I assumed it wasn't in his vocabulary.

But there it is, the word hanging in the air between us, a mark of his desperation. *Please.* Now I know the way he looked at me in the cave before he killed the Morrigan's wraith form wasn't for show. It wasn't to make the Morrigan think she had won.

She almost had.

"Very well," I say quietly.

The wraith shredded enough of my coat that it's easy to tear into strips. I press the longest one over my shoulder, securing it in place with another scrap of material that I knot with my teeth. I do my best to wipe up the blood along my back, scrubbing at it until my skin stings.

Then I toss the remains of my tattered coat into the fire and shrug into Kiaran's discarded one. It's so big on me that I have to roll the sleeves up.

I lift my arms with a slight smile. "How silly do I look in this? Be honest now."

I notice that a little tension leaves his shoulders. "Kam." He shakes his head with a small laugh. "You're adorable."

I grin. "My god. You just called me adorable in the proper context. And here I thought you only used that word for one terrible reason."

"Second reason, not terrible: You. In that coat. With that smile."

"What about my definition?" I push to my feet and start around the fire. "You. Me. Cuddling—"

"*Don't.*" Kiaran puts a hand out to stop me. I freeze when his pupils dilate. "Don't," he says again. "Stay there."

I keep still as I look him over. *How much time do we have until you're too far gone, MacKay? How long until I can't see Kiaran anymore?*

That's when I notice the wound on his arm: a long, jagged cut. Deep enough that blood is soaking through his rough wool shirt. The Morrigan probably injured him to help sever his control. With his powers bound, he can't heal it.

Slowly, I bend to pick up the strips of fabric I left on the ground. "Your arm is bleeding."

"I'm fine. Your concern isn't necessary."

He used to talk to me like that when we hunted together. It was the cold distance of teacher and student, expert and novice. A touch of condescension, a dash of superiority, and it always made me want to beat him over the head with a parasol.

I step toward him and he says my name sharply enough that I stop. "I don't want to hurt you."

I gaze at him patiently, because I'm going to wrap his goddamn arm if I have to hold him down to do it. "I don't care what you want. You've never experienced blood loss before. And you're not fine. You're pale, shaking, and you look like hell." When he glares at me, I cross my arms. "If you tried to attack me right now, I would wager a tidy sum on me having you on your arse in two seconds flat. Let me tend to that injury, or you risk passing out in a fight. Your choice."

After a moment's silence, he nods once. Good. That saves me the effort of finding a branch to beat some sense into him with.

I approach him slowly, my steps careful and even. When his fingers curl into fists, I pause until he relaxes slightly. Then I crouch beside him and put my hand out, palm up. Waiting for permission.

"Is this fine?" I ask, keeping my voice low, steady.

He nods again.

I push the tattered material away to get a better look. Unlike mine, his wound has already begun the early stages of the healing process, which means that even with his powers bound, his healing is much faster. It won't be instantaneous, but he's a lucky bastard.

I use one of the scraps to dab at his injury. Kiaran doesn't make a sound, not even when I wrap the cloth to bind his wound and start on the next one.

"Does it bother you?" I ask. "Knowing you won't heal as quickly here?"

"No. This is . . ." He goes quiet. "Sometimes it's easy to take life for granted when you don't have to worry about dying."

I turn the words over in my mind, wondering what it would be like to be immortal. That something as small as the sight of your own blood could be a revelation.

"I don't know," I say lightly. "I wouldn't mind going into a battle worrying a bit less about being mortally wounded. Sometimes I wish I were fae."

"No, you don't," he says with a bitter laugh.

I look at him in surprise. "You wouldn't want me to live forever?" *With you?*

Kiaran stares into the fire, his expression betraying a hint of unease at the thought.

"No." His answer is the twist of a knife.

"Oh." I don't want to see how much deeper that blade goes.

I turn to put some distance between us, but Kiaran's voice rings out behind me. "My kind hoard years because we're selfish by nature," he says, sounding almost angry. "We add each one to our collection until we've amassed so many that living no longer has any meaning. It becomes trivial, unimportant, and boring. Is that what you want for yourself? What you want me to wish for you? Because make no mistake, a human death would be far more kind."

I go cold inside. That's his future, his life, his existence. If I survive to find the Book and make it mine, he'll live on. My bones will be long in the ground and he'll still endure.

The fae don't truly live. They simply exist.

When my eyes meet his, the black of his outer irises bleeds over the lighter color again. I hate that small bit of darkness there, that reminder of his Unseelie nature, a separation between us.

The need to feel his skin on mine is overpowering. I just caught a glimpse of our separate futures, and now I'm reminded of how little time we have left. If we find the Book, this is it. If we don't find the Book, this is it. These small breaths between battles.

"I want you," I whisper, swallowing before my voice catches. I've never told him that before. Not ever. I glance at the space beside him. "May I sit?"

The blackness keeps spilling across his irises, and then retreats. He takes a deep breath and nods. I slowly ease next to him, pressing my thigh to his. He settles his hand on my knee, a gesture that's both familiar and distancing. As if he wanted it there to either touch me in return or push me away.

"Tell me to stop and I will." I press my palm to his cheek and he shuts his eyes. "Just say the word."

I lean in and kiss him softly, only once. "All right?"

Kiaran's grip on my knee tightens, but he nods again.

I dip my head to press my lips to the space above his shoulder. "All right?" I whisper again.

He's still. So very still. I hear him swallow. "Aye." The word is a plea on his lips, and I hear the blatant want there. The need. Just as much as I want and need.

I scrape my teeth gently down his neck and feel his soft, shuddering breath against my tongue. He seems more human than ever before. More vulnerable. Just . . . more. More everything.

When I slide my hand down to the bottom of his shirt, he seizes my wrist. I watch the struggle in his expression and understand that even if he feels human, he isn't. He's Unseelie. And I'm testing his limits.

When he opens his eyes again, they're clear. I can tell he's exhausted, that the battle to keep his Unseelie nature contained is beginning to take its toll.

"Sleep," I tell him. "For once, you need it."

When I start to get up, he doesn't release me. "Stay," he rasps out. "Don't go."

He pulls me down and presses a soft kiss to my lips, whispering the words again. *Stay.* Another. *Stay.* Another. He says it like it's all he has left to ground him. He says the words because we don't have years.

We hoard our minutes, our precious hours, because they're all he and I have left.

CHAPTER 30

WHEN I stir and pat the space on the ground next to me, I find it cold. Empty. Something crunches nearby and I snap my eyes open, my hand going for a blade.

Sorcha and Aithinne are leaning over me.

"You were snoring," Aithinne says, tilting her head slightly. "And pawing at the ground like a small dog. Humans are very strange when they sleep."

Sorcha snorts. "Are you capable of saying anything that isn't completely ridiculous?"

"I'll say something that isn't completely ridiculous when you say something that doesn't make the people around you want to rip your head off."

I sit up so fast my head spins. It's still nighttime in the forest—or perhaps it always is. The bonfire has long since died, but the moon still hangs full in the sky, bright enough to illuminate the spaces between the trees. I scan the woods for Kiaran, but there's no sight of him. The only indication he was here is the flattened grass next to me, his coat tucked around me like a blanket. He must have covered me before he left.

"Where's Kiaran?"

Aithinne straightens. "You were the only one here. We walked through a door and there you were. Snoring."

Why would he go off alone with the Morrigan still out there? My stomach knots with dread. I hope she didn't lure him away. She was able to manipulate his Unseelie nature in the cave far too easily.

"The Morrigan attacked us," I tell them, pushing to my feet. I shove my arms into Kiaran's coat and pick up my sword. "We need to find him. Now."

Aithinne looks confused. "You only fell through that hole a few minutes ago, how could—"

"Don't be a idiot, Aithinne," Sorcha says in irritation. "Time works differently here, depending on where you are. It's the same as in the *Sìth-bhrùth.*"

Wherever he is, Kiaran is injured, tired, and losing control. He could be in trouble.

I buckle my sword sheath to my waist and head for the trees. "If you're coming, hurry up."

They glance at each other, but follow. Aithinne matches my stride, looking askance at me. "You don't even know where you're going, do you? You're not walking into a fight, you're running into it at full speed with a blindfold on and your ears lopped off and—"

"*Thank you,*" I say. "That metaphor did not need to be extended."

I risk using a small pulse of power, a searching stroke in the trees around us. *Find Kiaran.*

Nothing. Not a stir, not a breath, not a whisper.

Aithinne waves a dismissive hand. "You know what I mean."

I shake my head once. "None of us knows where we're going," I counter. "Do *you?*" I glance at Sorcha, who is eyeing me warily—no doubt because I look half-crazed. "Does *she?*"

Find Kiaran. Find the Book. Kill the Morrigan. Focus on those three things with the iron will of someone who has everything to lose. Someone who may only have hours left.

If I worry too much about what's happening to Kiaran, I'll do something reckless. But I need him. To quiet my doubts. To tell me that I can do this, my final battle. It's my last attempt to make things right.

"Falconer." Aithinne's voice is patient. "We should plan our next—"

"I don't have time for that and you know it."

Aithinne grasps my arm to stop me. "Do you realize how you sound right now?" she says sharply. "*Mar theine beumach.* Like you're on a path of destruction. You're not thinking clearly."

"She's human," Sorcha counters. "Do they ever think clearly?"

I whirl on Sorcha, unsheathing my blade. The metal whistles in an arc, the tip pressing against her throat. "You know how to find the Book, don't you?"

"Aileana."

I ignore Aithinne, my gaze utterly focused on Sorcha. *"Answer me."*

Sorcha's green eyes gleam. "I don't like talking with a blade to my throat."

Her skin breaks beneath my sword and a small trickle of blood slides down her chest. It seeps into the red brocade of her dress, a perfect match. "And I don't like being manipulated. Did you find the Book?"

Nothing. Not a hint of an answer. Aithinne's gaze catches mine and I know she sees the question there.

She nods once. *Do it.*

I slice Sorcha across the arm. She cries out and backs away, but I'm too fast. My fingers close around her throat, pressing into the skin. "You seem to be under the mistaken impression that between Kiaran and me, I'm the weak one. Let me assure you, that isn't true." I squeeze harder for emphasis and she gasps for breath.

"Aileana . . ." Aithinne says uncertainly.

"Talk or I'll tear through your memories like gauze." Sorcha murmurs something, but it's too low to hear. "Louder. Before my hand slips and I crush your windpipe."

"Aye," she wheezes. "I found the damn Book."

"How? Where is it?"

Sorcha bares her fangs. "I don't remember."

A straight statement, no room for a lie—

No. She must be half-lying somehow. Sorcha is manipulative enough to figure out how to get around the truth. "I don't believe you," I snarl. "Last chance to tell me the truth."

She presses her lips together, her eyes narrowed into slits. "I. Don't. Remember."

I don't hesitate. I slam through her mind. Not like before—this time I'm careening through her thoughts in a loud, demanding crash. A struggle to find the right thoughts, the right images, the right memories.

Show me.

Sorcha isn't prepared for how frantic I am. For the urgent, desperate clawing and shoving through her mind. I am frenzied and determined as I sift past the images, of her and Lonnrach by the tree, of her running, of some girl with long hair and pale skin marked with something, but it's too dark to see.

I keep going until I come to a memory that makes me stop. An image so terrible I choke back tears.

Sorcha is in a bloody heap on the ground of a forest just like the one we're in. I don't know what I'm seeing; I didn't know that limbs could be turned all those different ways, bent, mutilated. Some no longer attached. Blood in a thick dark pool around her. Her breath coming out in a rough wheeze as if her lungs were partially collapsed.

She's singing in the fae language, the words catching in her throat. The warbled song of a broken girl.

How was Sorcha even alive? How? With her healing ability bound—

I have my answer a moment later when a woman with black hair and pale skin approaches.

Aithinne?

I almost drop Sorcha in surprise, but then Aithinne turns and I see her eyes. Blue eyes that shine as bright as cut sapphire—not the swirling, molten silver of Aithinne's eyes. This is the Morrigan in Aithinne's form. *Oh, god. The Morrigan kept Sorcha alive.*

She strokes a finger down Sorcha's bloody, tear-tracked cheek. "I like this song. You have such a beautiful voice, little bird." Then she seizes Sorcha by the hair and says, "Come along now. Let's put you back together and try something else."

The Morrigan drags Sorcha's broken body through the dark trees. Sorcha never stops singing.

CHAPTER 31

SHOVE AWAY from Sorcha and retch. After her memory, I doubt I could have held anything in. My mind keeps turning that image over and over again; Sorcha's broken limbs. Sorcha's disjointed song.

I was her entertainment.

"Didn't like what you saw?" she says mockingly behind me. Beneath it, I hear a tremble to her voice, a hint of vulnerability. "First lesson, Falconer: Don't break into someone else's thoughts unless you can handle them."

Aithinne grips my arm to help me up. "What did you see?"

Everything. I shut my eyes briefly. *Everything.* "I'm sorry."

I look up at Sorcha to find her clutching the trunk of a tree as if she were steadying herself. As if she were gathering the broken remains of what armor she has left and putting it into place. Armor I tore away like it meant nothing.

"I'm sorry," I repeat.

Sorcha's eyes flare with rage. "I don't want your pity." Her lip curls. "Do you want to know why I hate you so much, Falconer? It isn't your pathetic little romance with Kadamach. You're a girl with a passably pretty face and a bit of skill in battle, and he's a man and men are fools. No, I hate you because you believe yourself so far above my kind, when the truth is you're just as ruthless as the rest of us."

I have no retort for her, no clever response. Because it's true. I'm a war-hardened girl whose desperation is chipping away at my soul. I broke into her mind twice.

"Let me repeat what I said earlier now that I don't have a blade at my throat: I. Don't. *Remember*." She says the last word in a snarl. "When I came here the first time and the Morrigan captured me, she sent me to search for the Book since she needed my blood to open it. I found it. But I don't recall how or what it looks like. I just know that somehow I lost it, and the Morrigan found a great deal of delight in punishing me for my failure."

She sent me to search for the Book. "Do you mean to tell me," I say carefully, "that the Morrigan doesn't have the Book?"

Sorcha regards me impatiently. "Someone give this human a bauble for her detective skills. You're truly a wonder, Falconer." At my glare, she explains, "The Book was hidden here, and when the Morrigan came looking for it, the Cailleach trapped her. The Morrigan has been searching for the Book and an escape ever since."

The story that said the Morrigan found the Book was wrong, then. That means we still have the chance to claim it.

I stare at Sorcha, uneasy now after everything I saw in her mind. She's telling me the truth. I know it. I have so many questions, but first . . . "If you can't recall how you found it, then maybe Aithinne can—"

"No." Her lip curls. "If the Morrigan couldn't dig that memory out of my mind, what makes you think this incompetent simpleton can?"

"I'm not incompetent," Aithinne says easily. "I just hate you."

Sorcha rolls her eyes, grips her skirts and shoves past me. "Look, let's just find Kadamach and finish this so I can be rid of you both."

She doesn't get far before a loud *crack!* makes us all go still.

I grip my sword, my eyes scanning the trees. "What the hell was that?"

"What I wouldn't give for my powers," Aithinne mutters, turning sharply at another low rustle from somewhere I can't identify.

"How about a blade?" Sorcha says in a low voice. "I've already vowed not to shove it between your ribs—"

Pop! Pop pop!

We whirl, just as the massive oak behind us tilts forward. I lunge to the side, scrambling to get out of the way before it falls.

It doesn't. The damn tree is moving.

Branches reach for us like creaking, gnarled fingers. Roots wrap around Aithinne's ankle and yank her back. She drops to the ground and the tree drags her forcefully across the wet soil.

"Go!" Aithinne shouts. She slashes with her sword, hacking away to free herself. She pushes to her feet and breaks into a run.

We sprint through the dense forest. Our boots kick up mud and water; it's difficult to move through quickly. Slippery leaves on the ground further hinder our pace, but we keep going. We don't slow down. Behind me I can hear the snapping branches, a crash as a heavy root hits the ground.

I look over at Sorcha and see movement to my left. "Behind you!"

I'm too late. Branches wrap around Sorcha's torso, pulling her off her feet. The trees jerk her back through the mud, slamming her body painfully to the ground.

I can't help my fleeting thought: *Leave her there.*

But even if Sorcha can't help me find the Book, I still need her to open it. It's the only reason I'll bother to save her worthless hide. She's right: I am ruthless.

I charge forward, slashing into the tree. The fae metal slices through it easily—but a branch grabs me around the ankle. I hack at it, severing it before it has a secure grip. Then I lurch to seize Sorcha's arm.

"It's about bloody time, Falconer."

My blade whistles through the air as I cut her loose. "I considered leaving you."

"I thought you would."

I yank her with me as I break into a run. "This doesn't mean anything. I need you to open the Book. I still hate you."

"Believe me, Falconer, I understand your motives are far from noble."

Where is Aithinne? I look left and spot her battling with a massive, towering tree—and others are starting to close in. The Morrigan has brought the entire damn forest to life.

Aithinne vaults into the air to avoid a branch, but another comes right at her. She spins into a crouch, her sword slashing high. With a running leap, she joins us. Her expression is grim; her shoulder is bleeding.

We break through reaching branches, fighting and clawing our way out. The forest is dense—too dense. I can't see where it ends and this assault is too much, too quick. My limbs are burning, growing tired. When I slice through one branch, another takes its place. And another. Their grip is forceful, rough, leaving bruising red welts on my wrists and arms.

"There," Sorcha gasps.

Through the line of trees is a shining portal.

Aithinne's shout draws my attention. She slashes her blade, her movements fast. When she reaches me, Aithinne gives me a hard shove. "Go through the portal! Find the Book!"

Her silver eyes are bright. "Let me buy you time."

"But—"

"*Idiot*," Sorcha snarls, seizing me by the shirt. She pulls me hard and starts running. We sprint for the portal, the branches around us closing in. We're not going to make it. It's too far.

Too far.

No, we're almost there. *Focus. Find Kiaran. Find the Book. Kill the Morrigan.*

Just a little farther . . .

A branch wraps around my wrist and I cry out, hacking with my sword. Another yanks my feet out from under me. I slam into the ground and the branch ruthlessly drags me back, but I claw at the mud for my sword to hack it away. I manage to get to my feet, but now it has me again, with a painful grip on my arm.

Sorcha is there. She snatches one of the small blades out of the sheath at my wrist and smiles with a flash of her fangs. "I guess I'm buying you time, too. This still doesn't change a damn thing."

She slices through the branch, grabs me by the coat, and shoves me hard through the portal.

CHAPTER 32

THE PORTAL sends me to the edge of a dark, moonlit field. It takes a moment for my eyes to adjust enough to notice that there are figures on the ground. Shapes I can't quite make out—

Footsteps crunch through the grass behind me. The low murmur of Sorcha's voice drifts from the cradle of forest trees at the edge of the field. Then: "Ugh! Aithinne, would you let go of my—"

"Your arm is much less muscular than I thought it'd be."

"That isn't my arm, you *idiot*."

I turn just as they both stumble out of the trees at the edge of the field. Aithinne is plucking branches and leaves out of her hair and Sorcha is tugging at the heavy material of her dress. Her heels sink into the soft dirt of the field as both women head toward me.

"Glad you made it," I say.

"Of course I made it," Aithinne said cheerfully. "I'm amazing."

"You were stuck in a tree," Sorcha says with a snort. "I had to cut you loose and pull your heavy arse through the portal just as it closed—"

Aithinne nearly runs into Sorcha, who has frozen in her tracks. She looks past me and her breath hitches. "Oh, my."

I follow their gazes and a cold shiver runs through me. The figures in the ground I couldn't make out before are body parts. Thousands of them. None of them whole or attached: just a field of limbs and hearts and other organs growing out of the dirt as if it were a garden.

This wasn't a battle. This wasn't even a slaughter. This was for enjoyment. There is an organization to it, a perverse sense of pleasure in the way the field has been tilled and the body parts separated into their own distinct sections. Hearts. Limbs. Organs. Heads. The way one might separate flower beds and catalog each different type.

Each part is perfectly intact. There are no signs of rot, not even the scent of it. Like Derrick said, the *daoine sìth* don't decay. That's why they burn their dead, because otherwise they end up like this. I can't look at the pile of heads, at the features so pristine it's as if they were still alive.

There is only the stench of blood, heavy in the air. As if the Morrigan had fertilized the ground with it. It's so strong that I have to swallow before I heave.

I stagger back until my shoulder brushes against Sorcha. God, even through her dress and coat, I can feel her skin is frigid, alarmingly so. She hasn't moved at all.

"What the hell is this?"

Sorcha glares at me in fury. "What do you think it is?" she asks in a hiss. "It's every fool who's ever come to claim the Book. They were useless without the blood of my lineage to open it. The Morrigan plays with them for a few hundred years and eventually grows bored. Then she kills them and adds them to her little garden."

Beneath Sorcha's rancor is a slight tremble that hints at her fear. I saw her memory; Sorcha must have lived in terror of one day being added to the Morrigan's disgusting collection, of being torn apart one last time and not revived. Sorcha's voice must have been the only thing that saved her.

My pulse is loud in my ears as I look again. The field extends as far as an ocean. It must have taken thousands of years of faeries coming through the portal to form a field this massive.

"I thought they couldn't find the portal without your blood," I say.

Sorcha tears her gaze away from the sight before us. Her expression settles back into its usual one of smooth scorn. "How observant you are, Falconer. My ancestors would take other fae to the door, collect payment, and leave them there to the Morrigan's mercy. Why do you think I killed all of my relations? It wasn't just because I found them irritating."

"Except for me," says a low voice near us.

I freeze. His voice. That voice I heard for weeks in the mirrored room. Teeth at my skin, at my throat, biting me over and over. Leaving me to grow weaker each time until I stopped fighting him. Until I *let* him. And I'll never forgive myself for it.

Lonnrach. He's not in hiding. Not anymore. He's here.

When I reach for Aithinne's hand, her skin is cold and clammy. What Lonnrach did to her was worse. He tortured her for two thousand years in a faery prison beneath Edinburgh, killing her over and over again even though he never had the power to cause her permanent death.

Lonnrach did it just because Aithinne and Kiaran gave up their thrones and the kingdoms fell apart. Aithinne is the one who built the prison that trapped him and the other fae underground. He spent centuries getting his revenge on her for that betrayal.

"My Queen," he says lightly. Then: "Falconer. Back from the dead and fighting alongside the one who murdered you." He laughs, deep and rich, and the sound of it makes me shudder. "You've been busy, haven't you, Sorcha?"

I can feel him staring at me, as if he were whispering in my ear: *Look at me. Look at me now.*

I lift my eyes. He's beautiful, almost like a storybook prince, with salt-white hair, pale skin, and light gray eyes—but cold, hard, and bitter. Lonnrach is a devil in handsome livery.

Sorcha steps forward, slightly in front of me. I'm surprised at how almost . . . protective the gesture seems. "What the hell are you doing here?"

"I could ask you the same question." Lonnrach doesn't seem bothered as he steps casually through the field of body parts. "But I suppose I already know the answer, don't I? You came here for *him*." His lip curls. "Kadamach."

Sorcha reaches back behind her skirts and places her fingers at my wrist. I try not to let my surprise show when she starts easing my blade out of its sheath there, slow and careful, so he doesn't notice the movements.

So that's why she stepped in front of me.

"And you?" Her voice is stiff. "You're the last person I'd expect to find searching for the Book. You told me I was a fool for trying."

"I had a kingdom and a Queen to protect back then." He looks at Aithinne with disgust. "Now I don't."

"Ah yes, how things change." Sorcha has my blade out an inch. "One day you're a knight, and the next you have your fanciful delusions of being a monarch shattered by your own sister. So what conceited plot brought you here?" Another inch of the blade. Sorcha tilts her head as if deep in thought. "Did the Morrigan promise you a pitiful little kingdom of your own? No, she's much too selfish for that. An offer to be her consort, then." At his silence, she laughs. "Oh, you are *pathetic*."

"Better to be the Morrigan's consort than *this* bitch's knight." Lonnrach's eyes flicker to Aithinne and her expression shutters. He smiles when he sees how nonresponsive she is. "The Morrigan promised me I could have you. Don't you miss our time together in the mounds? I do."

Aithinne is panting hard. She shakes her head once, sharply, and I swear I hear her breathe a word. *No.*

"Shall I tell you one thing I've learned, brother?" Sorcha tugs my blade completely out of its sheath to hide behind her skirts. "Leverage is what keeps you alive. The Morrigan only needs one from our lineage to open the Book. So the other is going to have to die." She lifts the weapon and snarls, "And it isn't going to be me."

She throws the dagger and it sinks right into his chest. Lonnrach cries out, but I don't see if he goes down; Sorcha grasps me by the arm. "*Run!* If he's made a deal with the Morrigan, she'll be—"

Something grips my leg roughly, and I stumble forward. I look down in horror to realize one of the severed fae arms has me by the ankle, its fingernails digging into my clothes to hold me in place. It's alive. The goddamn thing is *alive.*

Sorcha seizes me and yanks me out of its hold. "*Aithinne,*" she snarls. "Stop staring, you lackwit. Let's get the hell out of here!"

The entire field comes to life like something out of a nightmare. The severed limbs writhe around us, reaching and grasping to bring us down. We race through the tilled dirt, each movement made more difficult by the sheer number of fae body parts; we're climbing over them, tearing our clothes to get out. A hand has a bruising hold on my arm and I pull free, but it's replaced by another, another, another. We won't get far like this.

A sound draws my attention to the line of trees on the other end of the field where there are figures silhouetted in the moonlight. The garden wasn't the entirety of her grave-yard. The Morrigan kept whole bodies in the woods.

And she just possessed an army of her dead faery victims.

Fae of every type stand in a line, each of them with vivid, sapphire-blue eyes. The same eyes I saw in the cave. The Morrigan's eyes.

She speaks out of the mouth of a female faery in the front. "There's nowhere you can hide that I won't follow. Surrender, little bird."

Sorcha almost backs into me. "*Never.*"

Sorcha whirls and runs, roughly pulling me and Aithinne with her. We shove our way through the field in earnest now, more desperate than coordinated. Here, in the deepest part of the field, those limbs reach for us with grasping hands and fingernails that rip through our clothes.

Aithinne crushes a hand with her boot, panting. "Does this fleeing involve a plan?"

"The plan," Sorcha answers, "is to get to the woods."

"*The woods?*" Aithinne's voice echoes as we careen through the field, kicking and slicing skin open with our swords. "Are they magical Morrigan-repellent woods?"

"At the moment I wish they were magical idiot-repellent woods," Sorcha snaps, breaking the fingers of a severed hand to pull herself free. "Falconer, why don't you make yourself useful and clear us a path?"

"I really shouldn't."

"What the *hell* does that mean?"

The army of fae are rushing through the field after us. Not a sound betrays them; no breathing to give away how far they are, or even footsteps in the tilled dirt. Just an unbearable coldness closing in, as if they were a massive shadow descending over the landscape.

A hand grasps Sorcha around the ankle and she plummets to the ground in a panicked breath. I grasp her arm and yank, hacking at the hand with my sword.

"It means"—I slam the toe of my boot into another limb and grasp my coat free—"these powers kill me faster every time I use them."

Aithinne joins in, slicing through the severed limbs to make a path to the trees.

"*Useless*," Sorcha huffs. "If we make it to that forest, I'm going to slaughter you both myself."

"Don't make me leave you behind, you ungrateful—" The fae are starting to close in on either side of us, fast. Too fast. "Goddamn it," I mutter. "*Fine.*"

I whirl, outstretch my hand toward the army of oncoming fae, and unleash my power. Not enough to permanently damage them—that would require too much energy—but just enough to slow them down. I make the garden into a swamp that pulls their bodies down into the earth. The fae begin to sink up to their knees, then to their thighs, in mud so thick that it becomes difficult to move through.

The blue eyes of the Morrigan meet mine and she says, "This won't save you."

I don't reply. I dart behind Sorcha into the line of trees. If this were any other place, the cover of the forest would be a relief—but the Morrigan can control the landscape. She has all the advantages, and we're just waiting for her to pick us off one by one.

"We can't keep running," I say.

"Quiet, quiet, quiet," Sorcha says, yanking her dress off a branch. "Stop talking. I know what I'm doing."

Aithinne and I let her lead us through the dark woods. We sprint over the twisting roots of the old trees, our breaths coming fast. Where is she taking us? We're so far into the woods that I can hardly see the ground in front of me, nothing except for a patch of light up ahead. Sorcha is heading right for it.

Almost there. *Almost there.* Sorcha shoves us into the clearing and we come to a sudden stop on the banks of a river, where a massive waterfall drops off a cliff into the forest below.

Sorcha smiles grimly. "Now we jump."

I jerk my head toward her. "Are you joking?"

"Do I look like the type to joke about this?"

Aithinne rubs her hands together. "Oh, thank god. I love jumping off high things. I hope I don't die."

Sorcha pinches the bridge of her nose. "Why Kadamach didn't kill you, I'll never know," she mutters. Aithinne grins and leaps off the edge of the cliff. She disappears into the mist at the bottom of the fall. "Well, all right, then." Sorcha looks at me with an eyebrow raised. "Now us. Ready?"

I shut my eyes and jump with her.

CHAPTER 33

LAND CLEANLY on my feet, shocked to find the
ground beneath me is solid. I open my eyes. I'm in a
cave—dry this time, thank goodness—and surprisingly warm.
A fire-pit has been set up in the middle with a pile of
kindling. More sticks and logs are stocked toward the back of
the cave.

The place is a room about the size of my living quarters
back in Edinburgh. But the sight of somewhere moderately
safe is such a relief I could drop to the ground and kiss it at
this point.

Sorcha begins gathering wood from the stack and placing
it in the pit. "Well?" she says. "Are you two going to sit down
or keep staring at the walls like fools? It's a cave. There's
nothing to it."

Aithinne slides her fingers across the walls with a frown.
"This place feels strange. Where are we?"

"A small pocket between worlds," Sorcha says, forming a neat pile of wood in the middle. "They exist all over the Morrigan's prison, and they're the only places she can't follow. Falconer, stop standing there with your mouth open and light this."

I ignite the fire with a small burst of power and sigh in pleasure as it sparks to life. I settle next to her, thankful to be able to rest. "Couldn't you have escaped here when she held you captive?"

She shrugs. "They're like the door. They move. And they're never any bigger than a human prison cell. Either way, I was still trapped."

"They move?" I stare at her. "Do you mean to tell me you had no idea if this cave would still be here when we jumped?"

"I assumed if we heard Aithinne fall with a splat against some rocks . . ."

"I should have known you were up to something when you didn't jump first to save your own arse," Aithinne says, sitting next to me. She shoves a hand through her dark, tangled hair. "Next cliff we come to, I'm pushing you over the edge."

Sorcha rolls her eyes and settles down on the ground. "If you'll excuse me, I'm going to embrace the calm, get some sleep, and not listen to either one of you idiots for the next five hours."

I sigh and look at Aithinne. "We should probably sleep, too." *Who knows when we'll have the opportunity again?*

* * *

In the night, I wake to find Sorcha sitting by the still-active fire, staring thoughtfully into the flames. I don't know how long I've been asleep, but Sorcha has dark smudges beneath her eyes that betray her fatigue. She doesn't glance at me when I sit up and quietly settle next to her.

"You should get some more sleep," I say. "You look exhausted."

Sorcha raises her eyebrow. "Concerned about me, Falconer?"

"For self-preservation purposes, aye."

Her smile is small. "I was wondering when you'd admit you only act out of selfishness, just like me."

"That's not true, though, is it?" I ask her softly. "You wanted Kiaran to be King. You could have claimed the thrones for yourself."

She lifts a shoulder. "It's not what I was born for."

We both stare into the fire and I realize then how many questions I long to ask her. How little I know about her and Kiaran's past. I only know what I garnered from that memory of her and Lonnrach, from the small bits of her conversations with Kiaran.

"Why do you love him?" I can't help but ask. "If he doesn't love you back?"

I thought Sorcha might be offended by the question. She just looks pensive, maybe a touch sad. "You wouldn't understand."

"Try me."

She doesn't respond in anger. Maybe it's her tiredness. Maybe it's the memories we've shared. Maybe it's something else. That's the only explanation I have for why she admits quietly, "There are some things that go beyond love. Kadamach is the only one who has never . . ." She looks away.

I swallow hard. "Never what?"

Her eyes lift to meet mine. "Used me."

"And yet you forced him into that vow." I keep my voice light, but can't hide the hint of bitterness behind it. *You still took away his choice.*

"He wasn't wrong," she says, staring into the fire again. "I am no better than my former master. I became the very thing I hate, I admit that."

"What does that mean?"

"Goodness doesn't last, Falconer. If enough time has passed and enough people hurt us, we all become cruel and heartless bastards." She stares hard at me. "So would you, if humans lived long enough."

I press my lips together. "Aithinne's not like that."

Sorcha snorts. "You think Aithinne is so special because she believes humans aren't completely useless. You might have seen her fight, but I've seen her in war. You believe she's incapable of being cruel? I've walked through whole battlefields covered in her victims."

I flinch and look away, toward Aithinne's sleeping form. "She was defending those she loves."

"Aren't we all?" Sorcha's tone is mocking. "We always try to play the hero first, Falconer. It makes it easier to justify the worst of our actions later." Then, after a moment's consideration: "Maybe I should show you."

She seizes me in a hard grip. Her palms are at my temples, and before I can stop her, her mind connects with mine.

CHAPTER 34

'M IN a cavern illuminated by the dim light of a single lantern on the ground. The first thing I notice is how vast the cavern is, how dark and endless, with shadows thick and pressing against my skin. The second is the stench, so strong I almost stagger. Death. Decay. The iron burn of spilled blood squeezes through my lungs. I press the sleeve of my coat to my face to stifle the odor, but it doesn't work—it's a memory. Not real.

A silhouetted figure is sitting next to the lantern, a bucket beside her. As I approach, I notice how small she is, slight enough to be a child. She hums as she stands up, a long strand of black hair escaping the hood at the back of her dress as she takes a few steps and leans down . . .

I jerk back when I realize that what I thought was a dark mound of rock just beyond the lantern light wasn't part of the cave at all. It's a huge pile of bodies. Hundreds. Thousands. They span farther than the light can reach, rows and rows of dead fae soldiers still wearing their armor.

The girl grasps a body by the arm and drags it off the pile. She makes quick work of removing the armor, moves the body into another pile, then hauls the armor toward the light. She picks a wet brush out of the bucket and scrubs the blood and dirt off the metal, her movements quick, efficient. Her fingers are as graceful as a pianist's, long and tapered. She drums them against the metal as she hums. The song is familiar; I heard it once, by the banks of a loch in the *Sìth-bhrùth*.

No, it can't be her. She's much too small to be—

But she is. Sorcha. Who else would it be? This is her memory.

I crouch next to her, watching her fingers move deftly over the armor as she scrubs and scrubs and scrubs. If I thought she looked ill in her memory with Lonnrach, it doesn't compare to this. Dark circles bruise the pale skin beneath her eyes. Her skin peeking out beneath the tattered, dark wool of her hooded dress is paler than usual, as white and ashen as a specter.

She's frail and fine-boned as a newborn foal, and just as unsteady. She sways slightly as she rises to her feet with the armor, dropping the heavy breastplate, helmet, and shining metals in their own piles on the opposite end of the cave. Returns. Picks up another body. Divests it of armor. Scrubs the metal clean. And again. And again. Every so often, she dumps the water and refills the wooden bucket from the underground spring. Again. And again. And again.

I wince as she hums through the work, even as her hands shake. Even as her voice grows hoarse. Even as her breathing grows uneven, ragged with exhaustion. She's so tired that she has to sit on the ground as she scrubs.

This isn't the work of a royal consort. This is the work of a—

Her song is interrupted by the metallic click of a latch. I look over as the heavy wooden door leading into the cave is pushed open. A man stands there, silhouetted against the brightness of the afternoon sun. Sorcha shuts her eyes at the onslaught of light. Sucks in a sharp breath. From the feel of her mind, I can sense her yearning to go outside.

She's been in this cave for so long. Scrubbing. Preparing the dead for their funeral rites. Salvaging their armor for new soldiers to die wearing on the battlefield against the Seelie. She's been among the dead for so long. For so long.

She's been in this cave for hundreds of years.

The man shuts the door and approaches Sorcha, a shadow of a smile on his face. Like the rest of the Unseelie, he's beautiful. The burnished copper of his hair glows in the soft light from Sorcha's lantern. His eyes are twin pools of black, sharp with malice and . . . something else. A satisfaction I don't understand.

She goes still when he flicks the crudely woven hood away from her hair and slides his hand down the long, shining strands. "You're making good time, *ban-òglach*. You do your work so efficiently. I'm pleased with you."

Sorcha remains motionless on the ground, but I notice how her eyes sharpen with hatred. The way her fingers dig into the dirt at her feet like she's holding back from hurting him. Why doesn't she? She's not chained or bound—

He strokes her hair again, as if he's baiting her. Something inside me twists with revulsion, with anger. For *her*.

"Have I not been fair? Am I not merciful?" he asks her gently. "I've given you four hundred years. When will you take your place by my side?"

Sorcha jerks out of his grasp and spits on his boots. "Not now," she hisses. "Not ever."

The faery's lips press into a cruel line as he plucks a kerchief out of his coat pocket and flicks it down to her. "Wipe it off."

With a growl, Sorcha snatches up the fabric and cleans the saliva off his boots. "Satisfied?" The word comes out like a curse.

"No." He grasps the blade at his hip and tosses it to the ground. "Pick up the dagger and press it just over your heart." Sorcha's hand shakes, but she does what he asks. Her eyes are hard, murderous. "Slide it in, girl," he says in a hiss.

I press a hand to my mouth as Sorcha pushes the blade through the fabric of her dress and through skin. Her breath comes fast, her eyes shut hard, but she never screams. I can tell she wants to. A small cry escapes her lips, but she bites her lower lip hard.

"*Stop*," the faery finally says. "Just there. One more push, and I can force you to end your own life. Every time you think of defying me, remember this moment. Remember it well." He orders her to remove the blade and Sorcha pulls it out with a rough gasp. "Shall I ask you again?" he asks her as she presses a hand to her wound. "Will you take your place by my side?"

She glares up at him. "I'd rather put that dagger through my heart."

The faery doesn't reply. He kneels next to Sorcha and grips her roughly by the chin. "You're even more spirited than your mother. A hundred years down here and she would have done whatever I asked. Some days I regret accepting your offer to take her place. I regret wanting you so badly to begin with."

Sorcha flashes her fangs. "*Good.*"

His fingers tighten around her jaw. "Then I think about how it will feel when you finally accept." With his other hand, he traces the line of her throat, down to the base of her neck where I see markings I didn't notice before. Markings Sorcha doesn't have now. I stare at her sharply. *A vow? To him?* "One day you'll look at this and no longer think of it as a burden. You'll come to me willingly."

Her laugh is rough, mocking. "One day this mark will be gone, and the first thing I'll do is slice open your throat."

His eyes harden. "You force me to be cruel. Fortunately for you, I am also very, very patient." He releases her and stands. "Another hundred years, then. This time, I won't even bring you a dying human to feed on. Let's see how long you last before you're willing to beg for one."

The door opens into the beautiful, beautiful sunlight and then cruelly slams closed to leave her in the darkness with the dead.

The memory shifts. The dark walls fade into a rich, opulent room in a massive tent. A large cot, covered in white silk sheets, looks minuscule at the back of it. The tent is composed of intricately woven tapestries depicting battles. Dark against light fae. Kiaran against Aithinne.

In the middle of the tent, taking up most of the room, is a wide, sturdy oak table. Kiaran is there, standing with Sorcha's master. No, not Kiaran. His eyes hold that same deep, dark, and hopeless gaze I've come to recognize. This is Kadamach.

He's staring down at a map that covers almost the entire breadth and width of the table, an intricate rendering of Seelie and Unseelie lands.

"If we send a fleet of ships," the other faery is saying, "we can take the port villages easily. Interrupt their supply lines from there and force a retreat."

Sorcha is crouched at Kiaran's feet, buckling a protective metal guard around his shin. Preparing him for battle. She works quietly, deftly pulling the leather strap through. Bloody hell, she looks terrible. Much worse than before. The purple smudges beneath her eyes have darkened, and those beautiful green eyes have dulled with hunger. She's so thin that she looks like one of Kiaran's victims, so close to death I don't know how he hasn't noticed.

When she moves to put the shin guard around Kiaran's other leg and he merely straightens his leg without looking down, I understand why.

She's a servant. He doesn't even see her.

Kiaran flicks a finger at the pieces on the map that mark their ships and strikes them down, one after another. "Is that what you think, Strategist? Am I wasting my time attacking the eastern front?" He looks up and I shiver at how cold his gaze is. "Tell me, why do you think I keep my soldiers at our shores rather than sending them out to sea?"

"Forgive me. I spoke out of turn." The Strategist's voice trembles slightly in fear.

"No," Kiaran says, "you didn't. Answer the question."

Sorcha reaches for the breastplate on the cot. Weakened from not feeding, she staggers under its weight and drops the metal to the floor with a heavy clatter. She freezes, her breath coming out in a terrified gasp.

Kiaran looks over at her, as if he's noticed her for the first time.

"You stupid girl," the Strategist snarls at Sorcha. He seizes her roughly by the arm. "This time I'll keep you in that cave until you can't even move—"

"Take your hand off her." Kiaran's voice is low, dangerous. When the Strategist hesitates, he adds, "*Now.*" Kiaran nods to the chair at the other end of the tent. "Sit there and be silent. If you make a sound, I'll cut out your tongue and make you swallow it."

Sorcha remains still, her gaze downcast, as Kiaran approaches her. "Look at me," he commands.

Her eyes meet his. Though she's clearly afraid, there's defiance in her features. As if she's saying, *Do what you will. Punish me. I won't plead for my life.*

Kiaran's lips twitch, and I know he sees it, too. "Why don't you tell me what my Strategist couldn't?" he asks her, almost gently. "Why do I keep my soldiers on our shores?"

Sorcha purses her lips. "The Seelie—" Her voice trembles, and she takes a breath before trying again. "They can speak to the sea, learn secrets from the water. They would know we were coming." At Kiaran's expectant expression, she explains with a hint of bitterness, "I have a brother. He's Seelie."

The way Kiaran's eyes gleam, I know she answered correctly. "What would you suggest instead?"

"I'm not a Strategist."

Kiaran waves a hand toward the map. "Indulge me."

I watch as Sorcha silently takes in the geographical features. Her mind goes over possibilities, attacks, counter-attacks. She plays out battle scenarios the way I plan inventions, as if it's second nature.

Finally, she slides her finger across the map and taps the mountain pass. "There. It's close enough to the sea that the Queen will consider her position an advantage. The cliffs on either side are high enough that our soldiers can pull the shadows to hide their true numbers." She looks up at Kiaran. "You might send some of the soldiers at our coast to lead the Seelie toward this pass."

"You're suggesting I sacrifice them."

Sorcha lifts a shoulder. "I told you; I'm not a Strategist."

Kiaran looks at the map, at Sorcha, at his Strategist. "I think you are. I think you've decided the victory would be worth their deaths." She says nothing as he sits in the chair next to the table and looks her over. His eyes take in the design around her neck. "You wear a mark of servitude."

Sorcha stiffens. "Yes."

"You don't strike me as someone foolish enough to make that vow without a convincing reason. Tell me."

"He tricked my mother into making it first," Sorcha says. "I saw what he did to her. How the mark forced her to obey his every command, no matter how badly it hurt her. She wasn't going to live much longer if she stayed with him." She lifts her chin. "So I offered myself in her place, because I *was* foolish. I was a child."

Kiaran's expression doesn't change. "He ordered you to kill her."

The other faery's lips tighten, but he doesn't make a sound. He isn't going to risk Kiaran making good on his threat.

"He did," Sorcha says, her voice trembling with anger this time. "Of course he did. She wasn't the one he wanted."

Kiaran's voice is almost soft when he asks, "When was the last time you fed?"

She draws a shuddering breath. "Almost two hundred years ago."

I can sense Kiaran's surprise. His face remains impassive as ever, but there's something growing in his gaze, something angry. Something ruthless. "Do you wish you could kill him?"

In the corner of the tent, the Strategist makes a low choking sound.

Sorcha's smile is small, a dagger's edge. "Every day."

Kiaran's eyes flicker to the Strategist. "Release her from her vow."

The Strategist's voice shakes when he speaks. "But, my King—"

"That wasn't a suggestion," Kiaran says coldly. "Don't make me say it again."

The other faery looks up at Sorcha and shuts his eyes in defeat. His words are barely spoken above a breath. "I release you from your vow."

Sorcha doubles over with a sharp cry as the mark around her neck glows red-hot as molten metal. The mark disintegrates to dust on her clothes. She straightens, her fingers feeling above her collarbone with an astonished look on her face. When she looks at Kiaran, it's with relief and gratitude. "Thank you, my King. *Thank you.*"

"Don't thank me. I don't do anything out of kindness." Kiaran reaches for the blade at his hip, pulls out the dagger, and hands it to her, hilt first. "You said you wished for his death. Take your revenge."

Sorcha's smile widens. "I plan to."

The Strategist is on his feet and making for the front of the tent, but Sorcha is there first. He never stands a chance. She falls on him, power barreling out of her with surprising strength to keep him still. Then she takes the blade and slices open his throat. She doesn't stop there. She stabs him over and over and over again, a scream erupting from her mouth each time. It goes on for so long that I shut my eyes to block out the sight.

By the time she's finished, she's breathing hard, her limbs shaking. She's covered in blood. Her eyes are wet with tears.

She doesn't even notice when Kiaran approaches her. "Tell me your name."

"Sorcha," she whispers.

"Sorcha." She closes her eyes, as if the sound of her name on his lips is a song only she can hear. "It appears I'm in need of a new Strategist. Are you interested?"

"Yes." Her smile is a flash of teeth, the one I'm familiar with. "Oh yes."

* * *

When Sorcha pulls me out of her memories, we're both trembling. Her eyes are wide, slightly wet. "Let me ask you something: If you could have killed me the night I murdered your mother, how would you have done it?" she asks. "Would it have been quick and merciful? Or would you have slit my throat and stabbed me a hundred times the way I did my master?"

I don't meet her gaze. I know which I would have chosen. She knows, too.

"You see?" she breathes. "You should be thankful he'll lose you before his precious Falconer grows into the ruthlessness I see in your heart. You'd become just like me if given the chance. Revenge makes us all monsters in the end. Remember that."

"Sorcha—"

"Enough." She stands and backs away. "That's enough. I'm going back to sleep."

I watch as she curls up at the back of the cave, alone.

CHAPTER 35

A FRANTIC SHOUT wakes me. "*Kam!*"

I sit up fast, my heart pounding. "Kiaran?"

Sorcha and Aithinne are still asleep by the dying embers of the fire. Neither of them has moved or stirred at the call. Did I imagine it? It was so loud, as if he were just outside.

"*Kam!*"

I lurch to my feet. Definitely not my imagination.

It might be a trick.

Kiaran's call comes again, so close, and it's laced with so much pain that my chest tightens just hearing it. I grab my sword belt off the ground and buckle it around my hips as I head to the mouth of the cave. He calls again, frantic now. It sends so much fear through me that I can't think straight. My instinct is to run out there and find him.

Just take one step out and if you can't see him, come back inside.

"Kiaran?" I call, stepping outside the cave. One step.

A portal opens, and I'm pulled right into it.

Suddenly, I'm in a ballroom. Men and women dance a close waltz all around me, just like in one of the fine assemblies in Edinburgh—

My breath catches in my throat. I *am* in the Edinburgh Assembly Rooms.

I recognize the grand chandelier that casts the room in a glittering glow. The stained-glass lanterns that float by the ceiling, scattering red, green, yellow, and blue light across the gold-textured wallpaper. Skirts rustle around me as gentlemen whirl their partners around the room, every one of them perfectly in sync with the orchestra's violins as they play a jaunty country dance. The one I remember from my nightmares.

The one that played the moment my mother was murdered.

Numb with horror, I look down at my dress. My dress. *The dress.* My fingers pluck at it to make sure—

Real. It's real. But it can't be real.

The last time I wore this dress, it was for my debut. Even the beaded rose slippers peeking out from beneath my skirts are the same. My breath catches in my throat.

"May I have the pleasure?" A gentleman's gloved hand extends into my view.

This isn't real. It's not real. It's not—

"My lady?"

The gentleman has a quizzical smile on his nondescript face. He seems harmless, but something isn't right about him. There's something unnatural about his features. His smile is a little too friendly. His skin a little too pale. A flash of color pulses in his eyes, gone so quickly I might have imagined it.

Then a flicker across his skin like a shadow passing across the surface of water. I wonder, for a moment, if I'm imagining him, but when I touch his hand, it's warm. Solid.

I hitch a breath. "I need to leave."

As I turn, he grasps my arm roughly. His fingers put a bruising pressure on my skin. "You're not going anywhere."

"Unhand me, or I'll break your fingers."

Without waiting for an answer, I jerk out of his grasp and dart to the exit. Another gentleman blocks my path, tall and blond, but with an equally forgettable face. The *same* face? "My lady, I believe I have this dance."

I have to get out of here.

"No," I say. "Let me pass—"

He seizes my hand. His grip is so tight that I cry out. "*Stop!*"

I struggle, but the gentleman yanks me into the middle of the dance floor. I lash out with my slippered foot, catching him in the knee, but it doesn't even faze him. He wraps his long fingers around my wrist and pulls so hard that I stumble.

"It's easier if you don't struggle." I almost pause at what sounds like a woman's voice beneath his masculine baritone.

Move!

I grasp his hand—I'll break every last one of his fingers if I have to—but he sweeps me into a waltz.

Just before I shove his fingers back, a painful jolt goes through me. Power, thick and oppressive and numbing. I have no control over my body. No matter how I try, my feet don't listen. They don't run. They don't kick, or thrash, or do any of the things my mind is *screaming* at them to do.

I dance like a compliant puppet. A pawn.

Am I the pawn? Then I think of Sorcha's words. *Maybe I'm the entertainment.*

I'm pressed so close to this stranger that I can feel his heat through my dress, and it isn't a normal heat. It scorches. Power burns so thick in the air that I almost gag. It tastes like smoke down my throat, coal fire in my lungs. I can barely breathe. I can barely think.

The Morrigan. She lured me here and I'm utterly, utterly alone. A fleeting image of Sorcha flashes across my mind. Of her mangled limbs and her trembling voice as she sang.

Let's put you back together and try something else.

"Stop," I whisper. "Stop."

"You want me to stop?"

The Morrigan's hands tighten at my waist, and I feel the unmistakable hint of claws scraping across the fabric of my dress. Her breath is on my neck and I feel the quick bite of teeth. It's gone so fast. A warning. A nip. One that says, *You're mine.*

"But I'm only returning the favor, little human. A small revenge for killing me in the cave. How does it feel?"

That's her voice now, clear and distinct. A raspy whisper that makes me think of destruction and looming chaos.

"Go to hell."

Her laugh makes my bones freeze. "How I've missed humans. So expressive and so painfully stupid." Her voice washes over me like a rising tide in winter. Quick, unmerciful. Cold. "Why are you here, Aileana Kameron?"

I risk asking a mocking question. "Can't you read my mind?"

"In glimpses. Like this ballroom and this dull reception. But unlike your friends, you still have the power to protect your thoughts." Her claws tighten at my waist. "Now tell me why you've come before I sink my claws into your gut."

"You know why I'm here. I want your Book."

"Everyone wants my Book for their own purposes. Power, greed, delusions of grandeur. What might your reasons be?"

I pull back enough to see her face, those dark sooty eyelashes framing fierce, bright sapphire eyes. "I want to save my realm."

The Morrigan's power rolls across my skin, sinking into my veins and brushing across my bones. Strong, so similar to mine. *She's the Cailleach's sister. Like calls to like.* "You already knew how to save your realm," she says. "It's part of my curse. All it took was for one of them to die. And instead, you brought them both to me. Such an unexpected blessing."

I shut my eyes briefly as her words sink in. I delivered them both—weakened, their powers bound, practically human—to their greatest enemy.

"Are you going to kill them?"

Her lips curl into a small smile. "I don't sacrifice my pawns until I'm certain I'm about to win."

I'm not a pawn, then. I'm the key. Always the key.

"What do you want from me?" I whisper. She wouldn't be here, dancing with me, if she didn't want something.

The Morrigan's eyes gleam. "You know the worst part of what my sister did to me?" she asks, instead of answering. Her thumb brushes down my cheek. "It wasn't that she betrayed me, or even that she tried to destroy me. It was how she left me: without a body. Not dead, not alive, stuck in this pathetic half-state." She leans in, her voice brushing across my skin like a whisper of silk. "What do I want from you, Aileana Kameron? I want your help. I want my Book."

Of course. She wants me to do what Sorcha couldn't: bring the Book to her. And if I don't . . .

Sorcha's words echo in my mind again. *I was her entertainment.*

If the Morrigan doesn't know where the Book is, there's still a chance to steal it, have Sorcha open it, and make it mine.

The plan still stands. *Find Kiaran. Find the Book. Kill the Morrigan.*

"I would advise you not to consider that an admission of weakness," the Morrigan says in a tight voice. "If you don't do what I want, I'll tear you apart. Easily."

"If you could harm me so easily, you would have done it already."

"I almost had your lover murder you in my cave."

"But you didn't. In the end you couldn't."

Now she smiles. It's like the edge of a razor. "What a clever little girl you are. I can see why my sister passed her powers to you and not to one of her useless children. Pity about your human body."

"Why ask me to find the Book?" I say, ignoring her jab at my mortality. "Because I have the Cailleach's powers? Just because she hid it from you doesn't mean I know where it is."

A flash of irritation crosses her features. "My sister? *Please.* She could never have got away with this on her own without me detecting it." Her voice is sharp. "It was *that girl*—my consort. I always knew she was too soft. She stole the Book, took it to my sister and they hid it here together. When I followed them, the Cailleach killed my body and trapped me." Her lip curls in disgust. "I hope my curse made her suffer."

Aithinne was right not to trust the stories she'd heard. Even the older fae she spoke with must not have been alive when the original Cailleach betrayed the Morrigan. A thought occurs to me: Perhaps Sorcha erased her own memory to *protect* it.

To make sure the Morrigan couldn't read her mind to find it.

I keep my expression even. "You didn't answer my question. Why me?"

Her fingers lift my chin and I meet her eyes. Their bright blue color doesn't make them any less deep, as deep as an abyss. There's something vengeful in that gaze, something that has been angry and building for centuries upon centuries. "My little bird was like you once. Stubborn, headstrong. She sauntered in with her garish wings and her wild song and I thought to myself: Those wings would look better painted the crimson of blood, and her voice would sound more beautiful from a cage of my design."

Sorcha. She's talking about Sorcha. *Little bird.*

Broken limbs like mutilated wings. A haunting voice like a caged lullaby. A broken shell of a girl.

"She was such a beautiful thing. I would have been happy to have her chirping by my side, under my rule. But she couldn't use my Book and that made her useless."

Couldn't use my Book. Her words roll around in my mind. Sorcha couldn't use the Book anyway. No wonder she vowed to give it to me—as if it were a concession, an exchange. *Kiaran for the Book.* She gave it to me so easily, and I never—for a moment—stopped to think why.

Because I'm a fool. An easily manipulated fool who had everything to lose. And when you have everything to lose, all someone has to do is choose which weapon to use against you.

I try not to let anything show in my face, but I must have failed. The Morrigan's lips twitch. "She didn't tell you." She throws back her head and laughs. "Oh, my clever little bird. Always so secretive."

I look away. "Just tell me why you're asking me."

"Of course." Her smile disappears as quick as the strike of a blade. "It was my sister's precaution: Only those in my consort's bloodline can open the Book, but they can't use it themselves. She never did trust anyone. Not something I knew until I read my little bird's memories."

"Sorcha told me they were erased," I say without thinking. *Don't concede information easily. Let her tell you everything.*

The Morrigan's eyes burn bright with anger. "Yes, that fool girl erased what she could. All I had left were fragments. Just her thoughts. Enough to discern that she tried to use my

Book, failed, and then lost it. I punished her at first, but in the end, I was forced to let her fly away. I never got over losing my little bird. She was my favorite."

Little bird. Mutilated wings. Haunting song. Broken girl.

Stop it. Focus. My mind is a cacophony of questions, but I can only ask one. "Why not find the Book yourself and use it?"

"Even if I found it, I don't have a body," she says shortly. "And possessing someone else's doesn't work. Another precaution to stop me using it." Her expression turns bitter. "I still need the blood of my little bird's lineage to open the Book, and I still need someone who can actually use it. *You.*"

"You could have asked Kiaran and Aithinne." When her gaze narrows, I understand why. "Ah, I see. You're afraid if one of them gets their hands on it, they'll become more powerful than you."

"You're human." The Morrigan sounds impatient. "You have my sister's power, and you're dying. You're the obvious choice."

"So I'm the person who has the most reason to help you." She doesn't answer that; she doesn't need to. "What are you offering me in exchange?" I ask, thinking of Lonnrach's deal.

The Morrigan smiles. "My, my. You've learned quite a lot from my kind, haven't you? Very well. What would you like?"

Something inside me feels raw, like I'm coming apart at the edges. *What do I want? Kiaran.*

Don't tell her that. "My world," I blurt, grasping on to the first fleeting thought in my mind. "Intact."

The Morrigan stares at me, as if amused. "The human heart isn't big enough to fit the space of the whole world. Whatever means the most to you is something small. Something worth dying for."

I set my jaw. "How do you know that?"

"We're all selfish creatures, little girl. Even humans." She leans in. "Here's the truth: You want the cursed king. And if you find the Book, he's bound to my little bird for eternity."

I say nothing. I look away, at the other couples dancing around us. They are like living puppets. The same faces, the same clothes, the same dresses in different colors. Just a setting for this meeting to show me that if the Morrigan wants, she can take things from my mind and use them against me.

The Morrigan grasps me by the jaw. "Pay attention." Her long claws scrape down my cheek, not deep enough to draw blood, but deep enough to hurt. "I can make him yours. I can lift his vow if you help me. I'll take away his curse."

"I'm not naïve," I say flatly. "You want something else. What do you want me to use the Book for?"

Her lips curve into a smile. "I can see why he loves you." She leans in. "Use the Book to resurrect my body. Do this, and I'll give you everything you desire. His curse removed. His vow to my little bird gone." Her eyes are sharp, searching. Assessing my weaknesses. "Immortality. Wouldn't you like that? To be with him forever?" *A human death would be far more kind*, Kiaran had said.

A kindness for me, but not for him. I have the chance to change that, regardless of what he wants for me. Sorcha's words echo across my mind. *You're just as ruthless as the rest of us.*

I am ruthless. War has made me crooked and sometimes cruel and not wholly human. Because I almost say yes. The word is on my tongue, on my lips, in my mind, and I open my mouth to whisper my fate in a single breath. *Yes. Yes, yes, yes.*

Until I remember Sorcha's mark on Kiaran's body. A sign of possession. *You're mine.*

We're passing him around like an object. Like he doesn't have feelings. Like he's a damn piece of property, a possession, a prize. I may be ruthless and I may be cruel, but I won't treat him like that; I'm not so much like Sorcha that I'd deprive him of a choice. I don't want him to be mine so badly that I'd give the Morrigan the power she once had. She can't be allowed to rise again. I won't be responsible for that.

When I speak, my voice is hard, decisive. "No."

The Morrigan's gaze is as sharp as a knife-edge. "Think very carefully before you tell me no."

"I did. Still no."

The Morrigan acts fast. She seizes my arm, throws her weight against my body, and dislocates my shoulder in a swift jerk. Agonizing pain explodes down my arm. A garbled scream erupts from my throat, and she slaps a palm across my mouth.

"Shh," she croons, pulling me tight against her. "I didn't say you could scream." Her lips are at my ear. "Give me my yes, and I'll heal this. I'll take away your pain."

When her hand moves from my mouth, I snarl, "*No.*"

My fingers fiddle with the blades at the wrist of my good arm. *Quickly.*

Her claws dig into my shoulder, sending another jolt of pain through me. "I'll destroy everything you love," she hisses. "I'll make you hate him. I'll break you in the end, just like my little bird. I'll make you say yes."

I coax the blade into my palm. "I'll find your Book," I tell the Morrigan. "And I'll use it to kill you." I ram the blade between her ribs.

The Morrigan in the gentleman's body crumples to the ground.

Run! I make a break for it, but the Morrigan is already in another body blocking my way. "You're going to help me," she insists, her eyes darkening.

I slash my blade across her throat and shove hard. In a running leap, I make my way toward the double doors, one arm hanging uselessly at my side.

Ignore the pain. Keep moving.

Another man pulls me into a waltz, his grip hard on my injured shoulder. The music swells with screeching violins that pierce my ears. I can hear nothing else, not my breathing, not my heart, not my thoughts. The Morrigan grasps my waist, her fingernails clawing to keep me in place.

She passes me off to another gentleman. Another. Another. All under her control, just puppets she's using to her advantage. Every time I twist away, I end up in another dancer's arms. I fight my way out and they catch me again. I'm trapped in a cage of human bodies. I'm spinning, my vision blurring. I'm too hot. I can't get air. I have to go, have to escape, but everywhere I turn there's another and another. Their laughter is the same as the Morrigan's. It's the sound of a blade scraping down metal. It's sharp and rough and inhumanly melodic.

"I'll leave you to think about it," the Morrigan says from another body. Then she grabs my arm and forces it back into its socket. Heals the injury with a quick pulse of magic. "Enjoy the dance. I'll break you again later."

I'm swept away in another turn. Firm hands prevent my escape. My breath comes quicker, panicked now.

Get out. Get to the exit.

Desperately, I look over the shoulder of the gentleman holding me, toward the door, and—

There's a girl standing right there.

CHAPTER 36

MY EYES had nearly slid right over her. She almost blends right into the walls. Her skin reflects the light. Her small, bony shoulders are slouched forward and her expression is skittish as if projecting: *You don't see me, you don't notice me, I'm not here.*

As I'm swung around in the dance, I nearly lose sight of her. I struggle through the crowd to glimpse her again.

There she is, standing by the exit. I notice her apprehensive gaze, the deep amber hue of her eyes.

She has a dancer's body, strong and lithe and athletic. The dress she's wearing shows off her form in a scandalous cut, the neckline swooping between her breasts down almost to her midsection. Even the sleeves are cut to practically nothing, leaving her strong, muscled arms bare.

I inhale sharply. Her skin is covered in ink. It's *her*. I saw the barest glimpse of her in Sorcha's memory, but the rest was blank. She has the same shape as the woman I saw silhouetted in the moonlight when I was in the cave.

Who is she?

When I'm passed off to the next gentleman, I don't resist. I don't want to take my eyes off her—off those strange tattoos that seem to glisten in the light—because I'm afraid that if I do, she'll disappear.

The girl's marks aren't like Kiaran's—they're not scarred or carved into her flesh. Hers are as dark as shadows, crawling in snakelike tendrils down to her fingertips. Something about those marks draws me to her. Without reason, without logic.

I just know I need to go to her.

Her eyes snap up and meet mine. What I see there startles me: She's afraid. I saw her, and she's frightened of me. *Why? Who is she?*

I'm swept up in another turn in the waltz, and when I turn back, I see a flash of her midnight-black hair as she sprints out of the room, like a deer bolting in the woods.

Find her. Quick. Now.

I start for the exit, shoving past a gentleman with his hands outstretched. But another grasps my arm hard enough to bruise. *I don't think so.* I smash my fist into his face and hear a satisfying *crack!* before his nose gushes blood. *Good.*

Get to the door. Go! Hurry!

I break into a run, but another gentleman blocks my way. I don't stop. I don't slow down. I snap my leg up and slam the toe of my slipper right between his legs. He staggers back.

My arms are seized by two other men. I shove them, straining hard, but they're too strong. I can't move. Their hands grip me roughly.

I claw my way through them. I bite, I punch. My cries go unheeded as they rush to keep me in place. It's a sea of blank faces in black eveningwear, puppets in the shape of men, here to keep me trapped, caged, until I say yes. Until I give my answer.

Desperately, I look for the exit. I try to fight them off. My fist crashes into flesh, and my stupid ineffectual slippers do what damage they can, but the soles aren't hard enough to inflict much real pain. I elbow. I break noses. I snap fingers. Still they keep coming, as if there's no end to them. Nothing stops them. I'm being crushed by the throng, and somewhere I swear I feel the Morrigan's eyes on me. *Say yes. Say yes.*

No. I have to find that girl. I have to get out.

Fingernails dig into my arms, biting into my flesh. The men laugh the melodic, inhuman laugh of the Morrigan and something in me snaps.

"Let. Go. Of. Me!"

Power bursts out of me, a ball of energy that blasts them all to ash. It feels as though the power is bending my bones, burning through my bloodstream. It's blinding light, a swirling stream of power with the force of a storm. I have to close my eyes against the onslaught.

When I open them, all the gentlemen are gone. My roaring heartbeat is in my ears. The silence is so thick that my swift, shallow breathing is the only sound in the ballroom.

A headache slams through my temples, painful enough to leave me gasping. My entire body is shaking so hard I can hardly stay on my feet. Something wet trickles down my lips.

I touch my finger to it. Blood.

You're dying. You don't have much time. Find that girl!

Desperately, I shake my head to clear it and hurry to the door she went through. My vision pulses before my eyes. I smack into the wall of the hallway and almost lose my footing.

Don't fall. You won't get back up.

In a limping run, I follow the hallway out to the back garden. It's nighttime. There are no sounds out here—or maybe I can't hear anything over the clamor of my pulse, a *bam bam bam bam* of a rhythm in my ears. A wave of dizziness hits me so suddenly that I have to slap my hand against the column of the building to steady myself.

Then I hear it.

A low gasp, caught in a scream. A familiar sound, one I used to dream about every night. One that Lonnrach forced me to remember in the mirrored room.

This is how my nightmare begins.

My heartbeat slows to a heavy, drumming cadence. I slowly walk along the path between the rosebushes, shivering in the winter breeze. It's all familiar. It's exactly the same, right down to the number of steps I take, the rustle of my skirts as I make my way to the back fence that borders the street.

As I approach the gate, my mind is screaming at me to find the girl I saw. To concentrate. To focus on something else. It is a constant beat of *Don't look. Don't look. Don't look. This isn't real. Don't look.*

But I'm compelled. *I have to look.*

I step forward and shove through the hedges.

There they are, my mother and Sorcha. Sorcha doesn't hold her tenderly, not like a lover, but the way a wildcat might hold a mouse: a violent grip, all fingernails dug into skin, lips at her throat. Then Sorcha throws back her head to catch her breath, her fanged teeth shining with blood.

"Stop," I whisper, unable to help myself. "*Stop.*" I shove open the garden gate.

I'm not that frightened girl who huddled behind the wall so the monster wouldn't see. I'm not the same Aileana who didn't put up a fight. I'm not the same Aileana who watched her mother die.

"*Sorcha!*" My power roars within me, ready to be unleashed—

Sorcha looks up at me. Only her eyes aren't the familiar green ones that gleam with malice.

No, they're the strange, bright sapphire eyes of the Morrigan. I see a flash of those uncanny irises, of a thin knife-edge smile, right before she tears out my mother's heart.

A choked cry erupts from my throat before I can stop it. My chest tightens and I can't get in enough air and it's happening again and it feels real and I'm here and the air is cold, and she's hitting the ground with a sickening *thud*—

Then I'm on my knees beside my mother. My power coils back painfully inside me as I hold her motionless body in my arms and her blood is warm and her eyes are sightless.

Just like the first time. Exactly like the first time.

The sounds of slow, soft breathing make me look up. *Sorcha.*

I watch as the Morrigan's blue irises seep away into green ones, and then Sorcha looks around, startled. "What the—"

The Morrigan possessed Sorcha's body and did this just to punish me. She must have caught enough glimpses of my memories back in the ballroom to re-create this: The memory that has tied me to Sorcha forever.

The memory of when her precious little bird shattered my life.

When Sorcha looks down at me—at my dead mother in my arms—she goes still. And I swear I see something akin to remorse in her gaze.

Then my arms go slack and light. When I look down, my mother has disappeared—the Morrigan's illusion gone.

It was a threat. A warning. *I'll kill everyone you love if you don't help me.*

I stay kneeling in the cobblestone street. I ignore the dull headache that is a reminder of my impending death, and I stare at the faery who took my mother from me. Who used me. Who manipulated me. Who stole from me. And now I know exactly how she managed to escape the first time.

In the end, I was forced to let her fly away. I never got over losing my little bird. She was my favorite.

"You made the Morrigan a vow, didn't you?" I ask flatly. Sorcha looks away and I have my answer. My laugh is rough and dry. "No excuses? No funny retorts, little bird?"

Sorcha's eyes flash. "Don't you *dare* call me that."

I rise to my feet, realizing I'm back in my hunting clothes. I'm wearing Kiaran's coat. The dress and the slippers are gone, and the blood has disappeared from my hands. None of it was real; she stole it from my memories, from Sorcha's memories.

"Why not? That's what you are. The Morrigan's caged little bird."

Sorcha slaps me so hard my face whips to the side. "I did what I had to," she snarls. "To survive. To get out of here. So I made her a vow that one day I would bring back someone who could open the Book. *You* were asking. *You* wanted this."

An opportunity presented itself, so I took it. Those were her words.

"And if she gets her hands on it, then what? She'll kill us all."

Sorcha lets out a sharp laugh, bitter. "I'm not a fool. You're my insurance. Why do you think I made you a vow? As long as she needs my blood to open it, the Book is mine. And I promised it to you. You have the most reason to keep it out of her hands."

"And I'm the one who would suffer the most."

Her hands fist at her sides. "Aye. I admit that."

"Then it must have been wonderful to have the Morrigan to replay your finest moment. When you took my mother from me."

"I have no desire to have my body used like some puppet. Especially not by *her.*"

Enough of this. I need to find that girl, and Kiaran, and Aithinne. "Where's Aithinne?"

"I woke up alone in the cave," Sorcha says tightly. "And I found myself here when I tried to leave."

I shove down my emotions. I can't think clearly if I feel too much, and the Morrigan will use that against me. Focus on the task at hand. That girl. "There was a girl who came out this way. I saw her in your memories. Small, covered in ink markings."

I swear, something flickers in Sorcha's gaze. Confusion? "I don't recall any girl."

"There you are!" I hear Aithinne's voice behind me. I turn to see her step out of the door of a building, relief plain on her face at the sight of us. She pauses. "I'm glad to see you both. Even you," she tells Sorcha. "Although I still hate you."

"Oh, thank god," Sorcha says. "For a minute I thought you might actually hug me." She sounds as acerbic as always, but I swear she looks almost glad to see Aithinne.

"I might still. Just to torture you."

"Aithinne," I say. "Did you see—"

The girl is slipping across the street right behind Aithinne, her dark hair glowing in the city lights. When she sees that I notice her, she lets out a soft gasp and bolts.

Before I can go after the girl, Lonnrach lunges out of the shadows between the buildings and grabs her.

CHAPTER 37

I RACE DOWN the street with Aithinne and Sorcha close behind me.

Lonnrach is trying to pull the girl through another building door—through what must be another portal—but she puts up a damn good fight. The girl slams her boot into his knee, wrenches herself out of his grip, and takes off running.

When Lonnrach sees us coming, he curses and sprints after her.

Aithinne grasps my sleeve. "What are we doing? Who *was* that?"

"I don't know," Sorcha pants. "But if my brother wants her this badly, we need to get to her first."

We race past the line of white-columned buildings in George Street and cut down a side street to come out near the gardens. The lights of Old Town are dark, the city eerie and shadowed as we come to a hard stop before the bridge.

"Aithinne, go that way"—I gesture to the west side of the street—"Sorcha, take North Bridge. I'll trail behind and we'll cut him off on the High Street. Go!"

We head off in our different directions. I follow Lonnrach past Waverley Bridge and into the winding, dark tenements of the ancient part of the city. The buildings here are high, all of them close together and built partially underground. If I lose sight of Lonnrach and the girl, I won't be able to find them again. This part of Edinburgh is layered in an elaborate maze of tunnels and wynds and closes.

As I follow Lonnrach down another side street, the buildings around us seem to grow darker, more shadowed. The Morrigan built the city from my memories. She has to be here somewhere, helping him along. Who is this girl? Is she another faery here to find the Book?

I see her just ahead, her long hair fluttering behind her like a veil. She darts through a dark close. She's trying to take advantage of the dim light and the mazelike streets of the Old Town. Lonnrach trails after her.

I follow behind, but the building starts to close in, as if it were—

It's moving. It *is* closing in.

The girl glances behind her with a panicked expression and speeds up. She whirls and presses her palm to the wall, pushing open a door I hadn't even noticed was there.

Lonnrach crashes through it and follows. When I reach the door, it seals and disappears. As if it were never there to begin with.

Damnation!

I rush toward the end of the alley, but the walls are so tight now that I have to turn my body to the side. Desperately, I reach out a palm and release a burst of power. It slams into the buildings and creates a hole for me to escape through.

I hurtle out onto the street just in time to see Lonnrach and the girl up ahead. I give chase, but they're too fast. I'm going to lose them.

Sorcha speeds around a corner and throws herself into her brother. They fall to the ground, striking each other. Sorcha smashes her fist into his jaw and slams his head into the pavement. By the time I reach them, Sorcha has him in an iron grip and the girl has disappeared down another street.

"She's gone," I pant. "Bloody hell."

"Who is she?" Sorcha snarls at Lonnrach.

His smile is mocking. "You don't know?"

She punches him in the face, a hard knock that splatters blood across the pavement. When he turns back, his lip is bleeding.

"*Tell me.*" She flashes her fangs. "I should have stayed behind to finish you off back in that field. I should have done it a long time ago."

Lonnrach launches himself at her, but I'm there first. I grasp him by the arm and turn it at a painful angle. His scream is so, so satisfying. He deserves it after everything he's ever done to me. He deserves more. He deserves to have his memory emptied. His hope destroyed. His will broken.

God, how I want to end him. My other hand is so close to my sword, all I have to do is take it out.

Then I hear footsteps behind me. When I turn, Aithinne is there, taking in the sight of Lonnrach on his knees and bleeding. Mortal.

He's not my kill. He's not Sorcha's, either.

"He's yours," I tell Aithinne. He struggles in my grip, but I hold firm. "Remember what I promised you. We'd do this together, but he's yours."

"Sorcha." Lonnrach sounds desperate now. "Sorcha. I'm sorry—"

"Now you're sorry?" Sorcha laughs, and her fangs glisten white in the darkness. Then, to me: "Falconer, when you saw my memories, I didn't show you that I asked Lonnrach for help to save our mother, but he refused because we were Unseelie." She lets out a growl, teeth bared. When she speaks again, her voice is cold and quiet and angry. "What was it you said, *brother?*"

Lonnrach presses his lips together and shakes his head.

Sorcha grasps him by the front of his shirt. "*Say it.* Remind me."

His whisper is so low, I barely hear him. I flinch at what he says, at the sudden memory of what it was like for Sorcha under the Strategist's control. Lonnrach told her that. He's her brother, and he abandoned her.

"That's right," Sorcha says with a smile. "How well I remember those words." She strokes a fingernail down his cheek. "Now allow me to return the sentiment: *You're not my problem.*"

Then she steps back and nods once to Aithinne. A silent message: she's not going to do anything to stop us.

Lonnrach jerks in my grip as Aithinne comes forward, but I shove him to the ground, holding him tightly. He's no match for my strength, not while mortal. *It's time. It's time to end this.*

Aithinne's breathing trembles as she stares at him, but when she speaks, her voice is strong. "If I were half as cruel as you, I would make this the worst pain imaginable. I would make sure you suffered as long as you made me suffer. Your death would take me two thousand years."

She slides her sword from its sheath and stands before him. She looks at me, a signal to release him.

I let Lonnrach go and he drops to his knees. When he tries to run, I shove him down again with my powers. Again. Again. Until he's panting with exhaustion and fear, kneeling before Aithinne.

"My Queen," he whispers.

"Am I that?" Aithinne places her fingertips under his chin and she looks almost gentle. "After everything, you'd claim fealty to me again?"

"Yes," he says, almost desperately. "Yes."

"Then consider this my last act as your Queen. I'm giving you a better death than you deserve."

She plunges the sword through his heart.

Sorcha and I give Aithinne a few moments to collect herself and retrieve her sword. I put my hand on her shoulder. "Are you all right?"

"No. But I will be." She looks over at Sorcha. "Thank you."

Sorcha is looking down at her brother's body with an unreadable expression. "I know what it's like to want revenge against the man who hurt me, and you showed him compassion. That was a kinder death than I gave mine." Then her eyes meet mine, and she murmurs a single word, and I know it's for me: "Different."

Different. Aithinne is different. She's not like Sorcha—not like me. I wanted to make Lonnrach suffer for the things he did; I wanted to make his death last. But Aithinne? She's merciful. Even when she doesn't have to be.

What does that make me, when a faery is capable of more humanity than I am?

The patter of faint footsteps distracts me. I look up and see the tattooed girl hurtling out of a building and into the street. She catches my gaze and without a moment's hesitation, she takes off again.

"*Wait!*" I sprint after her.

"Falconer!"

I don't stop. I have to catch that girl. Something about her calls to me.

A flash of her hair, just up ahead. My pace quickens. She enters a shadowed row of tenements and I go in after her. I'm gaining on her, close enough to hear her breath as she runs.

She heads around a building and I follow, calling out to her again. But just as I turn, I end up going through another portal.

I'm in a room. A room full of mirrors.

CHAPTER 38

TURN TO escape, but the portal closes. Mirrors surround me. *No way out.*

I'm not here. Aithinne just killed Lonnrach. *I'm not here.* I whirl and sprint down the long line of mirrors, hating my reflections. *Don't look. Get out. You have to get out.*

I slam against a mirror with a painful jolt, but I barely notice it. My pulse is racing, my breathing coming fast now. My vision is blurring.

This is an illusion. I strike the mirror with my fists. *I have power now.* I strike it again. *He's dead.* I summon the Cailleach's power, until it's a great whirling storm through my veins created out of exhaustion and absolute desperation. I throw all that energy out against the mirrors.

They don't break. They hardly even shimmer. A humiliating, pathetic cry escapes me. Then a deep, shuddering sob. *One more time. Then again if you have to.*

Again.

Again.

Again.

Blood streams down my face from my nose, my eyes, my ears, but I don't care. My vision wobbles and stars pulse in front of my eyes, but I ignore it. *Don't stop. You can't stop.* I lurch forward to strike the mirror with my power again. It doesn't do anything. Thoughts race through my brain. I'm too frantic to think clearly.

"You can still change your mind."

I freeze at the sound of Lonnrach's voice. My stomach knots with terror. My blood roars in my ears and I squeeze my eyes shut. "You're not real. You're *not* real. You're a memory. Aithinne just killed you and you're dead."

"Turn around, Aileana Kameron."

I don't. I can't. I can't look at him, not in this room.

"Turn around." His voice is sharp, commanding. *Don't show your fear.* I raise my chin and turn. Lonnrach's face is staring back at me, but instead of his stormy gray irises, his eyes are glittering twin pools of liquid sapphire. The Morrigan's eyes.

"I wanted you alone," she says, staring down at Lonnrach's hands. "I saw this room in his memories, what he did to you here. Lonnrach was such a clever boy, but too arrogant. Too demanding." Her lip curls in disgust. "He didn't even sing."

"So you *let* us kill him."

She blinks at me. "Of course. I gave him to you as a gift. Didn't you like it?"

I set my jaw. "My answer is still no."

"Is it?" Her eyes go cold. Without waiting for my response, she says. "Well. This is quite useful anyway. This place, this body. Since your powers shield your thoughts from me, his abilities will help tell me everything I need to know."

I just need to use your blood to see.

I jerk back. I know what she intends to do with him. With his body. "No."

I summon the power again. It swirls inside my core. It heats through my bones, through my veins—

Hot. Too hot. My vision blurs. Blood bursts out of my mouth and splatters across the vine-covered floor.

I'm too weak to hold myself up, so I fall. *Get up. Get up!*

The thud of boots across the ivy draws my attention. The Morrigan leans over me, her expression calm. The way I'd imagine Death to look before he takes your soul. "My sister's power is tearing you apart. Find the Book, give it to me, and I'll use it to save you."

"You have my answer." My voice is faint.

The Morrigan kneels next to me. "You're a foolish girl, Aileana Kameron. When I take that Book from you, I'm going to cage you. Just like my little bird."

She bares her fangs and seizes my arm. *Fight back.* My mind is screaming at me, but my body can't move. It can't fight anymore.

I shut my eyes as she bites down.

This isn't the same as with Lonnrach. The Morrigan doesn't slip into my mind easily. She enters my mind like a tidal wave crashing against rock, fast and powerful and destructive.

She tears through memories of Kiaran and me. She watches our hunts, watches us sprinting down dark streets under the stars. She watches us battle as if we were in a dance. She watches him save me. She watches him whisper against my lips, a chant of *I'm yours*.

She brings up the deep, dark secrets of my heart. My desire to live forever if I could—with him. About how we hoard our minutes, our hours, because that's all the time we have.

Because he's all that matters. Because he's everything.

Then the Morrigan takes her teeth from my wrist. When she looks at me, her smile is satisfied. A victor's smile.

When she speaks, I tremble with fear. "That, Aileana Kameron, is how I'll get my yes." Her laugh rolls over me like a cold shadow. "You've never told him, have you? You've never said the words."

The words. Three simple words that would change everything.

I love you.

I can't say it when I know he and I don't have a future together. Because even if I manage to survive all this, he'll watch me age, watch me wither, watch me fade. That's our fate.

I'd rather Kiaran think of me one day a hundred years from now—two hundred, three hundred, four hundred, five hundred—the same wistful way he thinks of Catríona, his Falconer, and I'll be remembered as a rueful smile. A lover's kiss. A *what if*. A *could have been*.

It'll make the memory of me less painful to bear than if he had heard those three words on the lips of a dying girl.

You were his butterfly.

As if she reads my mind, the Morrigan's expression hardens. "So many emotions. If you and he had no feelings at all, this wouldn't be so easy."

She almost looks like herself for a moment, I can almost see the shape of her through Lonnrach's face, the beautiful features that look so much like the young Cailleach's. "He'd give up everything, you know." She taps her temple. "I see it in his head. He'd give up his immortality to become just another filthy human. For you."

Then the Morrigan leans in. Her fingers reach up to graze my face. There's a clear threat in her touch, a promise of death.

Her hard voice is ice in my veins. "Say yes."

I shut my eyes. "No," I whisper.

When I open my eyes, she's standing ten feet away, her expression cold and recondite. "Our time is running out and I'm going to get my yes, little girl." The Morrigan smiles her slow, victorious smile. "One word. That's all it takes." She disappears like smoke.

I'm left alone in the room of my nightmares. And I begin to believe I never made it out.

It's so easy. Easy to fear and believe that I'm still under Lonnrach's control. When I stare down at the bleeding mark the Morrigan left behind, I have to remind myself that it isn't his. That I'm not there.

This is Kiaran's coat, I tell myself. *Remember? You ripped yours up after the Morrigan showed up as a water wraith and used it to bind your wounds. There, see? Feel your back. Those are her claw marks. Those are real.* You're real. You're all right. You're real and you're alive and this is *Kiaran's coat.*

I slip the coat off my shoulders and press it to my face, closing my eyes.

It smells like him. Even with all my blood, it smells like him. Like wind and rain and sea, something wild and untamed. Like salt on the air. Like running through the trees, wind through my hair.

Then I hear a sound across the room, and when I look up, he's there.

CHAPTER 39

MY FIRST instinct is to go to him, but something stops me.

Kiaran doesn't look the same.

The shadows linger around him a little too closely. Long tendrils of darkness rise from the ground and wrap like vines around his legs. His skin looks paler. Even with his powers bound, he seems lit from within, shining. Beautiful. Until I look at his hands.

They're covered in blood.

My eyes meet his and my chest tightens with dread. His irises are deep pools of black—not a hint of lilac in them. They settle on me and flash with hunger.

Are you Kiaran or are you Kadamach?

He shakes his head as if he's clearing it, and the ink in his eyes begins to recede until I step forward. "Stay back." His voice is sharp.

I put my hands up. "Are you all right?"

"No. You're hurt again." I hear his soft inhale. He can smell my blood. I doubt even a bonfire could hide the scent from him now. It's all over me.

"The Morrigan," I say, as if it explains everything. I look at his blood-soaked hands again. "Yours?"

Kiaran's fingers curl to form fists. "I don't know."

He glances around and catches sight of himself in one of the mirrors. Then he shuts his darkened eyes. He's getting worse, fraying at the edges.

"I don't know," he says again. "She made me kill you. I thought I'd killed you. I don't know what's real anymore."

I swallow hard. The Morrigan has been torturing him, breaking his control little by little. When he looks up at me again, his eyes are as black as a starless sky.

"How do I know you're real?" Kiaran strides toward me, boots pounding across the floor. "How do I know you're not *her*?"

Oh god. The shadows wrap around him in thick trails at his feet. He has the swift gait of a predator. Fast, so fast. I don't have anywhere to go. Nowhere to run.

I back up until I'm pressed against the mirror and he's still coming. "*MacKay.*"

Kiaran stops, inches away. His ebony eyes stare at me. The white of a fang glints between his lips. He tilts his head, a slight frown on his face.

"MacKay," I whisper again.

Something glimmers in his gaze, then. Has he recognized me? Is he too far gone?

His hunger will always win out. Always.

No. That won't happen. I can bring him back. I *have* to bring him back.

I murmur his name again, slowly reaching out my hand. My slick, blood-covered fingers meet his. He inhales sharply and for a moment I wonder if I've made a mistake touching him.

But then, with the little bit of him still left in control, he whispers, "How do I know you're real?"

"Do you want me to ask you irritating questions? Or shall I tell you another silly story?" I swallow back the tremor in my voice. "Because I can do that."

Kiaran's smile is small. Seeing it is like winning a war. "Doesn't matter."

I brush my fingertips across his cheek and tell him something I've never forgotten. "Ten months after the king and the girl met, they got caught in an early morning downpour outside of Old Town. It was midautumn and warmer than usual. They cut through the Meadows on the way back to the city, where the puddles were so deep that the water went up to their ankles." I slide my hand down to his collarbone, lower, until it's right over his heart. "The girl was so elated from their hunt she thought she would burst with joy. She took off her boots and ran through the grass. She whirled in the rain. She almost asked the king to dance. But when she glanced back at him, he was watching her with the strangest look on his face." I lean forward and press my lips to his. A soft kiss. Light. Careful. "She used to lie in bed at night trying to solve the puzzle of that look, but was never satisfied with the answer. She always wondered what he was thinking."

"The same thing I'm thinking now." Kiaran opens his obsidian-black eyes. "I love you."

Then he's kissing me, his mouth hard against mine. Demanding. Brutal. His kiss is darkness and love and grief and joy and a thousand different conflicting things because he's battling himself and I'm all that's left to ground him. His fingers leave trails of fire down my waist, my hips.

"I love you," Kiaran rasps against my lips, pulling me closer. "I love you."

His fingers tug at my clothes, urgent now. He whispers again that he loves me, an almost desperate chant. He shoves my coat down my shoulders. His fingers trace the arch of my spine and slide down the valley of my stomach. He worships me with small touches like he'll never get enough, like I'm the only thing that can save him.

He kisses me so hard that his fangs pierce my lower lip.

I jerk away with a sharp gasp. When I look up at Kiaran, he's staring down at my mouth, at where the blood drips onto my chin. And his eyes are dark and predatory.

Kiaran won't be able to help me like this. One more push from the Morrigan, and talking won't bring him back. I have to offer him the one thing I know he needs: enough of my energy to sustain him until we find the Book. Enough to sate his hunger and give him some control again.

If I go with you and I become someone you don't recognize, don't let me hurt you. Leave me behind if you have to. Promise me.

I lied. I knew it would come to this. I'm not keeping my promise.

I grasp the collar of my shirt to bare my neck. "I don't want to lose you."

Kiaran's eyes are unfathomably deep. As deep as the ocean, as deep as the darkest parts of space. His hand slides to cup the back of my neck as he draws me forward. When he looks at me again, it's with his last vestige of control. A wordless way of asking me, *Are you sure?*

"I'm sure," I whisper.

His lips are at my neck for the barest of kisses before he bites down.

Kiaran's bite doesn't feel like Lonnrach's. It's not brutal. It isn't violent. He holds me like he does when he kisses me. When we're in bed, and he's pressing himself close.

Then he sinks me to the floor and stretches his body over mine. The venom from his bite bursts through me and my body recognizes the pain. It recognizes what this is, and I go slack in his grip.

I shut my eyes.

It's not Lonnrach. This isn't Lonnrach. It's Kiaran and you're all right. You're all right. You're all right. You're all—

His control shatters and he bites down harder. I press my lips together so I don't make a sound. My powers are roaring inside me. I try to force them to hold back. But I'm getting lightheaded. My vision is blurring.

"MacKay," I whisper. "You have to stop now."

He tears more energy out of me and I have to bite my tongue not to cry out. "MacKay." I try to keep my voice even. I try to say his name to bring him back. It's not working.

My energy is leaving me faster than I can endure. I can't whisper words anymore, not his name, not anything else. Kiaran is killing me. And if he does, he'll break his vow to Catríona. He'll die with me.

I'm desperate enough to use my powers, but it's too late. I'm too weak to call them forth, to do anything. I can't even move. His name is a breath on my lips. But he doesn't hear me. He isn't listening. He's so far gone that there's no way left to reach him.

Across the room, I see a girl in the mirrors, the one with the tattoos. She's standing there as if she's uncertain what to do.

Her eyes meet mine. I'm desperate enough to mouth a word to her: *Help.*

Those dark amber eyes intensify and I swear I feel her connect with my mind. It's a tentative touch, a searching caress—and then a voice whispering across my thoughts in a light breeze: *I wish I had known earlier that you weren't like the others who came before. Your memories showed a safe place. I hope you find something like that again.*

Then she presses a palm to the mirror and disappears. A portal opens along the wall, and I see the fire of Aithinne's camp, my friends around it. Derrick is sitting on Gavin's shoulder.

"Derrick," I breathe. It takes all of my effort just to say it. "Derrick."

He looks up as if he hears me. "Aileana?"

The others don't notice when he flies past the fire, closer to the edges of the portal. He must see it as soon as he goes through the trees, because his eyes widen. "Aileana?" Disbelief, as if he doesn't understand what he's seeing.

I project the thought because it's all I'm capable of. *I need you.*

"Bloody hell." Derrick zooms past the trees and through the portal just a moment before it closes. He comes to a sudden stop as he takes in what's happening. Me on the floor. Kiaran at my neck. My hand grasping Kiaran's shirt as if that could make him stop. It can't.

Help.

Derrick yanks a wicked wee blade out of his sheath. "Get the *hell* away from her, you filthy—" He darts forward in a flurry of wings and slices Kiaran across the back. Kiaran lifts his head with a vicious snarl full of razor-sharp teeth. When his eyes meet mine, they're pitch black. Not a single part of Kiaran is in that gaze.

Then, with horror, I watch as his irises lighten to a bright, pure sapphire blue.

I freeze. *The Morrigan.* She's taking advantage of his lack of control to possess his body.

I'll make you say yes.

I only have a moment. I gather my powers and slam Kiaran across the room. I try to stand. Derrick is at my side, breathing hard. "What was he doing? What the bloody hell is going on?"

"Not. Him." I can barely form the words. Between my powers and the energy Kiaran took, I'm drained. My nose and neck are both bleeding. My skin feels sticky and hot and wet.

Derrick looks at me with alarm. "Oh, god," he says. "Aileana."

A wave of dizziness rolls over me and I have to lean on the mirror for a moment until my vision clears. I watch Kiaran get to his feet and fear knots my stomach. "MacKay, you have to fight her. I know you can."

"You want me to stop?" The Morrigan's voice threads with his. "Say yes."

"No," I snarl.

"Then I'll sacrifice my first pawn."

Kiaran comes at me in a running leap that I dodge just in time. I spin to face him, pulling my blade from its sheath. "Goddamn it, MacKay, don't make me do this."

Derrick lands on my shoulder. "Are you mad? You can't fight him. You can barely stand."

I don't have time to reply. Kiaran comes at me again, his sword swinging in an arc. My blade crashes against his with a hard smack of metal against metal. The force of it sends a painful jolt through my body that drives me to my knees.

Get up!

"MacKay, fight her!"

Sapphire-blue eyes flash as he lunges for me. He attacks me with his blade, each swing lightning quick. God, he's fast. His movements are smooth, elegant. Like a dancer with a sword, all graceful slashes and kicks and blocks. His blade sings. Its song is destruction.

He drives me back toward the mirrors. If I end up against one, I'm done. The Morrigan is trying to force me to kill him.

I don't sacrifice my pawns until I'm certain I'm about to win.

"You're losing," Derrick hisses in my ear. "If you went any slower, you'd have a limb chopped off."

"You're not helping."

Kiaran doesn't move before Derrick says, "Swing left!"

For once, I listen to him—just before Kiaran swipes with his sword. Our blades scrape together and I dart out of the way.

"Keep directing me," I tell Derrick.

Derrick sits on my shoulder, telling me how Kiaran will strike before it happens. The pixie can sense his movements, how his body bunches before an attack. Soon I'm driving Kiaran back, but my movements are slowing down, getting clumsier.

"Kiaran, *stop!*"

"Lunge!" Derrick yells.

I dive to connect my sword with Kiaran's, but at the last moment, he slams his fist into my face. I spin and hit the ground hard, fighting not to black out.

"Get up," Derrick tells me. "Get the hell up, Aileana."

Listen to him. Move!

Footsteps. Hard boots against the floor. The Morrigan's voice beneath Kiaran's, sounding triumphant. *I'm going to win.* "Shall I sacrifice my pawn? Or will you say yes?"

"No," I breathe. "No."

"Stay away from her," Derrick snarls.

Shall I sacrifice my pawn? I see the Morrigan's eyes gleam when she looks at the pixie. Derrick is flying toward Kiaran, his blade drawn and ready to attack.

Kiaran isn't the pawn.

"Derrick," I scream. "*Wait!*"

Kiaran snatches Derrick from the air and closes his fist with a sickening crunch. Then he tosses the pixie to the ground.

I don't remember saying anything. I don't remember screaming. I don't remember getting to my feet or stumbling to Derrick's broken body, lying next to his detached, mangled wings.

All I recall is picking up his broken, wingless body in my hand, and saying his name. *Derrick.*

He stirs. "Don't cry," Derrick whispers, his voice faint. "I don't like to see you cry. You're my favorite." He doesn't move again.

"Derrick? *Derrick!*"

I say his name over and over and over. He's not dead. He'll wake up at any moment with a stupid joke about how he fooled me and then he'll start plaiting my hair. He'll sew me a new coat. He'll threaten to make me another dress.

Because Derrick is immortal and the fae don't die. They live forever. *They live forever.*

Derrick isn't dead. He isn't dead, he can't—

His eyes don't open. His wings don't heal. His blood drips down my fingers.

I throw back my head and scream. Power bursts out of me, wild and furious and violent. Every mirror in the room shatters. Glass falls to the floor around me.

The room is quiet after that. There is only the sound of my breathing, rough and painful. I press Derrick's small body to my chest and finally notice that the taste of his power is gone. *He's gone and he's not coming back. He's not coming back. He's not coming back.*

"Kam." A choked whisper across the room makes me go still.

I open my eyes. Kiaran is standing there, his eyes back to normal. He's staring at Derrick's unmoving body.

But I feel nothing. Just numb. Derrick's body is losing its heat and I need to—I need to—I don't *know*. I don't know what to do.

"Kam," Kiaran says again.

I scramble to my feet and gather the remains of my power. The physical pain of it cleanses me. For a single beautiful moment, it washes away my grief, my despair. Everything. The pain is a cure. I feel it in my chest, through my veins, across my bones. In the shattered remnants of the mirror, I see my hair lift as if picked up by a breeze. My eyes are lit with the uncanny amber glow of something not quite human, not quite fae.

Derrick's wry voice rises from my memories. *Freaky eyes.*

I reach my hand out and light flickers between my fingertips. I gather the energy inside me until my body feels as if it will shatter with the gathering of it. *Hold. Hold.* I endure, because I have to. Because I'm not going to leave his body in this room. I'm not going to leave Derrick, just as he didn't leave me.

I search along the mirrors until I find the small remnants of the portal the girl opened to Aithinne's camp. It's barely more than a thin sliver, just enough for me to use. Enough for me to get out of here.

I release all the energy and blow open a massive, gaping hole to the outside world. And I stumble through it.

As the darkness closes in, I fall to the ground and pull Derrick's body against me. I hold him next to me where he's always been. Where he belongs.

His voice is the last thing I remember before everything goes black.

I wished for you. I spent two and a half months wishing for you. To see you one last time.

Before what?

I don't know yet.

CHAPTER 40

I WAKE TO a warm bed, the scratchy feel of rough wool blankets over my body. When I try to move, the pain is so agonizing it feels as if my skin is on fire. Sensitive to the touch, fevered and damp with sweat. *What happened?*

Images flash in my mind. Kiaran biting me. The tattooed girl. The Morrigan's bright blue eyes staring out at me from Kiaran's face. Derrick—

Derrick is dead. Derrick is dead. Derrick is dead.

Sudden hot tears wet my cheeks. A rustle to my left—just out of my line of sight—makes me open my eyes. Catherine leans over me, her long braid grazing my arm.

She's been crying. Her eyes are red-rimmed and wet. "Hullo, you," she says, voice hoarse.

"Where am I?" I croak. My throat aches.

Does it matter? Derrick is dead.

I push the thought away and try to raise my head, but the pain is too much. All I can see is the stonework of the inside of a cottage. The grass of a thatched roof. An open window on the opposite wall reveals lifeless tree branches outside. They groan as if the wood is rotting, shallow and ready to fall.

Beyond that, the sky has lost its luster. Even on cloudy days, the sky had a silvery glow mixed with shades of black and blue to break up the monotony. Now it is the dull, pallid gray of dead flesh. As if the earth were hanging on to her last breath. As if she were fighting to stay alive and failing. Just like me.

Catherine looks away. "You're back at the camp. You're safe. So are the others."

Not all the others. *Derrick is dead.*

I struggle against my tears. "How did I get here?"

Catherine draws in a breath. "We heard a noise like thunder. At first I thought it might be more land breaking apart, but it was you. You created a rift between the realms. You and the others came out, and you were bleeding everywhere. You collapsed onto the ground." She swallows. "Derrick is . . . he didn't make it."

Derrick is dead.

I shut my eyes.

Even faeries die.

"I'm not supposed to mourn him," I tell her. "He was supposed to outlive me. He was supposed to live forever."

"I know," she says.

"It's my fault." *I should never have called for his help.*

Catherine's gaze turns sharp. "He died doing what he's always done."

"What I asked him to do."

"Oh, Aileana." She sighs and grips my hand. "He wanted to save the person he loved most."

I reach up and touch my shoulder, feeling the absence of his wee body there like an ache. I wish I could stroke his wings one last time. I wish I could hear his voice. "He sacrificed himself for someone who is going to die."

"Don't be foolish," Catherine says gently. "He sacrificed himself for you so you would live."

I wished for you. I spent two and a half months wishing for you.

Derrick was probably the only creature on this dying, godforsaken earth who still believed that wishes held power. He might have lost his city and his family, but that didn't make him bitter. It didn't change the fact that he still had good in him. He was the one who taught me that not all fae were evil.

I'll never get to thank him for mending all the coats I ripped, the trousers I destroyed. For the silly dresses he made with their flounces and lace and ribbons, which I wore not because I give a damn about those things, but because he enjoyed making them. I'll never hear him sing bawdy jigs in my closet.

He saved me so many times and now I'll never, ever get to repay him for it. I'll never stroke his wings or listen to his stupid jokes. He'll never sit on my shoulder again.

It's empty. *I'm empty.*

"Catherine." My voice cracks. "I miss him so much."

Then her arms are around me in a crushing embrace and I'm sobbing into her shoulder. My tears are hot and wet and my body is shaking.

"We're all going to die, aren't we?" I whisper. "What do we have that's worth saving?"

What do we have left? A world full of monsters we have to hide from. An endless war. Nowhere that's safe. We'll worry the people we love will go into a battle and never come back.

This is our truth. This is what remains: a colorless place that's beginning to split at the seams; a life where we wonder how we're going to die and who will be next.

What's left?

"Us," she tells me. "We have us, and when we find the Book, we'll return everything to the way it was. We can end this. We can bring them all back."

"I don't think we can bring Derrick back," I whisper. When the fae die, there are no second chances. No coming back. Their souls aren't like ours.

"Maybe the Book can," she says, but I don't think she believes it.

I don't believe it either.

Catherine and I stay like that for a while. Quiet, lost in our own thoughts. The pain of losing Derrick is so raw. I've lost a part of myself and I don't have time to adjust. I don't have time to mourn him. I have to save my broken world and reverse all of this.

I'm going to give Catherine and everyone else their lives back. Everything stolen by the fae.

And for Derrick, I'll make the Morrigan pay. She'll wish she had never taken him away from me.

"I need to go back." I shove the blankets off my legs.

Catherine grasps my hand. "Rest first."

My time is running out. "I can't. Not until I've killed the Morrigan and used the Book."

"Aileana," Catherine says firmly. When she gets like this, it's difficult to argue. Catherine is every bit as stubborn as I am. "You're in no condition to go back into battle, and if you do—" She looks away sharply.

"What?"

"If you do," she whispers, "I'm afraid I won't see you before the end."

"I won't let that happen." *Tell me you believe me.* Catherine voiced my own doubt, my fear that I won't be able to defeat the Morrigan. *I need to know that you trust me.* "But I can't just lie in bed. Not when we don't have much time left."

She looks away with a sigh. "All right. Then I have to show you something. If you won't listen to me about resting, you need to see it before you leave."

When I get to my feet, the pain is so intense that I almost collapse. I've never felt so weak. Not even when Lonnrach stole my blood and my memories. Or even when Catherine had to nurse me back to health after being attacked by will-o'-the-wisps and I was bedridden for several days. Not even then.

It's not the same kind of hurt. This is the deep ache of my last breaths. The pain of knowing that I'm running out of time.

When I nearly fall again, Catherine catches me and slides her arm around my waist to hold me up. I lean heavily against her, flushing with embarrassment at how weak I am.

"I have you," Catherine says. "I have you."

We slowly make our way out of the cottage. I close my eyes against the outdoor light. A headache pounds through my temples and Catherine waits patiently until I move forward.

When I open my eyes again, I see Gavin and Daniel sitting next to the fire keeping an obvious eye on Sorcha, who looks unusually passive. Kiaran and Aithinne must have gone off somewhere. And Derrick . . .

Derrick is dead.

I remember this feeling. I remember how much it hurts. After my mother died, I would wake up and go into the drawing room, still expecting to find her sitting on the settee with her morning tea in hand. She used to look up with a soft smile and say the same thing: *Good morning, darling. What shall we do today?*

But she wasn't there. There was no smile waiting for me. No words of welcome. Just a cold, empty couch in a cold, empty room. Every day was a reminder that she was gone.

Just like this. Just like now.

Derrick is dead.

Catherine's eyes fill, as if she reads my mind. She leads me across the camp and down the path through the woods, until we reach the outer edges of the forest. I barely notice how long it takes.

Finally, she takes hold of my elbow and says, "Look."

I open my eyes and my entire body goes numb with shock. When I left to find the Book, this had been a forest so thick that the light barely penetrated to the ground. The trees towered into the sky, so high that I could barely see the stars. I remembered their lack of color, the way the forest looked as if it were a faded ink drawing instead of a real forest.

Now it's gone. It's all gone.

There's nothing left.

CHAPTER 41

ATHERINE GUIDES me through the last line of trees, and what I see there sends another jolt of horror through me. The forest has broken away and fallen into a massive crevasse like the one in the *Sìth-bhrùth*. It goes so deep that I can't see beyond the dark.

There isn't any land left on the other side, either. The escarpment here extends out of sight, as far out as an ocean. A deep black pit of nothing. It's as if the camp were the only place left in the whole world, an island dashed into a dark space.

And what's left of the camp? A few thatched cottages and a bonfire? "How much has gone?" The question catches in my throat.

Catherine shifts uneasily on her feet. "We're in the center of it. The only reason this camp isn't at the bottom of that pit is because Derrick put up a protective shield. With him gone"—she pauses—"I'll wager it won't last much longer."

"What about the mainland?" *Stay steady. Be calm.*

"Aithinne opened a portal and left a few hours ago to inspect the damage. She says everywhere she's looked so far is the same. Land crumbling, lochs drying up." Catherine steps away from me, her expression fierce. "I know you're grieving, but you have to win this fight. You have to."

"I will." I must.

Find the Book, kill the Morrigan. For Derrick. For this small, sad, scorched realm. So I can return everything to the way it was.

I back away from the cliff and my vision pulses as another headache slams through my temples. I sway on my feet and Catherine catches me. "You really should get some rest now. I'll talk to Aithinne about replacing your weapons."

Catherine leaves me by the fire. Gavin and Daniel have gone off somewhere, but Sorcha is still there, looking into the flames with an unreadable expression.

She glances up when I settle down on the log near her. She's lounging on the ground, her long legs crossed at the ankles. She's putting on a damn good show of appearing at ease. "You look ghastly," she says.

"Don't make me punch you in the face."

I swear she almost smiles. "Well, well. Someone is embracing her ruthlessness."

My laugh is dark, dry, and brittle. "Do you want to know how cruel I can be? There are moments when I think about what the Morrigan did and how much I want to punish her. I think about taking that Book and giving her a body just so I can torture it. Slit her throat, tear out her heart, and make her hurt. And then I realize"—I look up at Sorcha—"that's what you warned me about. It would make me just like you. And I'm still so tempted."

Sorcha goes still. Something about her expression is raw, open. When she speaks, her voice is rough. "The Morrigan and the Strategist both put me in a cage. He marked me and tried to make me his. She broke my body, stole my soul, took away my name, and forced me to sing until I had no voice left. She murdered who I was and left behind this . . . " She looks at her hands. "This shell. I know I said it was inevitable, but fight it. Don't give in and be like me. Don't let yourself."

I stare at her, turning over her words in my mind. "Why?" I whisper. *You said I was ruthless. I don't think I can be merciful, not like Aithinne.*

Sorcha looks away. "Because it won't give you purpose. You won't ever find relief. Those painful memories don't disappear just because you destroyed the one responsible. Killing just makes you empty."

She stands and strides off toward the forest, stopping only when I call her name.

"I can't forgive you," I tell her. "You took my mother from me, and you made Kiaran say that vow. And I can't ever forgive you."

When Sorcha turns her head, her expression is shadowed by the trees. "Forgiveness isn't something given," she says softly. "It's something earned. What could I do to earn it, Aileana? Nothing. I'd make the same choices. I don't deserve forgiveness."

A jolt of surprise goes through me when I realize she said my name.

She said my name for the first time.

Before I can reply, she walks away without another word.

Gavin steps out of one of the thatched cottages. He watches her retreating shadow and looks at me. "Do I want to know?"

"No," I say softly.

"Should I send Aithinne to threaten her?"

Haven't there been enough threats? Tears prick the backs of my eyes. *Forgiveness isn't something given. It's something earned.*

"That's not necessary." My voice sounds flat, unfamiliar to my own ears.

What do I know about anything anymore? I used to think all fae were evil. It was uncomplicated, easy. Now my thoughts and feelings are messy and chaotic. The one person who made things easy was Derrick.

And he isn't here.

Gavin settles down beside me. "Do you want to be alone?"

I stare into the fire. "No." I can't help the sob that erupts from the back of my throat. "Gavin, I'm not all right."

"Shh. Come here." Gavin gathers me against him.

"I don't think I can do this anymore."

I can't keep losing the people I love. I can't keep fighting. I can't keep going out into a battle with less and less of a reason to win.

Gavin strokes my back, and when I look into his eyes, they're wet with tears, too. "Since when do you ever admit defeat? You're as stubborn as Derrick was."

"And now he's gone," I whisper. "I watched the Morrigan kill him, using the person I love as his executioner. Just to make me pay for refusing her." I shut my eyes, trying to push away the memory of Derrick dying. "Look, can we talk about something else?"

Gavin is silent for a moment. Then: "I knew you cared about Kiaran. I didn't know you were in love with him."

That's not any better. Gavin is terrible at this. But I'll take any change of topic I can get.

"I'm not sure he knows either. I've never said the words."

Gavin squeezes me gently. I settle against him. Now that Derrick is gone, he's the one comfort I have left from home. Him and Catherine.

"I used to think the fae were incapable of loving anyone," he says. "But when I see him with you, I think—" His laugh is low, dry. "I loved you once. And I never looked at you the way he does."

Derrick's words from back in the pixie city flicker across my memory. *Like he wishes he was mortal.*

I shove down the memory of Derrick's voice. "You never told me you loved me."

Gavin shrugs. "I planned to tell you the night before I left for Oxford. I was going to say it when you sneaked me into your bedroom and kissed me."

"What made you change your mind?"

"I hoped you would ask me to stay in Edinburgh. You didn't."

Gavin never would have gone to Oxford and caught that illness. He never would have died and come back with the Sight and I wouldn't have gone to that ball at the Assembly

Rooms as a debutante. Maybe my mother wouldn't have been murdered that night. Maybe that one decision would have changed everything.

"So you left?" My smile is small, sad. "You didn't stop to think about how I was a sixteen-year-old girl, still giddy from her first kiss, and too terrified to say *I love you*?"

I'm still too terrified to say those words. Some things don't change.

"I was your first kiss?"

"Of course you were my first. I waited years for that kiss."

"I would have waited years to marry you," Gavin tells me. "I wanted to, long before we were forced into an engagement. If you wanted me, too. Not that it matters now."

I stare at the scars on his cheek, at the one along his collarbone. "I suppose nothing worked out the way we hoped, did it?"

"Never in a thousand years." His smile is quick, forced. "But I like to think if things had been different, we would have been happy. Don't you?"

When I imagine all that could have been, my mind comes up empty. My life has become so entwined with this war that anything else seems more dream than reality. I barely remember the girl I was.

I look down at my hands. Catherine washed the blood off, but I can still see it dried beneath my fingernails. Now that I think about it, my nails are hardly ever clean. They're always a reminder of all the fae I've killed.

I'm a creature of chaos and death and maybe this is how I'm meant to die. In a battle. At the end of a long war.

If things had been different and Kiaran had never come into my life, maybe I would have married Gavin. Maybe we could have been happy living in Edinburgh with our children.

"I don't know," I tell him honestly. "But I like to think so."

He stares down at his hands, too, as if he were thinking the same things I was. "If we manage to survive this, what will you and Kiaran do?"

Kiaran will be with Sorcha. She'll spend the next thousand years chipping away at pieces of his soul until there's nothing left of the Kiaran I know. An eternity of servitude given to her so I can have a book—a book that my friend lost his life for.

"I haven't thought about it," I lie.

"Aileana." He sucks in a breath to say something else, but I interrupt him.

"I'm dying." The words leave my mouth in a rush of breath. "I'm dying," I say again, lower this time. "Every time I use my powers, it kills me a little more. So I can't think about anything else. I have to find the Book, or—"

Something makes me look up to the dark line of trees. It's Kiaran.

His eyes meet mine, and I know he heard everything.

CHAPTER 42

I PUSH TO my feet. "MacKay. Wait—"

He doesn't look back at me as he turns and walks off into the woods.

I hurry after him. "Damn it, MacKay, *stop*." When the stubborn arse keeps walking, I say, "You can't go much farther unless you want to fall off a bloody cliff, so stop being a coward and talk to me."

That does the trick. Kiaran pauses, his back to me. "What do you want, Kam?"

I say the first thing that comes to mind: "I was going to tell you."

"When?" Kiaran turns. His face is so shadowed that I can't make out his expression. "When?" At my silence, he says bitterly, "Let me guess: as your last words?"

His lilac irises are blazing in the darkness. For a moment I can't help but recall the Morrigan's blue eyes. I'm assaulted by memories of Kiaran snatching Derrick out of the air to crush him. Like he was a dragonfly. A bug. A pest.

Shall I sacrifice my pawn?

As if sensing my thoughts, Kiaran looks away, his gaze ashamed as he stares out at the trees. When he speaks, his voice is so soft I barely hear the words. "I watched you die twice, Kam. I just got you back."

"I'm mortal," I say gently. "You have to accept that I won't live forever and I doubt the Book can change that." When he doesn't respond, I sigh. "What would you have said if I told you? Would you have tried to stop me from using my powers?"

He's quiet for a moment. "I don't know."

I can't bear our distance. I close the space between us and slip my arms around him. He lets me press my cheek against his chest and listen to his heart beat. When his arms circle me and he holds me close, I shut my eyes.

I want to forget everything. I want to stand here, with you, and forget the whole world. I want . . .

I tell him the truth: "I wish I had a thousand years with you. More."

"Not a thousand more years, Kam. That's time I already have. It's time I've already lived."

"What, then?"

Kiaran strokes a finger down my cheek, along my jawline, across my eyebrows. Like he's memorizing us just like this, little fragments for when I'm gone. For all the years he has ahead without me. "I want one lifetime with you. Not hundreds, not thousands, not eternity. I just want one."

When I lean in and press my lips to his, I notice the blackness of his outer irises has begun to creep back in. Not as dark as it was in the mirrored room, but dark enough that it looks like a shadow crossing a spring field.

His kiss is careful. So very careful. I know he's remembering the things he did. I know he's remembering his teeth at my neck, biting down.

How much time do we have? How much time do I have?

Why love a butterfly when it starts to die the moment it gets its wings?

* * *

Later that night, the bonfire burns high for Derrick's funeral.

Aithinne has scattered leaves, twigs, and branches—the only bits of nature we have left—across the ground in whirled designs that spread all the way around the camp.

There should be petals in every color, Aithinne told me as I helped her. *Flowers scattered for miles, like we did for you. So everyone would know that he was loved. He deserves flowers. He deserves better than this.*

She broke down in tears, and I held her shaking body until the thin edges of the shadowed moon rose in the sky.

As I make my way across the camp toward where Aithinne and the others stand around the flames, my chest aches again.

Don't cry. You know I don't like to see you cry. You're my favorite.

Sorcha isn't with the others, and Kiaran is gone. I should have expected the guilt would be too much for him. He killed Derrick's family. And Kiaran might have been under the Morrigan's control, but his hands killed Derrick, too.

How can you not hate me for what I did? Kiaran asked me before I left him in the woods.

Because that's what she wants me to do.

Aithinne rises to her feet when she sees me, and Catherine steps forward to put an arm around my shoulders. She murmurs soothing words in my ears, but I can't hear them. All my focus is on the small wooden box Aithinne is holding.

A box. *A box.* My friend, my companion, and now he's in a box.

Aithinne holds it out for me to take, but I can't. I can't move. Because once I touch it, this will be real. Derrick will really be gone.

Derrick is dead.

Catherine nudges me forward. "I'm here with you," she whispers.

I take the box, but I don't let my tears fall. The case is intricately carved, inside and out, with fae symbols along the wood forming small patterns that must have taken hours.

Aithinne says, "We didn't have petals. So I did this." She steps closer and lifts the lid.

His wee body is tucked under a silk coverlet. His eyes are closed, and he looks so alive. Like he's just sleeping.

He's not coming back, I remind myself harshly. *He's not asleep. He's not resting. He's not coming back.*

Wherever she goes, death follows.

I shut my eyes hard before the tears fall. *Stop. Please stop.*

"What does the box say?"

"It tells his story." Aithinne reaches her hand out to trace her fingertips across the markings. "His birth, his battles, through the ages until his death." She looks at me. "Would you like to see where you are?"

Without waiting for my answer, Aithinne takes my hand and places it inside the box. She presses my fingers to the wood, just where Derrick's body rests against the silk. The markings there are even more intricate and beautiful. As if he lived more during the events of those last few branches than he had in all the centuries that formed the others.

"You're here," Aithinne whispers. "The closest to his heart. So when he joins his family on the other side, they will see him marked with these words. With your name."

"What words?"

Her smile is small, sad. "*I lived for thee. I died for thee.*" She looks down at him. "We believe that when we die, we go to Tír na nÓg. The land of eternal youth. Where war doesn't exist." When she looks at me, there are tears in her eyes. "You'll see him there someday. We all will."

She gestures to the small platform she's put near the bonfire. When I set the box down there, the emptiness inside me grows. Aithinne steps inside the blaze—unburned—and lifts the platform to place it in the heart of the fire.

We all stand and watch as the flames consume the box, and we lose another of our own.

CHAPTER 43

AS THE first light rises in the pallid, dying sky, I don the clothes for my last hunt. I fought back tears when I saw them on the cot for me in Aithinne's cottage.

I knew what it was.

Make me a pirate costume.

Only if you save me a dance.

He had done as I requested and made this for me to fight in. Only Derrick wasn't content with just making a plain garment. It's the most beautiful thing he's ever created.

I miss you, I think, imagining him on my shoulder. *I miss watching you sew. I miss listening to your silly songs.*

The trousers are soft leather, warm to the touch. When I put them on, they fit closely, easy to move in. They were created to keep me swift and agile in a fight. Practical. Perfect.

Derrick's specialty was always the coat. That was where he put his greatest efforts.

I hold my breath and brush my fingers across the fine material. The garment is similar to the one Aithinne gave me, but it's the deep red of a summer sunset. It matches my hair perfectly. The front of the coat is covered with intricate gold threads that form hundreds of falling feathers. They span all the way across the chest to the back where they split off into stars. Constellations.

Each one is from my mother's lessons. *Polaris. Alderamin. Gamma Cassiopeiae.*

That's when I notice the inside of my coat. There's a scrap of material sewn over the interior pocket, where it would rest just over my heart.

My mother's tartan. The one that was destroyed with the pixie kingdom. Derrick remembered the design and re-created it.

As if that weren't enough, there's a note.

It's not the original, but I figured you ought to wear it.
Stop fretting over whether or not you're worthy.
You're being silly and you know it. —D
P.S. Don't destroy this coat on its first outing. Those gold threads
were a pain in my arse. No wonder pirates don't wear them.

Tears blur my vision. When I read the last line, I let out a choked laugh and lift the coat to put on. Derrick's scent overwhelms me. A sob rips out of my chest. I lower myself to the floor, press the coat to my nose, and savor the lingering taste of Derrick's power. Honeysuckle, sweetness, nature.

"I don't know if I can do this without you," I whisper.

Derrick would settle on my shoulder and say, *Of course not; you never could do your own sewing.*

That almost brings a smile to my face. I wrap my arms around his coat and inhale the scent of him again. "I'm tired," I whisper. "I'm so tired of fighting."

Derrick would know just what to say. *So what are you going to do about it? Sit here on your arse in my pretty clothes? Feel sorry for yourself until those powers finally kill you?*

I hear footsteps just outside the cottage and when I look up, Aithinne is standing in the doorway with her hands on her hips. "What do you think?" she asks me. "Shall we go for one last battle?"

I stare down at Derrick's note, and I imagine him speaking again. *Get up. Grab your sword. Find the Book. Kill that evil arsehole. Stop moping and take your life back, you silly thing.*

Because I have some advantages that the Morrigan doesn't have: I have Sorcha. I can use the Book and the Morrigan can't, not until she gets a new body. And she still needs *me* to create one for her. I just need to find that damn Book.

The girl.

The one from Sorcha's memories. She was at the ball. She was in the forest. I glimpsed her in the cave just after the portal formed.

She was in the mirrored room. And she opened that portal for Derrick to come through. She helped me.

"I know that look," Aithinne says with a smile. "That's the look of someone who has a plan." She frowns. "Dear me, it's not a stupid plan, is it?"

I don't reply. I get to my feet and shove past her. I need to find Sorcha right this bloody second. *Where is she?*

When I see the *baobhan sìth* by the fire, I stride right up to her. "You knew that girl."

Sorcha looks at me like I'm insane. "Excuse me?"

"The *girl*. The one with the tattoos that we saw in Edinburgh. I saw her in your mind before that. Who is she?"

For once, she seems speechless. She looks to Aithinne as if for help, but the other faery just stands next to me with her arms crossed. "I rather doubt that, since I don't remember her before we chased her. You're imagining things. Common in humans, I suspect."

"Oh, stop it. I'm not imagining things," I insist. "I need you to let me into your mind again."

Aithinne is frowning. "What are you thinking?"

"I'm thinking those stories never said a damn thing about what happened to the Morrigan's consort. That girl who helped me . . . I think she's the consort. And she knows where the Book is." I step closer to Sorcha. "If you let me in, I might be able to see something that can help us. Something the Morrigan missed."

Sorcha presses her lips together, somewhat impatiently. "So you're asking this time." At my nod, she sighs. "I hope this is the last time you go around digging in my head. Just hurry the hell up."

I place my hands on her temples and shut my eyes. My mind connects with hers easily. Now that I've been in her thoughts and seen her memories before, the colors and thorniness of them is less of a shock. Easier for me to navigate through.

Sorcha leads me through the stream of her memories as if she were guiding me by the hand. I go back to the events of her imprisonment. Sorcha's skin grows cold when the images of her torture go by. She trembles slightly. I gently nudge her forward, urging us to where I first saw the girl.

There. The image is so fleeting that I almost miss it. I go back and study it. The memory is only a fragment. The rest of it is blackened around the edges, like a painting that's been almost completely burned. Only a small impression of the picture remains.

The girl with her fingers beneath Sorcha's chin. Sorcha's head is tipped back, willingly. She had this memory removed willingly. The girl's long hair hangs between them, almost covering her eyes.

Her eyes are completely black; there isn't a bit of white in them at all. The tattoos on her skin glow, the light shining through the thin material of her dress. Her lips are mouthing something. A message. I only just catch some of it.

"—forget how you found me. Forget what I am."

How you found me.

What I am.

Not who. What.

I stumble back. My mind disconnects from Sorcha's. Aithinne catches me by the shoulders. "What did you—"

"The Morrigan's consort *is* the Book," I interrupt. "She's the damn Book. Those markings all over her must be the spells." *That's why Lonnrach wanted her. He must have figured out who she was. But without Sorcha's memory, he wouldn't have known what he almost had.*

The Book is the girl.

Aithinne stares at me. "Well, that's one way to hide it."

"No wonder she erased my memory," Sorcha says, rubbing her temples. "The Morrigan must assume she's still looking for an object."

And the girl is still trapped in there with the Morrigan. *Find her. We can find her and end this. Finish it.*

A part of me feels unhinged. Derrick isn't on my shoulder to advise me. I don't have a proper plan. My thoughts are a chaotic mess made worse by my urgency. Each second that ticks by is precious time lost. Each minute. Each hour. We have to do this now.

"What's your plan?" Aithinne asks.

"Go back, find the girl, and kill the Morrigan."

"Simple. Effective. Small chance of success." She smiles. "I like it."

"Well, I think it's suicidal," Sorcha says with a smirk.

"Do you have a better idea?" I ask her.

"I said it was suicidal, not that I had anything better. Once this place starts to go, whatever is left through that portal will go with it. Frankly, *suicidal* is our only option right now."

Aithinne glances at the edge of the forest, where the land is breaking off into the dark, endless pit. "We have to go soon. It's not going to hold. We'll have to take the humans with us."

Sorcha's laugh is sharp. "Humans fighting the Morrigan? That's not a death risk, that's a death guarantee."

"If you're not going to say anything of use, shut the bloody hell up," I say. I look at Aithinne. "Find Kiaran, gather the others, and whatever weapons you can find. We're leaving."

* * *

This time, it takes Sorcha many precious minutes to find the breach between worlds. The one I blew open had moved by the time we began the search.

Unlike when we were in Kiaran's endless palace, we only have our wee island on which to find a portal into the Morrigan's prison. Less than a few square miles. As far as I know, this is all that's left of our world. As it shrinks and falls apart, the portal itself becomes smaller and smaller.

Sorcha brushes her fingers against the trunks as she passes. "It's tiny," she says when she finally finds it. "Paper thin." Her hand presses to the tree harder and she shakes her head. "This had better work. Because the easiest solution is still for Kadamach to put a blade into his sister's ribs and spare us the trip."

"She doesn't help, does she?" Catherine asks.

"She's here to scheme," Gavin says. "Not help."

Kiaran crosses his arms. "And a much better solution would be to cut out your tongue so you can't speak."

"So hostile." Sorcha holds out her hand. "Give me your blade, handsome."

Sorcha slices the edge of Kiaran's dagger down her palm and presses her hand to the tree.

Through the portal is the Morrigan's version of Edinburgh. We're on Princes Street, the main shopping area in the New Town. The lamps along the thoroughfare are all lit up, but the city is a ghost town. Entirely silent, yet blazing with light. Every window in each building glows by either lamp or candlelight, from the white-columned shops of the New Town to the towering soot-blackened tenements of the Old Town. Even the gardens between the two parts of the city—usually closed up and dark at night—shine with an eerie, twilight glow.

Then I notice there are no stars. There is no moon. No clouds. Just an endless pitch-black sky. A great void of nothing above the shining city.

"My word," Catherine murmurs.

Gavin steps onto the pavement in disbelief. "I should feel at home, and yet I'm bloody terrified." He crouches to touch his hand to the cobblestones. "It's real."

"The Morrigan has a certain flair for the dramatic, doesn't she?" Kiaran says dryly.

I walk into the street and turn in a circle.

"She took this from my mind before." I gesture to the buildings around us, each one of them lit. "She's still using it to unnerve me." She's using it to remind me of what I'm giving up if I don't tell her yes.

"It would take ages to search through this for the girl," Catherine murmurs. "I hear those tenements off the High Street go underground."

Kiaran looks uncertain, too. "She's right, Kam. Maybe we should split up."

"I changed my mind. This isn't suicidal, it's just stupid," Sorcha says.

Aithinne rolls her eyes. "So negative."

"We're not splitting up," I say. "Catherine, Gavin, and Daniel can't endure the Morrigan's powers."

Sorcha flickers a glance at them. "I don't blame her if she kills them quickly. Humans are irritating."

"It must be difficult," Gavin says. "Seven of us left on this earth, and six of us hate you."

Sorcha curls her lip at him.

If Derrick were here, he could quickly search through the buildings for us. If he were here—

He's not here, and you have to focus. I try to block out the doubts, the low noise of the others murmuring to each other. I search the city with my senses, risking a small pulse of power. It travels through the landscape, combing the quiet, brightly lit streets. There is no hum of electricity, no birds in the trees, no horses. Edinburgh is entirely silent.

If I were her, where would I go?

My powers continue their search through the miles of mazelike streets. Through the layers of buildings and the vast underground network of tunnels. She must be here somewhere.

When my power lingers on George Street, I sense something. Small. Subtle. Music?

The Assembly Rooms.

I open my eyes. "Follow me."

I lead them past the shops in the direction of George Street. Past the beautiful houses of Charlotte Square; I keep my eyes straight ahead as we pass my old home. *Don't look at it. Don't get distracted.*

"Do you sense something?" Kiaran asks me.

"Music at the Assembly Rooms. It's where I first saw her clearly. When I was taken back to the night my"—I can't help but glance at Sorcha, my fingers curling into fists—"the night Sorcha murdered my mother."

I had almost said, *The night my mother died,* but why mince words? There's no need for politeness. Sorcha killed her. She knows she killed my mother.

Sorcha looks amused. "You certainly get straight to the point, don't you? If I didn't loathe you, I'd respect that."

The city is quiet, eerily so. I remember when I went out at night, it seemed as if the city held its breath until the moment I stepped out of my garden gate. When I ran through the streets with my coat in the wind behind me, Edinburgh pulsed as if it were alive. I'll never stop missing it; my heart is still here. It is a city of monsters, a city of secrets. No matter what happens, I keep ending up back here, right where it all started. It might be a hollowed-out hole in the ground in the human realm, but it still lives on through me.

The air is so still as we make our way past the empty shops on George Street. It's rare that the city would be this quiet, this lifeless. I'm used to there always being a breeze.

To the scent of hops and wood fires and a hint of whisky in the air.

But when I approach the Assembly Rooms, the chandeliers are all lit. The archways are illuminated, flickering with flames. From inside, I hear the melodic trill of violins playing a familiar song that stops me right in my tracks.

"Flowers of the Forest." The song they played during my mother's funeral. I didn't attend—I couldn't—but I stole out of the house to watch the procession at St. Cuthbert's. I swear that song echoed all over the city.

"Kam?" Kiaran's voice is soft.

"That song," I say. "I know that song."

I walk slowly to the entrance of the Assembly Rooms and push open the massive, heavy oak door. It's completely empty inside. The music has vanished, as if I had imagined it. The dance floor is bare; our footsteps echo harshly across the hardwood. The only indication I had ever heard it was the soft resonance of the song in my ears, calling, beckoning. A message? From the Morrigan or her consort?

"Well, she's not here," Sorcha says, looking annoyed. "Any other suggestions? Maybe she's gone to the pub."

"Do you actively *try* to be such an irritating pain in the arse, or does it happen by instinct?" Aithinne asks.

"I'm simply wondering when I can take one of these humans, tear open her neck, and drink from it until the end of the world." Sorcha eyes Aithinne. "Or you can fall on your brother's sword and the rest of us will hope we live to make it out into an intact world."

Aithinne presses her lips together and looks away. "I will. If it comes to that."

"No you won't," Kiaran says shortly.

I shut my eyes and think. When I was in the mirrored room, the Morrigan used Lonnrach's form to break into my mind. So if her consort was there hiding in the mirrors, she would have seen all my memories, not just of Edinburgh, but of my life here. Maybe the music was just a distraction for the Morrigan, or a message to me of where I first saw her.

Your memories showed a safe place. I hope you find something like that again.

Safe. Somewhere that's safe. Where would I go if I wanted to be safe? If the consort saw this city in my memories, where would she go to hide from the Morrigan? There aren't many places in this city where she would have seen me seek refuge. Just . . .

I have an idea.

I send a small pulse with my power again, searching just where I think she might be, and I find it. Small, barely noticeable, like a breeze rustling leaves. "I know where she is."

I'm already starting out of the ballroom of the Assembly Rooms with Kiaran close behind. "The last memories from the mirror were of us in Edinburgh. She would have seen the place I felt safest from the fae and hidden there when the Morrigan created the city."

"Where is she?"

I look at him. "My bedroom."

CHAPTER 44

SPEED BACK down George Street, barely registering the buildings on either side of me. I don't check to see if the others are following. My frantic, frenzied pulse thunders in my ears and something about it only urges me faster. Faster. I don't feel like myself. I feel like I did in the woods when Derrick found me, without any memories. Feral, savage. Desperate.

Find her. You're running out of time.

A thundering crash to my left almost makes me slow down before I reach Charlotte Square.

"Kam!"

I look over. Just behind Kiaran the buildings are beginning to topple, as if struck by something massive. Debris smashes into the street. Powder from the stonework bursts into the air as I sprint past.

The Morrigan? No, it's not the Morrigan. I don't feel her power, not yet. The realm is coming apart.

I race across the thoroughfare and into the center of Charlotte Square. My home is silent as I approach. The last time I saw this place, it was dilapidated, a partial ruin left behind from the Wild Hunt. When I battled the *mortair*, Aithinne's monstrous metal creation used by Lonnrach, the creature's weapon completely obliterated it. The real Charlotte Square house is ash now.

I jump onto the pavement and bound up the front steps to the door. Kiaran joins me there with the others close behind. I hesitate and look back at Catherine, Gavin, and Daniel. "If the Morrigan comes," I tell them, "don't engage her. Let the rest of us handle it."

Catherine opens her mouth as if to argue, but she only says, "Fine."

Sorcha is about to speak when Aithinne cuts her off. "Don't. My patience with you is very thin and I'm ready to stick you with the pointy end of my blade." Aithinne looks at me. "Go on."

It's unlocked. I push my way inside, but the house is so empty and still. A distant rumble reminds me that this place could go at any moment just like the other buildings.

Hurry.

I turn back to the others. "It might be best if I go in alone. If she's been running and hiding from the Morrigan for thousands of years, she might not trust anyone whose minds aren't safe."

Kiaran nods. "Be careful."

I head up the stairs. It isn't until I reach the top that I realize I'm holding my breath, trying not to make a sound. I hesitate outside my bedroom, then push the door open. The lights are off. There is no movement in the room, and for a moment I wonder if I'm wrong—until I see the slim line of light coming from the closet.

I swallow hard and grip the handle. This is Derrick's old home. Just the reminder makes my heart ache.

The house trembles. A great boom sounds in the distance. The foundations groan.

Hurry.

The closet door swings open to reveal the girl.

She looks younger than I thought at first, maybe younger than me. Her long black hair hangs straight past her shoulders to her waist. The strands brush forward as she crouches beneath a row of hanging dresses. The trunk that I keep there is open, and my mother's tartan is in her hands.

I suck in my breath at the sight. It was destroyed when the pixie city was demolished. The scrap sewed into my jacket is a replica.

The girl lifts the tartan to look at it better. "I pieced it back together from your memories. It's not quite the same. I don't believe I got the stitching right."

I clear my throat and crouch next to her. "You did. It's perfect."

"Good," the girl says softly. "I hadn't seen such a loving memory like that in so long. It means a great deal to you. I'm glad you're finally wearing it."

I swallow hard, the sting of tears in my eyes. "I still don't know if I'm worthy of it." *I have a ruthless heart. Sorcha was right about that.*

"Is *that* what you think?" The girl looks thoughtful. "I saw your memories. You believe you're a monster." Her dark, dark gaze rises to meet mine. Her eyes are as black as the space between constellations. "You don't look like a monster to me. When I saw your memories, I realized you were different from the others who came for the Book. Aren't you?"

Another distant rumble. The chandelier in my room sways. Something crashes just outside.

Don't frighten her. You don't have time to find her if she runs again. Be quick.

I take a deep breath to control myself. "Sometimes monsters wear the skin of harmless-looking girls," I say. And then I think of Lonnrach. "And sometimes handsome men. Maybe I'm no different at all."

A lift of her lips in an almost smile. "They would have come into this closet and seized me like a prize once they knew what I was. I know you want the words on my skin, of course. I can smell your desperation in the air. And yet you are waiting for my permission while the world caves in." Her smile is small. "Different." *Different.* What a little word. What an important word. Perhaps there's hope for me not to end up like Sorcha yet.

My laugh is dry, forced. "I know what it's like to be taken against my will. I just want your help to save my friends." *Help me save them all. Help me end a war.*

"My help?"

The house shakes and I have to brace myself against the doorframe or fall. I realize I don't even know what to call her. "What's your name?"

"Book of Remembrance," she says, as if she's said it every day of her life. A thing. Not a person. A possession.

"You weren't always a book. You were fae. You were the Morrigan's consort, weren't you?"

She jerks back at the reminder, something stricken flashing across her face. "Once," she breathes. "Before she became so powerful she had no use for a consort. Then I was just *mo laòigh*." Her voice is bitter. "Her fawn."

The Morrigan's fawn.

The Morrigan's little bird.

What's the easiest way to take away a person's identity and mold them to your will? Deprive them of the simplest thing: their name.

She brushes her fingertips down her arms. "When I wrote the Book on my skin, it became a part of me." She stares down at the marks on her arms, the squiggles of ink that form the words. "It was alive enough that I'm no longer who I once was. Like any object that has lived on past its time, perhaps I am no longer worthy of a name." She looks up at me, her eyes wide and dark and vulnerable. "But they used to call me Lena."

The house shakes again. The stone groans all around me. My heartbeat is frantic in my ears.

Hurry.

"Lena," I say. She closes her eyes, as if she misses the sound of that. I wonder how long it's been since she's heard it. "Can one of your spells truly reverse time?"

"With a few limitations." I worry about what she'll say until Lena leans forward with another smile. "I couldn't reverse the Book's existence, for one."

I smile back. "I also need information about the curse on the Cailleach's lineage. Do you know it?"

The curse that's caused so much suffering. Countless wars. Siblings killing each other, rather than ending the world. I can put it all back together again if only I can get this girl—this former consort—to help me.

Lena's smile disappears. "Those pages are why I betrayed the Morrigan."

"Could we destroy the curse?" I swallow hard. "Rewrite it?"

A violent *boom!* in the distance. Something falling and shattering downstairs. Kiaran urgently calling for me.

Hurry.

The look Lena gives me holds so much sadness that it's more than I can bear. "*As it begins in death, so shall it end in death, until the day a child of the Cailleach confronts their fate with a true lie on their lips and sacrifices that which they prize most: their heart.*"

"I know that." I try to keep my voice patient.

"Then you know what has to be done," she says. "What you have to do. It was clear from your memories."

I frown. "What are you talking about?"

Before Lena can reply, the bedroom windows shatter. Glass crashes to the floor and the whole building sways. I'm jerked back violently, my shoulder smashing into the wall.

Lena pushes to her feet, her expression frantic. She nearly loses her balance. "We have to go." Her eyes are deep, deep pools. "She's coming."

CHAPTER 45

I GRIP LENA'S hand and pull her down the quaking staircase.

Plaster falls from the ceiling and a sudden crack in the foundations almost makes me lose my footing. Lena pitches forward and I yank her back. The paintings sway on their hooks around us. Somewhere down the hall, a mirror shatters on the ground.

Kiaran looks up with relief as we enter the antechamber. Dimly, I notice the others aren't there; they must have stayed outside. "Cutting it close, Kam," he says.

"You know me. If it's not close, it's not exciting." I gesture to the girl with my head. "This is Lena. Lena, this is Kiaran. There's the front door. Let's get the hell out of here."

We rush out of the house and down the front steps. Alarm goes through me when I see the other houses in the square are falling, crumbling. One after another after another, like buildings made of sand instead of stone.

Bam! I look over my shoulder just as Number Six—my beautiful childhood home—collapses to the ground. Dust and debris explode around us. I pull Lena with me across the street where the others are waiting and watching with wide, frightened eyes.

They only look slightly relieved when they see us coming—except Sorcha, who looks irritated, but what else is new?

"You're just in time for the apocalypse," Sorcha says.

"She is such a treasure," Gavin mutters.

I tug a blade out of my wrist sheath and toss it to Sorcha. "Shut up and slice open your skin before I do it myself."

Sorcha is about to make a cut across her palm when she's shoved by an unseen force that sends her crashing into the cobblestones. I spin, but there's no one behind me but the others.

Catherine's wide eyes flicker to something beside me. "*Aileana!*"

Something slams into me. I'm thrown into the air, my body rolling and skidding painfully across the pavement. My arm smacks hard against a fallen piece of rubble. When I look up—stunned, unfocused, my vision blurring—I only see Aithinne.

When her eyes meet mine, they're the bright, vivid blue of the Morrigan. She's possessed Aithinne's body.

And she's heading right for Lena. "All I had to do was follow her until I found you," she says to Lena in Aithinne's voice. Lena cringes away, her back pressed against the lamppost. "All along I thought you'd just been here hiding with my Book. But I recognize my spells on your skin, my devious little fawn. How clever you are."

Kiaran lunges for the Morrigan with his sword out, swiping her across the arm—just enough to distract her. "Run!" he tells Lena.

The Morrigan smacks his sword away and slams her fist into his face. She holds him down with her powers. Lena tries to run, but thorny vines break up through the cobblestones, so quickly that she doesn't have time to flee. They wrap around her and pin her into place. Her eyes are wide with panic as she struggles against the vines.

At the edge of the square, Catherine moves to intervene, but Gavin and Daniel hold her back. I shake my head wildly. *Don't. She's too powerful.*

The Morrigan in Aithinne's body seems so much taller, larger than life. A goddess wearing the skin of a lesser being.

"You." The Morrigan's voice is sharp as she focuses on Sorcha. "I'll need your blood." Then she looks at me. "And you will give me my yes or I have three pathetic, frightened humans to sacrifice."

Do something!

I call the power inside me, pushing it through my veins desperately. I can't focus. My mind is screaming at me to act but it hurts so much. My power is going to tear me open, rip me from the inside out if I let it.

You can't afford to lose control. Breathe it out like air.

I shove all that power out and hurl it at the Morrigan, but she slaps it away, striking me with a bolt of power so strong that I'm thrown back again. I roll hard into the street, my bones aching as I get up. My lip is bleeding. My head is pounding. I fight not to black out.

You can't win. Not when you have everything to lose.

Kiaran is there, yanking me back to my feet. "Come on, Kam. Get up!"

"Go with the humans." My voice is rough, strained. "Get them out of here."

His grip on my arm is sure. "There's nowhere for anyone to go, and I'm not leaving you."

The Morrigan's power smacks him aside and I spin out of his grip. Kiaran hits the ground hard.

I hear her voice beneath Aithinne's beautiful laugh and hate her for it. "No hiding. I want you here to watch."

The Morrigan turns to Sorcha and uses her power to propel her forward. Then she seizes Sorcha's arm and twists it at a painful angle, dragging her over to Lena. Sorcha cries out when the Morrigan slashes the blade across her cheek. "Shhh. You remember, don't you? Don't scream unless I tell you to, little bird. That was my rule." She presses the dagger to the other woman's palm. "Now bleed."

Behind the Morrigan, Catherine breaks away from Gavin and Daniel. She picks up Kiaran's discarded sword and lunges for the Morrigan.

"Catherine, *no!*" Daniel shouts.

Catherine slashes the Morrigan across the chest, but it doesn't even faze her. The Morrigan reaches out toward Catherine with her fingertips.

All I hear is the awful crack of Catherine's neck breaking. I see her hit the ground hard. She doesn't move again.

A scream erupts from me. Daniel and Gavin stare at her crumpled body, stricken with disbelief and shock.

Catherine Catherine Catherine—

Bring her back. Finish this and you can bring her back.

I don't have time to mourn. Tears blur my vision as I strike the Morrigan with a hard slap of power. Her head twists to the side and she smiles. "Another pawn down." When she turns back, I see the quiver of blood on her lip. "Last chance, Aileana Kameron. Say yes before the other two go with her."

Daniel loses it. He attacks, but the Morrigan sends him and Gavin flying back with a flick of her fingers. They smack into the pavement in the center of the square.

I can't take it anymore. I can't watch them die, too. "Stop it!"

Her power brushes across my skin in a mocking caress as she tightens her hold on Sorcha. "Just give in. All you have to do is say yes. Who shall I sacrifice next? Will it be the King? You might be able to bring back your humans with my Book, but not him."

I swallow hard, staring at Catherine's body in the street. *Remember. Finish this and you can bring her back.* "No," I whisper, shutting my eyes.

She continues as if I had never spoken. "He looks at you like you're going to save him. His beautiful, dying human girl." Her sapphire-blue eyes bore into mine. "Say yes and my offer still stands. He's yours." She gives Sorcha a shake. "I'll undo the mark my little bird put on him. I'll give you immortality. All you have to do is say the word and resurrect my body. *Yes.*"

"Kam, don't!" Kiaran's cry cuts out as the Morrigan slaps her power through the air. When I look at him, Kiaran has a cut across his cheekbone, deep and long.

The Morrigan puts pressure on Sorcha's arm again. "Bleed." When Sorcha doesn't, the Morrigan snaps her wrist. Sorcha lets out a low choking sound. "I said, *bleed.*"

Sorcha wraps one hand around the edges of the blade, and, with an apologetic look to Lena, presses her bloody palm to Lena's ink-covered arm. Lena throws back her head in a silent scream. The writing all over her body glows and she pulses with pale silver light.

The Book has been opened.

The Morrigan is pleased. Her bright eyes lock with mine. "Aileana Kameron," she sings. "What's it going to be? A yes or a sacrifice?"

Sorcha looks up. "Don't do it. The Book is *yours* now—"

The Morrigan crashes her fist into Sorcha's face and she collapses into the cobbles. I lunge for her, but the Morrigan lashes out at me with her power. It strikes me with the force of a tidal wave. My teeth clamp together and the coppery taste of blood is stark on my tongue. I barely raise my own power in time to stop her from breaking every bone in my body.

"Say yes, girl."

Catherine's voice rings clear in my mind, warmth amid the pain. *We'll return everything to the way it was.*

And Derrick: *Get off your arse and finish this. End it, Aileana.*

"Aithinne," I breathe. "I'm sorry about this."

I throw my power into the Morrigan. It rips out of me like a lightning strike, tearing through my body with a pain that leaves me gasping. I fight through it and knock her off her feet. Our bodies collide. We slam into each other, fists and nails and hard, thrashing hits laced with power.

My body isn't immortal. My body is a frail, fallible thing of flesh and blood, and every punch makes me stagger back until she comes at me with a hard final strike. I'm breathless as I collapse onto the cobblestones. And I'm going to lose. I'm going to lose this fight because I can't throw everything I have at her. Because then I'll kill Aithinne.

"Kam!" Kiaran's call breaks through the haze of pain. "Use one of Lena's spells!"

The spells. Of course.

The Morrigan is on her feet but I tackle her back to the ground, my power slamming into her. The force of it is enough to make me see stars. I scramble over to Lena and throw up a shield to protect us from the Morrigan's attacks. It's clumsily erected, but it should buy us enough time.

Lena is slack against the vines. I grip her arm. "Lena. Give me a spell."

"I can't," she murmurs. "It'll kill you."

The Morrigan's power slams into the shield. Electricity crackles in the air, bolts of discharge that snap around us. The remains of the few buildings left around us are shuddering, falling. Gavin, Daniel, Sorcha, and Kiaran dodge falling bits of stone and use the Morrigan's distraction with me to leap inside my shield for protection.

"I say we mount one last attack." Daniel says grimly, his voice ragged. "Let's finish her off and be done with this."

"I agree," Gavin says. "Blaze of glory. Die with dignity."

"I'll help." Sorcha swipes at the blood on her face. "I didn't escape the Morrigan just to hide like a coward."

"And I don't run from battle," Kiaran says. "Especially not when the realm has degraded enough that I can finally feel my powers again."

The Morrigan's power crashes into my shield again. I wince, straining to hold it up. *Keep holding it. If we don't act soon—*

Catherine's soft voice in my mind reminds me: *This world isn't your burden. It belongs to all of us. Even them.*

"Wait," I tell the others. "Lena? What if Kiaran and Sorcha combined their powers with mine?"

Lena smiles. "Now that's an idea."

"Then it has to be all of us," I say, looking at them. We're all that's left. "Together. We have one chance."

Gavin's jaw is set, determined. "If you only have one chance, then you'll need a distraction." He looks at Daniel. "What do you say, old chap?"

Daniel nods once. "Aye. Time for your idiotic Plan B."

No. Everything in me is screaming to say no. *Don't let them go. What if they die and I can't win?*

But it's their choice. When Gavin's eyes find mine, I see the flicker of fear there. "Destroy her and bring us back," he says. "Or I'll haunt your arse forever, do you hear me?"

This world isn't your burden. It belongs to all of us.

"I hear you, Galloway."

I glance at Sorcha and reach out my hand, palm up. "This doesn't change anything," I tell her. "I still hate you."

"Of course." She puts her hand in mine with a quick smile. "I hate you, too."

At my other side, Kiaran's fingers thread through mine. "Now, Kam."

I let down the shield, and Gavin and Daniel hurtle toward the Morrigan. She looks at them like a hunter catching sight of her prey. Her powers build, ready to attack.

"Shut your eyes, Kam," Kiaran rasps. "Don't watch. Don't listen."

I close my eyes. Next to me, Sorcha begins to sing. Her beautiful, high, melodic voice fills my ears and blocks the sound. She gives me peace. One last moment of peace so I don't have to listen to my friends being slaughtered.

Lena presses her hands to my shoulders and whispers, "Say these words."

She whispers in my ear a language, a song. I meet the Morrigan's gaze as I sing with Lena. Our voices entwine with Sorcha's, then Kiaran's. The power builds and builds through our collective voices, through our bodies, our hands. I fight to stay with them. The song takes on a life of its own, surrounding us as if it were carried on the wind.

Then it hurtles toward the Morrigan. She fights against us, her voice rising in a song of its own. But I push back. I direct it.

Sorcha and Kiaran's energy crashes through me so hard and painfully that I almost fall to my knees. My veins are on fire. My bones are heavy. Blood begins to stream from my nose, my eyes. My voice strains, rasping in my throat, but I keep singing. I push all the agony down and use it to focus. I have to do this. For Derrick. For Catherine and Gavin and Daniel.

Derrick's amused voice rises from my memories. *Going out for a slaughter?*

Going out to save people.

A change of pace for you. I like it.

In the midst of everything, I almost smile.

I open my eyes just as Aithinne's body jerks. Her mouth opens in a wide scream and her back arches like something is being ripped out of her. The startling blue sapphire of the Morrigan's irises burns blindingly bright as power explodes around us in all directions. The buildings still left standing shudder to their foundations.

Then everything goes still and silent and calm.

Aithinne collapses to the ground, blinking in confusion. Her eyes are her own. The Morrigan is gone. She's *gone*. I can't feel her there anymore.

"We did it," I whisper to Kiaran. He catches me as I fall, easing me slowly to the ground. He orders Sorcha to go see to Aithinne, his voice sharp.

"You did it." His touch is gentle as he wipes the blood from my face. I rest my cheek against his chest. "Kam. Kam, keep your eyes open."

A startling crack draws my attention. Around us, the few remaining buildings are beginning to crumble, falling into the streets.

"It's almost done," Lena says quietly. "There isn't much time left to save your realm."

"Tell me what to do," Kiaran says.

"Not what you have to do. *Her*. She's the only one who can break the curse."

Me? But I'm not—

A jolt goes through me as I remember her words.

You have my daughter's blood in you, her powers. My blood, the Cailleach had said. I am of her lineage, connected by blood.

I'm a child of the Cailleach. A child of the Cailleach who can tell a lie.

Kiaran must realize it, too. When he looks down at me, his expression is determined. Decisive. "Lie to me, Kam."

"What?"

"Lie to me."

Sacrifices that which they prize most: their heart.

I try to jerk out of Kiaran's arms. "No."

I know what he's asking me to do. What he's asking me to sacrifice.

Kiaran holds me against him, his forehead pressed to mine. "Tell me a lie that can't be twisted to truth. We have this one chance. Just one."

"Please," I breathe. "I can't. Don't ask me to do this."

He's stroking my hair and I see how much he loves me. I can see it so clearly. "Tell stories about us, Kam," he whispers. "Tell people that when the faery king and the human girl first met, he saw how clever she was. How foolish and brave and magnificent. And he knew that one day, falling in love with her wouldn't be a choice. It would come to him as easily as breathing." His lips touch mine. "Tell people about how they stood at the end of all things and saved the world. Together."

He breaks off as the buildings around us fall. As the realm begins to crumble.

Another kiss, this one so very soft. "I've been alive for four thousand years and I've never once done anything that wasn't selfish. So let me do this with you. Let me do one good thing." He presses the hilt of the sword to my palm. "Now tell me a lie."

Taking the sword from him is the hardest thing I've ever done. I cup his cheek and tell him the truest lie I've ever said, one that shatters my heart. "I don't love you," I whisper, pressing my trembling lips to his.

Then I shove the sword through his chest.

CHAPTER 46

'M STILL cradling Kiaran's body as the world puts itself back together. As the Morrigan's prison realm dissolves away and reveals the remains of my world, the small island of rock still left standing at Aithinne's camp. As the land begins to form over the great black pit, rock by rock. Stone by stone. Tree by tree. Drawing together as if it were being painted by a deft hand.

The first rays of light shine through the clouds, and the sun rises up over the forest and spills through the trees. A breeze kicks up the beautiful fresh scent of pine and I shut my eyes and close myself off. I can't be relieved when I'm surrounded by so much death.

Here I am, the last human survivor in a war I never wanted and I'm shattering. I've lost too much of myself. I feel still and quiet. I am as empty as that pit when the world was breaking apart.

I hold Kiaran like I'm clinging to the last pieces of myself, a ruin of a girl. Beyond repair.

I love you. I should have told you I loved you. I should have said the words before I had to lie to you.

Footsteps jar me out of my thoughts. When I open my eyes, Aithinne is kneeling next to me. Her cheeks are red and stained with tears as she stares down at her brother. "After all this time you had to go and be a hero," she says to him. She strokes his hair. "Foolish *bhràthair*. You should have let me die."

"You're right. He should have." Sorcha stands over us, her hands clenched into fists. Her expression is grief and white-hot rage. She turns on Lena, almost accusingly. "Why am I still alive if he's dead? Why am I still here?"

"His sacrifice overpowered your vow. It's old magic, more powerful than a mark given under coercion."

Sorcha clamps her mouth shut. "That's—"

"Enough," Lena says sharply. She glances at me. "Give the Seelie Queen the Cailleach's powers before they kill you, Aileana." She reaches out a hand for me to take. "Come now. Don't let his death be for nothing."

I've been alive for four thousand years and I've never once done anything that wasn't selfish. So let me do this with you. Let me do one good thing.

My fingers brush across Kiaran's cheek. His skin is still warm. *Only for you. Only because this is what you wanted.*

I take Lena's hand and say to Aithinne, "After this, the spells are yours and Lena's. Together."

The spell whispers across my mind, the soft rustle of a song. For the first time since I inherited the Cailleach's powers, I'm not in pain. I'm not forcing anything. As the powers flow easily down my veins and into their new host, I feel lighter. There's a sense of relief I can't describe—as if my body is weightless, whole again. Except for my heart; the curse needed a sacrifice. I won't be getting it back.

Aithinne's hiss of pain is hardly more than a sigh. Her body goes slack, all the tension gone. Then she opens her eyes.

They're as clear and bright as melted silver. When Aithinne stares at me, it's with knowledge. It's with all the power of the Cailleach inside her, as ancient as the realms themselves. But unlike her mother, she isn't cold. She's warm and calm. If Kiaran were here, he'd say he made the right choice. She will make a better monarch.

"I feel as though I owe you a debt for saving my life," she says. "For trying to save his."

"No debts between us, Aithinne." Is that my voice? I sound empty. "You're my friend. You always will be."

She glances behind me, to where I know Gavin, Daniel, and Catherine are lying motionless on the ground. I can't look. I'm barely hanging on as it is.

I'm empty. I have nothing left.

"Then don't consider me reversing time to be a payment, just a gift. After everything you and they have sacrificed, you all deserve a second chance to live away from all of this. You deserve more."

With one of Lena's spells, Aithinne will alter the course of time and send us all back. As if none of this had ever happened. The others earned that.

But me? How can I pretend that I never went through all of this? How can I pretend I never met Kiaran? What would I go back to?

Aithinne's eyes are swirling silver. Deep with power and knowledge and, yes, sadness. "You can't spend your life mourning him, Aileana. He wouldn't want you to." When I say nothing, she continues, "No more fighting. No more war. Take this chance."

My heart thuds and I look at Lena. "Could you bring back Kiaran and Derrick?" I ask it even though I already know the answer. I just need to hear it.

Lena sighs. "Fae aren't the same. To bring them back requires a sacrifice. A life for a life."

A life for a life. I look down at Kiaran, stroking a finger down his pale cheek. I can't help my first thought—the first vestiges of my grief breaking through the numbness. *What will I return to if he isn't there?*

As if she reads my thoughts, Sorcha steps forward. "Don't," she snaps. "Don't you dare give up your stupid human existence to resurrect him." She swallows hard and I swear I see tears in her eyes. "He deserves better than that." She runs a shaky hand through her hair and laughs. I wince; she sounds like she's coming apart. "He deserves better than *this*."

She's right. And I promised Catherine I would see her again. I promised. I swallow hard and look down at Kiaran.

I'm going to have to let you go. Just like I let Derrick go.

"What will you do?" I ask Aithinne. "Now that you're Queen?"

Aithinne smiles sadly. "Create new fae. Build a kingdom with Lena's help." She glances at the other faery, who nods calmly. "I have a lot of work to do. If you should receive an invitation to a coronation one day, don't you dare refuse it. Or I'll show up on your doorstep and demand cake and dancing." She takes Lena's hand and leans forward, as if to touch me. "Are you ready now?"

I shut my eyes and nod.

Aithinne presses her fingers to my temple and murmurs words in her language that sound like the first notes of a lullaby. Lena's voice joins with hers, quiet and confident and lovely. I never feel the world shift around me. I don't notice time reverse.

I just hear Aithinne's last words to me over the dull pounding of my heart: *Live a full life, Aileana. The life he gave for yours.*

When I open my eyes, I'm sitting on the floor of my bedroom in Edinburgh—but not the teak-paneled bedroom I left behind. There is no map on the far wall that counts Sorcha's kills. No worktable of faery-killing weapons. No hunting clothes on the floor splattered in mud.

My bedroom is decorated as it was when my mother still lived, the buttercup-cream wallpaper, the gold curtains that shone in the sunlight. Back when my life was uncomplicated and . . .

And normal. Aithinne has reversed time to when I was seventeen.

I study my blue muslin day dress, then my hands—not covered in calluses. Not speckled with blood. A lady's hands. They never belonged to a warrior.

"Aileana?"

I go still at the voice calling for me. Tears blur my vision. "Mum?" I stand and start for the doorway, not certain if I heard right.

But there she is, coming down the hall outside my room. "Aileana," she says, "Don't forget we're having luncheon with—" She stops when she sees my tears. "Is something the matter?"

"*Mum.*" I reach her in two steps. I throw my arms around her and pull her into a crushing embrace. I hold her so tightly that I'm surprised she can still breathe.

She strokes a comforting hand across my back as I sob into her shoulder. "Shh. What's happened?"

"What date is it?" My voice is trembling. "What year?"

"Aileana." Now she sounds alarmed. "Do you need me to send for a doctor? Are you—"

"Date. Year. *Please.*"

"November sixth, eighteen forty-three." She strokes my hair. "Now tell me. Are you all right?"

Aithinne sent me back to a month before my mother died. *Maybe she could still die. Will that change, too?* "I don't know," I tell her honestly. "I don't know yet."

CHAPTER 47

A WEEK LATER, my mother asks, "Are you certain everything is all right?"

We're in the garden working on the ornithopter. The body of the craft is complete with a wing partially attached, but the flying machine is still far from airworthy. It would be another four months of tireless work before I finished it.

Mother tries catching my gaze, but I pretend to be distracted. I pull my coat closer around me. "Of course. Why wouldn't it be?"

"You seem . . . different." She frowns. "Quieter than usual."

Lately when I wake up, I have to remind myself where I am. I stare at the ceiling in my great bedroom wondering if I'm caught in a dream. If I'll open my eyes and the illusion will finally shatter, revealed to be a faery trick.

I duck my head under the ornithopter's wing, fiddling with one of the attachments. "Do I?" I ask, keeping my voice light. "I'm just distracted with all the assemblies planned."

"That's not it. Sometimes you look at me and . . ." Her voice trails off, as if uncertain.

"And what?"

She's quiet. Then: "You're somewhere else. You haven't been eating. You speak differently. Sometimes you look like you've lost someone important."

My eyes squeeze shut. Pulling in air is suddenly so difficult. "That's silly. Who would I have lost?" My voice is surprisingly even. "I haven't been eating because I'm not hungry. And blame my peers for my manner of speaking."

I need to go and see Catherine, Gavin, and Daniel. The four of us are the only ones with any memory of the fae purge that destroyed Edinburgh. Something Aithinne ensured so I wouldn't have to face this all this by myself. I would go mad if I did.

I drop my spanner in the toolbox before Mum can answer. "I'm going to call on the Stewarts. I'll return for afternoon tea."

I feel her eyes on me, but I leave without a backward glance.

* * *

My closet is empty.

Some nights I turn on the light, shut the door, and pull all of my dresses off their hangers. I lie in the tangle of silk and muslin and imagine a small body curled against my shoulder. I imagine wings brushing my cheek. I remember a bawdy song and a laughing voice calling my name. If I close my eyes hard enough, I can hear his voice. *Look at these terrible dresses. They don't have nearly enough ribbons.*

I smile. And then I open my eyes, and I remember he's gone.

* * *

One month after my return, I still run through the streets at night. I still look for monsters lurking in dark alleyways. I look for Aithinne. I look for Kiaran. I climb to the top of Arthur's Seat under the light of the moon and press my ear to the ground, wondering if this time I'll hear the underground drumbeat of a faery dance.

I walk through the city and listen to the sounds of everyone living out their lives; to them, nothing happened. The streets were never destroyed, and lives were never ended. Aithinne brought back every city that had been in ruins, every home, every town, every life. Scotland—and the world—is whole once more.

There are no monsters. There are no faeries. There is no music. I have nothing to fight.

Maybe the price of saving the world is forgetting how to live in it.

* * *

Catherine, Gavin, and Daniel are here for one of their biweekly visits.

"Christ, Catherine," Gavin is saying. "Why don't you just take all the tea cakes? Go on, just shovel them into your reticule like a thief."

I've come to cherish these moments of levity. I don't have to pretend with these three. None of us do. My mother still looks at me sometimes like she doesn't know who I am. I'm a battle-weary soldier in the body of her little girl.

The only people who remember the fae are sitting in this room. And we're trying to learn how to live with our memories of war. The truth is: The world might have been healed, but none of us have.

"Aileana," Gavin says, interrupting my thoughts. "Do you know Catherine has been stealing food from every party we've attended for the last month? She's hoarding desserts in her bedroom."

"Why are you so concerned about my eating habits?" She glances at Daniel. "If I gain several stone, so what? I haven't had proper tea cakes for three years. And Daniel encourages me, don't you, darling? You like tea cakes, too."

At Catherine's question, Daniel puts up his hands. "I am not getting in the middle of a sibling squabble. For my own survival."

Daniel came back to this reset time with a suspiciously convenient earldom passed on by some distant cousin he had never heard of—who probably didn't exist—and a sudden, astoundingly large fortune. Aithinne's doing. For a faery, she's quite the romantic.

Daniel and Catherine now have to remarry. In order to push for a quick engagement, Gavin had to speak with their mother and imply he discovered Catherine in something of a compromising position.

"Oh, for goodness' sake," I interrupt. I wave my hand. "Gavin, stop pestering Catherine and let her eat the bloody tea cakes. In fact, have five more."

Catherine stacks five more and looks right at Gavin as she stuffs one in her mouth. "Mmmm," she says closing her eyes. "Those extra stone would be worth it. I missed tea cakes. And tea. And shortbread."

I miss Derrick. I miss his songs. I miss having him sit on my shoulder.

I miss Ki—

No. Don't think about him.

It was slightly easier to breathe today. This morning, I was able to hold down black pudding and eggs. But if I think about him, I'll start to feel too much again. I'll get lost in my emotions.

"Not this again," Gavin groans and he tells me, "Catherine has this list of things she missed and it was about one hundred items long. She recited it at three in the morning and I haven't slept—" He presses his lips together at Catherine's sudden hard stare. "Sorry," he mumbles.

I look at her. "You're still having bad dreams?"

Catherine picks at her dress. "While I appreciate the cakes and the city and everything else, some parts I . . ." She swallows. "I sound ungrateful."

Daniel puts his arm around her. "It was three years, Cat. Don't apologize for not feeling right after one bloody month."

"I know. I just—" Catherine glances at the open door.

I rise from the settee and shut the door. We don't want servants listening to our conversations, not when we are all discussing what seems like a dream. A collective dream where the world burned to ash.

"I don't sleep either," I say. *More than that.* "Sometimes I still go out."

Gavin frowns. "What are you expecting to find? There are no fae in the city anymore."

"Thank you for reminding me. I'm aware of that." I say it a touch too sharply.

"Then why?"

"I don't know anymore," I lie.

* * *

Later, Gavin lingers as Catherine and Daniel leave. I'm standing next to the window, watching the sun shine through the clouds over the buildings across the square.

Gavin's shoulder brushes mine as he comes up beside me. "You're looking for him, aren't you?" he asks me quietly. "When you go out at night."

"Sometimes," I admit. "Sometimes when I'm in this house, I feel like I can't breathe."

I feel Gavin's eyes on me then, and I can't tell if it's because he understands or he's searching for something that isn't there. "Yes," he breathes. "It's the same for me. I suspect it would be the same for those two if they didn't have each other."

He nods to Catherine and Daniel, who are standing on the pavement outside of the house. Catherine laughs at something Daniel says, and the noise carries through the window. I look away. "How do you . . ." *Deal with this?*

"I lose myself in a woman." Gavin taps his finger distractedly against the windowsill. "It helps for a few hours." When I don't say anything, he sighs. "You can't keep living like this."

"How is what I do any different? We're both losing ourselves in something."

"True." He glances at me. "My offer still stands, you know."

"Marriage?" I shake my head with a smile. "You want to marry someone who is in love with someone else? That's no life."

"And what if I'm willing?"

I stare at Gavin. It's strange seeing him again as he was. His hair is cut and styled like a gentleman now, his facial hair shaved close. There are no scars on his face. No reminders of the life he lived, except for those in our memories, those awful things we can't forget.

I reach up and trace my fingers over his cheek, over his smooth skin. "Don't resign yourself to a life with me, Galloway. You deserve better than what I can give you. You deserve someone who loves you back."

He nods once in understanding. "What about you?"

My hand drops to my side. "I'll still go out at night."

⋆ ⋆ ⋆

Two days later it is the night of the debutante ball.

The night Sorcha killed my mother.

"What on earth has you so agitated?" Mother says as she helps me into the dress. This should be my maid's job, but tonight my mother insisted on helping me herself. Just as she did last time. She is wearing the gown I remember: the silk fabric dyed such a light pink that it's almost ivory. An unusual color for an Edinburgh matron, but it complements her pale skin and her upswept ginger hair.

The last time I saw that dress it was covered in blood.

Crimson suits you best.

I flinch. "What if we don't go?" My hand is trembling as I smooth my dress. "Would that be all right?"

Mother smiles at me like I'm being silly. "You're nervous, aren't you?"

"No. Mum—"

"There." She does up the last button and steps back to inspect me. "You look so beautiful. I have just one last thing and it'll look perfect."

Mother walks over to the dresser and picks up a wool bundle. My heart pounds when I stare at the familiar fabric. *Please no.*

She opens it up and there, nestled in the wool, are the familiar stalks of blue thistle. *Seilgflùr*.

My heart roars in my ears and my vision tunnels. I stare at the flower and memories flash in my mind.

My mother in the street, dress soaked through with blood. How I pressed my hands to her empty chest as if I could put her back together again. As if I could give her a heart—at that moment, I would have given her my own.

"Isn't it lovely? It'll be the only color on you."

It'll be the only color on you. The only color.

I jerk away from her, almost smacking into the vanity table. "Where did you get that?"

Mother looks slightly taken aback by the force of my words. "A woman gave them to me."

A woman. Not a man. The first time, Kiaran gave them to my mother for my protection. She wove them into my hair and their power allowed me to see Sorcha.

"Who? What did she look like?" I'm aware of the terror in my voice, but I can't tamp it down.

Mother looks alarmed. "I don't recall. Why does it matter?"

Sorcha said she'd make the same choices again. She'd kill my mother again. She made it clear she wasn't earning my forgiveness. And I'm not a Falconer anymore. I don't have any powers to fight her.

I'm just human.

Now the question is: Who was the woman? Was it Sorcha, or Aithinne?

"Aileana? Why does it matter?" she asks again.

"It doesn't," I say quickly. "It's nothing." I've lied to her so many times. About me. About everything. "I promise, it's nothing."

My stomach is in knots for the rest of the night. By the time we leave for the Assembly Rooms, I'm shaking so badly that I have to wind my reticule around my wrist or I'll drop it. My heart is slamming against my rib cage; I'm surprised no one else can hear it.

As we queue up at the front doors, my mother laughs and tells me that it's all right to be nervous. But I'm not nervous. I'm bloody terrified. I barely manage a nod when other people greet me. I don't pay attention to the dresses all around me, or the men dressed in fine eveningwear. It's all a blur of color, a burst of laughter and violins amid my panicked thoughts.

My memories are flashing too fast. The songs are the same. The dresses are the same. It takes the same number of steps to reach the ballroom doors and the same damn song is playing when we enter.

When my name is announced, I barely hear it over my heaving breaths.

A hand grasps my arm and gently but firmly leads me out to the center of the dance floor. I inhale the scent of cigar smoke and whisky. "Come along," Father says.

During the last month I've done whatever I can to bring us closer. Our progress has been slow, but encouraging. He doesn't speak quite as harshly, and now he's staring down at me with concern. "Are you all right?"

"Where is Mum?" I ask, searching wildly for her.

Nothing. I can't see anything beyond the blur of dresses and glittering chandeliers, the melding of colors as my father spins me around in a dance. Why didn't I insist we stay home?

My father's answer makes me go cold. "She had to go to the ladies' parlor to—"

"I'm sorry, but I need to go," I say, all propriety abandoned. I jerk out of his arms and back away. "I have a headache. I need to go."

I ignore my father's shocked expression as I shove through the line of dancers and hurry across the ballroom toward the double doors. People's conversations pause around me; they whisper amongst themselves at my behavior. I don't care. I slip out into the hallway and rush to the back entrance. My pulse is fast. I can't get in enough air.

Everything is happening in the same order as last time. With the exception of the person who gave my mother the thistle, it's all the same. It's *exactly* the same. I'm right back here and I'm going to watch her die again.

The door slams shut behind me as I exit into the garden. I don't even wait for the telltale gasp of my mother dying. I barrel through the shrubs, shove open the gate, and—

The street is entirely empty.

Breathing hard, I step into the pool of light cast by the street lamp where I found my mother's body the first time.

Not a sound, not a whisper, not even a breeze. I gaze into the cold, still night and no one is out here except me.

Until I hear footsteps behind me, careful and slow. Then a voice that makes my heart race.

"Kam."

I shut my eyes. *His* voice. I don't dare look until he says my name again, ragged and filled with longing.

I turn, and there he is. Bathed in the street lamp's golden light, only a few feet from me. God, how I missed that small curve of a smile, the way his beautiful dark hair sweeps across his forehead. When his bright lilac eyes lock with mine, he tilts his head as if to say, *Well? Don't just stand there.*

Is it you? Is it really you?

As I cautiously edge closer, I notice his skin doesn't glisten with uncanny fae light. A slight flush fills his cheeks with color and his chest rises and falls with the quick cadence of his breath—as if he ran here. It takes me a moment to realize what that means.

Human. *Kiaran is human.*

"This is a dream," I say.

He laughs and the sound is so lovely. "It's not a dream."

"I killed you." My chest aches and my voice trembles when I add, "You're dead."

"And you were dead twice," he reminds me. "I think I should have at least two more chances before you refuse to believe it's me." Then he moves forward and his palm cups my cheek. I shut my eyes at his touch. "Do you feel that?" he murmurs. "It's real."

"You say that in my dreams, too," I whisper.

"Then shall I prove it to you?" He sounds amused. "Is it my turn to ask the irritating questions?"

Tears burn my eyes. "I would love that more than anything."

"I only have one: How the hell did you keep up with me during our hunts? I've never experienced the discomfort of being winded before tonight."

I burst out laughing. It's him. *It's him.* I throw my arms around him and pull him in for a crushing embrace. "God, I missed you. How? How are you—"

"Lena told you," a voice calls from the shadows. Aithinne. "It requires sacrifice. A life for a life."

I look over and see Aithinne smiling at us as she leans against the garden gate. She's completely radiant in her brocade coat, an exact replica of the one Derrick made for her. The one I wore when I went in search of the Book. I suppose she'll get to wear it as a coronation garment after all.

"By the way, Sorcha wanted me to pass on a message," Aithinne says. "She said, *This changes nothing* and that she still hated you."

Sorcha. Sorcha sacrificed her life for Kiaran's.

He deserves better.

Sorcha's wrong. This changes everything. *Everything.*

Aithinne smiles fondly at her brother. "He could have chosen to remain fae, but he decided to be human with you. And he says he isn't romantic."

"Oh, he is," I tease. "He hides it behind glares and threats. I adore it."

"And I think—"

"Aithinne, don't you have somewhere to be?" Kiaran asks quickly. "Somewhere you said you'd go?" Then he mouths at her, *Go away.*

Aithinne grins. "Ohhh, right! I'm just going to go eat desserts and dance with humans. Can ladies dance with ladies? Never mind: I'll just go and find a lady, or some cake. But hopefully both. Leaving now." She hurries through the garden gate with her laughter trailing behind her.

"Oh dear," I say. "We're going to go back in there to utter chaos, aren't we?"

"Probably."

"Should we—"

"No. We shouldn't. Don't finish that sentence." Then he dips his head and presses his lips to mine.

I kiss him back with everything I'm feeling. I make promises with that kiss. I give messages. I tell him secrets. I believe in wishes now. Our kiss is filled with the thousand possibilities of a future entirely chosen by us. Him and me. Together.

Then I pull back and whisper against his lips, "I love you, Kiaran MacKay." I smile up at him, and my heart feels whole. "Will you dance with me?"

His answer is a breath between kisses. "Always."

As we spin around in a dance there in the street, I swear I feel Derrick's wings rustle my hair, the hint of his power in the fleeting winter breeze, and I smile.

Kiaran presses his cheek to mine and we dance together under the stars, with the glittering light of the city all around us.

ACKNOWLEDGMENTS

As I write this, I'm still in a state of disbelief that this series has, at last, come to an end. I've worked on these characters and this story in various drafts throughout most of my adulthood, and seeing it through to its final book has been such an immense blessing. It could never have come this far without the help of certain tremendous individuals along the way.

My agent, the extraordinary Russell Galen, who saw potential in the early draft I sent him of *The Falconer*—one I cringe just thinking about! I'll always be grateful to him for picking me out of his slush pile and guiding me throughout these years. And Heather Baror-Shapiro, my incredible foreign rights agent, for getting this series to publishers in other countries and helping to grow its fan base.

The team at Gollancz, my publisher in the U.K., and especially my editor Gillian Redfearn. I'm not sure what I would have done without Gillian's support, insightful suggestions, and gentle encouragements all these years. I consider myself profoundly lucky to have had her working alongside me for this long, and at times difficult, publishing journey.

The team at my U.S. publisher, Chronicle Books, for the immense efforts they've put into this series. My editor Ginee Seo's keen eye for description and detail has helped my writing and the story arc of this series immeasurably, and for that I'll always be grateful. To add, her ideas on the packaging of this series has created some of the most beautiful hardbacks I've ever seen, and I still can't believe they're for my words. I'm also so indebted to Lara Starr and the entire marketing team at Chronicle for going above and beyond in putting this book into the hands of more readers. Thank you so much.

I would have been a complete mess without the support my parents gave me while I wrote this series. I can't describe how difficult it is to live an ocean away from family, and those weekly phone calls keep me sane.

I can't say enough how much support from other writers means, especially when it comes to early drafts. Tess Sharpe, my amazing critique partner and friend, every day I wake up thankful for you. You're the most brilliant and beautiful person I've ever had the pleasure to know. And I can't express enough gratitude to Wendy Higgins and Laura Lam for their comfort and reassurance when I truly felt like I couldn't finish this. The truth is, I just couldn't have finished it without you.

And for Mr. May, I doubt I could put into words how much I love and adore you. But I know that regardless of what I write, you're going to give me your best and most gorgeous smile, and I'm going to melt into a puddle on the floor. So, in lieu of flowery words, come find me after you read this. I plan on kissing you.